A
MORAL SWERVE

A novel by

Annie Cook

*This book is dedicated to all of the young people
I had the true privilege of working with,
and for, in the criminal justice system.*

1

Thursday
- Alison -

As I walk up the garden path to my house, I'm congratulating myself that I've survived one of the most difficult days at work that I can ever remember, and I've managed to make it home without having a complete and utter screaming meltdown.

That's no small thing, to be fair, since I've spent the entire day trying not to lose it with a higher-than-usual number of whining, moaning idiots on the other end of the phone who use every ridiculous excuse in the world to worm their way out of paying their overdue bills.

Some people think credit controllers and call-centre staff were born yesterday, and it hasn't occurred to most of them that we've heard all their excuses before, and we actually *don't* have a bottomless barrel of sympathy, or the patience of a saint, for the mess they got themselves into.

I could probably write a bestselling book about it all. I'd probably call it something as ludicrous as its contents would actually be; something like *'Every Excuse You've Ever Thought Of (and Some of the Ones You Hadn't) For Failing To Take Responsibility For The Debt You Got Yourself Into When You Knew You Couldn't Afford That Sofa You Bought On Tick.'*

Catchy little title; it would go down a treat. I could look forward to a landslide of royalties. Then, maybe, I could give up my miserable job and forget the wretchedness of listening to endless of tales of woe for eight hours a day, five days a week. That would be lovely.

I'm home an hour or so earlier than usual, crying off with a headache that's been hanging around all day, coming and going and driving me mad. As I put my key into the lock, I'm mentally preparing for sitting out in my back garden with a delicious glass of cold chardonnay, with the condensation forming in glittery beads on the glass, on what will surely be one of the last nice evenings of the summer.

But alas, so often in the midst of innocuous tasks, like simply unlocking one's own front door, life-defining moments can steal upon us and blindside us completely, knocking us off kilter and sending us spinning in a totally different direction. So what I'm *not* prepared for, in the slightest, is the fact that within the next few minutes the notion that I'm safe from harm in my own home will fly straight out of a broken window, and my life will change forever.

The first thing I notice when the door swings open to a warm and slightly stuffy house is that Badger, my border collie dog, isn't there to greet me. At first I think he's probably still out with the dog walker, and maybe she's just late bringing him home, so I'm not too worried. I am home early, after all.

I have soft-soled shoes on, so there's no real sound as I leave the front door ajar to let some air into the hallway, and head towards the kitchen. But, as I make my way forward I hear two unfamiliar voices. Male voices. I freeze, horrified.

Somebody is in my house.

On the occasional table in the hallway is a heavy metal skillet, which I was drying with a tea towel at the weekend when the doorbell rang, and I came up the hall with it still in my hands. I put it down on the table to open the door and for some reason I didn't take it back to the kitchen afterwards. Forgetfulness; probably borne of another stupid headache. I've been having a lot of them lately.

The thought flies quickly through my mind, that I should probably book an appointment with my GP. Another thought quickly follows; that its weird what we end up thinking about sometimes, when we should be concentrating on something else that's probably a lot more important.

I pick up the metal skillet. It feels reassuring in my hand; like an unexpected gift; a weighty weapon to whack someone over the head with, should the need arise.

It's funny how much can go through your head in just a few seconds. In the short time it takes to creep down the hallway, I'm mentally wondering who would be in the house; running off a mental checklist of who's got keys, whether my cousin might be here, thinking it unlikely since she lives 140 miles away and hasn't called me; that sort of thing. As I tiptoe down the hall, the sound of two people laughing and chatting away to each other effectively masks my arrival.

As I near the door to the kitchen and look through the barely-open crack, the air is suddenly sucked out of my lungs by the sight of Badger, unconscious *(or dead?)* on the kitchen floor. Blood has seeped from his muzzle and, in a split-second, wariness and confusion turn to rage as I'm suddenly certain, beyond all doubt, that whoever is in my house is here for all the wrong reasons. The bastards have attacked my dog.

The sight of him lying there on the floor like that is too much to prevent me from screaming, as I fly though the door to confront what turns out to be two youngish males, who clearly didn't expect me to turn up just at that moment. They are calmly enjoying two of my beers from the fridge and having a bit of a laugh, at my expense no doubt, but the grins soon fall from their faces. They freeze, all merriment gone, as I roar into the room. My brain registers an open, scruffy holdall on the kitchen bench, with one bright corner of my metallic pink-covered i-pad sticking out of it, along with the silver filigree jewellery box my grandmother left me in her will.

One of these scumbags is about twenty or so. He's around six feet tall, heavily tattooed and solidly built, with longish, dark brown hair tied back in a shambles of a ponytail. He's clean-shaven, and his clothes are average; jeans, a dark t-shirt, and a pair of tan-coloured boots. He is also heavily tattooed.

The other lad is, I'd guess, around four or five years younger. Similarly dressed, he is unremarkable in almost every way too. He's a little shorter, his hair is a dirty-blond, and his face is full of bright, red, angry pimples. It's a total acne city, and that's the only thought I have, until the older lad pushes the younger one out of the way and sprints past both of us towards the French door which, judging by the broken pane of glass about halfway up, has been their point of entry. He yanks the door open and runs clean away, just as the front door slams shut from the backdraft, with a finality that leaves my teeth ringing.

I've had a *really* shitty day, my head is pounding, and I'm seriously upset about Badger, who still hasn't moved a muscle.

At this point I don't know if he is dead or alive but that cannot, for the moment, be my most pressing concern.

Scumbag Senior has run off, and Scumbag Junior wants to, but I can't let him. I really can't. I can't explain quite why, but stopping this lowlife from leaving has just become my number one priority.

I take a step towards him, without a truly formed intention in my head of what I am about to do, and then he moves to duck past me and head for the door. I swing the skillet and it hits the front of his head with a light 'crack'. It's not enough to knock him out, but he stumbles. He loses his balance and falls to the floor. The back of his head hits one of the chrome handles on my Rangemaster cooker and it obviously hurts because he lets his breath out in a big, quick 'owhh'. He's not laughing now, far from it. He looks at me warily.

'You came here to steal from me,' I say to him, flatly. He says nothing, so I kick his foot. He still doesn't respond. Instead, he stares at the skillet, then looks straight ahead and into the middle distance, in direct defiance. Perhaps he is hoping that if he ignores me I will go away, but *that's not going to happen, dickhead.*

I kick his foot again. 'What did you do to my dog?'

Silence. His jaw sets hard. He is determined not to respond.

'What did you do to my dog, you scab-faced, thieving fucking bastard?' I scream, *really* scream at him, so loud that it comes out in a surprisingly high-pitched screech that surprises even me. He flinches hard, but still says nothing. Then, still refusing to look at me, he shrugs. *He shrugs!* He is defiant, and seemingly indifferent, to the fact that he or his bastard mate may have just killed my very best, most treasured friend. A bolt of red-hot rage courses through me, and my banging head feels ready to explode right here and now. I try to blink the pain away, and I can hardly believe my eyes when Junior then tries to scramble to his feet.

Escape? I don't think so, mate.

I hit him again with the skillet, square across the left side of his head. This time the crack is just a little louder, just a little more satisfying, and this time it does knock him out. He crumples back into his sitting position on the floor. His head slumps forward, his chin hits his chest, and there is silence.

I leave him there on the floor and run to Badger, my beautiful boy. He still isn't moving, but his nose has stopped bleeding. It is wet and cold, but he doesn't respond to my touch. I sit on the floor, gather him into my arms and mercifully he begins to stir.

He's alive!

I'm shaking with rage, outrage, relief and disbelief; a hodgepodge of mixed emotions that swirl around, chaotically interweaving with my crippling headache, as I try to assimilate all that's just happened.

I breathe gently into Badger's face to bring him around, and he opens his eyes and looks straight into mine. He whimpers softly, and struggles to get to his feet, but he can't stand up. Fighting back rage and fear-filled tears, I feel along his big, shaggy body for anything untoward. There don't seem to be any broken bones, but I'm no expert, and without a proper vet check it would be impossible to know what his injuries might be. Together, we manage a half-drag and half-walk, till I get him into his bed in the corner of the kitchen, where I try to make him comfortable, and I put his water bowl next to his face.

I need to call the vet. I'll need a house call because I'm afraid to move him any further, in case I make his injuries worse. It's bad enough that I've had to move him at all, but I can't stand the thought of him being uncomfortable on the hard, cold kitchen floor. I move warily past Junior, who's still out for the count. I give his foot a kick for good measure, but nothing moves. I pick up the telephone handset and speed-dial the vet. Luckily, someone is still at the surgery and although they're about to close, they assure me that they can get an on-call vet to me within the hour.

So someone is on the way, and in the meantime, I have to decide what to do with Junior. I can't have him there on the floor when the vet comes. I don't want to call the police, either. I want to deal with this prick myself.

There are cable ties in the kitchen utility drawer, so I fish a couple out and tie up his hands behind his back, like handcuffs. I've heard somewhere that the police are using cable ties these days. I'm not sure if it's true, but it seems like a pretty reasonable option. I tie Junior's feet as well and, thinking on the fly, I drag him to the hallway.

There's a cupboard under the stairs, so I figure I can hide him in there until after the vet has been, because I don't think I could heft him all the way up the stairs, and since he has already defiled my home I don't want him up there again anyway. I could put him in the downstairs toilet, but what if the vet needs to use it? Too risky. No, I will put him in the under-stairs cupboard, and I'll decide how to deal with him after the vet has gone. Now, the first priority is my dog. I try to ignore this crushing headache I've got, and hold my fear and outrage at bay.

What the hell just fucking happened?

It occurs to me that I have no idea how long knocked-out people stay knocked-out for. If Junior comes to, while the vet is here, he could scream bloody murder. That won't do. There is duct tape in the drawer where the cable ties were, so I run back to the kitchen, pull it out, and cut a piece off it. Back in the hallway, I place it firmly across his mouth, taking care to keep his nose clear.

I open the door, and I have to pull out the vacuum cleaner and other bits and pieces before I can get him in there. He's not too big or heavy, so it's manageable; just. I heave and push, and all of a sudden he is in there. I have to fight to get the door shut after I pile everything else back in, but I manage it, and all of a sudden everything is quiet. No burglars, no thieves, no noise. My ragged, panicked breathing is the only thing that disrupts the blanket of silence that suddenly descends upon the house.

I clean up Badger's blood and the shards of shattered glass from the floor, wedge the French doors open so the broken pane will not be obvious from inside, and in a flash of inspiration I decide to put some music on; some light jazz, to dispel the crushing silence. It might also deflect any noises that might come from the under-stairs cupboard if Junior does wake up and starts trying to move about while the vet is tending to Badger. I don't want to have to explain anything.

I put the kettle on. The vet might want a cup of tea. Personally, in spite of this wretched headache, I feel a need for something stronger, but the chardonnay will have to wait. So will the summer evening. For now I need a shot of whisky. I pour it, down it, and feel the warmth spread through my chest. It soothes my jagged nerves, stops me from shaking, and helps me to focus. A second shot has me thinking coherently again, and when the doorbell rings, I feel fully prepared.

The vet is a tall, thin, thirty-something man with a serious expression, a receding hairline and rimless glasses. He has a kind smile, which transforms his face into something animated and delightful, and he listens patiently while, after closing the door to the hallway and moving us a little closer to the stereo speakers, I tell him that I came home from work to find my dog acting as if he had been hurt. I confirm that I have a competent, trusted dog walker, and that Badger hasn't been neglected or ill-treated; that he has in fact been loved and cherished every second of his life. I also confirm the details of our usual veterinary practice, and this vet makes a few notes. Then he kneels on the floor next to Badger's bed, and checks him over, slowly, gently, but very thoroughly.

'Okay, it's okay, boy,' he murmurs. Badger gazes at him with pain-filled but trusting eyes. The interaction touches me deeply and it's all I can do not to burst into tears. At length, the vet stands up, stretches his neck, and looks at me levelly.

'He may have a broken shoulder and a possible fracture to his nose. He has either been hit by a car or has been very strongly kicked by someone, and more than once. I think you need to have a chat with your dog walker to see if she can shed any light on what may have happened today, and let me have any information you get about it. I'd like to take him with me now to the surgery and have a good look over him, if that's ok? With sedation he should be fine to rest overnight. I'll x-ray him and we can take things from there.'

He sees my distress, and the tears welling up in my eyes. He places a hand on my arm. 'He'll be ok. It's painful, but it's not life threatening. It will all take time to heal, of course, and he may end up with a bit of arthritis in later years. But try not to worry. Can I take him now?'

As I start to nod, a small thump comes from the hallway; the sound of something having moved in the under-stairs cupboard. The vet raises his eyebrows at me.

'Vacuum cleaner,' I mumble. 'I'd left it in the hall, just put it away before you came.'

He seems satisfied with my explanation. 'I'm Simon Westrupp, by the way. Here's my card. The details of the practice I work at are on it, so you have the address and contact numbers. I'll take him now, and if you give us a call about ten tomorrow morning, we should be able to update you on his condition. We'll also contact your usual vet, get a report on his history, and let them know what's happening.'

With surprising ease, he lifts Badger gently in his arms, and heads towards the front door. I brush past him to go and open it for him. As I do it, I feel myself blushing. Briefly, from out of nowhere, I wonder if he is single, like me.

He drives away, with my beautiful best friend in the back of his estate car. I send a silent plea to any existing angels out there in the ether, to be with my dog and hold him safe until morning, and I close the front door.

I walk, zombie-like, to the under-stairs cupboard door. No sound comes from within. I know I need to deal with Junior, but right now I don't feel ready. My dog is alive and in the best possible hands, and that is all that matters, at this moment. Right now, I need another drink. I need to sit in a chair, with a drink, and contemplate what to do with Junior. He may be waking up already, and I need to have a plan for how to handle him.

The jazz CD finishes, and silence returns to the house. I pour another hefty whisky, and I sit. I think about Badger, and how lucky it is that those bastards hadn't killed my boy. The fact that they didn't was probably down to simple good luck and nothing more. They hurt him badly. They wouldn't have cared if he'd died, in fact I'm close to assuming that to have been their intention. At worst, intent to kill. At best, a lack of caring. Either scenario is so intolerable I can barely sit still. Every cell in my body roars with violation. I am quivering, and raw with rage.

I've never been squeamish about human pain. Show me a picture of dismembered, blood-covered body parts and entrails, and I'm more or less indifferent. Show me an animal in pain, or the victim of cruelty, and I want to rip someone's face off. I don't know what sort of person that makes me, and I suppose at some stage it might be cause for some self-examination about my level of humanity. But not now. Right now, as the whisky washes over me, I don't give a shit. And I hardly feel human at all.

2

Thursday
- Darren -

I didn't expect her to come home when she did. I'd been watching her come-and-go movements for fucking weeks, and she *never* came home before six. *Ever.* I'm not stupid enough to think it wasn't possible, but after weeks of watching, and never a day out of place, I just wasn't expecting her to come home right then. I estimated we still had a good hour and a half, to get clean away. If we hadn't decided to get cheeky and help ourselves to a beer, we'd have been away alright. It's that cheekiness that always seems to land me in the shit. My mum often says I push the envelope, and that's what'll always get me sprung, and she's right. She also said I never fucking learn. She's right about that too.

It's why we never rob people on a Friday afternoon. Sometimes they'll take an early dart from work for the weekend, and come home as early as lunch time. It's the one day you can never really bank on. But on a Thursday afternoon, just a random fucking day, after weeks of clockwork comings and goings? Nope. Didn't see that one coming.

I haven't a clue where Tommy is. It's been hours now and I haven't heard a fucking peep from him. I don't even know if he managed to pick up the bag of stuff before he got out of there. I expected him to be right behind me when I legged it out through that French door, but I was over the fence and two blocks away before I even looked behind me, and saw he wasn't following. He must have run a different way, but wherever he's ended up, he hasn't called me yet. I guess he will when he's ready, but I'm out of credit to phone or text him, so I'll have to wait. I expected him to have called me by now, but it is only his third burglary, so it's probably really spooked him, being sprung like that. He'll be lying low, I expect.

I feel bad about the woman's dog. I didn't mean to kick it quite as hard as I did, but it just wouldn't get out of the way, and then it started growling at me. The last thing I needed was for it to start barking, and draw unwanted attention to the house. The woman's pretty friendly with one of her neighbours, and we can always do without well-meaning mates wandering over to make sure everything's okay I had to shut the dog up, and nothing else was working, but I think I probably killed it.

It wasn't the dog's fault. I just couldn't take the risk. Collateral damage, we call it in the game, but it still feels like shit. I hope whoever is supposed to forgive us our sins will forgive me that one, at least.

Sometimes I wish I'd stayed on a positive path. I could have done more with my education, found another decent job, met a nice girl and all that. It's what every bloke wants; at least that's what they all say in prison. 'Wish it could be different. Wish I could start again, and do it all different.' Blah, blah, blah. Wish, wish, wish. If wishes were horses, beggars would ride. That's what people say. 'Make different choices,' as the prison shrinks all say, and you don't need to end up wishing.

I'm twenty-six, but I look a lot younger. Baby-face, my mates all call me. It's probably because I'm not doing the drugs like some of them. They might be in their twenties as well, but they look thirty or more. I once saw a poster on the back of the door at the local drug clinic, where I used to go with one of my mates to keep him company while he got his methadone. It showed a series of photos of a young girl, one of those progressive things; a different shot of the same girl every few months or so, while her drug habit got worse and worse. After two years she was hardly recognizable. A right bloody mess, she was, and it's really fucking sad.

But what's even sadder is it's the truth, and I know plenty of girls like that. They started off pretty enough, but they ended up with dropkick boyfriends; bad boys they thought were exciting, or sad, or mad. Blokes they thought they could 'fix.' What a waste of time and good intention. Most of those bastards weren't for fucking changing. They just basically took a good girl, introduced her to the smack, got her on the game, got her up the duff, all sorts of shit, and her lifestyle and looks just went down the fucking toilet. They're everywhere, those girls. If I had a quid for each one I'd seen, I wouldn't have to rob houses for money, would I?

There's nothing more tragic than a girl who used to be pretty, who's lost her looks and her self-respect because she didn't think enough of herself to go for something better than some tosser who ruined her life. If she's not slobbing around in filthy clothes and forgetting to drag a comb through her hair or have a bloody bath, she's at the other extreme, with her skirts up her arse, even if she's got terrible legs, and cheap, shitty shoes she can hardly walk in. Her tops are so low you can see pretty much everything, and she's slapped her make up on with a trowel. False eyelashes that look ridiculous, and enough lip gloss to send you skidding into the middle of next week. Who wants to kiss a girl like that? I bet half of those girls never even look at themselves in a mirror before they go out.

Girls like that are always trying to get my attention. Maybe they see me as a better prospect than the usual smack-heads they hang out with, since I'm really only into the drink, and nobody thinks that's as bad. My dad died of liver failure when I was sixteen and he would tell them different, but who really cares? Those girls just want to be rescued, and I'm no fucking Batman. I'm just a petty criminal who blew his chance at a decent life the first time he went to jail.

Because once you're tarred, that's it. There's few places to go when you finally managed to leave the school you hated and you just can't swallow any more authority. It's even bloody worse when you're not the best-looking bloke on the planet, despite what a lot of girls tell you, and you've managed to get yourself a criminal record. The only girls who want you are the slappers who've already been used and abused, and you end up being their lesser of a handful of evils.

I'm not interested in taking on someone else's kids either, and most of those tarts have at least one sprog they want taking care of as well. If I met a *decent* girl with a kid, or maybe even two, that might be a different story. But no nice girl is going to want to take a second look at me, is she? Not if she has any sense.

Tom should have got in touch by now. I suppose his mobile phone might be flat, like it often is. He lets it go flat because he can't stand his mum phoning him all the bloody time, wanting to know where he is, what time he'll be home, what he wants for his tea. She never stops hounding him.

Tommy's a really good kid at heart. He's pretty funny sometimes, and we have a good laugh. But he's a bit lost, like I was, so I took him under my wing a bit, teaching him the graft. His dad buggered off when he was three, so he's only ever had his mum and his sister, and maybe he sees me as a bit of a dad-like figure, even though I'm only 10 years older. That can seem like a lot to a kid. He failed all his GCSEs and ended up leaving school because he couldn't see the point in staying, and his mum never encouraged him to make anything of himself, so his prospects are even more rubbish than mine. At least I was able to get a job for a few years, back in the days when getting young men off the fucking streets and into work was a bigger priority than it seems to be nowadays.

Getting a crap start in life doesn't really help, and Tom's not the brightest spark off the anvil, so I do what I can. We never usually get a lot of money for what we've nicked, but it all helps. It pays for the booze and fags, some decent clothes now and then, and one time I made enough to have a nice night in a posh hotel with a girl I was seeing for a while. That was nice, and she was nice, but I got banged up for a job, not long after, and she left. She must have figured out that better prospects for a life of posh hotels would be found somewhere else!

But sometimes the stuff we get is more use by itself than the money we might get for it. A mate's sister's telly fell off its wall bracket, a month or two ago, and the screen smashed to pieces. I managed to nick her another one. Not quite as big, but it'll do her for now. Believe me, it's no piece of cake getting over a six-foot fucking fence unseen, even in the dead of night, with a forty-two-inch telly.

When I lost my job at the call centre, over six years ago now, I went off the rails a bit. I knew my mum would go spare about me ending up out of work again after getting such a lucky break so I didn't tell her, at first. I just used to go out and come home again at the normal times, so she'd be none the wiser. I'd spend my days at the pub, playing pool and dossing about with some blokes I'd known from school. They were wasters, and I knew it, but to be honest I didn't know what else to do with myself.

I was made redundant, and I was really pissed off about that, because it felt like I'd been singled out. I'd been there for a couple of years and others who had started later than I did still kept their jobs. Those of us who were let go all felt like there was another agenda, somehow, like we were the ones they really didn't want, but they never explained anything, or gave us a chance to be better at the job. Whatever the reason was, they just didn't want us anymore, and that was that.

Being made redundant at least meant I could get the dole straight away, so that's what I did. I signed on, and went to the pub, and that's how I filled my days, until one of the lads talked about getting some easy money from robbing some rich git a few streets over from where he lived. Some tosser with a big house and a seven-series BMW, and so fucking arrogant it made you want to kick the shit out of him.

That proposal was never going to help my prospects getting another half-decent job, but I never thought about that at the time, did I? Or about getting caught. It all just sounded simple, and I was so bloody bored with my stupid, messed-up life. I went for it, and lo and behold we got rumbled.

Overriding the bastard's alarm system was a piece of piss, but we never counted on him being a total gadget freak and having hidden CCTV cameras all over his house. Apparently he watched us on his i-phone, twenty miles away, while we raided his place, because one of his hi-tech cameras sent an activity alarm to the phone. By the time we'd grabbed what we wanted and made it to the back door, the police were there waiting for us, holding out the fucking handcuffs as we walked straight into them.

I did eight months for that, and it pretty much sealed my fate. Nobody was going to employ me after that, so I carried on claiming the dole, and doing a bit of robbing. Mostly I've been lucky, and I haven't got caught too many times. My sentences are usually only a few weeks, because it's always minor stuff, and I think they like my baby face, so I get away with lighter penalties more than the tougher, more brazen blokes do.

I don't go robbing as much as I used to these days anyway, because it's lost its buzz for me, if I'm honest. There's no more adrenalin rush. It's all about the relief of not getting caught now, and that's pretty much the long and short of it, but I do know the police are still never far from shining a spotlight on me. They only have to see me in the street now, and they'll find a reason to stop and search me. I'm a marked man. A common criminal. But I've made my bed, and now I have to lie in it. *C'est la vie.*

Was it my choice to be like this? I guess it depends on who you ask. I'm not even sure myself. All I know is I took the easy option at the wrong time and the rest, as they say, is history. I did pass all my A levels, back in the day. My grades weren't mind-blowing but they were pretty respectable, all B and B+. I could have done something with all that, but I didn't, and look at me now. Mister fucking Sparkling, the ultimate catch. I know my mum was upset that I didn't go to college or anything, but I was already fed up enough with school. I only ever went to get away from home, and with the choices I've made since I've more or less become unemployable.

Don't get me wrong. I don't *want* to just keep living on the dole, scrimping, penny-pinching, never being able to afford anything halfway decent, and living at home with my mum and her dumb-arse boyfriend because the dole won't cover the rent and bills on a decent flat. I'd only be able to afford some shithole with bunch of druggies for neighbours, and that wouldn't take me anywhere good, would it?

That's not a life. It's a basic bloody existence and nothing more, with fuck-all dignity, nothing to look forward to and nothing to aspire to, because you've shit in your own bed, so to speak, and you can't clean it up. It's there to stay, and you are what you are. Where you are is where you'll fucking stay. Prison taught me that.

Do I wish I could turn back the clock and make different choices? Yeah, of course I do. But I didn't, and that's it. If wishes were horses, as the saying goes. But a bit of robbing from time to time keeps me in decent boots or trainers, the odd bottle of good quality whisky, and the train fare to the seaside once a month so I can walk along a beach with a clear head and dream of a better life, and try to think of a legal way of getting it that I could ever afford. I keep drawing blanks, but I do keep trying.

3

Thursday
- Alison -

So… Junior – what to do? I know I should call the police, but I'd probably have a hard time explaining why I virtually hog tied him, gagged him, and stuffed him in a cupboard. They'd probably want to know why I didn't call them straight away, why I didn't report the crime of burglary in my home. And they'd be right to ask those questions. Problem is, I don't have any answers, other than to say I have no faith in the criminal justice system.

See, here's the thing. I have a very nice friend who was all over the news a few years ago for stabbing dead one of two young intruders to her home, a small hobby-farm on the outskirts of town. It wasn't their first visit. They'd robbed and terrorized her several times before, and the police had always said they couldn't do much. Remote cottage, poor responses, not enough resources, compromised evidence, yarda, yarda. They couldn't make any charges stick. The kids always managed to avoid any serious penalty and were always free to keep coming back, which they did, with depressing regularity.

One day, my friend decided she'd had enough of being terrified by intruders, then treated as irrelevant by the people who were supposed to protect her. So she took the law into her own hands. The next time those 'kids' turned up, she was ready for them. She stabbed one of them and killed him, in an act of defending her own safety and property.

And what happened next? She went to jail for it. They found my friend guilty of murder and sent her to prison for ten years. What a disgrace. Blame the victim? Send her to prison in return for her favour to the world of ridding it of a common, unscrupulous little thief? Where's the justice in that? Oh, and another thing. The police don't even come out to your house anymore, apparently, after a burglary. Unless someone is injured, they just issue you with a crime number over the telephone, for insurance purposes, and then they leave you to it. Not enough resources. Where's the reassurance in that?

So why would I call the police, then? What would they do? The damage to the house isn't enough to claim on my insurance. It's a broken windowpane, pure and simple, and I can take care of that myself. Badger's insured so that's covered too and the excess is something I can deal with. If I call the police, I'll be no better off, and this kid in my cupboard will walk. I know that as surely as I sit here breathing. Some fool funded by legal aid will argue that this little bastard's from a disadvantaged family (of course – aren't they all?), he needs a real break, he's a victim of his own sad circumstances, yarda, yarda. I've heard it all before.

Junior won't be punished for what he's done to me. He came into my house, with his scumbag friend, and they violated my privacy, with every intention of robbing me. Worse than that, they seriously injured my dog, my lovely, gentle, trusting Badger, who probably just wanted them to play with him. Instead they viciously attacked him and left him for dead.

Those two mongrels were in the process of stealing everything of true value from me, and they had the audacity to drink beer from my fridge, and laugh about it. Those aren't the kind of people who understand remorse. Why would I hand them over to the police, to be cosseted and protected? Even if they did by some miraculous turn of fate end up in prison, they'd have a better deal than most pensioners; warmth and company, flat-screen TVs, free dental care, three square meals a day, and too much time with other felons who will do little for them but help them hone their criminal skills so that next time they break into somebody's house they won't get caught.

It's the life of Riley, in prison. 'Deprivation of freedom' is the justice department's description, as 'punishment enough.' Who the hell are they kidding? Deprivation of freedom means *nothing* to people like that. In truth, most of them are probably better off in prison than they are on the bloody streets, but it's never for long enough to make a real difference, to them or to the public the system's supposed to protect. Prison's just a revolving door.

It's a joke. Except I'm not laughing, and neither is my injured dog.

No, the police will be a waste of time. My best option, I believe, is to terrorize this kid so thoroughly that he'll never dream of coming back here. I will scream in his face, slap him around, demand his name and address, find out who his parents are, take his photograph, and promise to plague him for the rest of his worthless life if I ever so much as smell him in the neighbourhood, ever again. If I give him a good enough fright he might learn something and he might leave good, innocent people alone. Fat chance, but it's worth a shot. I think it's my best one.

While the chardonnay continues to chill in the fridge, and while the sun sets on my lovely, abandoned summer evening, I finally acknowledge that I need to open the cupboard door and deal with Junior. It vaguely concerns me that there's been no sound from in there since the thump against the door while the vet was here. Perhaps he's being sensible and keeping quiet. Tied up or not, maybe he's even managed to manoeuvre himself into a position of attack for when the door opens. I need to be ready for that.

I stand up, shake myself down, and move to the cupboard. I bellow at the door and, channelling my still-simmering anger, I give it a hard kick for good measure. There is no response, but it doesn't surprise me. He had nothing to say from the very beginning. I guess he still thinks the silent treatment is his best weapon against what I might choose to do. My anger about Badger fuels me as I unlatch the door. There is still no sound, and no movement, but a strong smell of vomit hits my nostrils like a punch in the face.

I open the door wider and snarl into the darkness of the cupboard. 'Oi, pizza-face! You awake, you little bastard?'

There's no answer. The vacuum cleaner has fallen against the side of the door, so I pull it out. As I do it, Junior falls sideways out of the cupboard and his head hits the hallway floor. The duct tape across his mouth is spattered with vomit from his nose. His eyes, glazed, bulging and unseeing, stare up at me from his inert body. There is no life there. He is quite plainly dead.

I recoil in horror, as white noise descends. My back hits the wall as I stagger back in shock and sink to the floor. The blood roars through my ears as I take in the true meaning of what's happened. All I can hear is a hissing noise in my head, rising and falling in time with my pounding headache and heartbeat. My mind quickly casts its net, scrambling to piece together and explain what's here in front of me - the sequence of events.

Thanks to two blows to the head from the skillet, Junior is rendered unconscious with concussion. As he regains consciousness the concussion causes him to vomit but he can't let it out because his mouth is covered with duct tape and his nose isn't an adequate passage. This kid has choked to death on his own vomit in a dark, strange place with no chance to be heard. His short life, pathetic as it may have been, is over. And it's my fault. Whatever the little shit did, he did not deserve to die, let alone like this.

What the fuck do I do now?

* * *

I don't know how much time passes while I sit there on the floor in the hall. I sit, and sit, as the night starts to darken around me. There's no blood around Junior, just a bit of sick, and although it stinks, it's not much to indicate the passing of a life. I bring Badger back to my mind, my innocent but suffering dog, and I try to tap back into my anger, to find the fuel I need to rationalize this as okay, that Junior deserved this, that my dog could have died and I could have lost cherished family heirlooms so it was fair enough punishment. But who the hell am I kidding? Nothing can justify this. There's no way to make this okay.

I work to control my ragged breathing. The white noise eventually recedes, like the tide from a beach, leaving random bubbles of disbelief upon the sand. I can feel my bewildered brain gathering pace to clear the hurdle of the most vicious headache I've ever experienced, and land on the point where coherence can prevail. After a monumental effort to harness my hysteria, rationality returns.

I feel very cold, now. Maybe it's shock setting in. But right here, as the night slides by, while I sit here on the floor in the lengthening shadows, it occurs to me that I now have a very big problem indeed. The realization dawns that if the police weren't much of an option for me before, they're even less of one now.

My mind starts to scrabble for solutions. There's a really big old sea chest out in the garden shed. It's one of those battered old wooden ones that looks really cool, with sea labels on it, big, hefty hinges, and dents and travel scars galore. I bet that chest could tell some stories. I paid £100 for it at an antique store in an instant 'must-have' moment, and was planning to clean it up, fix it up, and have it in the house as a feature in my living room. I was going to store bedding in it. Now all I can think of is what a good temporary hiding place it's going to be for Junior until I can figure out what to do next.

Mobilized into action, I find the shed keys hanging on their hook in the kitchen, and I head out through the still-open French doors and down the path to the shed. There's a sack trolley in there, and I manoeuvre the chest onto it, to wheel it up to the house. I can't stop shaking, like I'm chilled to the bone. Shock. It has to be, since the night is still seasonably warm.

Back in the hallway, I have to lie the chest on its side so I can bundle Junior into it. He goes in without too much trouble, although I do have to bend his knees right up towards his chest to make him fit, and I then have to lever the chest back onto the sack trolley. The trip back to the shed takes somewhat longer, as I'm still shaking like a leaf and the dead weight I'm now pushing keeps threatening to topple, which leaves me no option but to go more slowly.

Down in the shed, as the dark mantle of night finally falls, I lever the chest and sack trolley back to where they were. Nothing looks like it has been disturbed. I take a quick look at the scene, but I don't linger. I don't want to be here. I have sick to clean up, in any case, and getting the stench of it out from the under-stairs cupboard is going to take some time. I need to get on with that.

An hour, a full bottle of bleach and several broken fingernails later, I'm done. The cupboard is clean, the vacuum cleaner is back in there like it had never been disturbed, and everything looks normal. It just doesn't feel that way, and I wonder if it ever will again.

On some level, I know that my life has changed forever. I have changed forever. And there's no going back from here, no retracing of steps with the option of doing anything differently. It is what it is, and I need to focus forward.

Sleep is out of the question, so it's back to the whisky. I retrieve my i-pad from the filthy bag on the counter. The filigree box comes out, as does my Tissot watch, the two hundred American dollars I'd had folded at the bottom of my underwear drawer (*the bastards went through my knickers?*) and assorted other little trinkets, more of sentimental than actual value, but important all the same. Only then, when I've emptied the bag, do I start thinking about Senior. The one that got away. Where is he now? Is he concerned about his friend? He didn't seem to be, when he took off like a bat out of hell from this kitchen, leaving Junior to face the music and the wrath of a screaming-blue-murder, skillet wielding woman, all alone.

And it's murder alright. Or is it? Murder requires intent, I remember that from stuff I read at Uni, too many years ago to count. For the charge of murder to stick, there has to be clear intent. I didn't intend to kill this kid – *or did I?* I wanted to, I really did. I was angry enough to want to take his life the way I thought he'd taken Badger's. But that's not the same thing as following through, is it? *Is it?*

It's up to the prosecution to prove intent, and up to the defence to rebut it. No intent equals manslaughter and people can get off that charge without formal penalty, under mitigating circumstances where compassion can prevail. However, if they've bashed their victim twice with a heavy hunk of metal, then proceeded to bind and gag him (cutting off his most important airway), before concealing him in a cupboard and leaving him there to die, it's a bit of a stretch to imagine any judge or jury viewing that with compassion.

As the contents of the whisky bottle dwindle and my head fills up with facts and fancy, I remain stone cold sober in just another example of justice being absent from the frame.

4

Thursday
- Darren -

So where the bloody hell's Tom, then? I'm starting to really worry about him now. I haven't heard a thing, and it's been close to five hours. Marla Findlay, his mum, keeps phoning me, and I keep ignoring her. I wouldn't know what to say to her, if I answered. The truth would make her go spare, so I'd have to lie to her and I'd rather not, at least until I know what the deal is with Tom himself. If the bastard's already gone to the cash-up with that stuff and taken off with the money, I'll fucking kill him.

Some people reckon that as robbers we don't have any scruples. Mum's boyfriend Pat calls me a waste of space. Not that he's any great shakes, himself. He runs a greasy chip shop, and he finishes late, then he goes to the pub, and he comes in as pissed as a fart most nights. I don't know what the fuck she sees in him, but he's nice to her most of the time, so I guess she's grateful for an easy life, as much as anything else. But he calls himself successful, that bloody drunk, and he calls *me* a waste of space. I think others would call that irony.

Victims and critics of crime have plenty to say on the subject too. They believe people who commit crime have no moral compass, but that's not true. Most people would be surprised to learn that we do in fact have our own code of honour. There's people we won't rob, others we won't wrong, and there's stuff we won't do to each other, like shag each other's women or run off with profit that should be shared.

Tom already knows the code. He wouldn't run off with my share of the graft. *Would he?*

Maybe there's something he wants bad enough to keep all the money for, but he's never said. If he does want something bad enough, he only has to say, and we'd work out how to do enough graft for him to get it. That's how it works, and he knows that too. If he wants fifty quid, we work out how to get a hundred, so we *both* get fifty. But running off with shared profit? Nah. He wouldn't.

So what's happened to him then?

If he hasn't been in touch by bedtime tonight, I'm pretty sure it'll mean something's wrong. But what? And what do I do? If he doesn't show up, what do I do?

Come on, Tom. This isn't funny.

You know, thinking about it, that bloody woman had a metal frying pan in her hand when she came into the kitchen, screaming like a banshee. What if she hit him?

Nah, she wouldn't have done that. *Would she?* People like her don't do that kind of thing. Too refined. Too 'civilized,' to actually smack someone with a frying pan. In any case, Tom's quick on his feet, he'll have dodged her and followed after me. But he might not have got the stuff. I think he'll have been lucky to have got away with that stash. We might have to write that one off, and hope like hell she doesn't report it or remember what we look like. I got out of there pretty fast. I don't know if she got a good look at me or not.

That's it! That's why Tommy's AWOL. He's probably embarrassed that he left without the stuff, and he's probably too bloody scared to tell me. That'll be what it is. I'm more worried now about demented fry-pan-bitch calling the plod.

I think I'll sneak back to that house tonight, now it's gone dark, and take a look around. Just to see how the land lies. I keep thinking about the dog. If the dog's dead then she'll definitely report it. And if she can identify us, we're screwed, not just for the burglary. Even though we may not have got away with anything, it's still breaking and entering, and I'll be back in bloody jail again. Tom's too young, he'd just get juvie if they convict him, but a stretch in a YOI is bad enough. And if the dog's dead, what will they charge us with, there?

That's the worst part; that poor dog. I can live with doing time for a burglary again. But what about killing someone's loved pet, for the sake of a quick few quid? It's almost as bad as mugging a cripple for the price of a bus fare, and it's another part of the general code we live by. We don't hurt people's pets. I do know some geezers case places with dogs, and they take drugged meat to knock them out while they do the place over, then after they leave, the dogs wake up and all is right with the world. Me, I wouldn't want to get that serious about it. I wouldn't know how much sedative to put in the food, anyway. That's serious shit, and to my mind it's still hurting them. Overriding burglar alarms is one thing, but drugging pets? I might be a bastard, but I don't want to start doing that.

Why the fuck did we pick that place? There had to be easier houses; what made me choose that one? In all the time I was watching it, I never knew there was a bloody dog in there! How did I miss that? And I love dogs. I truly do, and that was a beautiful dog. Under any other circumstances I'd have given it a cuddle.

I'm so sorry, little mate, I really am. If I could only take back one shitty thing I've done in my entire fucked-up life, it would be that.

So I have to go back. I have to see if that dog is alive. I have to see if that woman has called the plod, and I need to try and figure out where Tom went. I'm not sure how I can work all that out from just going back there and poking around, but I feel like I have to try. Marla Findlay keeps ringing and its driving me mental. So I'll take a look around, then whether I find something out or not, I'll have to take her call and tell her the truth, that I haven't seen him since this afternoon when we were hanging out together, and I don't know where he is. It's a half-baked, uncomfortable version of the truth, but it's all I can give her, for now.

I don't dare go over the fence again and into the garden, but when I look into it I can see every light in the house is on, and none of the curtains are drawn. There's no sign of the dog, in the kitchen or anywhere else. Moving around to stand in the shadows by the side of the house, I can see into the living room, and nothing seems out of the ordinary, but she's there on her sofa, sitting very still, staring at the wall with a glass of what looks like brandy or something, in her hand. She looks incredibly sad and I'm sure, more than ever now, that I killed her dog. I have to fight the urge to sob, because I can feel something like the worst kind of sorrow coming from her, and for the first time in my life

I feel completely fucking wretched, looking at the impact of what I've done.

It's official. I am the world's biggest bastard.

Swallowing down a lump in my throat for someone else is a first, for me. I don't usually feel much in the way of 'empathy for my victims,' as the prison shrinks always ask me. They're always disappointed when I shrug my shoulders, as if I don't know what they're on about. They then write their silly little notes in their silly little folders with their silly little pens, they smile sadly at me, and then they get up and leave. I know what they're thinking; that I can't relate to anyone's pain at the trouble I've caused them.

The loss of inanimate objects, the feelings of violation, none of that has ever made much sense to me, especially after one of the lads at the pub explained that most people, in the kind of homes we go and rob have insurance that covers their losses. Family heirlooms might be a different matter, I suppose, but I've never been that big on attachment to things.

We used to have lots of 'things' when I was a kid, but they all got sold, mostly to keep paying the rent my dad couldn't meet after spending all his wages at the pub and the bookies every week. When an antiques dealer turned up and took away the box of tin toy soldiers I got from my Granddad, I decided never to get attached to 'stuff' again.

Stuff comes, stuff goes. If its family heirlooms, it's a bit sad I guess, for people who are sentimental enough to have attachments to things, but if it's covered by insurance that's grand because the chances are that some poor sod we may have robbed of his laptop can get a much better, newer one off his insurance. If he'd been sensible enough to do what the experts always advise and back everything up, he'd end up better off. And if he'd been stupid and not done that, then it's his own stupidity that makes his life hard, not what I might have done.

But this feels very different. This was a living, breathing, beautiful animal that I've taken away, and I feel crushed. I feel absolutely blown *apart* by this, and seeing that woman looking so bereft and spaced out, I hate myself more now than I ever have in my life before.

But I have to snap out of it, and get away from here. I can see there's no clues anywhere as to what's happened to Tommy, so there's no point in hanging around. The longer I stay here, the greater the risk of being seen by someone in the neighbourhood, and with my face? One phone call and I'd be handcuffed and banged up by morning.

So I'm none the wiser, and after returning to the scene of the crime, I just feel like shit, in a way I never have before. Part of me wants to run up to the front door, bang on it, and tell that woman how sorry I am that I killed her lovely dog. I wanted to own up to it, take whatever punishment that comes, knowing nothing I'd say could ever make it right, but wanting to try, for the first time in my life, to make amends.

But the coward in me won the toss. I couldn't make myself do it. Instead, here I am walking away, hood up, head down, walking with purpose, like I have somewhere to go, like nobody would look at me twice and wonder what I was doing.

This estate is old and well established, but it's like a rabbit warren, and I'm a bit disoriented in the dark. Everything looks different at night so I head towards the noise of traffic on the busy main road, rather than rely on my instincts to get me round the back streets and out.

It's more than six hours now since I last saw or heard from Tom, and nothing looks to be out of the ordinary at that house, at least nothing that makes me think he got into any trouble there. It's a mystery. He's just disappeared, off the face of the earth.

Back on the main road, a car draws up alongside me as I'm walking, and it's the local fucking plod. Great, that's all I need right now. I try to keep a smile on my face so they don't clock how nervous I am at being picked up just a few streets away from the last bloody job, and on the same bloody night.

'Good evening, Mr Davies,' comes a bored voice, one I recognise from countless other run-ins, mostly just like this one, when I'm innocently walking down a road, minding my own bloody business. It's Constable Benning, and she always treats me politely, no matter what situation she finds me in. She's nice enough, for a plod.

'What has you out and about, miles from home, at this time on a Thursday night-cum Friday morning?'

'Just going home from visiting a mate,' I mumble.

The car has stopped and both coppers are out of it and walking towards me. So I stop and let them search me, and they find nothing incriminating, of course. It's not like I wander around with a fucking crowbar or a set of skeleton keys or something. *'Burglarious tools of trade by night!'*

'Get into the car please, Mr Davies,' Benning says, tolerantly. We'll drop you at home.'

'No thanks, officers. I'm happy to walk, don't want my mum going septic, seeing me come home in the back of a squad car.'

'It's not an option, Darren. You're making us nervous, wandering the streets after midnight, and you know we don't like feeling nervous. Get in.'

So I get in. The ride home takes just five minutes. In that time, I banter with Benning a bit, and to her credit she does respond, good natured-like. If you're not on the wrong side of the plod, most of them are actually okay. Basically they're just doing a job that some poor bastard's got to do.

'Any burglaries in the neighbourhood lately?' I enquire, as casually as I can.

'Either you're finally starting to get good at it Darren, or there's not been, for a few nights. Not that we're resting on our laurels, mind, so don't forget that. Yours will be the first door we come knocking on, if the situation changes.'

The living room curtains twitch as the car pulls up outside my mum's house. I thank the officers for their consideration in ensuring I get home safely, without running the risk of being mugged or murdered by a random, street-skulking maniac, to which they respond with sarcastic laughter. Benning's partner puts two fingers to his eyes and then points them at me. I do the same back, as they pull away.

They're watching me? Well, I'm watching them too, the bastards. I turn around and brace myself for the onslaught of questions my mum is going to ask, when I walk through that door. Most times, when I end up in a squad car, it's bad news for all of us. She might take some convincing that this time it's not, but right now I have bigger things to worry about - *like where the hell has my mate disappeared to, and why hasn't that bloody woman reported the burglary, or the death of her dog?*

5

Friday
- Alison -

I wake up on the sofa with a crick in my neck, as the sunlight fights its way insistently through a tiny chink at the top of the curtains where they don't quite meet as they should. I've never noticed that before. Do they always do that, or did I just make a poor job of trying to close them last night?

I'm disoriented for a second or two, vaguely wondering why I'm down in the living room and still in all my clothes, when the recollection of the previous night's events surges forward and crashes across me like a physical assault. I'd just laid down here in the darkness, hardly moving. At some stage, after hours of playing everything back in my head, over and over again in an effort to snap out of the numbness that had swamped me, I must have fallen asleep.

Shit. I glance at my watch, it's six-fifteen. The headache is back with a vengeance, and my mouth feels like the bottom of a dirty birdcage. I can still smell bleach on my hands, there's a strong smell of stale whisky, and I fancy I can still smell vomit, although of course that's probably just the olfactory part of my brain playing tricks on me. Knowing I'm in desperate need of a shower, I haul myself to my feet and stumble up the stairs.

Before I eventually managed to fall asleep, at whatever time it must have been, I spent a lot of the night trying to rationalize things as much as I can. Under the circumstances, I'm more sure than ever now that the police are not an option. There's no way I'll come out of this unscathed if I tell them what happened, because although my behaviour at the time might have been deemed by some psychologist to have been 'irrational,' killing a child and concealing the body isn't something that can be easily explained by an excuse of 'temporary insanity.' And, as much as Junior was a criminal, he was young enough to be classified as a child, in the eyes of the law. He couldn't have been more than fifteen or sixteen.

Irrational? For God's sake, I'm not insane, or even unstable! Most people would describe me as practical, down to earth, and 'reasonable' to the point of boring people rigid. I'm about as even-tempered as you'll ever get, until someone harms me or my loved ones, but who would be any different?

I'm a victim. *My* house got broken into, *my* dog got viciously attacked, *my* belongings were about to be taken out of the house to God knows where and probably sold for a pittance. *My* privacy got violated. But none of that counts for anything, does it, in the face of what's happened since? I know that, but I sure as hell do not intend to go to prison for doing what I felt I had to do.

The facts are pretty clear, even to my addled head. If I'd hit this kid, knocked him out and called the police straight away, I might have had a decent defence. But I didn't do that, so I don't have a scrap of one now. I made stupid choices. I didn't think things through, I let my anger govern my actions and now a young man is dead.

The bald truth is that I will have to suffer the emotional consequences, however difficult they may be, for the rest of my own life. I know that even once I've sorted this, gotten rid of any evidence that can tie me to Junior's death, there is no going back to the person I was just yesterday. This event has changed me forever, and it will haunt me for all of my days. That's my punishment; my cross to bear. I have to suck it up and get on with the practicalities of covering my tracks and learning how to live the rest of my life knowing that I've taken someone's else's.

I step into the shower, turn the dial to as hot as I can stand it, and scrub myself as thoroughly as I can. I check my watch again. It has just gone half past six, and the morning has started for most working people. Bill, my neighbour, will be out jogging, and ordinarily I'd be taking Badger for his early morning ablutions about now too. Bill and I often meet on the local towpath, exchange a greeting, and Badger gets an ear-scratch from him. Normal life that will probably never feel quite normal again, at least not like it did.

I miss my gorgeous boy this morning, the house is far too quiet without him, but its three and a half hours before I can ring the vet to find out how he is, so I'd better make those hours count. I can't just sit here staring at the walls.

I start by calling my work and leaving a voicemail message to say that I won't be going in to work today because I've been up all night with the same crippling headache that forced me to leave early yesterday, which still hasn't gone away. As I say the words, I realise it's the truth – *what the hell is wrong with my head?*

So rarely do I ever take a day off sick, I'm confident there will be no questions asked. A phone call will probably come later in the day from Daphne, my friend at work, to see how I am. I can fake it if I have to but if this damn headache doesn't dissipate, I *won't* have to.

At least it's Friday. That means I have three days to get to grips with this mess, and what to do about it, before I have to go back to work. Not having my head together by Monday morning is not an option, so I have a lot to do before then.

I wash the floors thoroughly again, to get rid of any traces of DNA that might be problematic if the shit does end up hitting the fan; a possibility I'd be stupid to discount. I remove, wrap and dispose of the rest of the glass from the broken windowpane, and clean up the kitchen like I normally do, with the usual cleaning paraphernalia. Nothing out of the ordinary but by the time I'm finished I'm as satisfied as I'll ever be, that I've done a thorough job. Just a homeowner cleaning her house, like everyone does, your Honour.

Next, I deal with the grubby holdall the terrible two intended to use to take my belongings away. It's filthy, scruffy, and one of the handles is fraying and threatening to come away from the main body of the bag. It's worthless and horrible, so I get the shears out of the utility drawer and cut it up into small pieces, before putting it in the grate in the living room, on top of paper and kindling, and I set it alight.

The pieces crackle and burn, filling the room with the acrid stench of singed fabric and burning plastic. It makes my eyes water so I light a few scented candles to help dissipate the smell. I shut the living room door so the fumes don't permeate the rest of the house, and I pray the neighbours don't question the fact that I've lit my fire at half past seven on a Friday morning in late summer. Wobbly and shivery, perhaps with a touch of food poisoning, I needed to light the fire to warm up a bit, your Honour.

Once the holdall has burned away, and only a small pile of smouldering ashes remain, I pour enough water onto them to put out the last of the smoke. It makes the smell a little worse, but only temporarily and once everything is reduced to a soggy, blackened pile of gloopy ashes I scoop it all out of the grate with the fireside shovel and slide the sludge into a plastic carrier bag.

Its bin day, and I'm just about to open the front door to put my soggy parcel in the bin and wheel it to the kerbside when I remember I'm supposed to be off sick. I race upstairs, hastily get undressed again and put my pyjamas on.

Back downstairs, I pick up the carrier bag, and have another small epiphany that it would be better to put it into the kitchen bin, then take the whole thing out, as normal. I do not want to draw attention to myself. This morning, I'm just a regular person, like every other in our street, who takes the kitchen rubbish bag out to the wheelie bin and wheels it to the kerb for collection. I'm in my pyjamas because I'm unwell, your Honour, but the bin needs to go out nonetheless, because rubbish lorries wait for no-one, sick or otherwise.

I check my watch again. It's still only eight o'clock. I have another two hours before I can ring the vet. I know they don't start until nine, and they'll need time to assess Badger again. But the minutes drag by in agonizing slowness, while I wait till the magic hour of ten, to hear how my beautiful boy is doing.

Badger came to me two years ago. He was only a puppy at the time, mad and crazy, like only Border Collie puppies can be. His owner was a neighbour of mine who'd been offered a job too good to refuse in Hong Kong.

I hadn't planned on having a dog, but my neighbour was so gutted to be having to re-home his pup, he was completely distraught and nearly in tears, and in a moment of weakness I agreed to take Badger on. I'd never had a dog before, so it was alien territory to me, but as it turns out, it was the best decision I've ever made. We love one another utterly and completely, Badger and I, and the thought of him not being around anymore is literally more than I can stand. I'm clinging on to Simon

Westrupp's assertion that his injuries weren't life threatening. He's a young, healthy dog, and he's in the best possible hands. If that doesn't turn out to be enough, I don't know what I'll do.

Wandering aimlessly through the house, I tick off my mental checklist. House, clean. Broken glass, gone. Holdall, disposed of. I glance at my watch, it's eight-fifteen. Glaziers might be at work by now, so I fire up my i-pad and Google who might be available to do a house call at short notice in my area. I find two with mobile numbers, and one firm promises a same-day service, so I give them a call. Late afternoon is the earliest time they can come, so I accept the time they offer, and I've bought myself a bit of time to come up with a story about how the glass got smashed. Kids with a ball? I might have to try and do better than that. The broom handle fell against it, your Honour.

A low growl rumbles through from my stomach. The last thing I feel like doing is eating, but since I didn't have a meal last night, I realise I need to eat something. Solids right now would make me heave, but I might be able to keep down a liquid breakfast. I whip up a smoothie, with a banana, a pear, two nectarines, and a handful each of grapes and spinach.

As I pour the milk into the blender on top of the fruit and switch it on to blend, it occurs to me how ridiculous this banal representation of normality really is, all things considered. I've just cleaned up my own crime scene, disposed of some key evidence and covered as many of my tracks as I am able thus far. I'm calling glaziers as if kids really *had* kicked a ball through my window, I've taken my guilt-loaded garbage out, and I'm standing in my kitchen blending fruit for a smoothie, like butter wouldn't melt in my mouth.

What nobody surveying this routine scene of domestic normality would see is the effort required to ignore the small matter of a dead body crammed into a shipping trunk, down in my garden shed.

I had plans tonight, but I'll have to cancel them. It's no big deal, just a dinner in town with a few work colleagues, to celebrate a couple of promotions. I send a text message to Daphne, stating that I'm poorly, sending regrets, but telling her to have fun. A text comes back within seconds 'No! Poor you! Will call you later x.'

More banal normality, except that if it was, I wouldn't be feeling so jittery and wired. Standing still takes effort, sitting down feels impossible, and sleep? Not a chance – although that's what I thought just a few hours ago, before my traitorous psyche decided it had other plans for me. I'm grateful for having the sleep, of course, but it makes me wonder what sort of person I must really be, to be able to simply go to sleep after taking someone else's life in a random, unexpected act of violence in my own home.

It occurs to me that while my world has tilted on its axis, everyone else's just carries on as normal. Nobody else has a clue. It's between me and whatever God is out there – and Junior too, of course. I've never been much for religion, but if I wasn't going to hell before, I'm pretty sure I've got a first class, gold-plated, Willy Wonka ticket now!

I reflect on what my original intentions were, with Junior. I'd planned to give him the fright of his life, off the back of my rage at what him and his scumbag mate had done to my dog, and the entitlement they seemed to feel they had, to ransack my home, drink my beer, and laugh at the fact. I briefly consider what that might have been like, just giving him a fright, but my brain refuses to go there. It's as if, somewhere in my pounding head, I know that 'what if's' will serve no purpose now, because what's done is done, and having to focus on what's next leaves no room for anything that might confuse what now has to be the clearest picture I've ever been forced to look at.

It's nine o'clock. Only an hour left to go now, before I can ring the vet. I spend the time going over what my weekend plans are, what I can change and rearrange, how much time I would need to dispose of a body, and how I would plan to do it. I cannot involve anybody else. This is my mess, and I alone have to clean it up.

I find myself properly sobbing now, for the first time since all this happened. Not for Junior; although he does deserve some tears I can't summon any for him, at least not yet. I'm crying for my dog, in pain and suffering. I'm crying for myself, and for the fact that I've so spectacularly fucked up my own life.

I have such a huge, horrible job to do now, and there isn't a soul in the world I could ask to help me. After all, you can't ask just *anybody* to help you dispose of a body, can you? It would have to be a really good friend, wouldn't it, someone you really trusted not to rat on you? And who in their right mind would put that good a friend in such a terrible position? It's an unthinkable prospect and at this precise moment I feel crushed by the weight of the knowledge, of just how utterly alone I really am, with this.

My mind darts back to a case I heard about, years ago, where a woman who'd been systematically abused by her husband for years and years killed him one night by accident. She put a sedative into his bedtime cup of tea, because she just wanted one night of not being raped and beaten, just one quiet night. But he didn't wake up. He died, and she got a couple of friends to help her conceal the crime and bury his body in the garden.

That's what got her convicted, in the end. That poor, panicked, desperate woman went to jail on a life sentence, in just another example of the farce they call justice. But her friends went to jail too, for helping her. Aiding and abetting, the courts called it, so several lives destroyed then, not just the two in the original frame.

It's hard to look into all that jumble of emotions and find the reality of the drive, the motives, the disbelief, the panic and fear, the desperation and the justification. It's all so complicated, but the law (which is an ass, of course) relentlessly seeks to simplify things and provide the 'fitting punishment for the crime.' You kill someone, you pay with your freedom, in all but the most extenuating circumstances. Battered women occasionally get treated with compassion, but that poor woman didn't, and neither did her friends.

It's half-past nine. So far I've come up with tomorrow night, for body disposal, under the cover of darkness. I can bring the chest up from the shed to the front door with the sack trolley. But I only have a hatch-back car, and while the chest will certainly fit in there, lifting it from the ground into the back of the car is more than I'm capable of.

So I will ask my friend and neighbour Bill. I'll tell him it's a chest full of heavy fabrics that my mum wants, and I'm taking it to her. He will help me lift it into the car. I just have to make sure the lid is closed and locked, and can't fly open. As for getting it out at the other end, well, I will have to figure that out once I've decided on a location. And that's the next challenge.

6

Friday
- Darren -

My mate Ginge has just phoned to ask if I want to go out tomorrow night. A bunch of the lads are off up town, but I really don't know if I fancy it. It's usually a brilliant night, a good laugh, but I'm really too worried now about Tommy to enjoy myself. It's been a full day, now, and there's been neither sight nor fucking sound of him.

This feels bad. I don't know what to think. All I know is that whatever stash we might have got away with from that house, it would never be enough for him to keep avoiding me for a whole night and a day, even if he had cashed it in. And his mum and his girlfriend are both going mental, because he hasn't been in touch with them either. I finally answered Marla's call this morning, and I told her I'd not seen Tom since yesterday afternoon and I'd tried calling him but just kept getting his voicemail. All of that was the truth. If I've called the bastard once, I've called him twenty times.

She said she'd rung the local hospitals, but nobody knew anything about him. It's like he's just evaporated into thin air. It's only been a day, but something is wrong; something about *all* of this feels dead fucking wrong.

I've been lying low all day today, thinking that Tom would sort himself out, willing him to, and get in touch when he was ready. I did think, at first, that he was just a bit freaked by being found like that, by the house owner screaming her head off and waving a fucking frying pan at us. It was bloody scary, obviously not something we planned on, and me running out on him like that wouldn't have helped. Neither would the prospect of the dog being dead.

And there's one other thing. The plod haven't been near me today, so far at least. All I can think is that the house owner mustn't have got a really good look at us both, because if she had reported it, and given them a proper description, they'd be all over me like a rash by now, especially after finding me in the neighbourhood last night. It wasn't the best of moves on my part, to go back there, but I just couldn't stop myself. If she'd reported anything, plod would've been hauling me down to the station on the off-chance, never mind giving me a lift home.

With my baby-faced mug-shot, there in the book and on the screen for all to see, if she'd got a good look at me she'd have picked me out easy. Not so much Tom maybe, although he was probably there for at least half a minute longer, which is actually a long time to be staring at someone. So she might remember his scabby mug a bit more than mine. But he doesn't even have a rap sheet yet, so even if she described him to a tee, he still hasn't been picked up because they wouldn't even know who they were looking for! The plod wouldn't lie to his mother, in any case. He's a minor. They'd have been battering her fucking door down if they had him, or a description of someone like him at a burglary, but clearly they don't.

So it looks like the woman didn't call them, maybe because nothing got taken, in the end. If Tom left empty-handed, she still had all her stuff, and if she hasn't filed a report, she must've had her reasons. It's not up to me to understand what they are, but to say I'm a bit baffled right now is an understatement.

The truth is, I can't make sense of *any* of this. I might come across to some folk like I don't have much between the ears, but I can string a few thoughts together, and I can work a few things out. I'm not as stupid as many might believe. But obviously I'm not that clever, am I, because something about all this makes me really nervous. Something's just not adding up, here, but I'm fucked if I can see what's not right.

After what happened last night, Tom would just want to go home to his mum, wouldn't he? He wouldn't be hiding away anywhere by himself for any reason, not for this long. He'd want to be around people who could make him feel better, like his dog, and his mum and his girlfriend. Maybe even me.

Tom, where are you? Just come home, for God's sake. My head feels like it's going to blow open.

People sometimes ask me why I hang about with Tom, since he's just a kid. Even his mum wants to know why I want to spend time with him. Truth is, all the lads I know around my own age are either decent blokes making good lives for themselves, who don't want to know me because I'm such a fucking loser, or they're drop-kick jail-birds exactly like me, and as I get older I'm starting to realise that I just don't enjoy being around them anymore. I'm fed up with listening to their stupid stories of who they've ripped off, who they've beaten up in a pub fight, what tart they've been shagging, or any of the other stupid shit that adds up to what their lives are all about.

Tom, to me, is like the kid brother I never had. He looks up to me, and that feels good, like I can make a difference. I'm not teaching him anything sparkling though, am I? Robbing people blind, but at least its teaching him how to survive, how to get by in a world where most of the good opportunities are never going to happen for him. Except I've let him down, haven't I? If I hadn't run off yesterday from that house like my arse was on fire, if I hadn't just left him, he wouldn't be missing would he?

Thanks to me, and my 'teaching,' he's disappeared. His girlfriend won't stop sobbing, and his mum's been going mental after ringing every human being she knows to see if any of them have seen or heard from him. She's drawn nothing but blanks, and she's now saying that he's never not come home before, or let her know when he had a plan not to. She has now filed an official missing person report, and she was kind enough to let me know that the plod are going to want to speak to me at some stage, probably sooner than later.

Add to all that, a woman's poor dog is dead, and we didn't even get away with anything close to making it worth it. The bag we stashed everything into has got my greasy paw-prints all over it too, so it wouldn't be hard to trace me. The plod have already got my fingerprints and DNA in their files. But that bloody woman hasn't reported the crime, and not knowing why is doing my head in.

Maybe I *should* go out tomorrow night. It might take my mind off things. I'm not usually much of a worrier. I'm usually okay at shaking things off, after they happen, but this time everything feels different. Maybe if I do go out, have a few bevvies and a bit of a laugh, I might feel better. Maybe it's that kind of normal I need right now, since worrying about Tommy isn't going to bring him home any sooner, and I can't do anything to undo what's been done.

I just can't get that image of the dog out of my head. All we wanted to do was make a bit of money. That woman didn't deserve to lose her dog. I'm the worst kind of bastard, and a few beers won't change that, but it just might let me forget about myself for an hour or three.

7

Friday
- Alison -

It's still not quite ten in the morning, but I just can't wait any longer. With shaking hands I call Simon Westrupp. The practice receptionist answers and puts me straight through to him. He answers with a warm chuckle, saying 'I thought this might be you! I suspected you wouldn't be able to wait.' His voice sounds calm, ordinary and reasonable. It's an ordinary day for him, of course. He sees dogs with injuries all the time.

Badger does have a fractured shoulder, but thankfully, his nose is just badly bruised.

'He's been kicked, I think, or hit by something heavy, possibly been glanced by a passing car. Last night I treated him for shock, and he's come through it very well. He's a healthy, robust dog, which helps a lot. I did the x-rays last night too, to be sure of what I was working with, and he's stable enough for surgery, which I'd like to do today, if that's okay?'

I ask what that entails, and Simon confirms it will involve a plate and screws. Badger's nose is fine, it looked worse than what it is, but it's badly bruised and painful and it might hurt him to eat for a while.

'I've given him some antibiotics and pain relief, which has kicked in. I'll do the surgery this afternoon, and I'd like to keep him here through the weekend, just to keep an eye on how he settles, but you can certainly come in and see him. I'm sure that would cheer you both up no end?'

I make arrangements to go straight down there. I realise I have to take a chance with the house being unsecured thanks to the broken pane of glass in the French door, but it's a chance I'm willing to take. I do stash the valuables under the stairs behind the vacuum cleaner though, before I set off. It would be too ironic to be robbed again within twenty-four hours of the first attempt.

Badger is pleased to see me, but he is, of course, a long way from his usual boisterous self. He raises his head, licks my hand and I hug him gingerly, not wishing to cause any more pain to my beautiful boy. I find myself weeping openly with the relief of seeing him in one piece. The memory of finding him on the kitchen floor, unconscious and bleeding, is one that will stay with me forever. That gut-wrenching, ice-cold fear that he was dead was a feeling I'll never forget.

Simon Westrupp chuckles initially at my display of emotion, which I'm struggling to rein in. The tears just keep on coming, though, and after half a minute or so of uncontrollable sobbing, he puts his hand on my shoulder. It feels warm and steadying, and it reassures me. He doesn't say a word, but I know he understands. He sees distraught pet owners all the time. He has to deal with them on a daily basis, so this is nothing new for him. He has no idea how much is really going on with these tears. I eventually get myself under control and by the time I do, a veterinary nurse has miraculously appeared with a cup of sweet, hot tea.

'Tea and sympathy! It's what we do here all the time,' Simon says. 'We provide tea and sympathy, and we do a bit of vet work on the side.'

He goes on to explain the surgery process, and I'm so relieved it can be done straight away, and with minimum fuss. He's such a nice man, a gentle soul, and I can tell his work is a true vocation. His touch with Badger is so caring, as well as competent. I've decided that from now on I want him to be Badger's regular vet. I tell him so, and he pulls a face. 'You might want to think again when you see the bill, I'm afraid.'

I assure him that the amount is irrelevant, and it really is, because no sum of money could replace my treasured boy, even if I didn't have insurance to cover the bills. It's only money. I have one last cuddle with Badger and say goodbye to him, with the promise that I'll see him again on Monday, after work.

Simon advises that Badger needs a cage to stay in, to curb his mobility while the break is healing, but he can sort that out for me, as they sell them there at the practice. All going well Badger should be able to come home by Monday evening. Simon will drop him off at the house, to save me from trying to wrestle with him on my own, with the injury. 'I can help you get him settled, then you two can take things at your own pace together from there.'

Simon locates and loads a suitable cage into the back of my car. But as I drive home, I find myself suddenly overcome with a wave of nausea so severe it forces me to pull over to the curb, open the car door and vomit all over the road. It is shocking, and random, and I'm left with tears streaming down my face from the physical and emotional impact of it. But maybe it's overdue; a symptom of delayed shock perhaps, after the events of the previous night, and seeing Badger in such distress.

It takes me a few minutes to get myself together, but I get going again, praying to make it home without another bout of vomiting. I go over the events of the previous night, again and again, for what feels like the thousandth time. By the time I pull into the driveway, I've switched my focus back to what still needs to be done.

It's a horrible feeling, unlocking the front door and my dog not being there to greet me. It brings home to me just how much I've come to rely on that wagging tail, that immutable surety that no matter how rubbish a day I might have had, there's someone that's thrilled beyond belief to see me come home. Today, the house feels empty and still, like time in suspension, where nothing happens and you wait for something, *anything*, that reassures you that the world is still turning, that life is still going on, that you haven't fallen into some suspended virtual reality where nothing is alive or real except yourself and your own demons.

From out of nowhere, it suddenly occurs to me that Junior may have had some kind of ID on him. Shit! I didn't even think to go through his pockets! He may have a wallet on him, a mobile phone, or some other thing that can readily identify him. That's something else I'll have to check for, before I dispose of his body.

That's the real biggie for me now; how do I do that? How do I get rid of his body? It needs to be done in a way that he will never be found, but my mind keeps drawing blanks. I push away all thoughts of his mum, other family members he might have, brothers or sisters, maybe a young girlfriend or boyfriend, grandparents, people who love him, who'll miss him, who rightly deserve a body to mourn.

I push away those thoughts because I have too much to lose, to allow myself the luxury of seeing him as a connected human being. In my mind I see the mother of the kid my friend stabbed to death, the little burglar. That grief-crazed mother was hysterical, screaming 'he was just a kid!' Well, not really 'just' a kid, right? A little scumbag bastard-burglar, in fact. A complete stranger to an honest day's work, with no regard for anyone but himself, and you can call me what you like but I find immaturity to be less of a mitigating 'excusable' factor than most people do.

In my opinion, anyone that age who is capable of terrorising a grown woman is a lot more than 'just a kid'. The implication of an innocence still there that was in fact long-since gone is simply an insult to most people with an ounce of intelligence.

It was the harm to Badger that pushed me over the edge last night. If they'd just taken my stuff, yes, I'd have been enraged, but not to the level where I wanted to do actual bodily damage to them.

Hurt my dog? That's something else again. Here I am, back to trying to justify the act of murder, or manslaughter, or whatever some legal 'expert' would seek to call it.

Do I have remorse? Of course I do! I'm a lot of things, but I'm not a monster. Until last night, I'd have laughed in the face of anyone who might have suggested I could be capable of *killing* someone, no matter what the circumstances might be. It only goes to show though, doesn't it, how quickly your life can crumble, on the back of a panic-filled decision you made, that changed it forever, and not just for yourself? I have irreparably scorched the souls of countless people, in doing what I've done.

So yes; I truly wish, with all my heart and soul, that I'd played a different game last night. But I didn't, and the facts are what they are. I robbed a young man of his life, and any chance he might ever have chosen, like rehabilitation or taking a different path, has gone forever.

But I'm damned if I'll go to prison for that. No fucking way. I *am* damned, and I *will* pay for my sins, but in a different and probably worse way than that. I have no doubt about it. My penance will likely be nightmares for the rest of my own pathetic life, but I'd rather suffer that than do God-knows how many years in an eight-by six just for some scumbag who tried to kill my dog as part of his miserable plan to rob me blind. Junior didn't deserve to die. But he was still a scumbag.

I cling to that thought, and make a mental note to check him for ID, and at first I think I'll do it when I'm ready to dispose of his body. But then I think again. What if he has a mobile phone that someone is ringing, and what if it can be heard at the bottom of my garden?

I quickly head down into the shed, closing the door behind me. I roll up my sleeves, take a deep breath, and open the chest. Junior's crumpled body is there, just as I put it, and I gingerly pat down the pockets I can reach, in his jeans.

My nose is telling me that he has shit himself a bit, as dead bodies are wont to do, once all the musculature holding everything together goes slack. Lovely! Rigor mortis has set in too, so it's not possible to pull him out and straighten him up. He is there, in the shape I put him in last night, and I have to work around it. I slide my hand under the body at the waist, trying to avoid the soiled area. I feel around on the other side of his jeans and, sure enough, I find what feels like a mobile phone. After much shuffling, levering and cursing, I manage to prise it free from the pocket, and I see that it's a cheap little flip-top thing, not a new smart phone as I expected.

I don't know why I expected he'd have a swanky new phone. I suppose it's because he was a thief; I expected him to have someone's really expensive, stolen smart phone. He has nothing else on him, no wallet, not even a piece of paper that I can find, so I still don't know who he is. I close up the chest again, and leave the shed, clutching the mobile phone.

Back at the house I flip it open to see that the battery is almost flat, and there are a total of twenty-nine missed calls, from five different numbers. I debate whether to listen to the voicemail messages, then I decide against it. I really don't want to know who loves and misses this boy. The less I know about him, the better. I switch the phone off, take out the SIM card, and cut it into tiny pieces. I wrap it in tissue paper and stuff it into my jeans pocket, with a view to disposing of it later, in some other place, a public rubbish bin maybe.

Then I call my lovely dog walker, to advise her that we won't be needing her services for a while, and by the way, did she have any idea why Badger came to be injured? Of course she is completely shocked, and quickly tries to reassure me that all was well with him when she brought him home. Knowing that to be true, I tell her I think he may have taken a tumble down the stairs. It's unusual, but possible, so we leave it at that. She assures me she is keen for progress reports so I promise to provide them.

I am covering myself. I'm amazing myself too, at how rational I am being, in the face of what I've done. I'm tying up loose ends with a lot more calm that I'd ever once have thought myself capable of, under the circumstances. It doesn't stop my hands from shaking, or my mind from jumping and skipping all over the place like a needle on a scratched LP. It doesn't stop my moods from swinging erratically between fear, anger, guilt and justification. It doesn't stop these infernal headaches or the occasional curious dwindling of my sentences before I get to finish them. Stress, logic, emotion, justification, all pinging around like ricocheting bullets in my overloaded head. I cannot seem to stop any of it. I know I need to get a grip. Like *now*.

The glazier arrives, and accepts my explanation that the handle of my broom hit the window and broke it, and that I smashed out the rest of the glass before disposing of it all in the trash, which has now been picked up by the bin men. Evidence gone, of both the window and the ashes from the holdall.

Replacing the pane of glass takes just twenty minutes, and the glazier leaves, having had a cup of tea and a chocolate biscuit. I'm a nice hospitable person, making him feel welcome in my home while he works. He has no reason on earth to suspect me of causing actual bodily harm to anyone. He makes no comment about a dog's bed and food dishes nestling cosily in one corner of the kitchen, and an obviously absent dog. I do have an explanation prepared, beneath my shallow breath, but it seems I'm off the hook.

The phone rings in the afternoon sunshine, and I almost jump out of my skin. It's my friend Daphne, enquiring how I'm feeling. I assure her that it's probably just a temporary thing, one of those twenty-four-hour bugs that blindside people from out of nowhere, and I expect it to pass over the weekend. She is disappointed that I won't be joining the crew tonight but she understands, commenting on how I really don't sound like my usual self. I tell her we'll have a rain-check for a drink and a bite to eat, and she is satisfied with that.

That done, I pour myself a triple shot of whisky and run a hot bath with plenty of bubbles. I sink gratefully into it, hoping it will warm me. I've felt chilled to my bones since the events of last night, and I suspect I may be suffering some delayed reaction. Well, I guess that does make sense, and it's proof that I'm human after all.

A text comes through from the dog walker, to see how Badger is. I send one back, to assure her that he is on the mend, but won't be out walking for a while. Bless her, she sends back a series of kisses and heart emojis. She asks if she can come and visit him sometime, and I tell her he'd love to see her.

Back in the kitchen, and feeling a lot warmer after my bath, it registers that I'm nearly out of whisky. There's only a couple of inches left in the bottle. As I look around, I can see that I'm out of a bunch of other stuff as well. I find my purse, grab the car keys off the hook in the hallway and head out through the front door.

I've always done things quickly. I make up my mind about most things very quickly, and I act on decisions quickly. Efficiency is in my nature; I've always frowned on ditherers who can't seem to make even the simplest of decisions. If I need food, I don't just sit there moaning about the fact, or *wishing* I had food. I simply go and get food. If something needs doing, I just get it done. It's the way I get through life.

It's rush hour, Friday late-afternoon pandemonium everywhere, with thousands of people all trying to make it home as early as they can, to officially start their weekends. Swinging into the parking lot at the supermarket is a routine thing I do at least once a week, and like most people I have my preferred location for parking; not too close to the exit, which is always an absolute zoo of disorganized comings and goings, and where more than a fair share of dents and scratches to people's cars occur. I like to park a little further away from there, and away from the entrance to the store, where things tend to be slightly less insane.

I'm lucky to find the perfect park, away from the harassed mothers with their shin-and-bumper-bashing trolleys, and oblivious, self-absorbed teenagers, welded to their mobile phones and sauntering in front of crawling cars, forcing frustration levels to skyrocket for most of the drivers. I swing into a parking space, lock the car, and rummage around in the inside pocket of my purse for the pound-coin-shaped token I keep in there, to dislodge a trolley from the stack close by. That done, I take a deep breath and head inside.

Meandering up and down the aisles, browsing for food, has always been a routine and usually pleasant enough job, but today it feels really strange. I'm engaging with the world, but I don't feel connected to it anymore. The banality of normal supermarket life is raging all around me, with the typical riot of shrieking kids and muttering grannies, but it's like I'm watching it from somewhere else.

I imagine that the guilt of what I've done must be written all over my face. It must be there in my body language too, for people to clearly see. But random strangers smile at me as I move around. They give way to me and my trolley, exhibiting the usual supermarket-stranger niceties and manners, as if me being there doing my grocery shopping is the most normal thing in the world.

Out of curiosity, I move my trolley towards the clothing section of the store, to check my reflection in a changing-room mirror. What stares back at me is not what I expect. All I see is a fairly normal looking woman, rather pale, with eyes hauled up from fine cheekbones, dark-ringed and slightly bloodshot through lack of sleep and a few too many shots of whisky.

She's neat enough, and tidy, and her hair is fairly nice. It's obvious she hasn't slept well. That's a good thing if anyone from work happens to see me though, isn't it? I'm ill, yes, but I need supplies, so I'm braving the throngs and not straying too far from the ladies' loo, your Honour.

The woman staring back at me simply looks tired. She doesn't look crazy at all. She doesn't look like a psychopath, someone others would cross the street to avoid. She doesn't look like the kind of person who would batter someone to death with a frying pan.

It makes me wonder, just who is walking up and down these aisles, who we pass in the streets, who we sit next to in cafes and cinemas. We have no idea if any of them are cold-blooded killers, or sociopaths of various sorts, all capable of being entirely personable in public, but astonishingly abusive in private. How could we possibly know who among them might have a ruthless disregard for the sanctity of human life, artfully concealed and bubbling below the charming, smiling surface?

Relieved but slightly unnerved by the normality of my appearance, I head back to the food section. Half an hour later, with not one but two bottles of whisky, half a dozen bottles of my favourite chardonnay and an assortment of food in my hessian bags, I leave the store and head for home. As I unpack the groceries onto the kitchen bench at the house, I'm again struck by how quickly the ripples in a pond settle down. In not quite twenty-four hours, everything and nothing has changed. Life goes on, for me and for others, and on the surface it seems as if nothing has happened.

But it has, and I still have the most important part of it to deal with.

I'm so tempted to use Google to help me find a solution. I'm sure there are dozens of sites that can give good advice about how to get rid of a dead body you don't want anyone to find. But the rational and calculating part of my mind tells me that if all this goes tits-up somehow (and my mind doesn't want to contemplate in just how many ways it could), I can't leave an obvious trail for some techno-whizz to find. Whenever someone is arrested, the police are always interested in a laptop or computer that might provide clues.

So far, I've managed to cover my tracks as I've been going along, although the small matter of the still-at-large scumbag Senior is one that I haven't yet figured out how to control. I'm sure that particular gargoyle is waiting in the wings to jump out and poleaxe me at some stage in the not-too-distant future. Senior is going to want to know what's happened to his mate.

I'll have to work on a plan for dealing with that later. For now, I have to focus on the somewhat burdensome issue of how exactly to dispose of Junior without leaving a single trace.

It's a harder conundrum than you think. Forty-eight hours ago, if anyone had told me I'd be sitting at my kitchen table trying to work out how to do something like this, I'd have laughed with incredulity. Now? I've never been so scared, so on edge, and so totally stumped for options.

I'm thinking of the obvious choices first. You know; the ones you see on telly? I could bury Junior. The choices there include the woods (remote and not often-travelled), deep and cold water (the kind that nobody ventures into) with enough weight attached so he never ends up bobbing to the surface or caught in a fisherman's net. I could put him on top of a coffin in an existing fresh grave (easy to dig but unutterably gruesome to execute), or into a building site cavity that's about to have concrete poured into it.

Those are the only options I can come up with. My mind won't take me anywhere else, and it really is too dangerous to use Google for other ideas. The last thing I want is for some lead-chasing detective to hijack my laptop and look at my surfing history. Even when you think you've erased anything incriminating, your hard drive is still at the mercy of experts who know exactly how to delve to its depths and pull up stuff you think you've long-since deleted.

Burying a body in the forest requires at least six feet of hard digging. A shallow grave's too risky. Rain can wash it out, animals can dig it up, or unwitting walkers can trip over fingers and thumbs that refuse to stay below the surface. Depending on the consistency of the soil, a six-foot slog could take hours and I'm not sure I have the stamina to dig all night. It's late summer, the earth is as hard as a rock, and the clocks still haven't changed so on sunny days it's still daylight until nine o'clock at night. As miserable luck would have it, the forecast is against me too; more fine weather through the weekend, which ordinarily would delight me.

For now though, I need it to be bucketing with the kind of rain that softens soil, renders even the hardiest of walkers and campers more inclined to stay at home, and obliterates tracks and other traces of human activity in remote areas where you wouldn't expect to find them.

Under the prevailing conditions, I wouldn't be able to even get started until after ten. Add to that, I'd have to drive to an appropriate, pre-defined location without drawing any attention to myself. I'd need headlights, and even remote areas have those annoying campers, passers-through, people who might notice something untoward going on in the middle of the night. Dark abandoned woods, heaven knows who or what lurking around in the shadows and not even Badger for company. Not an appealing prospect in the least.

Deep water, well there's none close at hand. I'd have to drive a long way and, weather depending, it could be late at night before I'd even be able to get underway. I'd need a rowboat. I'd also need weights to hold and keep the body down. If I went to the Lake District area, or to the coast, I'd have to have a good reason for being there. CCTV cameras with numberplate recognition are everywhere. Unless I had a pre-arranged reason to be there, it would be a major red flag if I were to be investigated, or required to provide proof of my whereabouts in the aftermath of Junior's disappearance. Even being there for 'legitimate' reasons might prompt some over-enthusiastic detective to start digging into everything and making correlations that wouldn't bode well for me.

Why would I go there? The only reason would be if I've hired a holiday house or booked a B&B, to get away from life for a long weekend, and why would I ever do that without my dog? I just wouldn't; nor would I go on holiday when he is at the vet's. Anyone who knows me would know that. So deep-water burial is too shaky a prospect and I strike it off my mental list.

Encasement in the concrete of a building operation is a great option, but I'd have to find concrete that has just been poured and was still in the process of setting, so I could get the body into it and the surface planed off again, before it set. But I might have to allow for body-mass displacement, which could complicate things. I also have no idea what's happening where or when, construction-wise, to be confident of being able to take advantage of the timing, in the time I have myself.

An existing, freshly dug grave feels like it could be a good option. People aren't usually in the habit of digging folk up once they've been put in the ground, unless an exhumation was in order, and I believe that to be quite rare. I wouldn't stretch to staking my pension on it but I'm fairly sure that in most cases, putting someone to rest means exactly that.

So I have to find a cemetery that's quite remote, far enough from a main road, where people wouldn't think to go to late at night. How many rural cemeteries have had a recent burial? I have no way of finding out, so it would be a case of driving around and checking, which could eat up half the night.

But I reason I can spend a night doing that if I have to, and hopefully I'd get lucky enough to get the job done before I had to see the sun come up. At worst I'd have to bring the sea chest home again and try again Sunday night, but that would be my last opportunity. If I didn't get the job done by then, my problems would be a whole lot bigger.

So it's cutting it fine, but it slowly dawns on me that cruising cemeteries, as long as it wasn't too close for comfort to where I live, is something I could do during the day. Collecting research for a short story I want to write, your Honour, for a competition I fancy entering.

I could case things out early, find the appropriate place, and then go back later. Right, so that's Plan A.

Early evening rolls around, and the setting sun is glorious. Determined, I open the fridge door, take out the bottle of chardonnay, pour myself a glass and take it to the garden, where I sit, listening to the birds. I make a Herculean effort to avoid looking at the shed, and shove the encroaching thoughts from my mind. I try to simply appreciate how nice the garden looks in the late stages of the season. Everything is over-lush and over-bursting, still colourful but just-past fresh. Summer is almost ending.

Just twenty-four hours ago, this small but important pleasure of appreciating wine and garden was to have been my joy, but there is no joy in it now. Somehow the colours don't seem as bright. The smell of the flowers seems to have a subtle rotting undertone and the birds sound somewhat shrill.

It's the earliest glimpse of just how surely and thoroughly I have tainted my own life, how nothing will ever be the same again.

8

Saturday
- Alison -

After spending most of the night lying awake with my mind whirring at a million miles an hour, considering other options, I'm still convinced that burial in an existing grave is the best one. I'm exhausted from the all-night mental. I feel like my limbs are weighed down. An overactive mind and an underactive body are not the best combination to be undertaking the dastardly plan, but I can't let myself be deterred by the grisliness *or* the physicality of it. It's a job that needs doing, and that's that.

Other options that went through my mind in the course of the long night included hydrochloric acid. I heard somewhere that it dissolves almost everything, including bodies. I think it's the stuff you pour down drains. But I decided I don't have a suitable container big enough to do the job, and I remember watching a movie where someone did that in their bathtub and the acid burned right through the bath *and* the floor underneath. I'd need so much of the stuff in any case, and I'm not even sure where to purchase it, or how long it even takes to work before it starts to burn the shit out of everything else around it too.

How does anyone do something like that, without drawing attention to themselves? It's not like I can phone a friend and say, 'Hey, how's it going? I've got a quick question… if I wanted to dissolve a human body, what would I use, where would I get it, how much would I need and how long would it take?'

I even found myself wishing too, in the middle of the night, that I had a friend who could get me access to an electroplating lab. When I was a child, I once went with my father to see someone about getting some car parts re-chromed. I can still recall the acrid, sour smell of the smoking, seething acid baths, all containing a sickening assortment of lethal chemicals that could literally dissolve metal coatings to create a surface ready to then accept new coating. The baths were huge, and the only way to them was by ladder access.

I remember the man my Dad spoke to telling me, as I looked at them wide-eyed; 'you wouldn't want to fall into one of those, dear. There'd be nothing left of you at all, in no *time* at all.' I was totally terrified at the prospect, as only kids can be, and I thought about that place a lot while I was growing up, always with the morbid but terrifying knowledge that a person could literally disappear forever in there. But I'd give the shirt off my back for access to a place like that right now.

Another thought was wrapping Junior in heavy plastic, taping him up and concealing him in one of the walls (or under the floor?) of my own house. That's one of the easiest of all options of concealment, really, because nobody else would inadvertently stumble across the body, at least as long as I live here in this lovely house I worked so hard to make beautiful, but two things steer me away from the prospect. It would mean tearing out walls and having to rebuild and redecorate, or tearing up floorboards and having to relay them. Huge disruption; noisy, dirty and hard to do quietly at the bottom end of a cul-de-sac of detached houses, even if I *could* do the work myself.

I've done a fair bit of DIY over the years, to get this house to what it is now. I'm handy with a hammer, and I'm not shy of taking on any number of light projects, but dismantling and rebuilding a wall is a bit more than I can feasibly tackle. And of course, logistics aside (even if I could deal with them), I couldn't keep living in this house with Junior here, lurking forever in the shadows of my walls and conscience. I'd never have a decent night's sleep again; not that I'm sure at this point I ever will anyway. If I sold up and moved away I'd always be wondering if he'd be discovered in some freak, random way by the new owners, when one of their renovation projects turned into the nightmare of the century.

I also considered cutting Junior up into smaller pieces and disposing of him in a wide variety of locations that would never be considered places to find dead bodies. But I rejected that possibility as soon as it came to mind, as I simply don't have the stomach for doing something like that. Or the time.

On a rational level, I know that would be the most logical solution, since a series of small parts are easier to dissolve or dispose of. If the distribution was carefully done the parts would never be discovered. But I literally could not make myself do that. For all my faults, which become more hideously overblown to me every day, I'm not cold blooded, and I think I'd have to be, to put that kind of plan into place and take the care and time needed to ensure it worked. That's dedication on a seriously sociopathic level.

At one point in my ruminations, I even acknowledged the fact that there are (sadly) no alligators, or piranhas in this country. The only other creatures widely known to make short work of flesh and bone are pigs, but there are no pig farms around here that I know of. I was amazed, as I lay there in bed at some ungodly hour of the morning, at how little I really know about so many things. But, I realized, I *could* Google organic pig farms, which could be explained away by the purchase of some pork or bacon from such an establishment. I needed to find an organic farm because I care about pig welfare, your Honour.

So, somewhere in the middle of the night, I reached for my laptop and fired it up. First, to set myself up for feasibility, I Googled slow-cookers, because I don't have one. Then I looked for recipes using organic pork joints. Then I searched for farm shops in my own and surrounding counties, and the next search was for pig farms.

I got the addresses of three, and hastily scribbled them onto the back of an envelope on my bedside table. From there, I Googled a few more recipe sites, just to cover my tracks. If my laptop was ever analysed, I'd have to simply say I'm just a woman making conscious choices for healthy food purchase, preparation and consumption.

I decided I could take Junior out to a remote pig farm after dark, and tip him into the pig pen, to be obliterated by animals that have no discernment when it comes to food. Everyone knows that pigs will eat whatever you give them, and they'll happily crunch bones to powder. Even if there was anything left, there wouldn't be much that would identify the victim. So, as night slowly gave way to a greying dismal dawn, that became my Plan B.

That plan does involve trespassing on farm property after dark, of course; running the risk of alerting dogs or other animals, and manhandling the heavy wooden chest with Junior in it, which would be no small feat. But I do have the sack trolley and the ground is hard from a long summer without much rain. I'd have to make sure the wheels are oiled, and that whatever farm I chose had the pen far enough away from the house and from the ears of sleeping dogs, for the noises not to be heard, of pigs going crazy over unexpected food.

So I need to 'case the joints,' like I do for the freshly dug graves, and all of that will take care of today. I reason that by lunch time I'll know which plan to plump for, and it will be all systems go.

I'm sure there are other ways to dispose of a dead body. However, without incriminating myself, I just have to run with what I what I've decided. Before I haul my protesting body from the comforting warmth of my bed and start this most miserable of mornings, I stare at the bedroom wall as if willing it to come up with a better answer.

The wall stares back at me in its usual stoic, rosebud-patterned silence. Eventually, I admit defeat and get up, mindful that when I turned off all the lights last night and crawled into bed, half blind with anxiety and exhaustion, and praying for some solace in sleep, my prayers went unanswered. There are no guardian angels listening to me or acting in my best interests. I really am alone, in this most terrible of crimes.

By the time the sun starts coming up, the late summer Saturday morning is bright and crystal clear. I'm exhausted but the adrenaline has kicked in now, and I'm wired, with the energy of ten horses. No time to mess about making breakfast; I resolve to stop at a McDonald's somewhere for coffee and a muffin on the run. There's a lot to do, and still a lot to plan, and I only have this day to pull the whole thing off, if I'm to make the right decision and do it at a comfortable pace.

A comfortable pace? I am struggling to believe my own thought process. There are no words, to describe how much I hate myself.

9

Saturday

- Darren -

It's Saturday morning and there's still no word from Tommy. I've hardly slept all night and I don't know what to do with myself. The plod haven't turned up here yet, and I don't see why I should sit around waiting for them. It might be hours. It might not even be today at all, when they rock up at the door.

I check my wallet, and there's just about enough cash in there for a trip to the seaside, so I grab a piece of toast on the way out the door, leg it to the bus stop, and jump on a bus to the station. A train is just about to leave for the south coast and I'm lucky that for once there's no long queue for tickets. I manage to get one and make it onto the train just as the doors are about to close. So, a smooth start to the morning without a lot of waiting around. It somehow feels like it's meant to be.

Although the day's bright, it's a chilly breeze that blows off the sea, and the tide is coming in. It's a perfect day for me, the kind I like the best. Wandering along the shoreline, braced against the cold wind, feeling it blow through my hair; I've found it's the one thing I do in this life that helps me clear my head.

Sometimes my thoughts crowd in and overpower me, and I can't think straight. A walk along the beach always helps. It's like the sea speaks to me, soothes me somehow. It's hard to explain and if I tried, if I told anyone that, they'd just tell me I was off my fucking rocker. Nobody would get it. So my beach trips are something I just keep to myself; my secret escape from a world I just keep getting more and more pissed off with. If I could move here, I would, in a flash. Fancy apartments overlooking the beach. No chance.

Surprisingly for a Saturday morning, there aren't many people around. The beach is more or less empty, despite it still being officially summer. There are just a few people roaming about on the sand with their dogs. A little kid is chasing a ball, screaming with fear and delight as he tries to outrun the waves that keep seeping under his feet. He's funny.

From out of nowhere, a red setter dog runs up behind me, chasing a stick being thrown, and he picks it up and runs towards me with it. I can hear a woman's voice, shouting the dog back to her, but he's not having it. He wants me to throw the stick for him instead. So I do, and he runs after it with his tail wagging.

An out of breath voice behind me says 'Thanks! I struggle to keep up with him, sometimes!'

I turn to see a woman about my age, Her long dark hair's being whipped by the wind. She's smiling at me, like I'm a real person worth smiling at, and as the dog runs back and throws himself at her she falls clear off her feet and onto the sand, into a laughing heap. I instinctively reach out to pull her up and as she grabs my hand I'm amazed at how light she is. She smiles again in thanks, and I notice how red her cheeks are, from the wind, and she has the bluest eyes I've ever seen.

'I like your dog. He's lovely.'

'Thank you! Yes, he is, isn't he? He runs me ragged but I wouldn't be without him. He's my best friend in all the world!' She smiles again, and the two of them turn away to go off back towards the car park.

My best friend in all the world. The dog at the beach is nothing like the one at that house on Thursday but it reminds me of it nonetheless, and the image of the woman just sitting there staring at the wall, floods back to me.

My best friend in all the world. That's what that dog probably was, to her. Have I ever had that, even in human form? No. I haven't got a fucking clue what it feels like, to have a best friend, and I've probably never been one either, except maybe to Tommy, wherever he is. And for the sake of a few quid I never even got, I killed someone's best friend in all the world. What does that feel like, to them? Losing your best friend in all the world must be a thousand times worse than wishing you even had one to lose.

I'm astonished to find myself crying, as I walk into the wind. I can't remember the last time I cried. I must have been a kid. Kids cry. Grown-ups don't. Even though the shrinks all say; 'it's okay to cry,' I've never felt the urge or the need. Until now. So what's this all about now? What the fuck am I crying for?

The tiny voice inside me that I always try to ignore, the one the shrinks all said I should listen to, is telling me something now. I'm crying for my own messed-up life, for the mess I've made of everything, for breaking my mum's heart over and over again, and for killing someone's best friend in all the world. And all of a sudden, in the midst of what somehow feels like the biggest mess I've ever got myself into, I find that it actually *is* okay to cry.

So all of a sudden, here I bloody am, a grown man, walking along a beach, far from home, with nobody in sight who knows me, crying like a fucking baby. But it feels alright to be doing it.

Crying gives way to outright sobbing as I keep walking into the wind, letting it whip the tears from my stinging, sand-scraped face. I reach the end of the beach, and find a rock to sit on, and I eventually manage to get a hold of myself.

As the tide rolls in, I realise that things have to change. My life has to change. I'm not a kid anymore, and I have to get my shit together if I'm ever going to make something of my time on the planet. Otherwise I'm just destined for more of the same; scrabbling to make ends meet on the dole, robbing for stupid amounts of money that make no real difference, and living at home with a mum who struggles, I know, to have any respect for me at all.

I don't know what to do or where to start, because I'm just a pathetic coward with a totally fucked-up moral compass. But sitting here, on this damp rock, with salty tears streaming down my face, it comes to me, that I just don't want this life anymore. I can't *live* this life anymore. I need to find something better, more meaningful, and I have to figure out how to make it happen. And if I can, once he comes home, I'll take little Tom with me, into that better life. I'll show him what's decent, and good.

Eventually the tears dry up, and my breathing returns to normal. One shrink told me that breathing is the 'foundation of wellbeing,' something to do with it being part of the ancient Sanskrit and Hebrew teachings, or some fucking thing. I didn't take much notice at the time, figuring that it sounded like a load of mumbo-jumbo, and I was already breathing alright, thanks, and there was nothing wrong with my health.

But her words come back to me now, and I find myself breathing properly, slowly drawing in a massive lungful of clear salty air, holding it, and slowly letting it out again. After the fourth time of doing it, I start to feel calmer again, and I feel like I'm on the threshold of something big, something new, but I couldn't describe what it is, even if you asked me. Something just feels different.

Eventually, I get up and walk back along the beach, the same way I came, back towards the station, but I stop for a cup of cheap tea in a greasy spoon along the forefront. As I sit down with my mug of tea, a voice pipes up, 'Hello again!'

It's the girl from the beach, the one with the red setter, her best friend in all the world. She's smiling again.

'Looks like we've had the same thought! A good hot cup o' char!'

'Where's your dog?' I ask her.

'Oh, I've put him in the car. I was gasping for a cuppa. That wind really gets to me sometimes.' She gets up from her chair and comes over, and plonks herself down opposite me. I didn't invite her, but I don't mind that she's invited herself. 'Are you okay?' she asks, matter-of-factly.

'Yeah, why?'

'Oh, nothing. I was watching you on the beach, that's all, and you seemed to have the weight of the world on your shoulders while you were walking, and sitting there.' That smile again, those blue eyes. She is so open, no agenda, just being friendly to a stranger, and for once I'm not suspicious. I like it.

We make small-talk while we drink our tea, and it's almost like we've always known each other. The conversation is simple and harmless. She lives locally, and she's a primary school teacher engaged to a doctor. Sounds like she's got her life all mapped out.

I confess that I'm a drop-kick with a dodgy past who's made a fucking huge mess of everything he's ever done and who's trying to figure out how to lead a better life. But, even to my own ears, for once I don't sound like the first arrival at a pity party. I sound matter of fact, honest and clear, with no hint of self-pity. It's a surprising first, for me, to be talking like this at *all*, to a stranger. The shrinks could never get me to say a fucking word.

Then, this lovely, sorted woman, the kind who would normally never give me a second glance, looks me in the eye and says, equally matter-of-factly, with a very elegant shrug;

'You don't look like a drop-kick, and you don't sound like one. You just sound like lots of other people who've lost their way a bit, that's all. It's a common enough problem. You just need to have a bit of faith in yourself. You're the expert on you. Trust yourself to find the right path, and get on it. And you will. If you really want to, you'll figure things out. And, when you have, everything else will fall into place and you'll do alright.'

And, in a few short sentences, she's done what several so-called 'experts' have failed to do, in *years* of trying to get me to fix my fucked-up life. She's summed me up, very neatly.

Next thing, she simply gets up from her chair and says goodbye. As she does, she tells me it was nice to meet me, and I believe her, because she sounds completely genuine and honest. She wishes me good luck, I say the same to her, and then she's gone, like she was never here at all.

Except she was. And she's right. I'm not a bad person. I might not be a *great* person, but I'm an okay person who's fucked up, like a lot of people do, and it feels like it might finally be time to accept that I'm actually no worse than that.

Maybe I'll still go to hell, if there is such a place, but maybe all I need really *is* to stop hating myself, to believe in myself for once, so that other people might too, and in that order, not the other way around. Maybe then I can find the ability to do better, and *be* better. Then I can start to live a normal life, one with some meaning. Maybe I can one day be of real help to someone like Tommy, instead of just teaching them to be a better thief.

I don't know what I can do, but there has to be something. Finally I can see, and appreciate, what all the shrinks were trying to do; what they were trying to get *me* to do. A girl on a beach, someone else's wife-to-be, someone I met for fifteen minutes, who I'll never meet again; that's who's got me here in the end.

My thoughts return to Tom. I need to go back and find out what's happening, because it won't stop eating away at me. And I'm not going out to get drunk tonight as planned. I think, actually, I might stay at home with my mum. Maybe I can talk to her about things. Maybe she can help me, and maybe, for once, I'll let her.

10

Saturday
- Alison -

After picking up a sausage and egg muffin, a couple of hash browns and a large cup of coffee at the local 'Macca' drive-through, I head out towards the villages on the outskirts of the county. There are many, and it is going to take some time to get around the various cemeteries. Fortunately, some are easy to survey from the car, without having to get out. Small graveyards, where it's obvious if there's a fresh grave. Others, I have to get out and wander about a bit, to see everything.

Just after midday, at the point of starting to despair of finding somewhere, I stumble across the perfect place. It's a smallish churchyard cemetery down a long driveway, quite a distance from the main road. There are no houses near it, and it's quiet and peaceful. The little stone church itself doesn't look as if it would hold more than around fifty people. There are two fresh graves, side by side almost; mounds of drying earth with mouldering bouquets of flowers, bent ribbons, and wilting cards strewn across the top of them, containing scribbled biro messages blurred by a few evenings' dew.

There's nobody about, so I take my time to visualise the route in from the car, with the sack trolley and the chest. There are no streetlights down here at all, and no lights in the churchyard itself, so I really would be doing this in the absolute pitch black of night, and I wonder if I could perhaps risk a small torch.

I decide I'm far enough away from civilization to make that possible, so I park that thought and check out the access route. There's a short path leading from the edge of the little car park to the wooden cemetery gate. On the cemetery side of it there is just a small patch of gravel, then grass with no discernible pathways in it, but the earth beneath the grass is firm, so the sack trolley shouldn't be a problem.

As locations go, this seems as close to perfect as I think I'm ever going to find, so I resolve to use this place, and I get back into the car. I try to analyse my feelings, as I drive away. I'm relieved that I now have a solid plan, but I'm also feeling sick to my stomach with fear. What if it doesn't work? What if I'm seen by someone, or caught in the act itself, or even just *suspected* of doing this? How will I cope? How will I ever be able to explain myself?

I tell myself to get a grip. I remind myself that I have to strive, to really *work* on being as cold and calculating as possible about what I have to do, because the alternative is to keep being drawn back to the edge of the abyss of total madness. I *have* to do this, and I have to focus on it. There will be plenty of time for self-recriminations later. Right now I cannot afford the time or the luxury of self-torture. I just have to step up, toughen up, get on with the wretched job at hand, and get the damn thing finished.

Traffic is light as I make my way home, all thoughts of pig farms forgotten, now that my Plan A is firmly in my sights. I go through the process in my head. Get the chest to the house, then get it (and the sack trolley!) into the car. Don't forget the spade. Remember the torch. Leave before dark, make a quick visit to my mother, probably stay for dinner (she will insist), and then leave after dark to head to the cemetery.

I arrive home again, and I am again struck by how deathly still the house feels without Badger. Nobody greets me, nothing moves, everything feels held in a silent suspension that crawls with condemnation. A profound wave of loneliness hits me and I brush it aside, and focus on the task at hand.

For a second time, I wrestle the sea chest on to the sack trolley and I wheel it up to the house. I set it down in the hallway just behind the front door, and I go to the car and put the rear seats down, to create space.

I think about the fact that I need help to manoeuvre the chest into the back of the car, and I get it as far as the tailgate before jogging across to Bill's place to ring the doorbell. My heart is pounding so hard in my chest. What if he isn't home? His car is in the driveway but he may be out running, and if so I will have to wait until he gets back. But he answers the door, and I ask him if he can give me a quick hand to lift a heavy chest into the back of the car. He readily agrees and sprints over with me to where it is sitting, on the ground at the back of the car.

'On the count of three then,' he says, grabbing the handle on one side. I grab the other and he counts and we heave. The weight of the chest seems ridiculous, but we manage to get it into the car without too big a struggle, and once it is in there he turns to me and says 'Fucking hell! Fabrics, huh? Feels more like a dead body!'

He then smiles while I struggle with all my might to retain a neutral facial expression. 'Kidding!' he grins, 'You look like you've seen a ghost!'

As humour goes, that all feels way too close to the bone but I smile back, as best I can, and explain that I've got a shocker of a headache, which is actually true. The pounding in my head has been going on for a week or more, since long before Junior rocked up and made it a thousand times worse. I really do have to find out what's causing it, before it joins the ever-lengthening list of things that shove me straight into the pit of insanity.

I mumble my thanks to Bill and assure him that I will be just fine getting the chest out at the other end. *Just go now, please!*

He nods and smiles again, and sprints back home. I take a deep breath, only now aware of how shallowly I've been breathing since he came out of his house. I lock up the car and head back inside to get ready for the evening's events, but I find nausea washing over me again, and I barely make it to the downstairs toilet before heaving the contents of my stomach straight into it; sick for the second time in two days. Is nausea a symptom of shock and fear? I've never had to think about it before, but probably.

I clean myself up, wait a few minutes until I feel less wobbly again, and I head back down to the shed. I locate a shovel, and back in the hallway I collect a torch from the under-stairs cupboard, where the smell of bleach still burns my nostrils as soon as I open the door. I decide to leave the door slightly ajar, in the hope that the fumes will dissipate with more air to evaporate into. It won't hurt the whole house, to smell of bleach for a day or two, and it would be nice if the fumes were completely gone for when Badger returns home in a couple of days.

An hour later, after I've called my delighted mother to announce my impending visit, I dress in old, faded black jeans, knocked-around old hiking boots and a plain black sweatshirt. All of a sudden, in too short a time, I'm literally ready to go.

I secure the house, making a mental note to get an alarm system installed next week. It's something I've been considering for a while, owing to the increase in burglaries in general in our neighbourhood, but the events of the past few days have strengthened my resolve to get it seen to as early as I can, in the coming week.

I carry the shovel out to the car wrapped in a blanket with a mop, making sure that only the mop head is visible. Anyone seeing me would perhaps wonder why I might be carrying a mop out to my car, but it would be a lot less alarming than seeing me carrying a shovel. The torch is stowed safely out of sight in my handbag. On the drive to my mother's house, I suddenly realise how much I'm looking forward to seeing her.

Predictably, she insists that I stay on and have some dinner with her. The last thing I feel like doing is eating but I surprise myself by actually enjoying her chicken casserole with jacket potatoes and salad. I half expected the food to taste like sawdust, but it's actually a really nice meal, the first proper one I've had in several days, and it's lovely that I don't have to fake my enjoyment of two full helpings.

Mum berates me for being so scruffy, and says I look like nobody owns me. It's one of her peculiar little sayings that has always confounded me a bit, but it's one that doesn't stand up to being unpicked and rationalized. Even if I tried to get her to explain the concept of being 'owned' by someone, and what I would look like under those circumstances, she would simply wave my questions away with the back of her hand and tell me, ironically, that I'm not making sense. She remarks that I look like I'm going to a funeral. I let that pass, and try not to choke on my chicken.

It's still broad daylight so I'm in no rush to get away, and she takes full advantage of the fact, enlisting my help with several little things that need mending that she struggles to do on her own. Her eyesight isn't what it was, bless her, and she has arthritis in her fingers, which makes things like sewing on buttons and mending hems a little difficult. She even struggles to thread the needle nowadays, so I help her with as much as she needs. I change a couple of light bulbs just as the daylight starts to fade and she's thrilled that she can now see her way down the hallway and up the stairs. Early evening dusk gives way to nightfall as I drink the last of my tea, and say goodbye.

We hug each other tightly, tighter than usual, and she remarks that I seem on edge and distracted. She asks me if I'm okay, and I reassure her that I am, explaining that I'm just having a difficult couple of weeks at work and my sleep patterns are a little out of kilter. I tell her about my headache and she pulls a sympathetic face.

'Get that looked at, sweetheart. Headaches are no fun. Maybe you need glasses, or something.' She thanks me for coming. 'I don't see you often enough! This has been lovely, and on a Saturday night too!'

She smiles and waggles a finger at me. 'You need a boyfriend to spend your Saturday nights with, not your old Mum! I'm never going to get any grandchildren at this rate, am I?' She giggles, to show me she's not serious, although I know it is her dearest wish to see me settled with a family of my own.

'One day, Mum, when I meet Mr Right.'

Surprisingly, Simon Westrupp's face flashes through my mind, unbidden, and I sweep the thought away. There is no room in my mind for thoughts of romance, as I leave my mother's house and make my way towards the car. The only space I have in my head right now is for the grim task that awaits me on this blackest of nights.

11

Saturday
- Darren -

Tom's mum Marla called again, just as I was getting on the train to go home, to ask if I'll help with putting up some 'missing person' posters for him. They're working on getting them printed now. I tell her of course I'll help.

I hope he turns up soon. I'll never forgive myself if he's done something daft or got himself hurt somehow. I've wracked my bloody brains for even the slightest thing, but I still can't get Tommy's disappearance to make sense. *None* of this makes sense.

He's a good kid, really, just a bit lost. He hasn't got a harmful bone in him. I struggle to believe he'd just go AWOL and freak his family out like this. Maybe the death of that dog sent him off the rails. God knows, it's doing *my* head in. I can only imagine how he's feeling about it. He's got a little dog himself! 'Button' the Jack Russell. It's as hyper as hell, and it's always yapping, but he loves the little fucker to death. Yeah, maybe that's not the best choice of words, under the circumstances.

According to Marla, the plod do still intend to speak to me about this, because I might have been one of the last people to see Tom, and I guess it's only a matter of time before they rock up at my place. Mum will go spare, but at least this time I'm not in any trouble I can go to jail for, at least I fucking hope not.

But I do have to get my story straight. I have to say that yes we were together, and at what time, and all that, but I can't say where we were, can I? I can't say we were robbing some woman's nice detached house over in the very posh neighbourhood of Topsham. I'll have to say we were at the local park, hanging out and dossing, doing nothing of note.

Nobody else can confirm that of course, but there's no CCTV up there that's still working. It was vandalised years ago, and the council have never bothered to fix it. I just have to hope the plod believe me. But it's the best I can do, and he's my mate so I don't want to dump him in the shit, and I *am* seriously worried about him, so I'm sure they'll be able to see that's genuine.

I'm nobody to be suspicious of, over this. I'm a small-time crook, but I don't hurt people. *Only dogs?*

When I get home from the beach, I find my mum crying in the kitchen. As I walk in, she looks up at me with such despair, I don't know what to say to her. Apparently the plod have already been round, asking for me, but they wouldn't tell her why they wanted to talk to me, and because whenever they come here they usually want to arrest me, she's pretty sure I've done something I'll be getting banged up for. She's more upset right now than I've ever seen her.

I try to reassure her that they only want to talk to me and it's because one of my friends has gone missing, but she's convinced I've done something, and she looks so hurt and sad. She doesn't even yell at me. She just talks, in a low tone, in a voice that makes me think she's all but given up on me.

'For fuck's sake, Darren. When are you going to grow up? You're twenty-six years old. When are you going to stop behaving like a complete dickhead and be a bloody man?'

What do you say to that? She's never asked me that before. She's always got angry and ranted a bit about my lifestyle, but she's never looked at me before, like she's looking at me now, and asked me that.

So I sit down at the table and we just look at one another. Then, to my own horror – and hers – I start to cry again. Twice in one fucking day, I've burst into tears. Mum's horrified. I don't think she's seen me cry since I was a kid. But she gets up, and she comes and puts her arms around me and she hugs me and starts crying again herself.

'What's happened love? Tell me.'

So I do. I tell her everything. It all comes spilling out, words all tumbling over each other, how me and Tommy were doing a job and we got caught and I ran off and left him and now he's fucking missing, how I've killed a lovely dog, and how shit I feel about my whole pathetic life.

All the time I'm talking and crying, she doesn't let go of me. She just hugs me ever tighter, and I realise that I can't remember the last time she hugged me, or even tried, or even when I've *let* her try.

'You have to hand yourself in,' she says, when I've run out of steam. 'Even if a crime hasn't been reported, you have to hand yourself in, because if you don't it will eat you up inside.'

I shake my head. Part of me suspects she might be right, but I'm a long way from being convinced.

What if I do hand myself in? It won't bring back a dead dog, it won't bring Tom home any faster or shed any light on where he's gone, and I'll go to jail again for certain. Whether not handing myself in *will* eat me alive is something I'll have to work out, and I don't feel it's the kind of decision I can make without sitting on it for a while and weighing up the options. It's something only a lunatic would do on impulse.

Even after confessing everything to Mum, I still have a really bad feeling in the pit of my stomach. I can't explain why I'm starting to think something bad has happened to Tommy. Some might say it's a sixth sense. Others might say it's just paranoia. Whatever it is, all I want is for the silly bastard to turn up. Doesn't matter what the excuses are, what he says, where he's been. None of that matters, but if I find out someone's hurt him, I'll bloody kill them. He's like a brother to me, that kid, and hardly anyone looks out for him. All I want is to see him again. I realise, with a jolt, that he actually is, and has been for some time, the closest thing I've ever had to a best friend in all the world.

So how would I feel if he never came back? Truth is, I'd be devastated, especially since I know if I'd stuck by him, or grabbed him and dragged him out of there with me, he'd be safe now. We both might be in the bloody bang-up, that's true, but he'd *be* here. His mum wouldn't be beside herself at the thought that he's dead in a ditch somewhere, his girlfriend might finally stop crying, thinking he's fucked off with someone else, and I'd have my mate back. Not that I deserve him. I left him. I put myself first, like I've always done. What kind of a prick am I?

That girl at the beach today, she told me everybody makes mistakes and I just have to figure things out and find the right path. But these mistakes, that dead dog and my missing mate, they feel like the worst mistakes, and the most stupid, that I've ever made.

What if Mum's right? What if I hand myself in? Rock up at the nick, and confess to breaking and entering, and everything that came after? Then what?

The plod would make the link to Tom being missing. They'd go round and talk to that woman, who maybe hasn't even reported the crime. She would I.D. me, I'd get locked up, and Tom would still be nowhere, the dog would still be dead, my mum would break her heart over me going to jail yet again, and my prospects would shrink even more.

I'm a coward, it's true. But honestly, if I genuinely thought handing myself in would do more good than harm to little Tommy, I'd do it in a heartbeat. I just can't see the positives, I just can't believe what my mum tells me, that it just might save my soul (even if it destroys hers), and I can't pretend it wouldn't. Maybe my soul is already beyond saving. Mum believes it isn't, and I'd like to think it's not, but I'm fucked if I know what to do.

Before I make any kind of decision that might seal my fate forever, I need to go back to that house again, to the scene of the crime. I need to see if there are any clues - any at all - about what might have happened there after I left.

I'll do it tomorrow night. I'm in no mood to sit around tonight with Mum all freaked out about things and haranguing me about what I should do, so I may as well go out with the lads as planned. I hit Mum up for a bit of beer money, grab a quick shower, make some toast, and I'm eating it on my way out the door before she can say any more about what we've talked about.

12

Saturday
- Alison -

The drive to the cemetery in the burgeoning darkness allows me time to focus on what I need to do. Unwelcome thoughts persistently storm through my mind, about someone else being there when I arrive, a courting couple perhaps, or youths drinking in a car. I push the paranoia out of my mind with all the effort I can muster. I can't let myself be scared away before I even get there.

The mind plays all kinds of nasty tricks when you're under pressure. I've noticed that before. The more focussed you try to be, the more the external 'what-ifs' seem to try and crowd your head, randomly tumbling into your consciousness, demanding space, and when that happens you can talk yourself into or out of almost anything. It would be so easy for me to simply turn the car around and head back, if I were to give any real head-room to the 'maybes' but then I'd be in an even bigger mess. Not being able to follow through with at least one plan is simply not an option, and I've run out of time to rethink.

Somehow it seems further, in the dark, but eventually I find the turn-off to the church and I switch the car's lights to park and creep forward as slowly and as quietly as I can down the lane. I'm more grateful tonight than I've ever been in my entire life for the fact that I have an electric car. There's no engine noise to splinter the peace of the night.

I'm almost all of the way down, within sight of the church and getting close to the car park, when I find that a chain has been extended across the lane, to stop vehicles from going any further. With my lights so dim I'm lucky I even saw it. Cursing to myself, I get out, grab the torch from my bag, and check it out. The chain is padlocked to a heavy metal post at each edge of the driveway.

Shit! Why didn't I see that when I was here before? I never even thought about night security!

Panic rises in my throat, and I struggle to keep from crying out in frustration. Looking around me, I see that there is literally nowhere to park off the lane, and my car is blocking it entirely. I take a couple of deep breaths and look again at the sides of the lane, which are small banks, about a foot high, and there are no fences at either side, so it looks possible to drive up, and head into the bushes a bit, which are not so dense that a car couldn't get through them with a bit of effort. I might have to pull some foliage out of various places on the car after doing it, but I think it is possible.

I listen intently into the night. The only sound is the plaintive hoot of an owl, off in the far distance. There are no vehicles, no voices, I am completely alone. Maybe I could even get away with leaving the car here in the lane. Chances are, nobody would come down here and see it. But do I really want to take a chance that big, when I have the opportunity to conceal it instead, behind some bushes at the side? Wasting no time, I get back into the car, reverse it a few feet, angle it slightly and drive up the bank. Luckily, the car obliges, and I manage to get through the bushes.

On the other side of them is a flat piece of farmland, just ten feet or so across, before a fence line. I can park here, and not be seen from the lane. Whether or not I can be seen from the other side of the field, I have no idea, but I can't see any lights beyond the opposite edge of it, so I don't let myself think too much about it.

I check my watch; it has just gone eleven o'clock. The night is completely still. It is cloudless but there is no moon and I am grateful for that, because the stars and the general cosmos are affording enough light for me to see what I'm doing. Extra light from the moon could be very risky indeed.

I decide to do a preliminary check of the lane. From there, I'm satisfied that my car can't be seen. I step over the chain and make my way down to the churchyard to check that out too, just to make sure I won't be setting off any security lights or alarms, and that nobody is at the church, and all that. It's about two hundred yards away, so not too far, and when I get there I relieved to find that no lights come on, and no sound can be heard. Nothing of note is happening here in the dark, unless of course you count my even darker mission of illegally disposing of someone I've more or less murdered.

I jog back to the car, satisfied that I'm quite alone here, and I can get on with the grisly job at hand.

I get to work, opening the rear hatch and dragging the chest out. It is stupendously heavy, as my friend Bill observed, and for a moment I let the balance-weight teeter on the edge of the car, before taking a deep breath and heaving it out. I hold it with my right thigh as it travels from the car to the ground, seeking to break its fall a little.

That works, and mercifully it doesn't spring open, which has been my biggest fear. The latches are sturdy; another thing to be thankful for. I haul out the sack trolley next and manoeuvre the chest onto it lengthways, to make it easier to balance.

Getting back down the bank is relatively straightforward and although the chest threatens to slide sideways off the trolley it does stay put as I move it down and into the lane. I get to the chain link, and I tip the chest off the trolley, lift the chain as much as I can, and push and shove the chest forward underneath it. I then lift the trolley over the chain and reposition the chest back onto it as before.

I make my way towards the churchyard, and the trolley wheels sound deafening as they bump across the top of the hard, mud-packed gravel. I stop at the bottom, having shattered the silence, to see if I have attracted any attention. The last thing I want is some curious farmer wandering down the lane with a torch, wondering what's causing such a ruckus down here. Stillness envelops me like a reassuring cloak.

I get the chest closer to the graveside before realising I've left the shovel back at the car. *Damn!* I have to sprint back to get it, leaving the trolley and the chest prone beside the grave. That rattles me more than I care to admit, but I don't have much of a choice.

By the time I get back, I'm out of breath and irrationally relieved to find everything exactly as I left it, just moments before. Thinking quickly, I pull my phone out and take a photo of the grave-top. I want to be sure that when I place everything back on top of Junior's body, it will look exactly as it did.

I set to work, taking the rotting wreaths, wilted bouquets and soggy sympathy cards off the top, carefully placing them to one side. Then I pick up the shovel and I start to dig.

After what feels like an hour of hard digging, but which is really only thirty minutes according to my watch, my shoulders and my arms are on fire, and I'm struggling to catch my breath. I've been going at a frenzied pace, mostly from fear of being discovered but also to keep my mind focussed so I can't be distracted by the true magnitude of what I'm doing. At the point where I estimate that I'm about three feet down, I take a two-minute breather to give my lungs a rest.

I've dug out a hole that is less than the full length of a body, since Junior's is bent and probably no more than four feet or so in length. It's easy enough dirt to dig. Having already been dug over once, it's not as hard going as it would have been starting from scratch, on packed-down, virgin soil.

I check around the location. Nothing is moving, and there are no noises, save for the mournful, far-away owl. Sounds can carry a long way across the night and I am acutely aware of how much of a racket I am actually making. I'm just fortunate that here, in this remote little graveyard at close to midnight, there is nobody around to hear it, apart from a few mute hedgehogs and the odd wary fox.

I resolve to dig another foot down, and I get back to work. Another half an hour goes by, and suddenly it seems as if the hole is finally deep enough, and wide enough, for me to put Junior into it and start covering him up. Feeling like a grave-robber must feel, furtive in the dead of night, I haul myself wearily out of the trench. Pulling the chest off the trolley I tip it sideways up, and spring the catches. Junior tumbles part-way out, accompanied by the putrid stench of faeces, urine and rotten teeth. I gag, nauseated, and take a couple of steps backwards as my lungs gulp frantically for fresh air.

As if the smell wasn't enough, a quick flash of the torch confirms that his body has indeed already started to putrefy in the late-summer, intensified heat of the garden shed. His face and hands are mottled with dark purple blotches, and his eyes and his tongue are bloated. It is the worst sight imaginable; hideous, sickening, and I know it will fuel my nightmares for the rest of my days, like a seared brand across my brain.

Even if I ever did manage to find absolution, certain images never fade, and I know that this will be one of them. It curls around and fits neatly alongside my headache. Both feel like permanent afflictions I will have to try and find a way to live with.

Although he is still slightly stiff, Junior is a lot more floppy than I remember him being last time I opened the chest to look for his phone. I'm hoping against all hope that I haven't got it wrong, that he will fit into the hole I've dug, now that he is not quite as stiff as I expected him to be. I thought rigor mortis was permanent. I guess I was wrong.

I tip him fully out of the chest and he lands on the ground face down. I gingerly pat him down again, one last time, to make absolutely sure that he doesn't have any incriminating evidence on him, like a wallet or some other kind of ID. Making physical contact with him feels vile. The act sickens me but, I have to do this right.

Satisfied, I push him with my foot, *kicking him into his grave!* It's a very slow process getting him to the edge of the gaping hole in the earth. I realise I've made more work for myself, by not tipping him closer. It's proof that I'm not thinking as coherently as I need to. It's too far to keep trying to lever him with my foot and I realise, with mounting horror, that I have no option but to get down closer and touch him properly this time, and roll him towards the black and gaping mouth of the grave.

As I inch him ever closer, I try to think of good things. My mind gropes around for any kind of memory I can hook into, to sustain me to keep going, to complete this hideous, hateful process; Badger, running joyfully through puddles, my mother's chicken casserole, my last holiday to Greece.

Eventually, after what seems like far too much time and pushing, Junior rolls without ceremony straight into the open grave. He lands on his back, staring up at me with his bulging, milky, unseeing eyes.

My breath is coming in sharp, hitched, ragged sobs and my hands feel like they're crawling with something unspeakable. But, I rationalize, it is slightly more dignified that throwing him in from the sack trolley, which I could have done. I could have inched the trolley underneath him and then wheeled him to the grave, and tipped him unceremoniously into it.

The moral conundrum catches me unawares. What's worse, in disposing of the body of someone you've killed? To kick him into his final resting place with your foot? To tip him in from a metal trolley, like bulldozers moving trash into a tip? Or to roll him in, as gently as you can, with your hands?

Somehow, as horrible as it was to do it, I'm actually glad now, that I've done it that way. It means that this boy received a human touch at the time of his burial, albeit from the hands of his killer. Somehow it feels like the best of the three options; the least callous. Doing it this way was disgusting, but it was right thing to do, and it is part of my penance, in atonement for my actions. *I'm sorry, I'm sorry, I'm so sorry!*

I give myself a minute or two to get my breathing under control, during which I take another quick check around to make sure nobody is standing, watching me from the silent shadows. Satisfied that I am indeed still all alone here on this terrible night, I scramble to my feet, pick up the shovel and set to work covering Junior. Tears are streaming down my face as I shovel heap after heap of cold dank earth over his body. I shovel and shovel until my muscles are burning, my eyes are stinging, my lungs are screaming, and I'm caked and covered in filth.

I heave the last few piles of soil onto what is once again a burial mound, packing it down so it doesn't look any higher than it did before, then I bring up the photo on my phone. With shaking hands I rearrange the decaying floral tributes and cards, in much the same way as they appear on the image, and once it is all done, I step back a few paces to survey my work. I check my watch. It is almost one-thirty in the morning. It has taken me more than two hours to dispose of Junior's body, but the job is done.

As relieved as I am that it's over, I do feel it should have taken me longer. Two hours, give or take, seems like such a short block of time to permanently dispense with a body. I feel like I've cheated poor Junior. He didn't get a proper funeral, the celebratory sort that would have lasted all day, quite possibly with laughter in equal measure with tears. Nor would he ever have one, if all went according to plan. I've robbed that boy of his life and his dignity, and so much more besides.

I've also robbed this innocent grave-dweller of peace in his or her final resting place. I don't even know if the person in there, underneath Junior, is a man or a woman. It's too soon for a headstone to be in place and I cannot bring myself to try and read any of the blurred cards that sit on top of the mound, sharing space with putrefying flowers, to find out. But whoever is in there has company now that they wouldn't want or expect.

I stand in the darkness, and I'm suddenly, acutely aware that I actually *don't* just have the stars for company, or the distant owl, here in this lonely churchyard. I'm standing in the shadows of the home of an all-seeing God. As surely as I stand here, shaking and crying in the heavy accusing silence, the notion of being judged and found wanting, by one I have so little knowledge of or belief in, is so strong I can hardly breathe.

I'm not a church goer or, as I say, even much of a believer in anything as specific as an omnipotent God. But I do feel the need to give Junior some kind of rite of passage to what may indeed be a 'next life'. At the very least he deserves a formal goodbye from *this* life, even if it's the most shameful person on earth that delivers it to him. So I whisper, tentatively, shakily, into the night;

'Forgive me, please, for taking your life. I don't even know your name, and that in itself is awful. I made a really stupid choice, and I'm so sorry. I know I've taken away your right to a future, and I'll be sorry for that for the rest of my life. I'm sorry it was me who was at this funeral, if you could call it that, and not your mum and dad; your family and friends. I'm sure you were loved, and I'm sure you'll be missed. Please be at peace now though, and be happy. And to whoever is in this grave, please accept my apologies for violating your resting place.'

I then recite the Lord's Prayer, because it's the only prayer I know. I stand looking at the sad mound of earth, for a few more moments, a few more heavy heartbeats, before closing the chest, putting it back onto the sack trolley, and wheeling it back towards the lane. If anyone were to see me I'm sure I'd cut the oddest figure, reminiscent of an olden-day grave digger in a horror film perhaps, wheeling a wooden chest through a churchyard in the dead of night, balancing a shovel on the top of it.

Back at the car, I heave the empty chest back in, along with the mud-caked shovel. I close up the car and tiptoe back to the scene, shining the light from my phone around, to make sure I haven't dropped anything, or left any other incriminating evidence of being there.

Everything looks clean, and I move the dirt around with my boot, to cover the evidence of busy activity around the graveside. Not that it would be questioned, since it's a fresh grave anyway, with plenty of visitors no doubt, who still want to keep a connection for as long as possible to their loved one. With two fresh graves fairly close together, a large amount of visitor activity would probably be normal, at this point.

I head back to the car, checking for tyre tracks from the sack trolley, but there are none. The hard earth, thanks to weeks without rain, has supported the trolley completely. By morning, with the sun having dried the dew on robust grass, any traces should hopefully be gone.

I check my reflection in the rear-view mirror. I look a mess. My hair is matted with soil and my face is filthy, from crying and wiping tears away with dirt-caked hands. I glance at my clothes which are covered in damp soil. I rummage around in the glove box for a packet of wet wipes, and I clean my face, hair and hands as best I can, with hands that shake like leaves in the wind.

Part of me wants to just sit here, letting the enormity of what's been done sink in. I want to sit here, lick my wounds, and let the silence settle me, for however long it takes. But the silence *itself* is unsettling now. Only a couple of hours ago, it was a reassuring blanket of safety, but a U-turn has occurred inside me. Now the silence is simply oppressive, with an undertone of menace that threatens and unnerves me. This is not the time or the place for self-indulgence. I need to get out of here.

13

Saturday

- Darren -

I'm looking forward to meeting the motley crew at the Fox and Grapes. I haven't enough money on me to get hammered though, so it looks like I'll be on the last bus home, but it's better than sitting at home with Mum bleating in my ear all fucking night, then Pat coming home and looking down his nose at me. And you never know; one of the lads might stand me an extra pint or two tonight. I've done it for them enough times, when they've been skint and I've been flush.

Predictably, it turns out to be no different a night from any other we've all been out on, but tonight I just can't seem to get into it. I've spent most of my money, and kept enough back for my bus fare, and I have had a couple of pints bought for me, but I can't seem to get a buzz on, so it's all been a bit of a waste of time and money.

Ginge, one of the lads, keeps banging on at me to go back to his place for some vodka shots after last orders, but I really can't be arsed, not least because it's a long walk home from his place to mine and taxis don't take buttons for payment, as far as I'm aware. Ginge is pissed already, and he plans to get even more pissed, and most likely incapable of doing anything with the hopeful, doe-eyed little tart he's managed to pull, who seems determined to follow him home, if her skyscraper heels will allow her to walk by the time she's finished that last pint.

Despite being an ugly stringy redhead, Ginge can pull the tarts like no-one else I know. Going back to his place, what's the bloody point?

So they're all booing me and calling me a piss-arse party pooper, and I'm watching the bloody clock waiting for last orders so I can have a last quick pint to run the course with them all, and then leg it for the bus. I don't give a damn what they do after that.

Party pooper? Well, I've been called a lot worse and it's better than getting smashed off your face, you silly bastards. You can have your fucking hangovers. I've got bigger things to worry about than how drunk I might have to get to stop ignoring the skinny, pimple-faced girl that's been smirking at me from the other end of the bar for the last two hours, and do anything with her.

Last orders gets called, I order my pint and I swill it down in five swallows.

'Right, you tossers, I'm off home.'

'What? You can't be, mate, the night's only just fucking starting!'

'For you, maybe, but I've got stuff to do tomorrow, so I'm off for the last bus.' *Good to see you, keep out of trouble, and I'll see you soon.* Not.

Howls of protest, chicken noises and name-calling follow, but to be honest they're all so shitfaced they'll have forgotten all about me in less than five minutes, so I'm not too bothered. They love me, really.

It hasn't been a bad night. But it's not what I remember our nights out being, probably because despite six pints I'm still as sober as a fucking judge and the lads all seem a bit pathetic in their rush to get hammered, throw punches and talk even more bollocks than usual. It also feels disloyal somehow, having a good time with those dole-dependent dropkicks, when I don't know what's happened to little Tom.

Or maybe I'm just outgrowing this raucous shit that passes for a social life. Maybe I just don't want to keep getting legless anymore and waking up in some tart's dirty bed, with a hangover from hell. I keep thinking about that girl I met at the beach this morning. Would she like a night out like I've just had? I doubt it. She'd be more into a few quiet drinks in a nice wine bar, or a meal in a cosy country pub with a log fire and good conversation.

And what's wrong with that? Nothing. Nothing at all.

Pat's little van is in the driveway at home, and the lights are all on, so I steel myself for walking in, to yet another glare from the man himself. I was hoping to watch a bit of late-night telly, as I often do when Mum and Pat have gone to bed, but tonight it doesn't look like they're in a rush to head upstairs. I don't even ask if they'll be up late, because I don't want to give him any chance to start moaning on at me borrowing off Mum to go to the pub. The less ammunition he can fire at me the better, so I poke my head around the door, say goodnight to Mum, then head straight upstairs.

As I lie in bed, with sleep eluding me yet again, I wonder how to go about telling the plod whatever I can about Tommy, without getting myself in the shit.

14

Saturday
- Alison -

I start the car and back up, with just the reversing light for assistance, and I continue backing up from the point at which I came in.

Look back at the bushes I've driven and reversed through, I can see there's a gap there now that wasn't there before so I get out of the car and go and drag a few branches back together to cover the hole, with just my park lights lending the barest level of illumination. I'm only partially successful, but there are no tyre marks where I went in and came out, so I simply have to hope for the best, that nobody will see that gap and wonder about it.

It's a bit of a trick to turn the car around in the narrow lane, but I manage it and head for home, inching up towards the main road, again with just the park lights on. Once I reach it I take advantage of the fact that there is no traffic on it at all, and I switch the headlights on and accelerate away. I decide to head home down the motorway so I can stop at the services to clean myself up a bit. I don't expect anyone to still be up in my cul-de-sac when I arrive home in the wee small hours, but just in case there are, I don't want to arouse any suspicion by looking like exactly what I am; a gravedigger.

I pull into the services and take off my sweatshirt, which is absolutely covered in dank soil. I head in, just in my t-shirt, jeans and boots, and I make straight for a disabled toilet, which is thankfully unoccupied. I run the hot tap at the basin and allow the heat of the water to seep into my chilled hands as it sluices the filth from under my fingernails, four of which are now ragged and chipped, to add to the ones I broke when I cleaned the understairs cupboard. My hands now look like I've tried to scrabble up a mountain face.

Twenty minutes later, I've achieved a presentable state. I've washed my hair and dried it under the hand drier, and rinsed my boots off under the tap and dried them off as best I can with paper towels. By the time I'm ready to leave the washroom, it's really only my jeans that look a mess.

I grab a much-needed coffee on the way out and, without even making eye contact, the night-shift assistant drones at me; 'have you had a nice day, Miss?'

After mumbling some remark about heavy gardening, I make my exit, determined not to glance into the eye of any one of the CCTV cameras which undoubtedly cover every public inch of the premises.

An hour later, I'm gliding gently into my own driveway. It's almost three in the morning and there are no house lights on anywhere at all. Everyone is in bed, hopefully sleeping. I leave everything in the car for what's left of the night, and head into the house. I don't put any lights on either, but as I close the door behind me I lean against it and listen for noises. I stand there for a long time, five minutes maybe, just listening for the slightest sound. The lack of Badger-welcome is profound, yet again.

All I can hear is a tap dripping, and a clock ticking in the bedroom. I love the sound of a ticking clock, it helps me to sleep. Some people can't stand it, but for me it's a soothing sound.

After satisfying myself that I haven't disturbed anything or anyone, I make my way upstairs and switch on the bathroom light. Swamped by the irrational relief that everything is exactly how I left it, I turn on the shower and step under it, as the room fills up with steam.

I overload on the shampoo and shower gel, using a nailbrush, a loofah and a heavily-scented exfoliation scrub in the hope that I will, at the end, feel clean. I crave the comfort of a pure cotton nightgown, so I rummage in my nightwear drawer to find one. I slip it over my head and, still warm from the shower, I snuggle down into bed, not caring that my hair is wet. I determinedly ignore my mother's voice in my head. She's told me a million times that one day, if I keep going to bed with wet hair, I will wake up completely deaf.

Will I sleep? Probably not, but I close my eyes anyway. I do at least need to make an attempt to get rest, if not sleep. It's been a long night. Since it's Sunday, and since I don't have to get up early to take Badger for a pee and a poo, I can stay in bed as long as I want to. I hope to be able to shed this God-awful, throbbing headache that really doesn't seem to want to leave me. It would be nice to feel something close to rested, rather than dizzy and sick, before I get to spend the day preparing to achieve some semblance of normality at work on Monday morning. Back to the whining debt-heads. Yay.

Maybe it's time for a change of job. It's been a long time since debt collecting was the challenge it started off as. My first ever 'credit control' job was working for a small, elite wine importing agency in the Cotswolds. I was living up there because I was seeing a bloke for a while who was at Cirencester University. When I first went to work at Baringford and Windy Ridge Wines, which was based in an old army barracks, the accounting system was woeful. It consisted of a simple, dog-eared rolodex with hand-written notes on it, as a record of who had bought what, and when, and whether or not it had been paid for.

It was the most pathetic and inept system of accounting I'd ever seen, so I set about updating everything, and of the forty-odd thousand pounds in unpaid debt that went back many months, I managed to drag in virtually all of it. Despite that, the owner and his wife, Mark and Annabel Fierce, decided that I didn't really fit into their ludicrously overblown culture of snobbery. Within six months of me getting those raving bloody toffee-noses back on their feet, they'd made me redundant with two weeks' notice.

They told me on a Friday morning, before I took a lunch break. I used it to sign up with a recruitment agency that offered me another job to start the following Monday morning. When I went back to Baringford and Windy Ridge Wines after lunch and told Mark Fierce, that I wouldn't be working a fortnight's notice, he blinked a couple of times and remarked that I didn't let the grass grow under my feet, and then his stupid selfish wife Annabel moaned at me because I was 'leaving them in the lurch.' That was the end of what bit of regret I felt, for leaving them in the lurch.

I was happy to go, and leave them to grapple with their list of wealthy clients who always wanted top quality wine but never wanted to pay for it. I knew they'd all be in the same silly mess in another six months, and I really didn't care. But the dice had been rolled for my future. It turns out I was brilliant at debt collection, and that was where I stayed.

I'm not sure at what point righting the company balance sheets stopped being a challenge and became just a wretched role instead, but I realise now, lying here in the dark, and shaken to the core of my being, that I don't want to do it anymore. I make up my mind to start exploring other options; maybe including writing that stupid book of 'stupider' excuses.

My mind keeps relentlessly dragging me back to thoughts of dirty soil, and the fight continues as I try to avoid it. In defiance to the horror of the days that have passed, I send healing thoughts to my beautiful dog, and I plan his homecoming. I'll make a meatloaf, complete with gravy. That's Badger's favourite treat, and something we can share.

I think about walks we will explore together when he is fully healed, and I do all I can to push away the thoughts that continually crowd my head, of the smell and taste of damp earth, the bottomless sadness at the loss of the life I've taken, and the sound of a lonely owl.

15

Sunday
- Darren -

It's unbelievable that after six full pints I'm still not able to get any bastard-bloody sleep! Everything keeps crashing around in my head and after tossing and turning for hours, I've realised that before I make any kind of decision about telling the plod anything at all, I need to go back to that house *again*, and take another look around. I need to revisit the scene of the crime to see if there are any clues – any at all – about what might have happened there after I left. I'm not naive enough to imagine I'll find one of Tom's trainers by the back fence, to indicate he's thrown himself over it, or anything so fucking obvious. But I have to reassure myself of something – *anything* – that can tell me this makes sense on any level.

I'll have to go under cover of darkness of course, and since I can't sleep for trying, I may as well go now. I look at the clock. It's quarter to four in the morning.

At the same time as telling myself it's a completely insane thing to be doing, at this crazy time of night, I get back up, get dressed again, and figure I can creep down the stairs and head out the front door quietly, without being heard.

No such bloody luck. Just as I get to the top of the stairs, Pat wanders out of the fucking bedroom and into the hallway, presumably going to the loo. He sees me, fully dressed and obviously heading out in the wee small hours of the morning, and he just stands there. We both just stand there, staring at one another. He says nothing, but the look on his face tells me everything. He thinks I'm skulking out to do a 'job.' To be fair though, given the hour (and with my track record), why would he think any different?

I consider telling him it's not what it looks like, but his face is so full of disgust, I know he'd never believe it, so I just shrug and make my way downstairs. He'll tell Mum, and God alone knows what she'll say back to him. I was hoping she'd keep our little chat about Tommy just between ourselves, but now, after this, I don't know if she will.

But I can't let that stop me. I have, as some would say, a very big bee in my bonnet, so I have to see this mission through before the sun comes up. Unwise, yeah, but the feeling that I have to do something other than just lie in bed is too big to ignore. I'll go fucking mad if I don't try.

So an hour later I'm back in Topsham, hovering around in the dark shadows like the thieving scum they all think I am. Loitering with intent. Or, 'loitering *without* tent' as Tom always loves to say, before bursting into uncontrollable fits of laughter. He has one of those infectious bloody laughs. The minute you hear it, you can't keep a straight face for trying. He's like a hyena on steroids, when he starts.

It comes right up from the bottom of his guts, that laugh, and he puts his whole self into it. If something's funny enough, he collapses like a house of cards, all his limbs go to jelly, and he literally rolls around on the ground, trying not to piss himself. How could you not join in with that? I can't wait to hear him laugh again.

But the truth is, now that I'm here at the woman's house, I haven't a clue what I'm looking for. Nothing looks even *slightly* out of the ordinary. The whole place is in darkness, and her car is in the driveway at the front, so she's probably home and asleep. The glass pane we broke has been replaced in the French door. Everything's quiet, as you'd expect in a neighbourhood like this, for the early hours of the pre-dawn morning; every well-heeled bastard snoring their fucking heads off.

The back garden looks normal. I've managed to pick the lock on her shed door, and I've used my mobile phone as a torch, but I haven't found anything helpful. It's just a shed, with potting mix, a mower, a few garden tools and empty pots, bits and pieces for a normal life. Nothing to indicate Tom's ever even looked in here, let alone hid himself here for any reason.

As I come back out I can see that dawn isn't far away from breaking now, which means I'm out of time. A security light comes on by the back of the house, so although I'm pretty sure I haven't been seen, I take off as soon as the light goes out, vaulting easily over the back fence.

Out on the road again, I take care to stick to the shadows, praying that the plod don't turn up again at this hour and notice me in the same part of town they found me just a couple of days ago, miles from my own house. That would ring every fucking bell they've got in their heads. And of course with a skinful of booze still in me, even if I do feel stone cold sober, it'll be all over my breath and they'll drag me in for bloody certain.

I'm none the wiser, after all that caper. Something's happened to Tom, but it doesn't look like it's been at that house. He must have left, and whatever's befallen him, it must've happened since.

I wish I didn't have to go back home, but I'm skint again, so I can't get back to the beach, and God knows what else I'm supposed to do at dawn in the city, without drawing attention to the fact that I'm out and about. I'm really regretting going out last night and spending every last penny on what didn't even end up being a decent night. And Sunday's a proper bastard of a day when you've nobody special to share it with. Sometimes on a Sunday I stay in bed until lunch time then watch the football on the telly. It's never been much of a day for me, really. It's a day for couples, families, friends, all to do stuff together, but I have nobody special to share the day with, and my so-called friends, those drunken fuckers from last night, are probably going to be sleeping off their hangovers until at least three o'clock.

So I just head home to go back to bed, and luckily there's no sign of Pat. As I make my way up the stairs I can hear him and Mum both snoring. What must it be like to share a bed with someone night after night, year after year, because you love them enough to put up with them rattling away like a JCB all night? I can't even imagine that.

I do drop off, this time, and the next thing I know, its noon. The sun's out, Mum's making Sunday lunch, which is usually ready about two o'clock, so I have a shower and straighten my room up a bit, then go downstairs to face the music, which will probably be frosty silence from Mum and being blanked completely by Pat. It also means I'll have to watch whatever he's watching on telly, since whenever I ask to change the channel I never get a response. Hopefully, he's watching the footie.

It's a kind of unwritten rule in the house that whoever's watching telly gets to keep watching their channel if someone else walks in. If you want to watch something different, tough. No point asking. I occasionally do, just to wind him up, but today I can't be arsed.

I did have my own telly in my room but it blew up after I spilled coffee all over the back of it, and I just haven't got around to getting another one. The main reason is that for me, replacing it means nicking one, and I know Mum would draw the line at having a 'hot' TV in the house. It also might send a message to her that I never intend to move out, and I don't want her to think that. I can't afford to move out, but that's not to say I don't want to. What bloke of my age still lives at home with his mum, for fuck's sake? Even if I had a girl, I couldn't bring her home. No nice girl would want to come here for the night, even if she was made welcome, and she wouldn't be; I'm sure of that. Mum might eventually get used to the idea if it was someone nice and steady, but Pat would never approve, and although it's Mum's house I don't want her ending up rowing with him over something I've done. Things are already bad enough.

For the first time, I'm starting to see just how empty my life really is, of anything nice, and if I want a better one I have to make some bloody big changes. But what do I do? And where do I start?

I promise myself I really will give thought to where my life is going, and what I can do about it. I just want to get Tom back safely first. That's the most important thing. I need him to come home to his family, and that includes me. I feel like his big brother, and I should have protected him, and I didn't, and all I want now is to see him, safe and well, back where he belongs. Right now, nothing's more important than that.

So I've made the decision. Tomorrow, I'm going to the plod, and I'll tell them everything I can, without incriminating myself. I'll do it before they pitch up here and stress my mum out again. That feels like the best place to start, and we'll see what happens after that.

16

Sunday
- Alison -

Last night turned out to be a bit disrupted, and that is putting it mildly. I woke with a start, just after half-past four. I didn't know what had woken me, but I was in a deep sleep after taking heavy painkillers to help me, so I figured it had to be something out of the ordinary. I lay there, holding my breath, listening intently for sounds, and after a minute or two I imagined I could hear a scraping noise in the back garden. Badger would have been barking his head off about anything out of the ordinary; he barks if a squirrel sets the security light off! But of course he isn't here to tip me off.

Every instinct screamed at me to stay where I was and try to ignore it, but curiosity got the better of me, and I quietly got up, slipped from the bed and padded into the third bedroom. I don't usually draw the curtains in there, as it's a lovely little room with a view of the back garden, which isn't overlooked by any neighbours.

I wasn't overly surprised to see that the security light outside the French doors had come on. Sometimes the activities of a neighbourhood cat are enough to set it off so I wasn't unduly worried to begin with, thinking that perhaps what woke me was a cat or a hedgehog knocking something over on the patio. I do have pots of herbs and flowers out there, and with all the dry weather we've had, they're not exactly heavy with waterlogged soil. It's possible for a big enough creature, like a fox perhaps, to knock one of the smaller pots down while brushing past it, and I'd almost convinced myself that it couldn't have been anything more sinister than that, when I noticed the door of the shed swing open, silently, on its well-oiled hinges.

I gasped inwardly and instinctively took a step back, away from the window, and off to one side. From my vantage point, tucked behind the curtain, I could just make out a tallish figure of a man as he stepped out of the shed and turned to close the door.

From what I could see, he wasn't carrying anything, so it didn't look like a theft in process, however his stance was furtive, stealthy, and it was clear that he didn't want to be seen. He kept looking around, obviously checking to make sure he hadn't been, and just in that split second before the security light went off, he turned his face toward the house. He didn't look up to the window but I could clearly see, in that brief, illuminated instant, the face of the man who was here in this house with Junior last Thursday, before he rushed past me and out through the French doors, into the wide blue yonder.

Senior!

As soon as the light went off, he moved with lightning speed. All I saw, in the insipid pre-lawn light, was the back view of him as he levered himself effortlessly over my back fence and disappeared off into the night. It seems that hasty exits are one of his specialities.

My breath came out in a rush. I was utterly stunned, and my heart was hammering. At half past four in the morning, a man who tried to rob me just days earlier was back on my bloody property, rootling around in my shed.

For what purpose? Was he really that desperate for something to steal? Was he emboldened by the thought that my dog is dead, so he can go about his business (*my business!*) without drawing attention to himself? Somehow, as much as I want to believe it's that simple, I know I'm wrong. He was looking for his friend. Or clues to his whereabouts, at any rate. The cheeky bastard must have broken the lock on the shed door.

I went back to bed, rattled beyond belief, but recognising that there was nothing I could do. Even if he'd still been in the garden, the last thing I wanted to do was confront him, or call the police. Imagine doing that!

Two hours later, in the stark light of morning, after fitful rest that could hardly be described as anything even *vaguely* resembling sleep, I note that the banging headache that's harangued me for more than a week is still there. It's actually making me feel sick now. I know I have to go to the doctor soon, about this. It's so debilitating, but I do wonder if it would have been a lot less of an issue if I hadn't allowed a child to choke to death, and then concealed the crime in the worst possible way. Maybe, without that, it would just be a 'normal' headache. And maybe Mum was right. I probably just need glasses.

The appearance of Senior in my garden has had a profound effect on me. Before now, I haven't allowed myself to dwell much on the fact that people will be looking for Junior. He could even be Senior's kid brother. Of *course* he is missed by now, it's been almost three full days!

I pad downstairs, make a cup of chamomile tea, find my laptop, and take both back up to bed. I switch the laptop on, and wait for it to power up before Googling missing persons in my county.

Results are quick to load and a number of sites come up. I scan through the one the local newspaper has put up, and bingo! Junior's face stares back at me, along with his details. He is officially reported as a missing person, and his name is Thomas Findlay. He is sixteen, and lives with his mum. He has a younger sister, and a young girlfriend. What they reported him as wearing when he was last seen are the same clothes he's buried in, in someone else's grave, in a small cemetery somewhere near the edge of the Dartmoor National Park.

The reality of this boy's life is suddenly here in front of me; everything I've been trying to avoid.

And, at the same time as an ice-cold finger of fear slides slowly down my back, I suddenly realise what else I've done. I've created a history footprint on my laptop with this search.

Damn! Fuck! Stupid, stupid!

Hastily I move to clear my cache and cookies, deleting my recent history. I'm aware that certain things can still be found by experts trained to delve into the deepest bowels of computer hard drives to glean information people thought they'd successfully deleted, but I'm hoping it will never come to the point where my laptop is confiscated and analysed. If it does, without a really good reason for conducting that search, I'm totally dead in the water.

I shake my head, as if to clear the thought, knowing that I will have to revisit it later. Maybe I need to get rid of this laptop, bury it somewhere too, and buy myself a new one.

My mind races ahead of itself, chaotic thoughts all jostling for position. If Senior is looking for Junior it means he is suspicious of what happened after he left. At the time, to be fair, I was white-hot with rage and wielding a very heavy metal frying pan. I'm pretty sure Senior was over the back fence and long gone before I hit Junior (Thomas) with the skillet that first time, *but I don't remember!* If he did see it happen, he couldn't have gone far. He'd have had to stay in the immediate vicinity; in the actual garden in fact, to have seen anything at all. I didn't even look up to see if he was still there, I assumed he'd legged it over the back fence, just like I saw him do early this morning.

But what if he was cheeky enough to have hung around? What if he *did* see something? What did he do when Junior didn't come out? How long did he wait? Did he see me hit him the second time? I'm not really sure if anyone can see into the house from the bottom of the garden, in the late afternoon sun, which would have been in his eyes anyway, if he'd stuck around.

The thought steals in to blindside me that he may not have been hiding at all! He may well have been simply standing there, in my garden, looking in at us. I wouldn't know, since my whole attention was focussed on Junior at the time. I simply didn't notice whether Senior had left the back garden or not! *Shit! Shit, shit!*

But I haven't had a visit from the police, and I'm absolutely certain they would have been here, hammering at the door by now, if I'd been seen bashing Junior's brains in with a skillet.

But then again, maybe not. Senior not reporting it may not be such a great surprise, since the two of them were in the process of robbing me, and he certainly wouldn't be keen to admit that. Whether he saw me or not, he doesn't know that I don't still have the filthy old holdall, and the beer bottle covered in his fingerprints and DNA, that could be enough to clinch a conviction. Was either of them wearing gloves?

I don't bloody remember!

If he didn't see, if he actually did leave the garden in his quest for self-preservation, then he has no idea that Junior (Thomas) is anything other than missing. He might have suspicions about what's happened, in fact his foray into my shed last night suggests that he does, but he will have no concrete idea that Thomas is dead, and buried, after a fashion. If that is the case, *do I have much to worry about?*

Whether he knows or not, that I'm responsible for this boy being missing, he was already sniffing around, in the wee small hours of the morning, trying to find out what he could under cover of darkness. It proves that he is worried. I've long since abandoned the hope that he was simply looking for something to steal. I don't know if the two of them had been into the shed before they came into the house. Even if they did, I have no idea whether Senior would remember a big wooden chest that was in there before, that isn't in there now. If he did, and he put two and two together, he may just make four. If he didn't, he has no real grounds for suspicion.

Anxiety gnaws relentlessly at my gut, dispelling all thoughts of trying to get more sleep, so I head down to the kitchen. Desperate to try and calm my jagged nerves, I make another cup of chamomile tea. I sit at the dining table until the sun starts to bathe the front of the house, flooding the living room with light. Then I get to my feet, open the French doors, and go down and check the shed door.

Not surprisingly, the lock hasn't been broken, but appears to have been neatly picked. It wasn't a heavy-duty lock; it was more of a lip-service attempt to secure what there was in there, which was in fact, all of very little value. Just a lawn mower, old and not really worth anything, a few small gardening tools, some old plastic pots, and a couple of half-empty bags of bark and compost. Not much to have to secure, apart from the wooden chest, which was pretty heavy and no mean feat for anyone to have manhandled out of the garden in any event. I'm so grateful I disposed of the body yesterday. Imagine if that chest had been still in there, for Senior to see!

The question had remained, flying around in my head, as to whether or not Senior had been in there before, to know if a chest had been and gone, but daylight brings clarity, and I realise that before and after I used the chest to hide and dispose of Thomas's body, the lock had been firmly in place on the shed door. There's no window, so nobody would know what had been in there, and the idea that Senior would have gently picked the lock, checked out the shed and then locked everything up again? Even I recognise that to be a stage too far in paranoia, and I let the reassurance wash over me that the presence and absence of the chest is not something that Senior would know about.

The day drags by, in a fog of failed attempts at remaining calm, and fruitless efforts to distract myself with reading and cooking. What I wouldn't give, to be able to take my lovely dog for a walk! Finally, late on Sunday evening, I fall into a deep, exhausted sleep in the armchair.

After the events of the past few days I thought I was damned, surely, never to sleep again but my jangling brain must have been overloaded to the point where it literally shut-down. I've gone over things in my head so many times now, it's like watching a video that involves someone else and not me. It's the stuff of TV drama when you think about it, and the brain must have finally said 'enough is enough,' and switched me off. Doesn't feel like it was great quality sleep though, and that's one thing I'm *not* surprised about, but anything is better than nothing.

I miss Badger so much. Poor boy, he has no idea or understanding of what happened to him, or why. He only knows he is in pain. I am so thankful he is alive and in the best possible hands, this lovely animal with the biggest heart. He knows nothing other than gentleness, he wouldn't hurt a fly. He's the dog who carries kittens gently in his mouth, who licks everyone who lets him, who nuzzles and snuggles, and shows nothing but love to anyone. He did not deserve to be attacked and left for dead. He is a true gentleman, who fully deserved to survive this trauma. And survive it he did.

In that instant, that moment of pure, undiluted gratitude to the universe, the clarity of what I have done does not disgust or appal me. It washes straight over me like a healing balm to my soul and, in that moment, I feel utterly justified and clean.

I've said before, to many a friend, that if anyone hurt my dog I would kill them and walk away with nothing on my conscience. A lot of people say that, but I wonder how many of them would actually follow it through, when push really came to shove? We all believe ourselves to be capable of murder, in self-defence, or in defence of loved ones. We all like to believe that if push came to shove, we really could cross that line, but I wonder how many people actually would? And, when they did, would they have any notion of what it would be like, to live with the consequences?

Well, I am starting to find out. And I guess that's what it all comes down to. If you do the worst thing imaginable to somebody else, can you live with yourself, after the fact? I don't have the answer to that yet.

17

Monday
- Alison -

My nerves are shot to hell, I'm jittery every time someone wants to speak to me, and even opening my emails is a daunting prospect, not that I'm expecting a sinister message along the lines of 'I know what you did last week.' But my ever-present paranoid thoughts keep pouncing on me, leaving me as tense as a tightrope with the effort of keeping them at bay. It would be so easy to succumb to having a full-blown melt-down.

I take a shower and get ready for work, heartened by the fact that Badger will be coming home tonight. I need to keep focussing on that thought. I'm counting on it to get me through without thinking too much about the past few days, and running the very real risk of losing it completely in front of my colleagues or, God forbid, on the phone with some whining punter who's trotting out yet another excuse for not making his fifth monthly payment for the new Mini Cooper convertible he must have *known* he couldn't afford.

As if on cue, the phone rings, and its Simon Westrupp, the on-call vet, checking to make sure I'll be home when he drops Badger off, at seven o'clock tonight. We chat for a minute about his progress, which is good, and I end the call feeling a lot more encouraged, with the anticipation coursing through me, of seeing my lovely boy at the end of the day. It's the first positive feeling I've had since Thursday night when my life started unravelling at the speed of sound, thanks to the two scumbag burglars who entered it and smashed it off its axis.

I finish getting ready for work, and resolve to turn as many of this day's moments into positives as I can, and get through them, one at a time. All I have to do is just get through this first day of supposed normality. It will be a benchmark going forward, I hope. 'Fake it till you make it.' If I fake it hard enough I just might be able to convince myself and everyone else that life is as normal as usual. It shouldn't be too hard, since I'm not known at work for my warm and cordial nature anyway. I'm aware that most people see me as a bit remote, and work-focussed.

I've never been a touchy-feely kind of woman. It takes me a while to get to know someone, and even when I do, I'm not the demonstrative type but when I warm to someone, I really do. I am a really good, solid, unshakeable friend, who happens to have really good, solid, unshakeable friends. They're just not my debt-collecting colleagues. Other than Daphne, who I've known for years, long before we ever started working together, I don't go out of my way to socialise with workmates. In my opinion, work and leisure shouldn't overlap. Like that old Offspring song that said; 'you gotta keep 'em separated.' It makes life a lot less complicated. I've never been interested in a work-weekend of Team Building, so convincing people at work that all is well shouldn't be too much of a stretch. Convincing Daphne is another matter. I'll play that out as it rolls along, as the day goes forward. I can wing it with her.

Enabling *myself* to feel like I'm functioning normally is going to take a lot more work. But I have to do it. I simply have to apply myself. Oh, the irony of that, reflected back from the comments of my teachers on my school report cards; *Alison will do just fine if she applies herself!*

The most challenging task of 'applying myself' is getting out from under this dark, persistent fug of foreboding. That's going to take many more long nights of logical reasoning and self-assurance that I've covered my tracks after doing the only thing I could realistically do under the circumstances. If I'm to have a life to look forward to, I need to get on with that process.

Everyone looks up when I arrive at work. I know I look like shit, and I guess everyone else sees it too, because a few people ask how I'm feeling, and everyone seems to want to hear the answer, which isn't normal behaviour for them. I assure everyone that despite still feeling a bit wobbly, and not having had a lot of sleep, I'll live if they don't expect too much of me today.

I'm greeted with smiles, and the general unspoken assurance, borne of long-standing teamwork ethics, that everyone will pull together to ensure I don't get overloaded on my first day back. It's what we all do. Like geese. One flags, the others rally round. There's no room for piss-takers of course, and everyone's had enough experience with those to be able to spot them at forty paces, but generally we're a pretty tight bunch, and we all pull our fair share of the weight.

The morning drags. Lunchtime rolls around, after what feels like three full days instead of just three hours, and a group decide to head to the local pub for a quick 'cheap and cheerful' bite. I'm invited to go along, but I automatically decline, preferring my own company to the raucousness of the crowd. They don't drink alcohol at lunch time, unless it's someone's birthday, but they do tend to get a bit boisterous, in a welcome release of the morning's tensions.

Nobody can blame them for that. Monday is our busiest and most tedious day. Everyone who owes us money gets their overdue reminders, threats of repossession, et cetera. on a Friday or a Saturday, so they're all on the phone first thing Monday morning, bleating away with their abuse and excuses. We tend to call the place A& E, and that's why. Abuse or Excuse; it's usually one or the other.

I started off in this job feeling sorry for the people who'd let their bills pile up to the point where they got themselves into hot water. For the first month or so, I used to go home feeling pretty low and hanging out for the weekend, when I'd have two merciful days of respite from the abuses, excuses, and tearful pleadings for extra time. If it wasn't a death in the family, it was redundancy, short-paid wages, an unexpected bill that had to take precedence. There was never a shortage of stories. It had got to the point where we started asking for evidence, such as a death certificate, a copy of a payslip, letter from the bank, and other proof of 'poverty-stricken status.' Even where people said they had a funeral to pay for, we now asked to see the bill before we'd grant them any leniency.

It used to really get me down. It wasn't just the genuine plight of some of those people. It was also the fact that others were outright lying about the worst of human circumstances just to get out of paying their bills, and the fact that we had to demand proof from even the genuine ones; effectively asking people to throw their dignity and right to privacy out of the window. Going home seriously questioning my ongoing suitability for debt collection started happening too many times to count.

One day was particularly brutal, and I found myself uncharacteristically heading straight for the pub at the end of it. When I got there I found half a dozen of my colleagues, all with the same idea, sitting staring dejectedly into their pints. Only one seemed chipper, and I asked him what the secret was: how did he not let it smash him.

'You have to toughen up and get over it, sunshine,' he told me. 'It's just a job, and someone has to do it. These people all had the opportunity to *not* buy stuff on tick, or pay up on time when they could, or negotiate with their debtors when they couldn't. Their coping skills, or lack of them, are not something you can control. You can't rescue them. They got themselves into the mess they're in. Regardless of how they got here, it's where they are, and it's their problem, not yours. You've got to let it slide like shit off your shoulders. End of.'

His words were blunt, but his tone was kind, and I knew him well enough to know that he meant it in the best possible way. And he was right. So that became my mantra. 'Do the job, and then forget it. Go home, and leave it in the office.'

I realised that if I couldn't do that, the job would eat me alive. So I toughened up as much as I could, while still being as human and compassionate as I could, and opportunities eventually led me to the position of Team Leader, and then to Senior Executive. I distanced myself emotionally from the punters and their stories, while still being able to appreciate their circumstances, and I simply organised solutions that would work if they were followed, for all concerned. Part of the deal was very clearly spelling out the consequences of failure to comply. As much as I sympathized with the awful plight of many, we did as an agency have to make sure they all got the point, that the responsibility for consequences was theirs alone to bear.

By the time I was offered a partnership, three years into the job, I had designed and implemented an operational system that had been extrapolated across the board. I even wrote and ran the training courses for new staff. I was as close to the top of my game as I was ever going to get, outside of running my own agency, and the thought had crossed my mind. I wanted to find workable solutions for the *punters*, not just for the staff, something that often seems to get forgotten in the relentless quest for getting payment and meeting those all-important KPI's that drive us all so hard. It was an imbalance that I really felt compelled to try and change. Compassion and solution-focussed attitudes are things you can't readily teach, but you can look for them in the people you want to hire.

But I've become very jaded in the last year or so; tired of everything, the same old shit I keep hearing and I'm genuinely starting to feel that staying in this industry at *all* is the last thing I want, let alone running my own show.

That decision is coming, and I will have to deal with it sooner or later, but the only thing I want right now is a bit of peace and quiet, to keep my diabolical headache under control, and my scrambled thoughts from unravelling and affecting my behaviour in ways that might raise red flags for my colleagues. If that means being the killjoy who won't go to lunch, so be it. Nobody is particularly surprised, since I still have all of the work from Friday still sitting on my desk, and the 'dodgy tummy' plea helps, but next time someone asks, I'll either have to be fully prepared to socialise without an apparent care in the world, or keep coming up with excuses until I run out.

I need to get it together, and fast.

Daphne hangs back, quite obviously torn between a much-craved 'top-off-the-pressure-cooker' lunch and her loyalty to a friend.

'You go,' I say, waving her away with my hand. Off the hook, she grins, tells me she will have a cup of tea with me at three, and then bolts for the door. Silence descends. There's a bit of keyboard tapping coming from the main floor, where some staff are working through, munching sandwiches as they plough through seemingly endless piles of files, but for the most part it's quiet.

I close the door to my office, and sit, staring out through the window. I have a nice view; on a clear day I can see out to the Exe river, and all the way over to the hills.

I suddenly remember the promise I made to myself first thing this morning; I promised myself I'd try to make each moment a positive experience where I could. So I jump up, grab my handbag, and head for the door. If I walk fast enough, I can catch everyone up. This will be my first test. A pub lunch, a positive event, and my first full attempt at normal. I power-walk to the pub, arriving just in time to sit down with the others, even though they've already all ordered at the bar. I grab a passing waitress and ask her if I can order, and have my food arrive with everyone else's, and she nods, all smiles. I order a gentle flavoured soup and sandwich, remembering that I'd forgotten to make my lunch that morning anyway.

Daphne is delighted, and swaps seats with someone so she can sit next to me. 'Glad you changed your mind,' she says with her usual big, warm smile.

I love Daphne. She's always a ray of sunshine on the worst of days, and I'm more grateful for her friendship than ever today, as she starts telling me about her weekend, deflecting the spotlight away from me having to make up some story about my own. She's been single for a few years, after a messy divorce, and she's recently started seeing a guy who makes her feel fabulous.

Concentrate on what she is saying, I tell myself, and once I do, it becomes easy to listen, ask questions and catch her enthusiasm. It lightens me in a way I didn't expect, and I am absurdly grateful for the diversion. It makes me wonder what I routinely miss, when I don't listen fully to people. She's thrilled that I'm interested and answers my questions with all the glee of a teenager in the flush of first love. It looks like it *may* be love, with this new guy, and I am genuinely happy for her. After too many nights to count, of sitting with her while she cried over her ex-husband's infidelity, and trying to reassure her that one day her world would mend and she would trust and find love again, it seems we are finally here.

The opportunity to think about something other than myself, Badger, Junior, and the desperately miserable events of the weekend, is beyond wonderful. It feels like a gift, and all of a sudden I'm doing it! I'm turning the day's moments into the best kind of positive. Daphne notes that I have six broken fingernails, and she jokes about it, but doesn't ask me to explain how I got them. As we all walk back to the office, I wonder if it might not be as difficult as I first thought, to have something resembling a normal life again.

I manage to get out of the office by five o'clock, and take a shortcut that most people don't know about, which takes no end of back-street turns but circumvents most of the rush hour madness. That means I'm home in twenty minutes instead of the usual forty or so. I tear up the stairs, take a shower, then spend far too long trying to decide what to wear for when Simon Westrupp arrives with my beloved dog. I decide on a simple coral frock. It's sleeveless, with a row of tiny pearls sewn across the top of the neckline, and the richness of the colour complements my dark hair. I have nicely toned arms, and I still have some summer tan left on them, so I think I do look nice. I blow-dry my hair and apply a bit of mascara and lip gloss. I don't want to overdo it, but I don't want to seem like I don't care what I look like either. That fine line between trying too hard and not trying enough.

I don't even know if Simon is single. He might be married with eight kids, but I want to be presentable for other reasons too. My dog is on his way back to me, and I want to make the effort, to welcome him home. I also want to feel like there's more to me than just jeans, a grimy sweatshirt and mud-caked boots. So, given there's a handsome vet involved, I decide it doesn't hurt to get a little more tidied up than usual. Perfume feels like a slight step too far though, so I don't bother.

Not that things feel *right*, of course. Far from it! I'm still like a cat on a hot tin roof. My headache and occasional bouts of nausea are all still there, hovering around the edges of my consciousness, and I feel as if my face betrays my actions, but if I needed any proof that that's not the case, I had it all day at work. Nobody looked at me sideways, nobody asked me why my hair was standing on end, because it wasn't. Nobody thought I was behaving strangely, as if I'd killed a child and dumped his body in someone else's grave.

It's not quite half past six, so I have half an hour. I decide to have a glass of wine, to calm my nerves. I'm having flashbacks again, unbidden, of seeing Badger on the floor, unconscious and bleeding, and of the feel of a metal skillet in my hand, and the sound it made when it smacked Junior's forehead twice. My hands start to shake, and I'm feeling tearful, but a couple of gulps of wine do help. I put some music on, some ragtime jazz, and it lightens things a bit. I'm nervous, but I'm also excited, and I'm sure that once I see my boy I will also be weak with relief.

The past few days have been such an incredible rollercoaster of emotion. Fear, white-hot rage, dread, confusion, incredulity, determination, anticipation, grief, sadness, remorse, resolve; you name it, I've felt it. I didn't realise I was even *capable* of such a range of emotions, all those things and more, in a few short days. I've met myself coming round a corner, had the chance to survey myself from a critical angle, and I hate what I have seen. There are parts to me that I didn't know existed. Now I know what they are, and exactly what I'm capable of, how do I live with myself?

I have no doubt that time will show me.

Time. Life's great healer. But does it heal everything? You look at some people whose lives are crippled and blighted by the ghosts of the past. They haven't healed. Sometimes, even those who want to, find they can't. Is that the life I'm destined for? Will I get over this? Will I have a day, a week, a month, a year, a significant plane of time in the future when I don't see that young man's face and feel like dropping to my knees and howling like a tortured dog? Will I ever be able to visit a quiet country churchyard? Will the sad stench of damp dirt and the acrid smell of household bleach always make me want to cry?

The clock ticks quietly on the wall, edging closer to seven o'clock. I try to pace myself with the wine, resisting the urge to gulp it down. I don't want too much gone from the glass when Simon arrives. I plan to offer him a glass, just to be friendly. He might not even drink. He is driving, anyway, so I don't suppose he will want one, but I do have to be polite and offer. Funny how, in the midst of the worst emotional turmoil, I can still be mindful of my manners.

Inevitably, seven o'clock arrives, and then so does five past. There is no sign of Simon, and when quarter past seven approaches I start to wonder what's held him up. I start to pace the floor, with all sorts of images going through my mind, of a car crash, Badger not surviving, of sudden complications that mean he cannot be brought home. I force myself to get a grip, take another gulp of wine, and as I set the glass back down on the kitchen bench, Simon's car finally pulls into the driveway.

In a flash, I'm on my feet, and I don't even wait for his knock. I fling the front door open as he is still getting Badger from the back of the car, and he sends me a quick look of frustration. In an instant, my anxiety is gone. The look on his face tells me he would have been here on time if he could. Somehow, I just trust that look. Even though I don't really know the man, there is something so fundamentally honest about him, in the way he conducts himself. He just radiates basic masculine honesty and goodness.

What you see is what you get, I think to myself as he makes his way to the front door with my shaggy, gorgeous boy in his arms. What a shame it is, that the same cannot be said of me.

'Traffic,' he mutters, as I put my face to Badger's. 'I'm so sorry. There's been an accident on the ring road, and I had to take a detour.'

I assure him that it is fine, no problem, in the midst of burying my face into Badger's warm fur. It feels so good, to do this, to feel and inhale his Badger-ness. I love my dog so much, there are simply no words to describe it. My love for him engulfs me. Having him home again is the best feeling in the world.

Remembering my manners, I step aside and allow Simon to enter the house, telling him that Badger's bed is all set up in the new cage, in a corner of the kitchen. He carries him through and lays him gently onto the floor, onto his bed in the last of the sunshine that filters through the French doors.

I'm immediately on the floor, nuzzling Badger's face again with my own. He licks my nose, gently. In that instant I am crying again, this time with relief and the pure and simple joy of having him home. This poor man, Simon Westrupp, must think by now that I'm simply a basket-case who doesn't know how to do anything but cry. But he chuckles, and allows me the time I need to recover my composure. Badger is quiet, but happy to be home.

We sit at the dining table and Simon goes through Badger's healing regimen. There are antibiotics and pain killers to administer, and I need to be prepared for a few toilet accidents in the coming days as we work on his mobility to get him to the garden. He needs to be carried to and fro, so that he can conduct his toilet. That's not a problem. It does mean I'll have to race home at lunchtimes for a couple of weeks, and I can also get the dog sitter to look in on him while I'm at work, to make sure he has food and water, and is not in any distress. She's paid by standing order anyway, so she may as well keep earning her money.

Overall, it seems to be a manageable regimen, and of course if Badger heals the way he is meant to, it won't be a long inconvenience for either of us; me or my lovely boy.

I offer Simon a glass of wine, since I've seen him glance a couple of times at mine. He smiles, that lovely smile that lights up his entire face, and says 'Why not? I'm driving, but I'm not on call this week, so a little one won't hurt.'

So we sit at the table and chat about his work, about my work, and the general state of the nation. The conversation is easy and light. We don't touch on any really personal stuff, like if either of us is seeing anyone, but somehow there's no pressure to find all that out. Half an hour rolls by, and when Simon's wine glass is empty, he prepares to make his exit. Part of me is relieved, but another part is longing for him to stay because not only is he a genuinely nice guy, but he also represents *normality* in a way that sitting here alone with my empty wine glass, reflecting on the events of the last few days, will never be.

'If you don't have to rush off, I can throw together some pasta and salad,' I offer, out of the blue, surprising even myself with my sudden forwardness. I guess the need for normality beat decorum to the post.

Simon looks uncomfortable and makes to hasten his departure by sweeping his jacket off the back of the chair and shrugging into it in quick, decisive movements, and I immediately regret my offer. 'I'm sorry!' I mumble now, mortified. 'I didn't mean to cause any offence...

He cuts me off with a shake of his head, saying 'No, no, none taken. It's just getting late, and I should get off.'

'Right then,' I say, trying to sound bright about it, and wondering if I've embarrassed the poor man, who quite possible *does* have a wife and eight kids waiting at home. We walk to the door and he steps outside. He nods curtly, and tells me that if I have any concerns about Badger's progress, I should feel fine about getting in touch. I thank him again for all his help, and he unlocks his car and gets into it quickly.

I don't wait until he leaves the driveway, like I would for most visitors, waving them away with a smile as they drive off. Truth is, I'm so glad the whole embarrassing scenario is over, it's a relief to simply shut my door. But I'm slightly sad. I don't know what I was really thinking; I just wanted to share some of my meal with him. I really had no thoughts of anything beyond that, but it was abundantly clear that he didn't really want to spend any personal time with me.

I pour another wine, grab a cushion, and sit on the floor beside Badger's cage. I give him another reassuring stroke, bury my face in his shaggy warm fur, murmur comforting sounds to him, and hug him as best I can. I'm so thrilled to have him home again and in some small way, seeing him so incapacitated, a glimmer of justification briefly sparks in my chest.

He is my dog. My beloved. He relies on me. It's just as much my job to protect him from harm as it's his job to protect me. It's my job to punish those who harm him. For one brief moment, that spark of justification flares and burns bright before it quickly dies away, leaving a taste of damp dirt in my mouth.

Five minutes tick by, while I work to stave off all thoughts of dinner-for-one, stinking soil and filthy fingernails, and an undetected corpse beneath a chill mound of earth.

All of a sudden there's a knock at the door. I startle so hard I almost spill my wine, and I sit there, frozen for a second, while the end-of-summer shadows steal around the edges of the room. The knock comes again, and I think to myself *there are no lights on, I can pretend I'm not home.*

'Hello? Alison?' comes a voice through the letterbox. It is Simon's voice, I realise with surprise, and since he knows I'm here, I really have no choice but to answer the door.

'Please can I come in for a minute?' he enquires in a rush of words. I swing the door open and indicate to invite him in. The very second he crosses the threshold he turns to me with a frown on his face, shakes his head and says; 'I'm so sorry. I was unbelievably rude to you just now. You issued a very kind invitation to me, and I was just bloody rude. I've had to come back and apologise for that. Please, please forgive me.'

I start to protest, seeking to reassure him that it is in fact perfectly okay for him not to want to have dinner with me, however informal, but he raises his hand to silence me.

'The thing is, I've been on my own since my divorce a couple of years ago, and it seems I have lost the ability to be gracious when a lady invites me for dinner.' He grins, sheepishly. 'Will you forgive me my appalling manners?'

'Well, I'm not sure I'm really much of a lady,' I say, with a smirk, 'but forgiveness might depend.' He raises his eyebrows at me and I tell him that I will only forgive him if he changes his mind and can be mannerly enough not to condemn me to eating alone.

'Alright then, when you put it like that,' he says, and the frown disappears, to be replaced with a cheeky, relieved grin.

We go back to the kitchen and I set about making a simple tomato and herb sauce, and setting pasta to boil, while he leans on the counter and regales me with tales of neurotic dogs and their even more neurotic owners. He does a great 'outraged falsetto' of a woman whose pug had eaten a corn cob and couldn't digest it; 'he didn't even ask if he could have it.'

As we sit down to eat, I'm struck by how comfortable it feels, to have him here. It's easy, relaxed and fun. He is kind, he is funny, and he is seriously good looking when he smiles. Fuelled by three glasses of wine I tell him so, which only serves to make him outright chuckle, which truly transforms his face. He compliments me in return, and the evening turns out to be one of the nicest I can remember.

I tell him that too, as he is leaving for the second time, with a far nicer atmosphere around us, and he nods in agreement. As he departs, he bends and kisses my cheek, thanks me for a lovely time, and heads to his car. This time I do keep the door open, until he has backed away and his taillights have disappeared at the end of the road.

Only after he has gone do I realise that there has been no mention of another meeting. Not that it seems to matter a lot. Somehow I just have the feeling that I'll be seeing him again, and it's not as if I have nothing else to do but sit by the phone.

18

Tuesday
- Darren -

The posters are up. They're on lamp posts, in newsagent windows, and being handed out on the streets. It's only been a few days, but I was kind of hoping that somebody would have come forward, to say they've seen Tom somewhere. Not one single lead has come to light yet, about where he may have gone, but I know for absolute certain that if he was okay, he'd be home by now. I've been back to that house twice, although I only looked at things from the street, the first time, and when I went into the garden I didn't see a single thing that would help me work anything out.

Surely there has to be some clue, somewhere, about what's happened to Tom? People don't just fucking vanish, do they, without *someone* knowing *something* about it? Part of me wants to just march up to the front door of that house, ring the doorbell, and ask that bloody woman what happened after I legged it last week. But the bigger and more cowardly part of me just says 'what the fuck are you thinking?'

As I'm sitting here staring out the window, waiting for Mum to come back from her cleaning job around the corner, an idea starts to form in my head. I stick the kettle on, to make a cup of tea for her when I hear her come in, and it's ready for her when she comes into the kitchen. Her face lights up. 'How lovely! Thanks!'

She sounds genuinely surprised and thrilled that I've made her a cup of tea. It's such a small thing to do, but it means so much to her. How blind have I been? She doesn't want much. She doesn't *need* much, to be happy. Just a bit of consideration, a bit of support. Why have I never noticed how sad and weary she always looks? I *have* seen it, if I'm honest, but it's never properly registered. Neither has the fact that I could do something about it or - more to the point - that I might just be the bloody cause of it.

'Sit down, Mum. I've got an idea.'

She looks at me suspiciously, not sure how to respond. She sits, and starts sipping her tea. She reaches for some sugar, and it occurs to me that I made her a cup of tea without even knowing that she likes sugar in it.

'Mum, how would you feel about going to that house we tried to rob, where I went with my friend Tom, and talking to that woman?'

She looks at me as if I've just spoken to her in a foreign language. She takes a deep breath, as if she's trying not to lose her temper, and asks me if I'm off my bloody head. It was the reaction I expected, but I ploughed on.

'Mum, you could pretend to be someone from a charity or something, just talk to that woman, suss her out, get into the house if you can, just to see how things are. I just need to know if there's anything in there that might give a clue to where Tom might have gone, or if she says anything about being burgled, or about her dog. Anything, Mum, anything at all that might help. Please!'

I sound desperate, even to my own ears, and I realise I really *am* desperate. Not just to find out if the woman knows where Tom went, but to find out if she's reported the crime or has any plans to. I'm also desperate to know how she's coping about losing her dog. For some reason that just keeps on coming back to me, that vision of her staring like a zombie at her own fucking wall.

'Darren, you must be stark raving mad! How the hell would I get a complete stranger to talk to me about anything important on her doorstep, let alone invite me into her bloody house?'

'I dunno, Mum. but if we could think of something, would you try? Would you?'

She looks at me for a long time, saying nothing. She finishes her tea, stands up and says; 'Have you thought any more about handing yourself in?'

'Yeah. It's all I've been thinking about.'

'And?'

'I haven't ruled it out, Mum. I really truly haven't. I will talk to the plod, and I'll do it today, but I can't tell them everything yet; not all of it. I just can't. It's not me being a coward; it just doesn't *feel* right. None of this feels right. I'm not saying I won't come completely clean at some point, but I need to know more first. I have to get a few things straight in my own head, before I make that decision. I don't want to go to jail again, Mum. Not if I really don't have to.'

She nods slowly. It's the second coherent conversation she's had with her son in two days, after years of grunting, shouting and silence. I can see that she is weighing a lot of things up in her own mind.

'You need to go out, love. I need some time to think. I'm not saying I won't help you, and I'm not saying I will. I just need time on my own to think about what I can do, and if there is anything – and I'm not saying there is – the next question is whether I'd be prepared to do it. And that's as much as I can say about it for now. So you need to go.'

'Thanks Mum.' I get up and start to leave the kitchen, and I hear her say, quietly 'I love you Darren.'

'I love you back,' I say, and then I leave.

As I close the front door behind me, I'm wondering what the hell to do with myself for the rest of the day. I know the plod want to talk to me, and I know they won't back off until they've had the conversation they want, so I decide to pre-empt them coming back here looking for me and getting my mum all wound up again. She's been upset in the past when they've turned up to arrest me, and taken me away in handcuffs. I don't suppose anyone wants to see that happen to their kids, however old they might have got, or however responsible they should be as grown-ups.

I start walking towards the station. I figure I can at least tell them I saw Tom on Thursday.

When I get there the place is pretty quiet. Not much happening at all, even though it's almost lunchtime and by now there's usually at least one shoplifter and a couple of prozzies waiting to be processed. The plod must have had an easy night and morning, since there appear to be no bang-ups, no drunks or smack-heads shouting the odds from the cells. Some of society's finest are probably still sleeping something off. Others are no doubt queuing for a court appearance at the other end of town, and some will already be back on the bloody streets after their bail hearings. I know the systems in here well enough.

I recognise the copper at the desk, and he recognises me. He raises his eyebrows, smirks a little, then says 'Well, well, well. Look what the cat dragged in. Good morning, Mr Davies. Bit unusual, seeing you walk in here of your own accord with no handcuffs on you. And before lunchtime, as well!' I just look at him and I stand there, saying nothing, forcing him to ask: 'What can we do you for, Darren?'

'I heard you lot want to talk to me, Sarge, about Tom Findlay, that lad that's missing. Thought I'd wander in, save you the task of turning up at the house unannounced, and upsetting my mum again, you know, like you're so fond of doing?'

'Well, Darren, let's not argue about who's responsible for your Mum being upset when the police come knocking. It's certainly never *our* intention to wind her up. Can't say the same for you, of course. Seems like you don't need our help with that. We're only ever just doing the job, of course.'

'Of course,' I say in return, with as much sarcasm as I can find. I want to knock the bloody teeth straight out of his smirking fucking face, but of course I resist the urge.

'Well I'm here now, so does anyone back there want to talk to me or not? I can fuck off as easily as I came.'

He tuts and rolls his eyes. 'Sit down. I'll get someone out.'

After a half hour's wait, I'm called through to an incident room, where I'm told to sit. Again. Like a trained bloody dog. After a few minutes, a couple of plod come in, and I know one of them, but the other I've never seen before. They don't smile but they're not unfriendly. One of them prepares to start writing everything down.

They start by asking me how I know Tom Findlay. I tell them he's a friend, and they ask me what a bloke like me is doing with a kid like him. It's a fair question, it's the same one that most people ask, so I give them the same answer I give most people.

'I just always knew him from around the town, like. He doesn't have many friends, and neither do I anymore, because I'm sick of the assholes I used to hang out with, so Tom and me, we just knock about together now and then, have a laugh and a natter. He's a good kid.'

They then ask me when and where was the last time that I saw Tom, and I tell them it was on Thursday afternoon of last week, up at the rec ground at the back of the town. I bite my tongue slightly as I say that.

One of them looks at me. 'There's no CCTV up there, so we can't check that. Is there anyone you know who can corroborate it?'

I dunno,' I answer, shifting in my seat and trying not to look down and to the left, which I've heard is a dead giveaway to the plod when you're lying. 'I'm not in the habit of telling people where I'm going, and I dunno if anyone saw us up there or not. You'd have to ask around.'

'What were you doing up there?'

'Like I told you. Same as we always do. Moaning about our families, talking about who we're shagging, what we'd do if we won the lottery, that sort of thing.'

'Were you drinking? Taking any drugs up there?'

'No, mate. No fucking money for that.'

'And what happened after that? Did you see where Tom went? Did he tell you where he was going?'

'No. We parted company. I don't know where he went or what happened to him after that.'

I left him! I don't know where he went or what happened to him after I fucking left him!

'Well, thank you Mr Davies, for coming in to see us. We may want to talk to you again, so don't be surprised if that turns out to be the case.'

'Just call me, alright? Ask me to come in and I will. Just don't come to the fucking house again. It upsets my mum. And will you let me know if you find out anything about Tommy? He's my mate and I'm worried about him.'

'We will. Thank you for your time, Darren.'

Within seconds of all that, I'm out on the street again; turfed out of two places in the space of one bloody morning. I'm wondering what to do with the rest of the day, since Mum's made it clear she doesn't want me in the house while she mulls things over. No money, as usual, so I'm walking the streets again. It's like that's all I've done, since last Thursday.

I feel a bit better, even though I've lied about what we were doing. At least they know Tom was alright on Thursday afternoon. If they believe me. They didn't give me any indication that they thought I was bullshitting them, but you never can tell with the plod. They've got faces like smacked arses, most of them. Good faces for a poker game. You can't read them. Must be part of the training, learning to look blank.

I spend the afternoon bumming around the town, window-shopping and chatting occasionally with people I know, and by 5pm I'm wondering if it's safe to go home yet, because I'm fed up with just walking about, when my phone rings. It's Mum, summoning me home.

When I get there, she's got sausage and eggs on the table for me, and a fresh pot of tea. As I tuck in, she sits opposite me and says 'I've thought of a way I might be able to get into that house. I didn't ask you what sort of house it was, though, and that matters.'

I tell her it's a posh mid-forties detached, down a cul-de-sac in a well-established area, and she visibly relaxes.

'I thought you were going to say it was a new-build, and that wouldn't have worked.'

I look at her with my eyebrows somewhere up near my hairline, and with a huge sigh she carries on; 'I thought I could go and say that my parents lived in the house before I was born, and would she mind if I had a look through it.'

Genius! Unless of course the house had been handed down through family for generations, then the woman would know it was bullshit, and when I ask Mum about that, she just shrugs and says 'well, then she'll tell me I'm mistaken and I'll just apologise for having my wires crossed, and go.'

'We can probably check on a website like Rightmove, actually, to see when it was last sold. That might indicate it hasn't been handed down through the family? We can probably also get a floor plan off that, for you to know where things are. Might make it more convincing, when you're there?'

Mum nods. 'Yes, that's a good idea. But if there's no information and she does calls me out, or seems suspicious, I'll look a bit confused, and apologise and leave. It's not much of a plan but it's the best I can come up with, son. It will either work or it won't.'

She still doesn't look at all convinced but the fact that she's thought about a plan that really might work and is prepared to see it through for me is more than I deserve or could have hoped for.

For some reason I feel like crying again, but I manage to stop myself. I seem to be turning into a complete wet fucking lettuce. I hardly recognise myself, and if anyone had asked me a week ago, I'd have said I was the least emotional person I've ever known. Now? I'm fighting back tears more often than my menopausal mum, or some weepy adolescent girl.

Mum doesn't drive, so she plans to take the bus, and I give her the address. She goes and gets herself ready, and after half an hour she comes down the stairs in her best respectable suit, with her face fully made up. Her hair is nicely done, and she's got her best shoes on. It's so long, since I saw her all dressed up like that, like she's going somewhere nice.

'I didn't mean you had to go today, Mum!'

'If I don't go now, I'll talk myself out of it altogether,' she says simply, and I know this to be true. If there's one woman who can talk herself into or out of anything at all, it's Mum.

'If I'm going, I have to go while I've still got the daring in me. I should be over there by half past six. Hopefully home by half past eight. Wish me luck.'

I do, as she goes out through the door without another word or a backward glance. As I sit there at the table, with the last bits of my fry-up going solid on the plate, it dawns on me that I didn't have chance to tell her I'd gone to the nick to tell them what I knew about Tom. Sitting there, I'm conscious of the grandfather clock in the hallway, its pendulum ticking heavily as the seconds, minutes and hours of the evening roll by.

19

Tuesday
- Alison -

After a quick lunchtime dash back to the house to check on Badger, the rest of the day passes in a blur. It's been another manic one, and I wonder if that's going to become the new normal, with the current cost-of-living crisis crunching at the heels of people who once would never have dreamed of ending up in the debt they're drowning in now.

So I haven't had much time to dwell on anything but the work at hand. Having an absorbing distraction from my jangling thoughts and nerves has been wonderful, but I'm still more grateful than I've ever been in my life to get home at the end of the day, even though it's to the place where my life has actually fallen apart. There's a note from the dog walker to say she's looked in on Badger too, this afternoon, and he is doing okay.

There's also a voicemail message from the security company I phoned yesterday asking for quotes about getting an alarm system installed. They want to arrange a time to come and look at the house.

I take Badger into the garden for his early evening ablutions, and it's a slow, limping process. I have endless time for my dog, so it's not a problem. It's a bit uncomfortable for him, but he manages alright, and I bring him back into the house, get him settled back on his bed in the cage, and I'm just putting the kettle on, when I hear a knock at the front door.

I freeze. Who the hell could it be? This time last week, if there was a knock at my door, I'd have simply assumed it was someone I knew, and would have had no hesitation in opening it. Now, I don't even want to even *go* to the door, let alone open it. I'm not expecting anyone and Bill normally just texts me if he fancies a run. It occurs to me that I still haven't told him about Badger, and I make a mental note to pop over later, and let him know we won't be meeting him on the towpath for a while. He's the sort that would worry if he just doesn't see us for a while with nothing being said.

The knock comes again, and I steel myself, walk up the hallway, and call 'who is it?' through the door.

'Hello?' A woman's voice pipes up. 'My name's Barbara Davies. May I please have a word?'

'What about?' I can't believe my own paranoia!

'Sorry, I just want to ask you a question about this house. My parents used to live in it.'

I open the door to see a fairly short, middle-aged woman standing there, quite nicely dressed, and I can see that she is incredibly nervous. Her eyes are like saucers and her face looks weathered, like she hasn't had an easy life. There's a sadness; a weariness about her, that I can't quite define.

'Hello,' she says again, and meekly offers her hand. 'Barbara Davies.'

'Nice to meet you,' I say, raising my voice a little at the end, as if to ask *what do you want?*

She just stands there, fidgeting slightly and offering no eye contact, so I properly prompt her. 'How can I help you, Mrs Davies?'

Her words come out in a bit of a rush. She says she is very sorry to trouble me, and she looks like she really means that. 'Rabbit in the headlights' is the phrase that comes to mind; she is almost shaking with nerves. She explains that her parents lived in this house before she was born. Since they've both died she was researching a bit about their early lives, and her own family tree, and she'd discovered they'd lived here. She has obviously rehearsed this little speech in her own head before saying it; a number of times, I would guess.

She takes a deep breath and says, 'I wonder if I could trouble you to make a time to come back and have a quick look inside the house? I know it's really cheeky, and I know you're probably very busy right now, but it would mean a lot to me if I could see just for a few minutes, sometime when you have time to show me? I could come back when it suited you?'

She looks so miserable, like she's about to cry, and I get the feeling she's not used to asking strangers for favours, particularly such intrusive ones. It must matter to her then, this visit.

I stand there looking at her, thinking for a minute. Then I think to myself, *why not?* Why not give this poor scared woman something she really wants, an opportunity to connect with a past that obviously means so much to her. Why not do something nice for someone? It won't mitigate the enormity of my sins but it couldn't hurt to let her in for a minute or two, could it? She's just a mousey middle-aged woman. She doesn't look like she has an axe in her handbag.

I ask myself, *is this part of my penance? To be suspicious of even the most harmless of people, for the rest of my days?*

In the absence of an answer, I shrug off my once-more burgeoning headache, swing the door open, and invite her in. She looks stunned, obviously she wasn't expecting me to say yes so readily and invite her in on the spot.

'I have a few minutes free now, so since you've made the journey, you may as well come in now, if you like.'

'I came on the bus. It's taken me ages,' she admits. She smiles and crosses my threshold. *Into the lion's den.*

From the look on her face, she is thinking exactly the same thing. Now that she's inside, she's probably thinking twice about asking something so reckless of a complete stranger who may just have an axe in her *own* handbag! Well, luckily for her, I don't plan to make murder my on-going recreational activity.

I usher her down the hall, through the side of the living room and through to the kitchen where she immediately claps eyes on Badger, deeply asleep in his bed, inside the cage. She turns to look at me with a questioning look.

I sigh, deciding to tell her some semblance of the truth. 'I was burgled last week and my dog was badly injured. I thought they'd killed him, but he only has a fractured shoulder and a very painful nose, thank goodness. He'll be okay in a few months, but he has to stay in that horrible cage to confine his mobility, and he doesn't understand why.'

My voice catches a little, as the relief of Badger's survival hits me all over again, and this Barbara Davies reaches out and tentatively pats my hand, her way of reassuring me that she understands.

She thinks for a few seconds then asks me if I'd called the police. I tell her I didn't, and when she gently asks why, I explain that I just didn't think it would do any good, I didn't think the police would be interested, since the thieves didn't get away with anything, and my dog would heal, in time. I also tell her I'm getting a security system installed.

Keen to move the conversation to a safer topic, I offer to show her the garden. She smiles politely and we go outside. She looks around, and I assume she is thinking about how her parents lived here, and what they might have done in the garden.

I explain that the house was a lot plainer than this when I moved in, and that in the past nine years I've pretty much redecorated the whole place, replaced all the windows and ripped out the back door and replaced it with French doors that lead onto an outside patio I laid myself. I tell her I also had the downstairs bathroom installed, and that's my cue to bring her back inside, show her upstairs, and then gently manoeuvre her back towards the front door. I ask her if I can be of any more help, and she assures me that she has no further questions, reiterating that she simply wanted to see where her parents started their married life.

'What were their names?' I ask, conversationally.

She looks flustered for a moment, which surprises me, and I decide that she's probably just a private person who ironically doesn't want to give too much away about her own past to a stranger she's just asked such a huge favour of, herself. I don't press her any further, having regretted asking at all, if it's made her feel uncomfortable.

'June and William Fairweather,' she says quickly. She smiles again, as nervously as ever, and as I open the front door she thanks me again for letting her come in without any warning.

'It's the least I can do,' I mumble. I wish her all the best with her searches, I bid her goodbye, and I watch this strange little woman of so few words scuttle up my front path and out onto the road, presumably towards the bus stop at the top.

Just as I'm about to shut the door again, I hear Bill calling me from his own front door. I call back, telling him I'll pop over.

I resolve to do just that, and once I feel Badger is fully settled, with his latest round of medications administered, I pick up a bottle of wine and head across the street, for a catch-up with my friend. A slice of this kind of normality is exactly what my addled head needs right now.

Bill introduced himself to me as soon as I moved in here. He made it his business to introduce me to everyone else in our cul-de-sac too, all of whom were welcoming and have been friendly ever since, even though we can go for weeks without seeing one another. They are all the best of neighbours. Concerned and caring, but not intrusive. I realise I have a duty to warn them all about burglars in the area, and I ask Bill if he can spread the word.

He is shocked when I tell him what happened; that people broke into my house and badly hurt my dog. I tell him they didn't get away with anything, that I must have disturbed them coming home unexpectedly, but I didn't see who was there. They must have legged it when they heard me arrive. Again, I'm asked about the police, but I tell Bill I just don't want the intrusion. Nothing was taken, Badger will be fine, and I am getting an alarm system installed within the week. I'm starting to feel like a parrot.

He tries to talk me into contacting the police but sees that I am adamant. It's funny how everyone else's automatic reaction would be to inform the police, when my own automatic reaction was *not* to.

'It's really shaken you up though, Alison, hasn't it?' Bill observes.

'What do you mean?'

'You seem very on edge, a bit brittle. It's to be expected I suppose, and it will help when you get that alarm put in. Bit of peace of mind I should think, woman alone like you are, love.'

I nod, and agree that I will sleep better once the security system is in place. Bill and I chat about all kinds of things and, as the conversation progresses, I remember that he has lived here in this house for all of his life. He was born here, he grew up here with his parents and when they died he inherited the house, almost forty years ago. A retired drama teacher, he is now content to potter about in the garden, work with the local amateur dramatics club, and go jogging most days. He's been on his own since his wife died, before I ever moved here. He knows this neighbourhood like the back of his hand.

'I had a visitor earlier,' I remark.

'Yes, a woman. I saw her leaving as I called over to you.'

'She just turned up, out of the blue. Her parents used to own the house before she was born, and they've both died, so she's piecing together her family history. She wanted to take a quick look inside the house, so I showed her through. I think she was only here ten minutes.'

Bill's eyes narrow slightly, as if he is thinking. 'What did she say her name was?'

'Barbara Davies.'

'Who were her parents?'

'A June and William Fairweather, she said.'

I hear my mobile phone beep in my pocket and I pull it out to find a panicked-sounding text from Daphne 'Call me. Urgent!'

'Ah, Bill, I'm sorry. I have to make an urgent call,' I say rising from my chair. 'Can I catch up with you again in a day or two, when I'll have more time to sit and chill?'

'Course you can, love,' he says. 'You go. Take care of yourself, and that lovely doggy-boy. I'll pop around with a treat for him soon.'

I give Bill a quick hug and leave quickly, worrying about what's up with Daphne. As I enter my own house the phone connects, and she is far from upset. She's delirious. She's just got engaged, and she's wondering if I will be her maid of honour in a year's time!

I'm thrilled for her. It's wonderful to have some really nice news like this, and we chat for a while about the embryonic wedding arrangements already being drawn up. I promise to go over at the weekend and help her to plan.

As I hang up the phone, I can't help but smile, and for a few brief moments it seems that all is blissfully and perfectly right with the world. Everything is turning as it should, on its axis, and for a few brief moments while I bask in the pleasure of someone else's joy, I manage to forget about the shattered shoulder of my suffering dog, an undetected corpse in a wrongful grave, and the unhappy prospect of a lifetime of haunted dreams.

20

Tuesday
- Barbara -

My feet are killing me. I should never have worn these bloody shoes. When I stuffed my feet into them back at home I'd quite forgotten that they crippled my feet. It's that long since I last wore them, or any heels at all for that matter, I completely forgot how much they throw me off balance and give me back pain and bloody blisters.

Well I'm remembering now alright, and it's too late to do anything but grin and bear it until I can get home and get the bloody things off. Not that I feel much like grinning. I've just stood in front of someone, a perfectly pleasant stranger, and lied through my bloody teeth. I've just coerced someone I don't know from Adam, into letting me into their house on a false pretext, and I can't believe I did it. I can't believe I even *thought* about doing something like that, let alone actually going through with it.

I'm not a devious person by nature; what you see is what you get, which isn't all that much, but it's usually not dishonesty. I don't often lie to people. It's an uncomfortable feeling, and I understand how folk can get themselves into a right bloody tangle over telling lies. Nothing good can come of a tangle of lies, you mark my words.

It's over at least. I'm surprised how easy it really was, looking back. Is it always like that? Do complete strangers just swallow a story and act on it like that? I could have been anybody! I could have been there to kill her, and she just let me in, on my flimsy story, and swallowed it like it happens all the time. That's how some people get robbed, I suppose, like oldies who let the gas man in without thinking to check if it really is the gas man, then it turns out it's not; it's someone who threatens them or batters them, or worse, for their valuables. You read about it all the time.

People are just too bloody trusting. The woman did grill me a bit before she opened the door, I'll give her that. But the minute I started to speak, she just swallowed it all and swung the door open to let me in!

Do I really look so bloody harmless? I suppose maybe I do. I'm no spring chicken, and I've an honest face. Maybe it's why grannies get through customs carrying all sorts of drugs and the like. They look like the last people in the world to do any smuggling so nobody thinks to search them. I've looked innocent since I was a child, in fact, and it got me out of a few scrapes here and there while the other kids took the rap, but I've never exploited my innocent face as an adult. Never, until today.

I hope the bus isn't packed, I really do need to sit down. This one's going into town so it probably won't be, but the one I have to catch in town to get home again might be. Damn these God-forsaken shoes!

Darren will want the full blow-by-blow, and I've a good mind to tell him I never went, that I bottled it and turned around and came back home without seeing anything at all. I really want to do that, but it's just more lies, isn't it, saying that? Then where does it end, the lying? It feels bad enough already, lying to that woman just to get into her house, after she's been burgled already, and her poor bloody dog's been injured. At least the poor thing's not dead, like Darren was dreading. He'll be very relieved to hear that.

It's that bit of the whole thing that's been wracking him with the most guilt, not the act of stealing from someone, which to my mind is just as bad. It's a strange moral compass to have, isn't it, caring about what you do to animals more than what you do to people? But Darren's always been a bit of a mystery to me, the way that mind of his works at times.

The bus is here and there's plenty of seats, thank God.

When he was a kid, Darren used to bring home broken birds, and other little animals with injuries. He was so keen on fixing broken creatures, so gentle with them, that I fancied for a while that he might go on to be a vet, but that didn't happen. It wasn't that he didn't have the brains. He was clever, when he chose to be. He just didn't choose to be, that's all. He did well enough at school, and he could have done so much with his life, but he hasn't. He's a petty thief, a 'dosser' as my dad would have called him.

Dad would never have let me go courting with a dosser, never in a million years. He'd have chained me to the bloody bedpost before he'd let me walk out with a bloke like Darren. I know times have changed and parents don't have the same kind of authority they used to, over their daughters, but I'm still not surprised that Darren's not met a nice girl and settled down. Modern girls, they know their own minds, don't they? They can certainly think for themselves and they do know when a bloke's not got much to offer. You can't blame them for not hanging around.

I'd like to see him settled though. If he had a family of his own, I think it would set him straight. That's all it would take, I'm sure. If he could find a decent job, the right girl would soon come along. A couple of kids and a cat and a dog, a family to be responsible for, and he'd be just fine.

He'd love his own kids, would Darren. His Dad was no great shakes, and Lord knows we had too many years of ups and downs. I feel bad, like it's my fault he's the way he is. I should have done more than I did, to balance the influence his dad had, which wasn't good at all. Looking back, I probably could have been of more help, but I just didn't know what to do.

It's easier nowadays, there's a lot more support for struggling families. Back when I had him, I wasn't much more than a kid myself, knowing nothing about the world, or how to take proper care of my own new family. Working out how long to boil a bloody egg for was all I could do, back then. I'll never forget the day someone gave me a cabbage, and I took it home and sat the whole thing in the biggest pot I could find. I didn't have a bloody clue how to cook a cabbage!

What else could I have done, back then? Who would I have turned to for support? Who could I have confessed to, that my life wasn't turning out the way I dreamed it would, that my kids weren't having the life I wanted for them, that their father was a bloody drunk who never thought that paying the rent was important?

The last thing I could ever have done was gone and admitted to my mum and Dad what a massive mistake I'd made, and what a bloody mess it had all turned out to be. So I did what I could on my own, for Darren and Michelle. I know my son's not sparkling, but he could be a lot worse. He could have *had* a lot worse. At least he can't say I haven't loved him. I love him with all my heart, and I always will, and despite his attitude, and the life he's chosen, he does know that.

Michelle turned out okay, thank goodness. She got married a few years back, to a Spanish bloke whose family live in Barcelona. She moved there after the wedding, and I don't see much of her now, or the grandkids, but we talk on the phone. She rings every Sunday night, like she always has, regular as clockwork. She's happy, which I'm grateful for. It seems like a good marriage, so far at least. She always asks about her brother but we never spend too much time talking about him.

What do you say? After saying the 'same old, same old,' every week, there's nowhere else to take the conversation where we haven't taken it a hundred times before, and in the end it all just gets repetitive and bloody frustrating, because there's never any answers. No solution that I can see. None that Michelle can see. It has to come from Darren himself, and I've all but given up.

But I do have to say, I have seen a bit of a change in him over the past few days. Since that bloody burglary he did with that young lad; the one who's apparently gone missing. I didn't know Darren was hanging about with a kid like that. Sixteen, he is. What's he doing with a twenty-six-year-old? Why can't he hang around with friends his own age? And what the hell's Darren doing, taking a kid on bloody burglaries? I swear to God, my son's life just keeps on getting more and more complicated and harder to fathom.

I've got a twenty-minute wait for the next bus, the one to take me home, so I've bought a cup of tea at the bus station cafe. It's tasteless, like they've shown the teabag to the water for all of three seconds, but it's hot and wet, and that's all I need. I resist a sticky bun; a lifetime on the hips and all that. Just looking forward to getting home now.

But what to tell Darren? I have to be honest. I'll tell him about the dog, of course, and that will relieve him. But I'll also have to tell him the truth; that there's nothing else to report, other than to say the woman was friendly if reserved. She's a clean-freak because I couldn't see a single speck of dust, the place reeked of bleach and there was nothing at all, about her *or* the house, that made me think anything was even remotely wrong in there.

She was just a woman on her own, house-proud, and she confessed to being burgled. She got upset, when she was telling me how she thought the dog had died, so it obviously affected her, like it would affect anybody. But there was nothing else. Nothing at all, that I could see or feel about her, that would give Darren any reason to be concerned about his missing friend.

I don't know that woman though, do I? I don't know if she's always like that, or whether she's acting out of character. How would I know? It makes a laughing-stock of the whole mission, really. I mean, what was I expecting to find, a smoking gun on her kitchen table? A dead body propped up in one corner of a room with a lampshade on its head, or a pair of boots sticking out from behind the bloody settee?

What *I* think is that young man left her house after Darren did. *I* think, if something really has happened to him, it happened later that night somewhere else. Maybe he was at the pub and got into a fight. Sometimes boys get taken into the pub, someone will invite them in, ply them with drink and they think it's bloody wonderful. Then, all of a sudden, they're blind drunk and something happens to them.

I once read about a young boy, sixteen I think he was too, that got lured into a pub by someone, and he ended up being raped and murdered. They found his body under a bridge, all bare and battered and covered in blood. Tragic, it was. Bloody tragic.

Anything could have happened. But Darren seems different, because of all this. He seems worried, yes, but something's *different* about him. He really talked to me on Saturday, like he hasn't talked to me in years. I hated seeing him upset, but he had to get something off his chest, and while I could hardly stand what I was hearing, I did feel that something had changed with him. It's like I caught a glimpse of the man I've always hoped he could be, not the man he is right now.

Was it just wishful thinking? It's too early to say for sure. This might just be a turning point for him, although I don't know what will happen if they do find that poor lad and something horrible has happened to him. That might just send Darren spinning completely off the rails.

Here's the bus, thank God, and it's quiet too so I can sit down until I have to get off. I'm throwing these shoes out when I get home. I wouldn't wish this kind of pain on anybody, so forget the flaming charity shop! They're going straight in the bloody bin.

I'm afraid though, if I'm honest. I'm scared of what might happen in the coming days. It's like waiting for that first bolt of lightning, that first clap of bloody thunder, that tells you the storm they've been promising all week is finally here and about to unleash all manner of hell. I feel there's a big storm coming, and I'm not sure if I can hide from it, or what part I've played in it by getting involved where I shouldn't.

Lying to that woman; I'm not proud of that at all. Like most people I suppose, I've done a *few* things in my life that I'm not proud of. Staying for too many years with a drunk. Being too afraid to make anything of my life when I had the chance. Not doing more for my kids, that sort of thing. Oh yes, I have plenty of bloody regrets.

But coercing that woman today, that was a new low for me; a proper run off the rail, as my dad would once have said. If I didn't feel it was important, that what I did might somehow help my son to get his life together, I'd never have even *considered* doing something like that. But he seemed so desperate. It's a long, long time since he last begged me for anything, in fact I can't remember a time when he *ever* did, and that's probably why I felt I had to try, just in case it turns him around. Maybe my help in this will do what nothing else I've tried to do has ever done before, to save him from himself.

I couldn't save my bastard bloody husband from himself, could I, despite my best efforts? I nursed him until his ale-sodden liver finally gave up the ghost. It's the one thing I could do, in the end, so it's what I did. In some way I felt it would make up for the resentment I felt for so many years at being bloody stuck with him. I hated him, towards the end. It's the honest truth, but I've never admitted it to anybody, that I couldn't wait for him to die, that I nursed him, cleaned up his shit and his sick, and smiled through it all in spite of my shame, only because I thought it was the only way God would forgive me for hating the man I'd promised to stay with, through thick and thin.

In sickness and in health? Well, we had the bloody sickness, alright. Cirrhosis of the sodding liver! For richer or for poorer? We certainly knew what it was like to not have two pennies to rub together. Towards the end, I couldn't have loved him to save my own soul. I don't like myself much for that, I feel like I let him down, for not being able to love him, and I think that let the kids down too, but it was what it was, and we are where we are today. There's nothing I can go back and change, is there?

I love my kids with all my heart and if I had my time over I'd do it all differently. If I could go back, I'd have left that drunken bastard to it, years before. I'd have swallowed my shame, *and* my pride, and gone back to my mother's with the kids. I now believe my mum and dad wouldn't have judged me. At the time I was just too embarrassed and too afraid of making yet another mistake, still hopeful I suppose that things would come right and by the time it dawned on me that they wouldn't, mum and dad were dead and bloody buried. But now?

I'm a mother myself now, to a grown-up girl, and if Michelle showed up here distraught, saying she couldn't live with the man she'd married, I'd take her in with open arms and not a scrap of bloody judgement. Of course I would. I do think you have a duty to try and get them to work things out, but sometimes things just can't be worked out, and you need to know when it's like that. I'd do anything I could for my kids and grandkids, if it would help them.

But I don't want do anything like I did today, ever again, even out of love. I can't stand the thought of doing anything like that again; standing on a stranger's doorstep with my heart about to burst through my chest, trying to breathe without gasping, trying to look convincing while I'm shitting myself inside, steeling myself to lie and going through with it. Darren needs to know that I won't do that again. I need to tell him. I've betrayed my own principles to help him on this, and I don't like myself for it, and I do have to live with myself.

Most people would say compromising your own integrity's what anyone would do for love, and I suppose plenty of people have done it in one way or another, but that's no excuse and I can't sell my own soul to try and save his. What I did today was morally wrong. It was unfair to that poor woman, as well as to me, and it was just plain wrong.

Darren has to sort *himself* out, that's the long and short of it and as for me, well, I have to try and put this behind me now and get on with things as best I can, and whatever will be will be.

I might just send flowers to that lady, with a simple note that says, 'thank you for seeing me.' She won't know it's an apology but it really would be, from me. Maybe that's the best I can do, to try and put it right. I'll see what we've got left in the kitty after the next round of house-keeping.

I get home to find Darren pacing like an expectant father, up and down the hallway. When I open the door his shoulders literally crumple with the relief of seeing me, and I find myself wondering what he thought might happen. Maybe he thought I'd go into that house and get swallowed up and never come back out. I look at him and I say nothing. I just push past him and go to the kitchen, put the kettle on and take off my coat and, mercifully, these bloody horrible, feet-strangling shoes.

I want him to fully realise what I've just done for him. I've lied my way into someone's home, under completely false pretences, gaining their trust about a non-existent errand and worming my way into their most private space, which gives me a terrible sense of shame. I want him to feel how big it is, what I've done. I don't want to make it smaller somehow, which I feel I really would, if I started to speak first. I want him to speak first.

It takes him a while, as he seems to sense that I need a few minutes to collect myself in front of him, but he gets to the point where he can't contain himself for a second longer, and he asks. I know he has a million questions, but he asks just one.

'How did you get on, Mum?'

His tone is gentle, respectful. There's none of the usual impatience he always seems to have with me these days. He's asked his question and he seems to be alright about me taking the time I need to answer it.

The kettle comes to the boil and I make a pot of tea, lay two cups out, and he gets the milk out of the fridge. He also gets the sugar bowl out of the cupboard, and I fish a teaspoon out of the cutlery drawer. Routine tea-making, like any other normal day, except it doesn't exactly feel like a normal day, and not just because my son never usually even thinks about a sugar bowl. It feels like I'm watching things play out from afar, like it's not really me that's here.

We both sit down, and as the tea starts to draw, I start to speak.

'I went. It wasn't difficult, just very strange. She believed my story, and she showed me around the house.' I take a deep breath, and I plough on. 'Her dog is badly injured with a fractured shoulder, but it's alive Darren. You didn't kill it.'

He looks at me and I see the tears spring to his eyes, the second time I've seen a vulnerable emotion from him in less than a week, and I'm surer now than I've ever been, that something hard inside him has finally started to crack. I don't know what, or why, but I can see a glimmer of a break-through, just hovering there beneath the surface. He says nothing, just looks at me with those glistening eyes; tears that threaten to fall, but don't. Not yet. Something inside me softens too, seeing how relieved he is, and knowing that this is one thing, at least, that he can stop torturing himself about. Maybe doing what I've done today was the right thing after all. The lioness protecting her cub.

'She admitted to being burgled, and she was very upset about the dog. It's having to stay in a bloody cage until it's broken bone heals, and she probably has a right game, trying to look after it and get it to the toilet and everything, but she said she didn't report the burglary because nothing got taken and her dog survived.

'She said she didn't think calling the police would make any difference because they wouldn't take it seriously. She seemed to have a real aversion to the police. I guess she has her reasons, and it's not for me to speculate on what they might be. But it seems your off the hook. So that's everything you wanted, isn't it?'

I take a sip of tea, and Darren still says nothing. He just keeps looking at me, waiting for more. So I sight, and tell him all I can.

'The house is nice, Darren. I couldn't see anything amiss, not with her, or with the house. It's as neat as a pin and clean as a whistle. Not a speck of dust anywhere. She seemed fine. A bit reserved with me as a complete stranger, but that's probably to be expected, since she's just been bloody burgled and her dog's been hurt. The poor woman's probably as rattled as hell.'

Darren has the grace to look ashamed.

'But I don't know her, do I, son? I can't say whether her behaviour was normal or not. I don't know what her normal is, do I? She seemed alright, but what would I know, really?'

Darren asks me if I saw the garden, and I tell him I did.

'I saw the whole house. She was gracious and polite, but I don't think she wanted company. I was in and out of there in just a few minutes.'

'Did she rush you out?'

'No, she was very kind, but it did feel like once I'd seen the house, there was nothing really to hang around *for*. She didn't offer me a cup of tea or anything, not that I expected her to. She didn't ask about my family, apart from asking me their names.'

'Please tell me you *didn't* tell her?'

'I did, Darren. It would've been difficult not to.'

Darren grimaced at her. 'Okay, I guess we just have to hope she doesn't go checking. Could be a warning bell, if she does.'

We sit in silence as the clock ticks on in the hallway. Neither one of us seems to know what to say now, but I look at my son and I can see all kinds of conflict on his face. He's never been that great at hiding his emotions. You can always tell what mood he's in, though not so much the nuts and bolts of what he's thinking.

After a time, after we've sat as long as we can with our own thoughts, he clears his throat.

'I'm glad the dog will be alright, Mum. If I'm going to hell, at least it won't be over that. I'd never have hurt it, normally. I love dogs.'

I tell him I know that. I've always known it. What he did was completely out of character. Panic makes people do stupid things, and I tell him that too. He nods, and then sighs, as if he's releasing a million years of worries in it.

'So we're back to square one then, about where Tom might be.'

I draw myself up and shake my head. 'No, Darren. *We* are not anything. *You* are back to square one with this. I want no more of it; I won't be doing anything else. This has been hard enough for me, lying for you, betraying someone's trust like I did. Whatever happens from now on, it's your mess to deal with. I want no part of it. Do you understand? I'll support you as best I can, but I won't be doing anything else that involves telling lies and being furtive.'

He says nothing, and looks into his tea.

'Do you understand me, love?' I repeat.

'Yeah. I do, and I'm grateful for what you did. The dog thing was tearing me apart.'

'I know it was, and that's why I did it. So you could know, one way or the other. But it was hard for me, Darren, doing that, and seeing that poor dog in so much pain. And you're lucky, is all I can say, because if the poor thing *had* died I'd have told you the truth, and you'd have to deal with it, whichever way you could. But if there's anything else you're tearing yourself apart over, Darren, I can't help you. You're on your own.'

It hurts me to say that, because I really want to mean it, but I know in my heart of hearts that despite what I've said, I'd lay down my life for him in a heartbeat, if it came to that. He probably knows it too, but you have to put the boundary there, so that over-stepping it is a last resort for them and even if they try and do it, they'll *know* they're trying to do it, and that might be enough to stop them.

Some people spend their whole lives working to have something to leave for their children. I've nothing much to show for a lifetime of scrubbing floors and penny-pinching. I've nothing real to leave either of my kids, so doing what I can for them while I'm here is the next best thing. But there are some things you just shouldn't ask for, even from your nearest and dearest.

He surprises me by getting up, stepping around the table and giving me a quick hug. He hasn't done that since Christmas. I look up into his sad face. It's a handsome face, though he's never believed that. Too many years accepting what his bastard dad kept telling him, that he was too ugly and too stupid to get anywhere in life.

Am I getting you back? Are you finally coming back to me? I pray I'm right but, as I say, time will tell.

'Thanks again Mum. It's late, and you've had no tea at all. I'm bloody starving too. Should I get us some fish and chips?'

'Good idea! I can't be bothered cooking at this time of night. Pat will give you some, so don't go to the local chippy. Walk the extra, down to the shop, and tell him I sent you. I'll text him to let him know you're on your way.'

I can see by the look on Darren's face that he doesn't relish the thought of asking my Pat for anything, especially something for nothing, so I raise my eyebrows at him, daring him to give me cheek over it. He opens his mouth to say something then thinks better of it and just shrugs.

'Okay. See you in a bit then.'

As he goes out, banging the front door closed behind him, I let out my first proper breath since coming home. I get up and chuck my silly shoes in the bin and as I sit back down to pour myself another cup of tea, I think of how bright and cheery that lovely house was today, all that light paint and pretty wallpaper keeping everything looking fresh.

'I think it's time I redecorated,' I announce to the teapot. 'It's time for a lick of paint around here, and maybe even some new second-hand furniture. I think we could do with a bit of a freshen-up.'

It'll give Darren something to do. That's what he needs; a project - something to get his teeth into for a bit, that he can finish and look at with pride. I don't know why I never thought of it before. I don't think we've decorated for a decade or more and now as I look at everything, it all seems so dated and drab.

Paint is cheap enough, in fact I'm sure we've got something down in the shed that would do. If not, we can get something cheap and cheerful from one of the discount suppliers. One of the chains of charity shops in town always has nice furniture on offer, so perhaps we can have a new sofa as well. Curtains too. Maybe a make-over is exactly what we need.

I pull a couple of plates down from the cupboard, and get the tomato sauce out of the fridge. My mind works hard and eventually I manage to stop thinking that it might just be the last supper.

21

Tuesday
- Darren -

Shit. I'm no further ahead when it comes to finding out what's happened to Tom. I'm so glad that dog isn't dead. A fractured shoulder. Not the best outcome, but I'm so grateful it wasn't any worse. A fractured shoulder will heal, but it will take a long time, and it's still traumatic for the dog, and for the woman. But I didn't mess up totally. I find myself wishing I could take on the pain myself, away from the dog. I gladly would, if I could. Poor little bastard.

I'm relieved, but I'm not off the hook, am I? I've still caused a massive amount of pain to an innocent animal, and to its owner, and my mate is still missing and fuck-knows where.

I'm looking at lamp-posts as I head to Pat's chip shop, and I'm seeing posters of Tom on every second one. They're in all the shop windows too, and there's a bunch, held by string, dangling from the edge of the notice board on the wall in Pat's chippy.

I don't mention it to him when he gives me his usual tight-lipped, barely-tolerant smile. After all, me and Pat, we don't do the small-talk thing, so what would I say?

'Hello, Pat. Nice, to see you've got posters to give out about my missing friend?' I don't think so. He'd look at me like I was bonkers, and he'd immediately assume that if this kid was my mate, him going missing would somehow involve me.

He asks me what we want, me and Mum, and I pick a random assortment of things, and step back to wait. The shop's busy. Pat is serving, someone else is throwing the chips into the fryer. As I watch, I can see that a lot of the people who come in here are locals, they obviously come in often, and Pat greets some of them by name, and always with a smile, and it's a genuine one, as if he really is pleased to see them. He's never smiled at me like that, and I suppose it's because I've never given him much of a reason to smile at all. I'm probably the one person in his life that he's never happy to see, and I can only guess at the conversations he has with Mum sometimes, about me. He calls me a waste of space. He's dead right. I bloody am. Or at least I have been, up until now.

I realise, standing here watching him doing what he seems to do best, that he must really love my mum, to put up with me living there with them. I've been looking at his faults all this time, the things that piss me off about him, because we've never had a conversation or a moment in time when we've seen the best of one another, anything to hang any hope onto, that we could ever be anything like a family. He fucking hates me and I've decided not to like him *because* he hates me. And I suppose that's the vicious circle we're all living in. He hates me and he shows it, so I don't like him and I show it, so he hates me even more. Mum just sits on the sidelines, wringing her hands and making excuses for me, and that must piss him off as well.

Pat's chip shop is nice. It's the first time I've been in here to order anything, and I'm surprised how big it is. It's clean too, and there are a couple of tables to sit and eat at. There are lots of flyers on his notice board about community projects, missing cats, an upcoming autumn school play, appeals for donations of all sorts to the local hospice shop, and collection boxes for various other charities on the counter for spare coins.

Everything shows a real community happening around here that Pat's involved with. It's the first time I've thought about him as being connected to the community he cooks chips for. But he is, and he cares enough to provide a notice board to support those who need help.

He hands me the package of food, and turns away without a smile. 'Thanks Pat,' I say. He doesn't turn around but he stops, and he nods, then he carries on with his work as if I don't exist. It's as if me being civil to him gave him a shock. When did I ever say thank you to him for anything? Probably never. So I step forward again, and I call him back. 'Pat?'

He comes back to me, with a sour look on his face. Determined to ignore it I just say to him, 'Pat, thanks for taking such good care of my mum.'

I want to say more, as he stands there staring at me like I've just spoken at him in French, but I haven't a clue what else to come up with so I just nod and leave the shop. My face is burning and I feel like a bit of a tit, but I'm still glad I said it. I meant it. I really am glad Mum has someone who looks after her and I wanted him to know that.

I've always told myself it's just a greaseball chippy, hardly the fucking Ritz, and I've always sneered at it, and at him. I've always thought of him as not much more than a lazy-arse who gets pissed every other night. But it occurs to me now that maybe he feels like has to do that. Maybe he feels that if he's had a few to drink, it helps him to put up with *me*.

I'm starting to think I might've been a bit unfair to him. Going there just now, I didn't see a greaseball chippy. What I saw was a clean shop and a hard-working bloke very much liked by his punters, who handed a parcel of food to someone he hated, because the person he loved wanted him to.

By the time I get home, Mum's got the table set up for the chips, and she's on what looks like her third or fourth cup of tea. I've never known anybody drink tea like she can. She can drink it to championship level. It's the one thing we've never been short of. We might have had pretty lean pickings for an evening meal a lot of nights, when we were growing up, but we never ran short of tea. Mum and dad both used to smoke, but she gave up after Dad died, and we had even less money to make ends meet. She had to start making every penny count.

I've never smoked. I just never fancied it, probably because I grew up in a nicotine fog; it was everywhere, all through the bloody house. Over the years the smoke made the wallpaper go brown, except for at the very top where it met the ceiling. There was a clear white strip right at the top, about an inch deep, all the way around the room. I always wondered about that strip, about why it stayed there, stayed white, why the nicotine never made it all the way to the top. I still don't know why it did that. But I used to go into the toilet after mum or dad had been in there, and it's true that you can smell nicotine in someone's shit. It's the worst smell in the world. I hated it, worse than anything else about living at home, living with that stink, and all my clothes reeking of smoke, my hair, everything. They even smoked in bed, and to this day I can't believe the place never went up like the Towering fucking Inferno.

So I ignored the taunts and the teasing, all the kids at school calling me a fucking wimp 'cause I wasn't fagging my head off like there was no tomorrow. Cancer sticks I called them, and I think my mum dodged a bullet by giving them up when she did. Smoking just wasn't for me. I couldn't go out with a girl who smoked either. I've snogged a few girls who did, and every time it's been like licking the inside of an ashtray. Proper disgusting, it was.

For all my faults, I do like things to be clean. I can't stand people who aren't clean. There's no excuse for it, apart from mental health. If people are doo-lally to the point where they can't keep themselves clean, that's a different story, but most people are capable of taking care of themselves. I smell blokes on the bus with the worst cases of BO, and I see other passengers wrinkling their noses, but nobody has the guts to say anything. They just pull their stupid faces, look at one another and roll their eyes, as if that will change anything. It's even worse when it's women. Dirty bitches, some of them, like they wouldn't know a stick of deodorant if you shoved it up their arses.

I've been thinking a lot about that girl I met at the beach. She was a nice girl. A normal girl, clean, happy and sorted; the sort of girl any bloke would be lucky to have. No trophy, just pretty, and honest. That's all I want. She doesn't have to be Miss fucking Universe. She just has to be nice, scrub up alright for a night out, but just a normal girl. Folks reckon there's someone for everyone. I hope my 'someone' will turn up, and when she does she won't be a slapper or a mental case.

I'm beyond starving, in fact I could eat a scabby horse and go back for the fucking rider! It looks like Mum's ready to do that too, so we tuck into the food and neither of us says anything for all the time we're eating it.

'I haven't had a spring roll in ages,' she says, eventually, licking her fingers with real delight. 'I used to love these!'

'I know. You used to always order one. Friday night was chippy night, wasn't it? Same order every week, a fish and a sausage each, two fish for dad, and enough chips for us all to sink a bloody battleship, but only a spring roll for you, and you always said you only wanted six chips but you always ate dozens.'

She laughs at the memory. It's nice to see her laugh. She needs to laugh a lot more, and I tell her that.

'Well love, there's not been much to laugh about lately, has there?'

My thoughts go to Tom, and I suddenly feel guilty for even thinking about laughing. It's been nearly a week, now. He's in trouble, I just know he is, and I can't begin to imagine where he is or what might have happened. I can't laugh anymore, it feels disloyal. It feels like a betrayal somehow, and like making something bad even worse, like smearing tomato sauce on pristine white chip paper, or a bloodstain on pure white snow.

What if Tom never comes back? What happens then? Will I forever be haunted by the thoughts that if I hadn't fucking left him, he wouldn't be gone? That if we hadn't gone to that house everything would be normal? That if I hadn't been such a smart arse, trying to show him how to do alright on a life of crime, he'd be safely at home with his mum tonight? Or will I get to a place where it doesn't torment me, the fact that I ran out on him? The fact that my yellow-belly cowardice may be the sole cause of whatever's happened to him?

The dog is alive. That much I can be thankful for. But Tom's disappearance feels so bloody big, so much bigger than the life or death of a dog. It's like someone talking nonstop, telling you a story, and you're listening to every word, then they just stop, mid-fucking-sentence, and you wait for what comes next, but nothing comes. You keep waiting, and waiting, and eventually you just give up, and you find your own ending to the story, and it might be the wrong one, but it doesn't matter because you just have to have an ending.

What's the ending to *this*? Will it be Tommy turning up laughing, with a lump on his head? Or will it be his body, by fair means or foul? Or will there be nothing at all, just a space, a voiceless, endless space where he used to be?

It's the powerlessness that eats away at you. I've been powerless before, like when my tin toy soldiers got taken away. I knew I'd never see them again. It felt like a betrayal of my Granddad, to let them go, but I was powerless to stop it. The only power I had was over whether or not I cried. And I chose not to. Not on the outside at least.

I feel like that little kid again now. I'm powerless. I don't know what to do, where to look, who to talk to. Mum's been banging on at me about handing myself in, but what if I do that and it just draws another fucking blank? Why should I do it if it wouldn't help find Tom? How would me admitting to being with him at a burglary lead to finding him?

Mum's finished her dinner, and I'm still picking at mine, but she's still sitting at the table so I ask her if I can talk to her about everything. She looks at me warily.

'Don't ask me to get involved anymore, Darren. I've already told you I can't.'

'I know, Mum. But my head's about to blow off. Please, you're the only person I trust.' And, as I'm saying it, I know it's the truth.

She straightens her shoulders and settles into her chair. 'Go on, then.'

She doesn't take her eyes off me, all the time I'm talking. I tell her about going to the police, about telling them that Tom and I were up at the rec when we weren't. I admit to her that I lied, and I tell her how sick I feel inside, knowing that what might have happened to Tom could be my fault, and I feel sicker still when she doesn't interrupt me to tell me I'm wrong to feel that way. Her silence tells me I'm right. I tell her I'm confused, sad, worried, panicked, that I don't know what I'll ever do, how I'll ever live with myself, if he never comes back, or if he does and he's damaged, or he rocks up dead.

When I've spilled my guts I just sit there, with the grandfather clock ticking away in the hall. It's never sounded heavier, or louder, than it does right now.

After a time Mum clears her throat.

'I can see why you don't think handing yourself in would help. But look at the facts, Darren. You did a burglary with Tom, you got caught, you ran away, and Tom's now missing. Those are the only facts that matter around him disappearing. The rest is just theory; what *might* have happened. You don't know.'

She continues, 'The only things that could have happened to him are something while he was there, or something after he left.

All I can say is that everything at that house seemed fine, *she* seemed fine, *ordinary,* when I went there. I probably could have asked more questions, but I didn't want to start ringing any alarm bells. What I think though, for what it's worth, is that he got out of there. I think something's happened to him since.'

'You don't think she did anything to him, do you?'

'Like *what,* for goodness sake?'

'I dunno, Mum! Maybe she hurt him or something. She didn't report the burglary, she told you that herself. Why not? Why would she not report it?'

Mum and I look at one another for what feels like a long time, without saying a word. The hair starts to prickle at the back of my neck when Mum's eyes go wide.

'No! She wouldn't. Surely to God she wouldn't have done anything, would she? What would she have done?'

'I dunno, Mum. But something's not adding up. I know she said she didn't want the bother of the police, but maybe there's more to it than that. Maybe she hurt him. He could be wandering around out there badly hurt, or something. She was screaming her head off with that frying pan in her hand. It was fucking terrifying. I ran from fright, without even thinking he wouldn't be straight behind me. But he wasn't. I dunno if he did make it out of there. And, if he didn't, what happened?'

Mum looks away and stares into the middle distance, still saying nothing.

'Mum, I have to talk to her. I need to go around and talk to her, and if she calls the police then that's what she fucking does, and I'll have to take the consequences. If I showed up at her house, she'd only call the police if she had nothing to hide. And if she has nothing to hide and she does call them, then this is on me and I'll have to take whatever happens on the chin. But if she does have something to hide, she is not going to call the fucking plod, Mum.'

Mum is absorbing this information, and I can see she's struggling with it.

'If you do go to that house, Darren, and you give her your name, she'll make the connection with me. I gave her my real name. I had to, I couldn't bring myself to lie about that, as well as everything else. But I could end up on a bloody charge for something, now. You need to think very carefully about going round there. You need to be prepared for whatever the consequences might be, for yourself, for her and for *me.*'

Getting my mum in the shit over this? Is that an option? Of course it's not! Is making things even more difficult for that woman if she *hasn't* done anything wrong an option? Not really, no. What a fucking mess.

'I've been round there, twice now, lurking about. And you've been once and actually spoken to her, and we're none the bloody wiser for it, Mum. I have to talk to her. Confess, apologise, and ask her what happened after I left.'

Mum is shaking her head to the point where I wonder if it's going to fall off her shoulders. 'I don't like it, Darren. I really don't. I have a really bad feeling about you doing that. Bad for all of us.'

'I have to do it for Tom, Mum. I owe him that. He's my mate. I let him down, and I need to fix it. I need to find out what's happened, and I know I won't rest – I *can't* rest – until I do, even if it means getting sent down again.'

Mum closes her eyes.

I get up and go to her, to give her a hug. She is as stiff as a board, and I know how anxious and unhappy she is. 'I'll sleep on it Mum. I promise you, I won't do anything without thinking good and proper about it first.'

She nods and pats my hand. She looks so tired, bless her. Can I load any more worry onto her shoulders? *Can I?* Is going to talk to that woman the answer, really? I go over it in my mind, like I've been doing for hours already, but this time looking at it from my mum's point of view.

It can only go one of two ways. She'll either talk to me or call the bastard plod. But if she does talk to me, she's not going to admit to doing anything, is she? She's not going to stand there, at her front door, saying 'yeah, sure, I snotted him good and proper with the fry pan.'

And even if she had done that, what happened afterwards? If she'd really hurt him she'd have to have called an ambulance, wouldn't she? So if she hit him, she couldn't have hit him hard. I think Mum's right. The most likely scenario is that he legged it behind me, whether he'd been hit with a fry pan or not, and he went a different way. And somewhere, somehow, he managed to get into trouble after that.

It's not about trying to convince myself that me leaving him wasn't what got him into trouble. That's not working so well, as it happens, since I know full well that if I'd dragged him with me or stuck around, he'd be safe now, like I am. But I really do want to believe, with all my heart, that he's out there somewhere and trying to get home because, if he is, that means he's got a chance of making it back and it's just a matter of when. I just hope that when he does come home, he forgives me for being such a cowardly bastard.

Tuning back in, I realise Mum's banging on about redecorating the living room. She wants me to do it. Is she for real? I haven't a fucking clue about painting and wallpapering, and I remind her of that, but she shakes her head and tells me she thinks it would be good for all of us to have a fresh room, and that the cheapest way would be for me to do it. She seems insistent so I agree to give it a go. Anything for a quiet life, and it's not like my appointments diary is jammed, is it?

'Let's make a start in the morning.' she says. I move to speak, but she puts her hand up to stop me. 'Just redecorate the bloody living room for me, Darren, and after you've done that, if you still want to talk to that woman, go *then*.'

I realise she's trying to stall me, and it pisses me off, but maybe she's right. Maybe I just need to get my head out of all this for a day or two, think about something completely different, and everything else might look different after that. Tom might have come home by then, and all this might feel like just a bloody bad dream.

'Okay,' I say, and suddenly Mum's all smiles. I have to admit, it's a long time since I did anything really nice for her, and this place does look pretty scruffy, so while I'm sure I'm no great shakes at decorating, I'll give it my best for her. She rabbits on a bit about the wallpaper shop, and heading down there in the morning to look at what they've got in the sale bins so I agree to go with her, and also to the charity furniture shop. Something about a new settee and curtains.

She seems happy, dreaming away and prattling on, so I leave it at that and tune out to her again, as best I can, while I try to settle my own jumbled thoughts.

As the night drags by, we try to watch a bit of telly, but nothing grabs my attention. Mum's all distracted with colour schemes and curtain styles, and flicking through channels to find a makeover programme to watch. I'm trying to focus on getting my head into a different place or even just slow it down a bit, but nothing works, so at half past ten I make an excuse and head to bed. Sleep doesn't come and I don't expect it to, but I don't want to be in the living room when Pat comes home from the pub.

I think there were little inroads made today, for me and him, but I don't want to push the point. I'll let Mum tell him whatever she wants about what's going on, and we'll see what happens after that. He'll probably just keep looking at me with the usual disgust, like I'm something he dragged in by mistake on the sole of his shoe, so I'm not holding my breath.

Just for the hell of it, I try Tom's mobile phone again. As expected, it immediately goes to voicemail, so either he's on it and yabbering away to someone, or the battery's dead. I don't think he's on it. There've been enough messages left on it now, from me, his mum and his girlfriend, and that's just the people I know who are worried about him. There's bound to be tons more. He'd have got enough messages by now that everyone's freaking out, and although he's still a kid, he's old enough to know what panic sounds like. If he could have picked up a call, he would have. If he could have made one, he would have.

It's the worst feeling in the world, when you want to do something but you just don't know where to bloody start. I *want* to do something, to stop feeling powerless yet again, but everything I think of has either been done, or it's fucking futile, like roaming the streets looking for him, calling his name like so many people must do who've lost their bloody cats, like the ones on that notice board in Pat's chippy.

I guess those people must wonder about the fate of their cats. I don't want to think about what might have happened to some of them at least. Or to Tommy. But it's a fairly safe bet that if I wandered the streets crying 'Tom!' he wouldn't bloody answer. Needles and haystacks, and all that, and I'd probably end up like the feline version of the bloody pied piper with all the neighbourhood cats named Tom running along and yowling their prunes off behind me. And there's every chance I'd be picked up by the plod too, which is the last thing I need right now, so I just have to swallow down the pure unadulterated joy of being restless.

The plod say they're doing everything they can, and 'pursuing different lines of enquiry', as they put it. I hope they bloody *are* doing everything they can. It's a first for me, having to depend on them to do something positive, something significant. I've never been in a place before where I've *hoped* they'd do their job!

For me, it's always been about the punishment they dish out, not the help. I've always known they help people, that's what they're there for, mostly - to help people avoid or overcome being victims of crime.

Punishment is only part of what they do, and they actually don't even do that, when you think about it. They just find the criminals. Then they charge them and hand them over to the courts to do the punishing. You could say that being charged is being punished, but it's what you have to expect if you do the crime and get caught. You expect to get charged. If they've got the bloody evidence, it's what they *have* to do. After they've charged you, and bailed you, or kept you overnight for a morning magistrate's hearing, their part of the job is done.

So I'm lying here hoping that the plod are onto this, in the best way possible, and they'll find my missing mate. But hope's not the same as faith, is it, and that's one thing I don't have. Not in anyone, really, but certainly not in the plod. I always got away with a lot more than they ever caught me for, and I don't think I'm that fucking clever, so it's hard to be convinced they're much good at finding *anything*. I just think that maybe they're not so clever either, and that's not what you want to feel when you're depending on them to bring someone home who's missing.

22

Thursday
- Alison -

I can't believe how quickly the time has disappeared in such a blur. It's a full week since I killed that boy, and I'm astonished to realize that I haven't actually had much time to dwell exclusively on the fact, or on what happened after. As terrified as I was that it would plague my every waking moment (and most of my sleeping ones too) the truth of the matter is that I've been a bit distracted with work being crazy busy, and with also focussing as much as I can on helping Badger from day to day, to function and heal.

Daphne has been commandeering a fair bit of my time too, both at work and out of it, to talk about endless wedding stuff. To top it all off the on-call vet, Simon Westrupp, called me out of the blue today to enquire about Badger. He ended the call by asking me out to dinner tomorrow night.

Flustered a little, I said yes, because I was in the middle of something really important, with no time to make up a suitable excuse to fob him off. So now I have to face the prospect of having dinner with a man who is far too nice for me, and trying to behave normally in yet another setting I'd rather shy away from.

I weigh up the idea of calling to cancel but decide it would be too rude at this late stage. He seems like a lovely man, sticking his head above the parapet for probably the first time since his divorce, and he doesn't deserve to have it so brutally knocked off, so I resolve to go with the arrangement we've made. The sane part of me says that it may indeed be a nice, normal, pleasant evening. The other part of me, the part that continually threatens to become hysterically unhinged, starts to argue that this nice man definitely doesn't deserve to be breaking bread with a fry-pan wielding, homicidal maniac.

I push that thought away and start thinking about what to wear. It's just another normal decision in what would look and feel like a normal week to anyone else but which has taken on, for me, the most surreal of contexts I couldn't dream up if I tried.

But all through the manic events of the week, I've been continually almost-conscious that there hasn't been much time for reflection, or to truly process everything that's happened. My traitorous body has allowed me to sleep, albeit with a couple of glasses of wine and at least three shots of whisky at night to help me on my way, and in spite of the headache from hell that still persistently plagues me.

So I haven't had the 'luxury' of even a couple of sleepless nights to give me any real thinking time. While lying awake mentally flogging myself all night is not what I really want, I'm desperately aware that everything will, as soon as breathing time permits, storm back into my consciousness and demand to be processed, in whichever way I can reconcile or not, at whatever time of day or night it chooses. My brain is its own buzzard, picking away as my conscience, at the carcass of my crimes.

Last night, after I got home from work, I finally got the axe out and chopped the wooden chest into small pieces. Aside from the fact that it had Junior's decaying DNA all over the inside of it, I couldn't bear to look at it again. It could never claim a place in my home now, so it definitely had to go. I burned it in the big metal drum in the garden with some old, dried bush cuttings that had been lying in a big forgotten pile behind the shed. It was just time to clear the garden of mouldering leaves and branches, your Honour. I was grateful for the fact that nobody was around, to see me cry my heart out as I did it.

Maybe I could go 'antiquing' again soon with Daphne, or my mother, and find another chest. I wouldn't want one that looked too similar of course. But I do need something, to do the job that chest was destined for.

My thoughts race on. Controlling what has become a continuous stream of consciousness is getting tiring but I can't seem to slow anything down. Even the ibuprofen I've been taking, to the point of virtual overdose to try and get on top of this horrible headache, hasn't served to dull the edges of the tumbling waterfall of perpetually roaring thought.

Badger is healing well. He is slowly getting his mojo back; wagging his tail properly again when I come in, and the dog walker says he does the same for her when she visits to check on him. He is getting the sparkle back in his eyes. He doesn't appear to be too traumatized by what happened to him; the best hint I could have that his inherent good nature will prevail.

I'm relieved about that, because if the attack on him had altered his personality, that would have been too much to bear. He is a trusting animal and I want him to retain that. It wouldn't hurt for him to be a *little* more wary of strangers, as I've always been quite concerned that he's so friendly he would pretty much walk off with anyone. So having a bit of reserve wouldn't hurt him, but I wouldn't want him to end up being afraid of people, or his own shadow. I hope he'll bounce back okay.

I prepare a salad with some leftover chicken and rice, and I just sit down to eat when there's a knock at the door. Bill is standing there. He looks a little agitated, and he pulls an apologetic face.

'I'm sorry to disturb you; I can imagine you're having your tea about now love, but I have to go out again tonight, and I wanted to see you before I went. I've been busy with different things and it was drama club last night, so it's the first chance I've had to pop over.'

I open the door and invite him in. He stands in the hallway and declines my invitation to food or a cup of tea.

'What do you need then, Bill?'

'Oh nothing, love, but I wanted to tell you about something that's been bothering me a bit since you came over on Tuesday night. You know you had that visitor, the one who told you about her parents living here?'

'Yes, the Fairweathers, I think it was?'

Bill looks at me and frowns. 'That's the thing, Alison, and I don't want to alarm you love, and I don't know what it really means, but since you've had the break in and all, I think I should just tell you.'

And Bill goes on to explain that there has never been a family called Fairweather living here. This house was owned and lived in from the day it was built, by a Ronald and Sylvia Bartlett, who had an only child; a son, named Edward. He grew up here, then moved away to get married, and then he moved back into the house when he inherited it after Ronald and Sylvia died. Teddy Bartlett raised his own family here, and then he sold the house to me.

It takes me a minute to absorb what Bill has said. Then my mind starts casting randomly around for an explanation. The woman (Barbara Davies?) must have been mistaken. She did seem sure it was this house, but it obviously wasn't. Bill has lived here all his life, and he knows his neighbours like the back of his hand. If he says there have never been Fairweathers in this house, I believe him. And he'd not forget if another William, or Bill, had lived anywhere at all in this street.

I realise I'm gaping at him, and he is starting to look uncomfortable.

'Um, well. I guess she must have been mistaken then, Bill. How weird.' I force a neutral expression onto my face and shrug my shoulders as nonchalantly as I can.

'I thought it was a bit strange too. But people do get things wrong sometimes, don't they? And that's probably all it was, but I just wanted you to know. I hope you don't think I'm interfering.'

'Not at all,' I reassure him. 'We all have to look out for one another, don't we?'

He tips his head and goes, and I head back to my dining table, my mind in a frantic fog. My meal no longer seems appealing, in fact it tastes like ashes in my mouth.

One of two things has happened here. That woman, Barbara Davies, she was either mistaken about this house, or she was lying. If she was mistaken, and simply had the wrong address for her parents, her showing up here just days after I'd been burgled is nothing more than a random coincidence; the kind I should just shrug off and think no more about.

But what if it's *not* a coincidence? What if she *was* lying? If she was, it means something altogether more sinister is going on here. If she was lying, it was purely to get into this house for reasons other than what she said. Why would a middle aged, nondescript woman show up out of nowhere and want to see inside my house, and lie about her reasons? Who would do that?

Is it just a coincidence that she turned up here just a few days after I'd been burgled? Or are the two events connected? I've lived here for nine years now, and in all of that time no stranger has ever knocked at my door before, asking to come inside my home. The fact that it's happened less than a week after someone broke in and attempted to steal from me, and left my dog for dead; *is* that just a random coincidence? Am I just being paranoid because of what I've done, in wondering if it's something more than that?

I don't know, but I can't just assume anything. I'm badly rattled. I fire up my laptop, all thoughts of food abandoned, and I wait for the internet to connect. As soon as it does, I type in 'Barbara Davies' and press search. I don't suppose in a million years that she would have used her real name if she was here under false pretences, but she would have I suppose, if she was genuine. This may be a way of finding out. All I want is to put my own mind at rest, so I can get rid of the cold, clawing fear that grips me now.

More than a dozen Barbara Davies links come up. It's a pretty common name. One is a journalist, another's a doctor. There are a couple of solicitors, and a housewife from San Diego who writes blogs about children with epilepsy. Facebook has several Barbara Davies profiles but none has a photo that links the woman who came to my house. Two have profile photos of pets, but they are listed as being in Australia and Scotland, and my Barbara Davies definitely did not have a Scottish accent.

Google has lots of images for people of that name, but after trawling through, I cannot find even one that links that name to her face.

I'm about to admit defeat and acknowledge that she has very probably used a false name when finally, on the fourth page of trawling, I spy a link from a local newspaper. I click on it, to find a court report from three years ago.

It is simply a citation, naming a Barbara Davies as the mother of one Darren Peter Davies, aged twenty-four, who was evidently bailed to her care while he awaited trial for burglary.

The hair prickles at the back of my neck. Burglary. Darren Davies. Aged twenty-four or, as he would be by now, more like twenty-six or twenty-seven. But Senior, the man in my kitchen, the one that got away, surely he couldn't have been any more than twenty. I'm about to write it off as a dead end when something stops me. Instead, I search for Darren Davies on Facebook, and several pop up.

To my absolute, utter dismay, one of the first profiles that comes up carries the picture of a face I've been dreading to find. It's Senior, the man who was here in my kitchen, calmly and jovially drinking my beer after robbing me while my beloved dog lay crippled on the kitchen floor. It's the man who ran out of here like a scalded cat, leaving his young accomplice to face the music all alone. I guess he thought his mate would be right behind him. It's the man who prowled around my garden just a couple of nights later, in the dead of night.

Darren Davies. *So that's who you are.*

I'm beyond stunned. All I can do is sit here staring at that profile. He has his privacy settings set quite high, so I can't find out much about him. I can't even get a look at his photos. But it's definitely him. His profile picture suggests him to be much younger than his age, unless the court report was wrong. I'd never have picked him as being in his mid-twenties.

My mind scrambles to actually believe that this man's mother came here to case this house, lied to me through her teeth, and actually *used her own name!* He had to have put her up to this. Which means, then, that she knows what he did.

I'm no gullible fool. I do get the measure of most people fairly quickly. I've built a career doing that on the phone, and I can certainly do it with someone who's standing right in front of me. The woman who came here seemed like a decent sort. But an uncomfortable truth gnaws away at me as I sit here at my table, while the light leaves the day, and the gentle snoring of my dog quietly breaks what would otherwise be a blanket of deafening silence.

Barbara Davies was casing my house. She must have been looking for clues. No wonder she was nervous! Now that I think about it, when she saw Badger and I told her what had happened, *she asked me if I'd contacted the police!* Is that what she was here for? To find out if I'd reported her son?

Or is there more going on here? Does this Darren suspect I'm connected to the disappearance of Tom Findlay? Is that why he sent his mother here?

My heart is hammering, my breathing is shallow, my headache is threatening to render me unconscious, and I realise I'm on the verge of spinning out.

I have to get control of myself, *right now*. I cannot let this roll me over. I have to get a grip, concentrate, figure out what this means, and work out what I can do.

I put some lights on, grab a pen from the sideboard and some paper from the printer, and I start to write everything down. To hell with the fact that it could incriminate me; I will dispose of this evidence in good time. But for now, I need to see things in black and white. I need to sort out the facts from the jumbled, incoherent mess that my brain has become, where tangled thoughts tumble over and over themselves like too-hot clothes in a dryer, and nothing at all makes sense.

A dozen deep breaths later, and I'm focussed. First, I list the facts of what has happened, in chronological order. Next, I jot down the theories, listing the other people I know to be in the mix, and second-guessing what they're thinking, wanting or doing. After that I look at it all and try to determine whether there's any basis to any of what I've written down, as it relates to the facts. That's a good start. It will help me to separate the truth from the paranoia.

After an hour of scribbling, I have a kind of mind-map forming that starts to make sense to me. I've always been a fan of mind-mapping. Sometimes I have so much in my head, it's impossible to get a clear focus on what the priorities are. It's no wonder I have a monster headache that doesn't want to leave me! *Is this what the unrelenting stress of a crippling guilty conscience does?*

Getting everything onto paper is the one thing that seems to straighten it all out; at least that's what works for me. Others talk things through with trusted friends and that's worked for me too, on occasions, but who could I ever possibly talk to about this? Whose world could I mess up completely by delivering knowledge to them that would haunt them for the rest of their days, whether they turned me in or not, whether they abandoned me or not?

I've been a list person all my life. I write things down so I can keep them all clear. Paper trails, points of reference, looking forward or looking back. I don't keep a diary anymore though, and I'm unutterably glad I don't have the self-discipline to commit all of my personal thoughts to paper in such a way anymore. I kept a diary for a while I was in my teens (it's what we all did, as I recall), and when I looked back on it, years later, I found myself cringing with mortification, at the things I'd considered important back then; how over the top I'd felt, expressing extreme reactions to the most ridiculous things, and what certain people meant to me at the time. The hormonal ramblings of an adolescent schoolgirl; who wants to look back on that? All it did was remind me of how pathetic I'd been. I burnt that diary and never thought about it again.

Even if I did keep a diary now, this catastrophe is far too shameful to ever put into written form. But I do have to make sense of it and what my options are and where I go from here and what to expect and how to manage certain situations that might realistically crop up like what people might say or ask or do or see or guess and how I can pull my life back together as if nothing had happened and how I can sleep at night going forward and look people in the eye and give to charities as if I care about the dignity of others. And mean it.

My mind keeps clicking into chaotic overdrive. But, I breathe again, ten more long breaths. By doing that, then refocusing on the mind map, I manage to fight off the overwhelming urge to lapse into full-blown hysteria and start screaming at the top of my lungs, and never stop.

Certain facts are clear. Some of them are facts that only I know, and those are the most important ones to be clear about, in terms of who knows what, or who could guess what, so that I'm not jumping out of my skin every time there's a knock at the door or the phone rings.

Barbara Davies and her son know nothing of what really happened here that night. All they know is that Darren Davies was in this house with his friend, and they got separated after being sprung in the middle of a burglary. Davies legged it and no doubt assumed his friend had too, and he didn't check. If he knew what had happened here he would not have come back here in the middle of the night to sneak around, nor would he have sent his mother here on a false errand. If either of them knew what had really happened here that night, they would both have acted differently, whether self-incrimination came into it or not.

You're assuming they're more moral than you are then, my dear.

If they knew I'd killed Tom Findlay and disposed of his body, I think it's pretty safe to say I'd be in custody by now. But I'm not, am I?

I have cleaned up all the evidence that was ever in this house and disposed of it permanently. There is nothing here, in or around this house, that can link me to the disappearance of that boy.

There's a body, yes. But even if that was discovered, how would they link it to me? Nobody saw me do anything and Bill, who lifted what he thought was a chest full of fabric into the back of my car, has no reason in the world to suspect me of anything untoward. My mother, whom I visited, has unwittingly provided me with the perfect alibi, and I am one hundred percent confident *(really? Are you? Really?)* that nobody saw me enter or leave that churchyard. All lights were off here in the cul-de-sac, and nobody was about, when I rolled silently down and back into my driveway in the middle of the night.

My biggest concern is about is the CCTV and numberplate recognition cameras at the services I stopped at on the way home from disposing of Tom Findlay's body. But it's a big stretch to imagine they'd be looked at, unless a chain of events that linked that part of my miserable plan prompted it. And, to the best of my knowledge, there is no chain of events that *anyone* can pinpoint or describe. It feels like the perfect murder, if you could ever really say such a thing.

People are always looking for the perfect crime, aren't they? The one they can get away with, whether it's robbing a bank or doing away with someone they want gone from their lives. But few people ever get off Scot free. Something, somehow, always pops up to dash their hopes of getting away with it. They overlook some clue, make a miniscule, random mistake that a diligent detective picks up on, then the string simply starts to unravel until it leads straight to the villain. These days, with the technology and science that forms the foundations of the analytic process, it's pretty hard to get away with anything for long.

But I may just have managed it and, quite possibly, only because Tom Findlay was unknown to me. Most people say that, most times, killings are committed by someone known to the victim. When someone's found murdered, a routine round of questioning usually takes place among the friends and family first, and then the victim's acquaintances are examined. Some statistics suggest that around eighty percent of murders are committed by someone known to the victim, so of course it makes sense to start there.

So I'm in the twenty percent bracket, which puts the odds of not being discovered substantially in my favour.

Nobody knows it's a murder yet, though. Boiled down to its nuts and bolts, it's actually a manslaughter, but if I go on to be discovered it's going to be very difficult to prove that and, even if it weren't, I can't bring myself to try and minimize the enormity of what I've done by seeking to trivialize it with a semantic technicality.

At this stage, if we push things a little further, it's still only a missing person case. It's not a death at all. Without a body, it might be weeks, months or even *years* before Tom Findlay's disappearance is treated as a death, if it *ever* is.

I know families have to try to come to terms with the loss of one who leaves and never comes back, and in most cases acknowledging that their loved one is probably dead is a place many can't force themselves to go to. Hope remains burning, blazing brightly in the deepest part of their souls, that their cherished one will return one day, waltzing through the door with excuses or reasons for why they've been gone, and they can all begin to pull their lives back together as a family again.

I read about a little boy who went missing, out of the blue. Nobody knew what had happened, but it turned out his estranged Dad had abducted him from the legal guardianship of his maternal grandmother, and taken him abroad. He was found after nine years, and I can only imagine the rollercoaster that poor grandmother went through, until he was safely returned to her.

Until then, she'd been forced to contemplate and try to accept the worst. What must it have felt like, in that moment, when she was told he was alive and well?

Everyone hopes for something like that, or a 'fugue state' scenario, where someone somehow forgets who they are for a while. The eternal flame of hope is compounded by so many cases coming to light nowadays, where people *have* come home after years of being missing. They've had an injury, amnesia, have started life somewhere else as someone else, only to one day have the memory return of the life they left behind.

Others come home after police searches, sometimes transcontinental, where young men and women are returned home from being trafficked or used for sexual slavery, either abroad or closer to home. Young women are sometimes abducted to be used for sex, and concealed so well in basements even the next-door neighbours never knew. Or *said* they didn't, at least. I've always found that hard to believe, but now, having seen for myself just how much goes on under my own nose that I'm more or less oblivious to, and what I've managed to do without my own neighbours being aware, I can understand a bit better how someone even in close proximity to the worst kind of human behaviour may actually fail to notice it.

There are even TV programmes about that kind of thing now, usually based on reality, where people are found and returned home to their loved ones, to pick up their lives as best they can. But all such attempts at 'entertainment' really serve to do is perpetuate the hope, for countless bereft families, that they will one day be reunited with the ones *they* lost. I don't know the statistics for those who get their wish. I don't imagine it's very high, which makes those TV programs all the more insensitive and brutal to the ones who remain bereft.

I expect Tom Findlay's mother will be feeling like that. Bereft, and frightened for her son. I hate to think of her sitting there, night after night, year after year, staring at her clock or calendar, remembering the last time she saw her son, and wondering if and when she might again. If Tom's body is never discovered that poor woman will go to her own grave never having understood what happened, and never having known how to properly mourn the loss of her child.

I lost Badger once, for two hours, and I almost lost my mind with worry. It wasn't long after he'd come to live with me, but we had already bonded and I was already madly in love with his shaggy, doggy gorgeousness. We'd been to the park, and I'd let him off his lead to sniff around the trees for a while as I walked along chatting to Daphne, who'd met us there. After five minutes or so I called to him but he didn't come. Daphne and I spent the next two hours running around the park and nearby streets, calling and calling and calling, to no avail. Chilled fingers of fear kept clutching at my heart, and my mind kept racing with possibilities, all too hideous to dwell on, but there all the same, until my mobile phone rang and Bill told me Badger was sitting at my front door.

I believe that the absolute worst of visions are reserved exclusively for those who love with all their heart. You let your dog off the lead, and all of a sudden he is missing, and you're thinking he's been stolen, taken to be used as bait for dog fighting or tortured in some other way for someone's sick pleasure, or he's been hit by a car and crawled away to an unknown place where you'll never find him, to die alone in fear and pain. The pain *you* feel is beyond description. The remorse you feel, for not having looked after him better, is crippling.

What must it be like for parents then, when the possibilities are so much worse, so much harder to contemplate or live with? Where humanity and the observation of another being's dignity are the things they pray for the hardest, but come to doubt the most?

That's what I have done to this woman. To this boy's family. That's where I've put them; in that place of fear and dread, all tangled up with hope and expectation. That family, like so many others, will run the gamut of human emotion in the coming days, weeks and maybe for the rest of their lives, if my crime is never discovered. Nobody on this planet will ever see Tom Findlay alive again, and it's all my fault.

Suddenly my stupid mind map becomes meaningless. Its significance no longer matters. Its support fades to nothing, beneath the dark, desperate shadow of what I must somehow, in one way or another, find a way to atone for.

23

Friday
- Darren -

Bloody decorating! It's been driving me mad these past few days, but I'm finally starting to think we might be getting there. Stupid me, I thought we'd be all done and dusted in a day or two, but it's going to take a week before we're finished. We've got some good wallpaper that Mum likes, but we've had to strip off what was already there before we could put it up. That wasn't as easy as it bloody sounds, since there were four fucking layers that had all been painted over. It took two days just to get it all off. Then I had to 'size' the walls, with some watery shit you have to put on to make new wallpaper stick, and that took care of another half a day.

By the time I finally started papering, just this morning, I was losing the will to live. But it's starting to look alright, I think. I've never wallpapered in my life before, and it's a patterned paper. Red poppies on a white background with black and yellow bits in the middle of them. Very cheerful. It took me a couple of goes to get the hang of matching the bloody flowers up, and must've wasted half a fucking roll before the penny dropped on how to do it properly, but I'm well underway with it now.

After we picked the paper, Mum dragged me to the charity furniture shop, hoping to pick out a new sofa. As luck would have it, we ended up with two that matched, with a footstool as well. Lemon leather with chrome legs. She's made up; proper pleased. Got them for a bloody song, and just as well. Even on sale, that wallpaper was expensive. Mum got Pat to agree to pick it up in his van so I didn't have to hike around town with it all, and she arranged to have the sofas delivered at the weekend, to give me time to get everything finished and her time to get rid of the old suite. She advertised it on Marketplace for sixty quid and some geezer wants it. He's picking it up next Tuesday night and paying cash, so I'll have to be here to help load it all, because Pat will be at the chippy working. He only has Monday nights off.

I've never been so knackered, but it's a good feeling, I have to admit, looking at the work. It's shaping up alright, considering I've never done it before. Mum's after black curtains and cushion covers now, and a red rug to match the fucking poppies. She's put a shout out on a local Facebook for-sale page, so she's hoping someone will help. I told her she could just dye the curtains we already have, and she thought that might work, if all else fails, but I think she's just excited at having a bit of 'new' stuff. I'd love to win the lottery, so I could buy her everything she wants *brand* new, instead of someone else's cast-offs, but I'd have to buy a ticket first and I never seem to remember until I'm seeing the bloody draw on the telly.

Pat came home tonight straight from the chippy, which was a bit of a surprise for a Friday night. He usually goes to the pub and pitches up some time after midnight, but tonight he was home by eleven, and actually said the decorating was looking alright. He said it like he couldn't believe it, and I wanted to ask him why he was so surprised, but I decided against it. I'm getting a buzz from seeing Mum happy if I'm honest, and that wasn't going to last long, was it, with me picking a fight with Pat?

Finally I've done something he approves of. He made a cup of tea and he actually asked me if I wanted one. Another fucking first. Maybe that's all it takes, for him to make an effort – me making one first.

All the way through this I've been thinking a lot about Tommy, where he might be, and going to see that woman, but it hasn't taken me over like it threatened to before I started with this project for Mum. Now, it's like I'm considering it from a different place, like it's not me, but someone else thinking for me. I feel less anxious about it, until I start to think about it proper, and that's usually at bedtime, when everything's been put away for the night. That's when the thoughts suddenly start rushing in because I don't have something else to fill my head with, like paint and matching poppies.

So my nights have all been restless, rehearsing over and over what I plan to say, and it feels as though I've already made up my mind to go. I'm a bit more settled about it, though, not as panicked as I was when I first thought about doing it.

Just one more day of papering, and it should be finished. Mum's decided she wants the bastard bloody skirtings and windowsills painted now, and I told her we should have done that first, before the paper went on. I think I can still do it though, if I'm careful, and she says there's some paint down in the shed that would do, so that will finish the job off. A couple more days should crack it.

Mum is so happy I think she's going to burst. For once I find her excitement quite funny, and not pathetic like I usually do. She's like a little kid, all thrilled that her living room is starting to look so different and she has a few nice things coming. I've surprised myself, for having the patience to do all this painting and papering properly, and for making such a halfway decent job of it. If you don't look too closely at the corners, where the curves went into holes a bit and had to be repaired, it's a pretty reasonable job. Pat thinks it's alright and Mum thinks it's wonderful, so who am I to argue?

It'll be nice when it's all finished and the furniture's arrived, and she has her bloody curtains and what-nots. Maybe she'll shut up for a while and just enjoy it, but I do have a niggly old feeling it won't be long before she's banging on about getting some of other rooms done. Best gird my loins for that one. It's only a matter of time. I just hope to fuck she doesn't have the bright idea of having a new kitchen. I might have to draw the line at trying to do that.

24

Friday
- Alison -

Driving home from work, I decide I'll wear a simple, short-sleeved white linen dress for my dinner with Simon. I'll team it with a pair of powder blue suede wedge sandals and a matching cashmere cardigan. The evenings are still warm, but a chill has started to creep into the air after the sun goes down, so the warm cardi will ward off any evening shivers, without the need for a jacket or coat. It seems a shame to resort to that just yet.

I'm very much a summer person. Winter depresses me. I even have a UV light-box that I plug in from time to time, over the winter months when the sun doesn't make it through the clouds, just to stop my mood from sinking.

As I make my way home, unwanted thoughts storm in and settle like oversized frosted holly wreaths hanging on heavy church doors, like thick blankets of pristine snow on chill-filled graves and headstones. Despite the late summer day, my mind seems mired in winter.

I pull into the driveway, seeking to shake the mantle of gloom that seems to overshadow my every waking thought, and I see there is a small bouquet of flowers on the doorstep. My first thought is that they must be from Simon. How lovely.

I unlock the door and open it before picking up the flowers and as I take them inside and set them on the hallway table (where that skillet sat, just eight fateful days ago) I notice a card pinned to the cellophane. Still imagining they are from Simon, it's his name I expect to see as I pull the card from the envelope. But instead, the inscription reads:

'Thank you so much for your kindness in showing me your home this week. All best wishes, Barbara Davies.'

You've got to be fucking kidding me!

The card falls from my hand and I take a step back, blinking at the little bouquet. Of all the things that have happened to me lately, or the things that might happen in the future, I was not expecting anything like *this*.

Confusion clouds my head. What is the woman trying to do? Is she taunting me, playing mind games? She really didn't seem to be that kind of person. Taken at face value, the note is simply what it says; a thank you for a kindness shown, with best wishes offered. Does she know that I'm aware I was duped? If so, this must be her way of apologising for it, so perhaps she is a decent person after all, one with a conscience. If not, it's just her way of trying to make *herself* feel better about what she did.

There was a time when I used to try to see the best in people; a time when I believed that most were inherently good, and that those who didn't appear so must have had a good excuse. I used to give people the benefit of the doubt. I always found it hard to accept that any person could really be rotten right through. But too many years as a debt collector, listening to the endless excuses people continually came up with for their inability to deal with their own responsibilities has stripped me of my rose-tinted glasses. That, and being let down and disappointed too many times to count by people I've cared about and trusted over the years, has severely dented my initial will to always look for the best. Nowadays I'm probably one of the most cynical people you'd never meet.

I greet Badger and help him with his toilet, then sit at the dining table. I close my eyes and I concentrate, trying to comprehend what may have been in that woman's mind when she ordered these flowers and wrote or dictated the note. I try to put myself in her place, in her head, as she seeks to justify what she did; to herself, to her son, and now it seems, to me.

It's a real stretch to second-guess her, and I can't discount the fact that I may be way off base, and she may well just be completely off her head. But I reason that she didn't have to reach out to me with a gift, with a message of thanks, after she'd lied to me and violated my privacy, unless she felt bad for doing it. That would fit with her general demeanour, of nervousness and almost an apologetic approach. She just didn't seem like the sort of person who would play games. She looked almost miserable to be here, and I didn't think too much about it at the time.

But now, as I grope back through my memory to connect with how she was, it seems significant. She was clearly here on a mission she didn't want to be on (is Darren Davies a bully?) and this little posy of flowers is the clearest indication I could ever get, that she felt bad about it afterwards.

It in no way excuses what she did, and I still feel outraged at the barefaced bloody cheek of it, but I do find solace in my overriding feeling that this was a small gesture of atonement from a woman who regretted what she'd done. And I'll wager that it hasn't erased her guilt completely. Not if she has a decent moral compass.

If only I could send a bouquet of flowers to Tom Findlay's mother, to atone for what *I* did. If only everything were that simple.

Today is Friday and Barbara Davies came on Tuesday, so if she had any suspicions about me, or what might have happened here in this house, there would have been consequences of some sort by now. I haven't had a visit from the police. Nobody else has been or called here, in fact the ripples in the pond have settled down to the point where it largely feels like any normal day or week, apart from the unrelenting viciousness of my ever-present headache, and a constant, crippling fear of my crime being discovered.

A quick glance at my watch tells me I have just one hour now, to get ready for Simon. A quick shower and another bout of dithering over what to wear, and finally I'm sorted, in the outfit I originally planned. While I'm waiting I sit on the floor with Badger for a while, stroking his silky ears and murmuring softly to him.

I hear Simon's car and I'm on my feet and at the door before he has chance to knock. 'Hello,' he smiles and leans forward to give me a quick peck on the cheek as he comes in. he hands me a small bunch of flowers. 'How are you? You look lovely. How's Badger?'

'Come and see. I think he's doing okay, but I'm keen for you to see him.' Simon follows me through to the kitchen, remarking on the other bouquet of flowers on the hallway table and asking if there's any competition he should be worried about. I grin and shake my head.

From his bed in the corner of the kitchen, Badger lifts his head and gives a short bark in greeting. His tail thumps the floor, showing his delight at seeing another friend. Simon looks and feels him over, and proclaims him to be doing nicely, which reassures me a lot. We make him comfortable before heading out.

In the car, Simon talks about his week, I talk about mine, and the conversation is easy and light. He pulls into the car park of a canal-side pub which has recently had a big makeover, and I'm pleased and very keen to see inside for the first time.

'The Bow and Stern! Simon, what a delight! I used to come here a lot before it got refurbished. Although it was a bit run-down, the food was always really good. Let's hope that hasn't changed!'

'It hasn't. I came here a couple of weeks ago with my sister. It was her birthday so I treated her and the kids. I can vouch for the food, and I've booked a window table so we can watch the narrow boats come and go. Friday night's busy one, with weekend boaters setting out. So if you find me a crashing bore, at least you can look at something else while we eat.'

I turn to him, slightly unnerved, to find him grinning from ear to ear. Somehow I don't think he's going to bore me. It will probably be more a case of me boring him. When did any man last find me interesting? I really don't remember.

We order drinks at the bar; a pint of cider for Simon and a glass of chardonnay for me, and we sit on an overstuffed sofa to wait to be called to our table. A hostess scuttles up to assure us it will only be ten minutes, so we relax and talk some more about work.

Simon tells me that his family are working class but he excelled at school and he went on to study to be a vet after an uncle died and left him enough money to enable him to pay for university.

'We couldn't have afforded for me to go, otherwise, and not end up in debt for a decade or more with student loans. That just seemed like more than I could cope with. Then the inheritance came, and I knew I had to use it wisely. It's what my uncle would have wanted me to use it for, to set myself up in a worthwhile career.'

I admit to him that I understand what a profound life-changer a legacy can be if the right decisions are made with it, since I was incredibly fortunate myself to have been left not one legacy but two (from my father and my grandfather) which enabled me to buy my lovely house with no mortgage to worry about.

Simon also wasn't aware that I'm a debt collector and he's as fascinated as most people are, to know the mechanics of how we get people to pay, so we talk about that for a few minutes and I manage, without betraying any confidentiality, to recite some amusing stories about the antics and attitudes of punters, clients and colleagues.

We're called to our table, and spend some time looking at the menu. I decide on prawns in garlic butter sauce for an entree, venison in red wine with mashed potatoes and garden vegetables for a main course, and I defer a decision on dessert for the moment, deciding to wait until later to see if I will even have room.

Simon is not so reticent. He orders an entree of mushrooms on wild rice, a main of steak and ale pie with lashings of chips and gravy, and a stack of profiteroles to finish. I cannot help smiling.

'Perhaps you might help with the profiteroles.' he chuckles. 'I'll order two spoons.'

We chat away until our entrees arrive. The prawns are delicious and Simon assures me that his mushrooms are equally so.

'Tell me more about your sister,' I prompt him.

'Well, she's four years younger than me, so she's thirty-five. Single mum to a teenage lad, who's a bit of a handful, and a sweet daughter who's just turned twelve. She's been on her own with them more or less since the outset, and that's been hard for her. She's never had an easy ride of it, and she struggles at times to make ends meet. There's not much left over every week, and she finds it really hard to accept help, but she mostly does okay.'

Simon pulls a wry face. 'She doesn't want me to interfere, especially financially, but I do what I can for her. She didn't inherit from my uncle, which I've always felt bad about, so I've always tried to do a bit more for her and the kids, to make up for that, although I do have to find creative ways of helping at times because she can be a bit bristly about it.'

A kind of hunted look comes over Simon in that moment. A shadow passes over his face, and suddenly I feel there is a crushing weight on him. The lightness has simply evaporated from his manner. He looks sad in that moment, and desperately uncomfortable, as if admitting to hardship in his family has sapped him of his happiness.

'I'm sorry,' I venture. 'I didn't mean to pry.'

He shakes his head. 'No, it's fine. You're not prying. It's just normal conversation, isn't it?'

But somehow, he has literally transformed before my eyes to something a long way from normal. The joy has just left him. He is noticeably fidgeting now, and my mind goes back to that first time I asked him to stay for dinner, how he bolted like a frightened rabbit, and then came back to make amends.

I think he is just painfully lacking in confidence with women, and I decide to let it ride until one of two things happen. He will either snap back out of it, or the evening will end before it has really begun.

The minutes tick by without comment from either of us. We both concentrate on our food to try to dispel the awkwardness, and the headache that has left me for a few hours has come crashing back, and is now throbbing quietly. I look at Simon, who doesn't meet my gaze, and I suddenly feel sad. He's now on the verge of speaking, and I think I know what he's about to say. I think he is about to suggest taking me home, that this is a mistake, that he's not ready to start seeing anyone, it's not me, it's him, the usual spiel trotted out by those who suddenly discover that they really don't want to be on a date with someone after all.

He clears his throat, toys with his dinner fork, and continues to concentrate on what's on his plate.

'It's alright Simon, if you want to leave, we can leave,' I say gently. I manage to keep my voice even, so the disappointment doesn't render me incoherent.

'I'm sorry if I've said something wrong. If you want to just take me home, that's fine. It really is, I promise.' *You don't deserve to be with a nice man, you murdering bitch, and here's the proof!*

He looks up at me, finally making eye contact, and he bites his lip.

'It's not that, not at all. Alison, I really do want to be here, please believe me. There's just some really bad stuff going on in my private life, with my family, that I'm not handling very well, and I just don't know if it's fair to you, to expect you to be around while all that's happening. I don't know if I can give as much time as I really want to, to getting to know you.'

Relief washes over me, at not being rejected in the way I thought I was going to be. I decide to take a leap of faith.

'Simon, I have some bad stuff going on in my life too, like you wouldn't believe, but I want to be here too, here with you, and if I can help I do want to, even if it's just to listen.'

This delightful man has the weight of the world on his shoulders, and I can see it, and I find I really *do* want to help. I want to shove my own monstrous stuff aside, for a few merciful moments, and concentrate on listening to him while he offloads his.

He looks at me for a long moment, while my heart skips a couple of beats, then he grimaces, and takes a deep breath.

'Okay, well then; here goes. We're all in a bit of a state, right now. My sister's boy, my nephew, went missing last week. He's just vanished, without a trace. There are no clues, no reasons that any of us can come up with. He's gone. Just like that!' Simon snaps his fingers, and it sounds far too loud in this quietly muted, civilized place.

'Marla, my sister, is out of her mind with worry, so is his little sister Jenna, my niece. I am out of my *own* mind with worry! None of his friends know where he is, nobody has even the slightest idea of what might have happened. It's like he's literally evaporated off the face of the earth, and I haven't a clue what to do. I feel so helpless, so inept. I want to be able to find the answer, I want to find him and bring him home to Marla and Jenna. I want us all to have our family back the way it was, but I have this feeling, this horrible sick feeling, that he's gone for good.'

I'm horrified to see tears springing to Simon's eyes. I pray with all my heart that he can hold them at bay.

'I think something truly terrible has happened to him, Alison, and he isn't coming back. I don't know why; it's just a horrible feeling I've got. But I can't say that to my sister and my niece, can I? I have to be a rock for them. But I'm falling apart myself. I need a rock myself, and there isn't one for me, and I don't know what to do. He's just a kid. Sixteen. The police don't have a single lead to follow. We're all out of our minds with worry.'

Blood pounds through my head, and my mouth goes dry. I take a gulp of my wine to free up my strangled vocal chords.

'Last week? He went missing last week, you say? What's his name?'

I hold my breath. Time in suspension, all sound gone from the room, everything frozen, nothing leaking through but the sound of my own blood, rushing madly through my head, surging like a waterfall and cascading away like rapids, as if it wanted to go anywhere, be anywhere but here, flooding the spaces in my brain. My headache blooms like a blue hydrangea, growing and seeping into the furthermost corners of my crowded head.

'Tom. His name's Thomas Findlay.'

I look down at my plate. One prawn remains, plump and succulent, but I couldn't eat it if you put a gun to my head. As sound returns to the room, I feel myself slowly sliding off my chair and onto the floor. I'm suddenly spinning, faster and faster, into the deepest, darkest pit of oblivion, clinging blindly to the last conscious thought, of the sound of sliding plates, and feeling everything falling on top of me.

* * *

I wake up on a sofa, with fog still drifting around my brain. As it clears, I realise it's the same sofa I was sitting on with Simon before we went to our table. A white wicker screen has been artfully arranged around us, to shield us from curious glances from other diners and drinkers. Simon is crouched on the floor next to me holding my hand, and two of the restaurant staff are hovering close by, waiting anxiously for me to indicate that I'm alright, which I try to do by raising an arm that feels leaden, like it doesn't belong to me at all. One of the waitresses is holding a mobile phone, and asking Simon if he wants an ambulance called. I shake my head, mumbling.

'No, no ambulance. I'm fine, really.' My words come out slurred, like I'm drunk.

Simon leans forward, his face full of concern. 'Alison? What the hell happened? Are you alright? One minute we were sitting there talking and the next you just fainted clean away from me!'

I lie there for a couple of heartbeats, blinking, until I remember what he said to me just before everything went black. I say to him, in a wobbly voice; 'we were talking about your nephew.'

Even to me, my voice sounds hollow, fake, like its coming through a reed-thin pipe from a hundred miles away. I sound small, and I feel small, infinitely so, as I sit here, swamped with knowledge that would, if I shared it, simply shatter this poor man's heart.

'That's right, we were.' Simon looks at the waitress with the phone, and shakes his head at her. The lady is coherent. All is well.

I move to sit up, and he helps me, propping a cushion behind my back. The waitress with the phone has disappeared, but the other staff member, probably the manager, is still hovering. He hands me a glass of water, and enquires whether I really am alright. He assures me I can sit for as long as I need to, and he asks gently if there was a problem with the food. I assure him that the food was fine. He wants to know if we'd like to continue with our meal, and I shake my head. I'm unable to look Simon in the eye. Being able to sit here in the restaurant and continue having a meal with him is unthinkable now.

'I think I just need to go home. I'm sorry, Simon. I don't know what came over me. I've been having some brutal headaches lately, but I'm not usually a fainter.' *I've never fainted in my life before. Is this what guilt does? Is this what I can expect for my life now, to conk out every time I fly too close to the flame of guilt?*

Well, you *did* faint, my dear. So I'm going to have you checked out at A & E, and I'm not taking no for an answer. I'll bring the car up to the door.'

As he stands to go, I make a move to stand also, and find it doesn't work. My legs feel like jelly. I have no choice but to sit back down and wait for him to bring the car around, and help me into it.

Neither of us speaks on the way to the hospital. Simon looks over at me occasionally and smiles gently, and at one point he reaches for my hand and gives it a small squeeze. There's a knot in my chest, so huge I can hardly breathe. I can't respond to his smiles or his touch. I've lost the ability to engage with him at all. He senses this, and stays silent, as he pulls into the parking lot at the hospital.

He helps me in, and explains to the desk staff that I've had a blackout or some kind of seizure. Suddenly, the normal A & E crazy Friday night crush and queue ceases to exist for me, as I am swiftly put into a wheelchair and taken through. Heart attacks and head stuff always get prioritized. I may have had, or still be having, a stroke or a fit of some kind, and they need to act fast to rule it out.

The last thing I see, as I'm taken behind a curtain, is Simon's worried face, and it literally breaks my heart. Discovering that I have in fact killed this lovely man's nephew, and realising just how widespread the heartache I've caused is starting to become, I'm acutely aware of all that I deserve, the last thing on that list ever being his kindness or his love.

Alone in my little cubicle, with the flimsiest of curtains separating me from the brutal reality of what might await me in the outside world, I try to refocus.

Simon has no idea why I fainted. Will he connect it to what he was telling me? He doesn't know me well enough to know. I could tell him anything, I could say I suddenly came over all queasy, that the prawns were off, that the room felt too hot, that the chardonnay had gone straight to my head. I could offer any excuse at all, in fact, and he'd have no choice but to accept my words, even if he didn't believe them. He has no idea I was even burgled, so how could he have the slightest inkling that I might be involved in the disappearance of his nephew?

I'm a middle-class career woman. I have a social life, of sorts. I have an animal to care for, an extended family that I belong to, and as far as outward appearances go, there is nothing whatsoever that could connect someone like me to the disappearance of a young criminal like Tom Findlay. I don't know if Simon even *knows* Tom was a criminal. He didn't say as much.

I try to recall the conversation but it feels fragmented; like waking up and scrambling, in vain, to hold on to the evaporating edges of a disappearing dream. I can't recall every word, but I am certain that nothing was mentioned about Tom being involved in crime. Simon actually got to say very little, before I hit the deck like a crumpled sack of blue cashmere and white linen potatoes.

But I am fine, now. I just have to get out of here, go home, and regroup my scattered thoughts. Sadly, the medical team seem to have other ideas; they are not about to let me walk out. In the current climate and the state of the nation, they are probably too concerned about being sued or at least pilloried for poor diagnosis and inadequate care. There goes the cynic again.

After taking my history, asking me a few questions and doing a few visual tests with light-pens and fingers, the doctor decides he is not convinced I'm well enough to leave. I assure him that I feel absolutely fine, apart from my headache, which I try to pass off as nothing more than the residual effect of fainting in public, even though I'm not sure I believe that myself.

However, the good doctor is not to be swayed. He wants to take a closer look at my head, so they decide to give me a CT scan. Apparently this will take some time to set up, so they suggest I may have to be prepared for being here most of the night.

I'm frustrated by this turn of events, and by what feels like wholly unnecessary measures, but I'm impressed. After everything I've heard recently about the burdens on the health service, and how tough it is to find beds for the sick and dying, I'm amazed that I'm being fast-tracked in this way, and I tell them so.

I ask to see Simon. Looking him in the eye is the hardest thing I've ever had to do, but I manage it, and I ask him if he will please call at Bill's, my neighbour, and see if he will tend to Badger until I can get home later tonight or tomorrow morning, I'm not sure at this stage which it will be. He protests, says he wants to stay with me, for however long it takes, but I reject that. I can't tell him I just don't want him around me, but I really need to be alone right now, to process what's happened tonight. I tell him I'm exhausted, and need to sleep.

'Alright, if you're sure you don't want me to stay. I'll certainly get Badger sorted out for you. Does Bill have a key?'

'Yes, he does. If you can advise him, he will know what to do.' I really don't want my poor injured dog to spend a night alone, on the floor, waiting for me to come home when I may not, and Simon picks up on that.

'I'll see if he can have him at his place for tonight. I can carry him over, if so.'

I murmur my thanks, beneath my heavy blanket of self-loathing, and Simon bends down, kisses my cheek and pulls a face.

'Not the best start, but we'll pick up where we left off, another night, I promise. Call me when you're done, no matter what time. I can come and get you. And don't worry about Badger, I'll makes sure he's cared for, either by Bill or by me. Good luck with the scan. And *call* me. Okay?'

In another instant he is gone. It occurs to me that my dress is covered in garlic butter sauce, and I have no way of cleaning myself up. I mention this to the nurse who assures me, as she hands me a hospital gown, that I mustn't worry, this kind of thing happens a lot, and they can certainly provide me with a toothbrush if I want one, and other basics as required, albeit nothing fancy.

Time ticks by as I wait to be taken up for my scan, and I think of how funny this story might one day be, if I can ever fight my way to a place where I can laugh again freely, and without restraint. Woman goes for dinner with very nice man, faints in the middle of the starter course for no apparent reason, and ends up in A & E.

What a great first date! If we were ever to get married we would talk about our first date for our whole lives. Our best man would refer to it in his wedding speech. We'd go on to regale our children with the story, and our grandchildren too. It would be one of those family legends that lived on, long after we'd left the world.

But there will be no wedding for me and Simon. Not that I thought at this embryonic stage that anything could lead to that. One date does not a lifetime of wedded bliss foretell. But even if that might ever have been on the cards, there will never be a chance of it now. If he were to learn what I've done, he would loathe me for the rest of his days. Better to get it nipped in the bud now. I can never see him again. Ever.

It all feels damned, and I know it's because of what I've done, that I can never confess to him, or to anyone else. He seems intent on being around, has even offered to come and collect me no matter what time I'll be ready to go. I need to put him off; I can get a taxi home. With any luck, I'll only have to have contact with him one more time, to say thank you for all that he's done, but I'm not ready for a relationship, thank you all the same. It's not you, it's me. You deserve better. All those platitudes I thought just a few hours ago I was about to hear from *him*.

That's the thing about platitudes and clichés, though, isn't it? However much we deride them, or however much they make us cringe, they all come from a sad place of truth.

A nurse comes to get me, to take me to my scan. She sits me in a wheelchair to take me up to the next floor, which feels faintly ridiculous, but I comply in silence. Doctor knows best.

The scan is straightforward, but that's not the end of things. Apparently, they now want to do an MRI scan of my noggin. I suffer a little from claustrophobia, so I'm not looking forward to lying perfectly still for half an hour, but it seems I have little option, other than to walk out of here with questions left unanswered. Since I'm here, I may as well get some clarity. No point in wasting an opportunity. It would be good to know if my headaches are anything to be concerned about. I don't have to worry about much else, I don't think. I'm sure a guilty conscience and a video-chip-like memory of the terrible things people do don't show up on their brain scans.

It takes another hour of waiting around before I'm taken for the MRI. When we get there, to the room with the massive tunnel-like chamber, a nurse asks me what sort of music I like. I tell her I love jazz, so she hooks me up with earphones and before I know it I'm flat on my back, gliding gently into the tunnel, with Benny Goodman for company. I force myself to concentrate on the music in an effort to drown out my clamouring thoughts.

25

Saturday

- Darren -

Bright and bloody early, Mum's banging on the bedroom door and shrieking. She's had a text off the delivery bloke to say the sofas are due to arrive within the next half hour, so I dive into the shower and throw a bit of breakfast down my neck, and bang on time the doorbell rings, and yes indeed, there's a bloody big delivery van outside.

Within minutes we've loaded the sofas into the living room and waved the driver goodbye. It all happened pretty fast, and I was impressed. I have to admit, as well, that the sofas do look nice. We play around for half an hour or so, putting them into different positions, and where Mum ends up deciding to have them means I then have to move the fucking telly and the bloody great cabinet it sits on. That takes care of another half hour, but by the time we're finished it all looks pretty good.

Mum's managed to track down the black curtains and cushions she wants, but the woman who has them can't deliver, so it's a bus trip into town, then another one out to the suburbs on the other side of town, and then the repeat reverse process. Mum was happy enough to go on her own, but I've nothing better to do until tonight, so I told her I'd go with her. She was all smiles about it. It's so good to see her happy, and it hasn't taken all that much, when you think about it.

I never thought much about her being unhappy, when me and Michelle were growing up. We were just kids, getting on with our stupid kids games, and school and the like. I can't speak for my sister, but I never took much notice of Mum as a person, in all those years. She was just my mum, and she fed me, washed my clothes, walked me to school and then brought me back again. She was always there, at the school gates, waiting for us at the end of the day. We never had to worry about her not being there to meet us.

Like clockwork, she'd march us home and make us do our homework before we were allowed to get changed out of our school clothes and go outside to play for an hour or two before dark. Then when we came in, either together or separately (as happened more as we got older and we each found friends of our own to hang out with), our tea was always on the table. Sometimes it wasn't much, but we never went without a meal of some sort. Mum always made sure we had *something* to eat.

It was later, when I got a bit older, that I started to realise just what a hard time she often had with my dad. He was the biggest, first-class, A-rated asshole you'd ever fucking find. If he wasn't away, doing God knows what, he was just staggering around the house blind drunk. He never hit any of us, but he used to shout and scream, and call us names. I was a useless piece of shit, Michelle was a dirty little scrubber, and Mum was an ugly, washed-up old tart that nobody else would ever fancy. According to him we were lucky to have him. He used to say that all the time and I dunno who he was trying to convince, us or himself.

I grew up hating the bastard, and so did Michelle, but Mum stuck by him, through thick and thin. I never understood why, and thinking about it, I guess I didn't have much respect for her because of that, and because she never stood up to him, not even when he was roaring and screaming at me and Michelle. There were a lot of nights when I lay in bed, fantasizing about finding the balls to pick a fist-fight with him, and then beat seven shades of shit out of him and shut the fucker up for once and for all.

We were just kids, and our Mum and Dad were supposed to love us and take care of us, defend us from harm and all that shyte. I knew *he* didn't give a damn about us, but I got to thinking Mum mustn't have cared all that much either, if she could just stand by and let him say all those nasty-bastard things and spend all his money at the pub or the bookies before we could even get the rent paid, or any decent food on the table.

Emotional abuse they'd call it nowadays, and all those prison shrinks asking their stupid bloody questions - *tell me about your childhood, Darren* - then banging on about having choices, like not having to become what you've been labelled. If only it was that bloody simple.

Most of those dickheads meant well I suppose, but they didn't have the first fucking clue about hardship, with their posh degrees, fancy painted fingernails and stupid, false expressions of empathy. Oh poor man, did you have a rough start? Ah well, we can help you turn yourself around! Yeah, well, you don't know the half of it, and I don't intend to bloody tell you, so you can fuck off, thanks very much.

But our Dad hurled endless verbal abuse at us, for years, and Mum just sat back and let it happen. I never knew why he hated us so much but that's less important to me now than why Mum *let* him treat us that way. So, since we're sitting here on an almost empty bus with nothing much else to say (and both avoiding the elephant sat in the opposite seat, of little Tommy's disappearance and my proposed plan to go door-knocking where I probably shouldn't) I decide to ask her.

'Mum, can I ask you something?'

'Course you can, love. Ask away.'

'Why did you stay with Dad? Why didn't you leave him, years before he died? He'd have deserved it, you know, if we'd left him.'

She doesn't speak for what feels like two bloody miles, and I'm starting to think I've really pissed her off. I'm about to give up on it when she finally answers.

'Yeah, I know, he absolutely *would* have deserved it. And I wanted to, Darren, and that's the God's honest truth. He didn't deserve any of us. We were *all* too bloody good for him. I really did want to leave him, more than anything.'

I decide not to prompt her, because somehow I just know she's struggling to choose her words, and she needs time to find the right ones.

'It was a combination of things, love. First, I had nowhere to go, and no money to support myself somewhere with you two. Looking back, I probably could have gone home to your Nan and Grandad's, but at the time I was too ashamed. Your Grandad didn't like your dad, always said he was trouble, he'd make me bloody miserable, and I shouldn't marry him. Going back there and admitting he was right? I just couldn't make myself do it, Darren. My stupid bloody pride got in the way of everything.'

'And fear too, Mum? Fear of being judged?'

She heaves a great, weary sight, the likes of which I almost never hear her make. It's like she drags that sigh all the way up from the bottoms of her feet.

'Yes. And fear of being judged. So I stayed. But what most people don't know is I didn't like your dad, not even a jot, towards the end. In fact, I hated him almost as much as you did, but not *quite* as much, because every time I looked at him I still remembered what he was like before he got all bitter and twisted. But you never had that memory of him, did you?

'He was lovely in the beginning, but he turned into a bastard before you were old enough to realise anything had changed.

'I'd made a commitment, Darren. And, you know, there's nothing in wedding vows about it being okay to forsake someone for bad behaviour. It was all 'for better or for worse,' back then. Later on, the way he was, you'd call it mental cruelty, and you could get a divorce because of it, if you could prove it. It was harder back then, though, to be taken seriously.

'If he'd knocked me about, if I'd had bruises and black eyes and the like, it would have been easier, I'd have had a bit more support. But back then, what they couldn't see, they couldn't act on, so I was trapped, I suppose. I stayed because I couldn't see any other options, and because of the other vows 'in sickness and in health.

'Your dad was sick, Darren. He had cirrhosis of the liver, and nobody else would take care of him. In spite of how he was, I wanted you and Michelle to know him. I didn't have the right to just take you away from him, even if I could have, and he was the sort of bloke who'd have fought me tooth and nail for custody of you both, even if he didn't bloody want you, just to prove he could win.'

'But I feel like you threw us to the wolves, Mum. He was such a bastard, always yelling, telling us we were useless wastes of space. He hated us, and we never knew why. For years, you just let him tell me I was useless, and I ended up believing it, Mum.'

'Yes. I hold up my hand, Darren. I failed you both; you and Michelle. I know that. I should have taken you and left. That would have been the beginning of a different kind of long battle, but it would have protected you more. I'm so sorry, love. I just felt like if I gave you enough love, myself, it would make up for how he was. That's very naive, I know, but I was a lot younger then. I felt so trapped, so alone, so I just resolved to try to make the best of things, and for a long time I thought we were all managing. But then Michelle left home to go and live with a school friend and never wanted to come home even for a cup of bloody tea. She just wouldn't set foot in the house again, while he was in it.'

Now that she's said it, I do remember that. I remember Michelle leaving, hauling her suitcase down the bloody stairs, and out through the front door, with Dad screaming 'go then, you filthy little tart, and don't come back.' And you know what? She never did. She never came back to our house again, in all the years he was alive. She didn't even go to his funeral.

I did. I wanted to make sure the bastard was dead and fucking buried, and I'd have danced on his coffin if I could have.

'You were doing alright to start with,' Mum carries on; 'You got all your A levels and then with that call centre job, I really did think we'd made it through the storm but then when you started going off the rails I realised that in staying with that miserable bastard I'd only made an even bigger mess for you and your poor sister to work through. She managed it, but you didn't fare quite so well, did you, love?

'I stuffed up big-time, Darren, and I'm sorry. I truly am. I should have known better, I should have *done* better, for both of you. Me and my stupid pride, and thinking I was better than I really was, at making it work.'

Mum looks proper fucking miserable now, with big fat tears rolling slowly down her cheeks, and for the first time I realise that what she needs more than anything else in her whole life right now is not a redecorated house, or a pair of second-hand curtains. Right now, more than anything, she needs to be forgiven.

And I find that I have – forgiven her, I mean. So I tell her that. And I tell her I remember all the afternoons she sat with me trying to help me make sense of my homework, how she always made sure we had hot water bottles on winter's nights, how there was always some kind of food on the table, even when it was really hard to find anything decent with no money to feed two growing kids who never thought about much else but their bellies.

'Darren, he never hit any of us. And I want you to know that if he ever started with that kind of bloody nonsense, I would have gathered you up and left. I absolutely would have, no questions asked. But a lot of the time I was *afraid* he would, if I tried to intervene, because he was just so bloody angry all the time.

'I never knew what would set it off, and I didn't want it to boil over, so I tried to keep the peace before it ever got to the violent stage, but I never knew how big a toll it was taking on you until later. And I know you didn't have much respect for me. I don't blame you for that, love. You were just a boy. How could you have understood?'

I lean over and put my arm around my lovely mum, who's still crying but now pretending not to. I give her a squeeze, but I don't know what to say to make her stop, so I don't try, and that seems to be alright for her.

'We survived him though, didn't we?' I smile at her. 'We survived him, Mum, and we're doing fine.'

She looks at me, with her red-rimmed eyes. 'Are we? *Are* we doing fine? I'd like to think so, but you need to sort your life out, love. You can't go on living this way. You need to find a way to be happy, and robbing other people, bouncing in and out of bloody jail, that's not going to make for a good life. You need to grow up, Darren, and make something of your life before you end up like him, all bitter and twisted and angry at the world because you got short-changed, and all the while it was your own bloody fault.'

We both stare out of the bus window as it trundles along, each lost in our own thoughts for a minute or two. Then she says something that truly surprises me.

'And just so you know? Your dad didn't hate you. He loved you. He just couldn't handle being a father. The weight of it crushed him. When you were really little, too small to remember, he used to idolize you. Then, when Michelle was born, he buckled under the weight of the pressure of having *two* kids and a wife to take care of.

'Don't get me wrong. He wanted you both, every bit as much as I did. But when the chips were down, he just couldn't handle the responsibility. He was never the most responsible sort, and my own father could see that, even when I couldn't. Your dad didn't start out as a dosser, though. You need to know that. He did manage to hold down a job for a long time, in the beginning, and he wasn't a bad husband back then.

'But he couldn't sustain it, Darren. He buckled under the pressure and he let us all down, and it was *himself* he hated, and *me*, for 'trapping' him, for having expectations he wasn't man enough to meet. But he never hated you. Resented all of us and took it out on all of us, yes, but one thing he never had was hatred for his own kids.'

Mum went on to tell me that when I was a toddler, Dad used to sit on the end of my bed almost every night and watch me sleeping, and whisper to me about his dreams for me. He wanted me to be a big-shot lawyer or something, anything grander than himself in his working-class life. He wanted great things for me. And as I sit there on the bus watching the miles roll by, while Mum trances off again with her thoughts of curtains and cushions, something suddenly slots into place.

We didn't let him down; his own mind did. His own shortcomings did. His own weaknesses did, and I find myself praying to a God I'm not even sure is there, that I have more of my mother in me than I have of him.

I want to build a better life. I'm more sure of that now than I've ever been. Where to start is another matter, and for the moment I have more pressing things to deal with. I can't contemplate my future, or if I'm even to have one, until I've been to see that woman whose house we burgled, right before my friend just disappeared into the fucking great blue yonder.

Mum's right, though. I'm in very great danger of going the same way as my dad did. But, as they say, knowledge is power. And now, through the knowledge, the most precious gift I've ever had from my mother, I know that the sane part of my dad wouldn't have expected or wanted this pathetic life for me. That part of him would have believed in me, so maybe – just maybe – my life can end up being something positive in spite of the man he became, and not something negative because of him.

26

Friday
- Alison -

So, a brain tumour then. A *glioblastoma multiforme*, to be exact, which is the most aggressive form of tumour a girl can get. Lucky me.

It's a Grade 4 astrocytoma, which means its terminal. It explains the headaches I've been having, the random bouts of nausea and vomiting and, of course, the black-out I had at that restaurant, right after learning that Simon Westrupp is Tom Findlay's uncle.

On being confronted with the concept of six degrees of separation neatly whittled down to two, my immediate and entirely coincidental response was a full-blown seizure, slightly more dramatic than a simple swoon. I've had two more seizures since, fortunately in the company of people who know what to expect, and it seems I can either look forward to a lot more, or start taking the anti-convulsive medications to prevent them.

I hate taking drugs of any kind. It's all I can do to persuade myself to take a pain killer when I need one. It's probably why the headaches got so vicious. I didn't want to mask anything that might get worse if I didn't keep an eye on it. How ironic. Nothing I could have done would have prevented the tumour that is blossoming in my brain, like a mushroom cloud rising in slow-motion, in the aftermath of a nuclear bomb.

But, since I live on my own and it's not like my dog can pick up a phone and call the emergency services, I probably have to take the drugs. And the tremors that have started in my right hand mean that sometimes filling the kettle is a challenge, let alone holding a hot cup of tea and getting it safely to my mouth. So drugs it is then, and Mum is coming to stay with me for a while, to make sure I don't do myself an accidental mischief, and to keep an eye out for any adverse side effects.

Isn't she a lucky girl too!

It's no comfort at all, to learn there was nothing I could have done, or avoided doing, that would have prevented this from happening to me.

As with most brain tumours, the cause isn't really known. Everything under the sun gets blamed, from 'brain-frying' mobile phones to too much marijuana, or other life hazards such as head injuries, passive smoking, chemicals in toiletries and fluoride in the water. Most of the suggested 'causes' don't in fact have any scientific basis, however, and the general consensus is that while the responsibility may simply lie with unlucky genetics, they really just don't know.

What's possible, in my case, (according to the 'experts'), is that an earlier melanoma I had removed ten years ago could have been the culprit. We got the little bastard, or so we all thought, but the tail end of it, quite literally, may well have kept cruising, eventually finding a home it liked the look of in the left-hand side of my brain.

Not that it matters. It is what it is, and what can be gained, really, in harking back and wishing I'd done something differently? Even if lying in the sun and baking my flesh as a teenager *did* unwittingly cause this thing to pop up in my head now (and there is no certainty of that either), what would be the point in dwelling on it?

Do I not already have enough to flog myself to death over anyway?

Well, eventually, its seems that my little uninvited friend will rob me of my speech and various other neurological and motor functions, which roughly translates to stealing away like a thief in the night with whatever dignity I may still possess as the end draws nigh, in just a few short months from now. And let's not forget about the additional threat of paralysis, or 'hemiplegia' to quote the medical term, starting to stalk me as the weeks go by.

How ironic. I've spent almost every waking minute of the last few weeks wondering how I can ever live with myself for killing Tom Findlay and throwing his body into someone else's grave, but it seems that I don't have to. Nature has intervened and decided for me.

Oddly enough, I'm not as upset as I once imagined I might be, at being told I didn't have long to live. Most people think about it, I suppose; the prospect of being told they suddenly have finite time, and they wonder what they'd do. They probably draw up a 'bucket list', make amends with people, plan to secure the future of any dependents left behind, get their financial affairs in order, that sort of thing.

All of that comes in due course, I suppose, but that kind of focus usually only comes after the initial shock, and the inevitable grief process that follows. By the time you get to resolution, if there's any time left, you resolve to make the most of it. If you can. If you're not too incapacitated.

For me, there was certainly the shock. I don't know how long it generally takes for that to subside, but for me it wasn't long; a day, possibly two. I'm sure for most other people it takes a lot longer than that. But then, most other people haven't already monumentally stuffed up their own lives, taken someone else's, sought to cover their tracks in a way that's given them no peace, and reached the point where they're not even sure they're capable of living in any case, with the torment of what they've done. Maybe, for people like me, the prospect of an uncomfortable death is preferable to an uncomfortable life.

After the MRI, I was sent home from hospital, with the experts remaining tight-lipped about what they might have seen. I'd been back at work for three days, in fact, when I got the first call inviting me into the hospital for an urgent biopsy. From there, apparently, they had what they call an MDT; a Multidisciplinary Team meeting, where the surgeons, oncologists and neurologists all sat around and discussed my condition, along with potential interventions and prospects, before deciding who was going to be landed with the terribly jovial job of informing me that my days on Earth were ending.

All that week, I had a funny feeling of foreboding. Somewhere in my gut, I just knew things weren't going to go well and, when summoned forth and told what it was, what could be done and what I could expect going forward (which really wasn't much at all), the small but growing part of me that was already buckling under the burden of my shameful secrets just wanted to laugh out loud. A glioblasto-*what?*

It seems that my head is riddled with 'secondaries,' too. When my GBM turned up (see, I'm already 'hip' with the jargon!), it brought a load of its mates along, and they're all having a voracious orgy in my head now, going forth and multiplying like good little tumours in a grotesque, time-lapsed parody of star-shaped cauliflowers blooming.

I am grieving now, in my own way, for the fact that my life will soon be over. There is a profound sense of impending loss, deeper than I've ever felt before, even when my dad died.

At first, when I got the news, all I really felt was empty. I had this horrible hollow, scraped-out feeling inside me, like everything of substance had been ripped from my body, like everything had stopped and wasn't going to start again. A weird, post-apocalyptic silence descending solely around *me*, as the earth continued to turn, and life lurched on all around me. My tide rolling out and staying out, exposing pits and hollows and the jagged, uneven rocks that symbolize the seabed of my life. My tide disappearing, and never coming back in.

For the briefest time, in those first few moments, I felt suspended - frozen in time and completely removed from the world; probably because I was there on my own, being given the worst news imaginable to pop onto the passenger seat and take home with me, on what would no doubt be one of the last times I'd ever get to drive.

The consultant asked me if I would like to have a chat with Rachael Barnes, the hospital chaplain, before I left. I declined. What would I tell her? If she sat here in front of me, all kind and serene, with her love of her God shining through her, could I ask for absolution? *Could I?*

It would probably mean confessing, but it's all too horrible to utter. I can't even imagine the words coming from my own mouth. In any case, I'd feel like a fraud, even if I could confide in her, because I don't even know what my belief system is. I've never given it a lot of thought. I guess somewhere in the back of my mind I just thought it would evolve somehow, when it was ready; that what I believed in, if anything, would become clear in its own good time by way of maturity and my own experiences. I know I'm not religious, but I also know I'm not an atheist, and that's as far as I've ever got with it all, really. It never seemed important until now.

It's a bit like the concept of judgement. In my own mind, especially lately, I've made many references to that. But the truth is I've never had any clear idea of the origins or context of judgement, or of the consequences, good or bad. But if there is a judgement, it's coming up fast. I've never believed in hell, or heaven, and I'm not at all sure about *any* kind of afterlife. I have always wondered, on some vague level, if there's a good place to go after dying. But if there is, surely (through the equitable balance of natural law and order) there must also be a bad one? But I can't imagine either place, or what each would feel like.

Now, thanks to circumstances of my own making, I do believe there is a hell but I think it's the result of what we weave for ourselves and others, right here in this conscious life. Theoretically then, through the same counterbalances of natural law and order, there's also a heaven on earth that we can create for ourselves, and I suspect that's more about attitude than environment.

At any rate, I've never experienced that kind of nirvana, and there's little point in dwelling on it now. I said goodbye to any chance of heaven on earth when I robbed someone else of *his* right to find it.

Personally, I think my lack of clarity on any belief was heavily influenced by the most catastrophic event that occurred in my life, at least until Tom Findlay turned up and proved to me that something worse really could happen. I was just seventeen when my dad died in a car accident one rainy night on his way home from work. He was killed outright by an out-of-control lorry that failed to give way at a stop sign. It must have felt like being hit by a freight train, at the point of impact, and that's what I felt had hit *me* when I was given the news. A runaway freight train that slammed into me as hard as anything could have without killing me outright too. Now, I'm wishing it had.

My dad was my world, like most daddies are to their doting daughters, and one night he was there and the next night he just wasn't. No warning, no time to prepare, just one big roadside bang and he was gone. I found myself asking, at the time, what sort of just and benevolent God would rob a child of her father, and a sweet kind woman of her husband? My father was a really good man, for all his faults, and he didn't deserve to lose his life at forty-two. The outrage, the senselessness of it, completely overwhelmed me.

Having no fully formed belief system at the time, which could arguably have given me some comfort, my grief process ended up being very long and very muddled. I was so angry for such a long time, and so lost, like a rudderless ship that wanted no safe harbour; that really only desired to dash itself up onto the rocks, again and again, until there was nothing left but jagged shards and splinters. I felt that breaking into a million irreparable pieces would be a thousand times better than trying to batter my way through what felt like an impenetrable wall of grief.

In the days that followed Dad's death, a victim support counsellor asked me to describe myself, and I found that really hard. If you asked me that question again now, all these years on, I think I'd still find it almost as hard. I guess I've never really thought much about who I am, what I need or what I even really *want*, from life. And any fledgling belief I might ever have had in a just and benevolent God was gone for good with my father.

Daphne will have to find another chief bridesmaid.

What a madly random thought! Where did that come from? Out of the blue, in the midst of self-reflection, I'm thinking about letting my friend down. Maybe it's the tumour influencing my thought patterns, although I have to say that apart from the small matters of murder and concealment, ongoing lying and my futile attempts at finding oblivion in the bottom of various bottles, I don't feel I've behaved irrationally at all.

I've never been a bridesmaid, much less a bride, and I was looking forward to Daphne's wedding, watching her find the kind of happiness I never imagined for myself. After all, with virtually no self-awareness, there's little chance for self-love, and without that, who else could you expect to love you? I've certainly had my share of boyfriends, but never any truly meaningful connections. I've always thought that if you're going to commit to being with someone, it shouldn't just be because you can imagine yourself living with them. It should be because you can't imagine living *without* them. And I never met that 'one.'

Would Simon Westrupp have been The One? I felt a frisson of something, but who knows what it really was? Plain and simple chemistry? Desperation? My biological clock sending me a subconscious message? We'll never know, now, will we? Is that a tragedy? If I dwelt on it, I may get to the point where I think so, but it never helps to ruminate on things you cannot change.

Not long after I got home from the hospital I rang Simon, as promised, to tell him what was happening. Predictably, he was devastated, and he wanted to come right over, but I said I wasn't ready for visitors and probably wouldn't be for a while. He asked if we could keep in touch by phone, and I agreed, but whenever he rings me the conversation isn't very long, because he doesn't know what to say about my brain tumour or the fact that I am dying, and I can't bring myself to ask about what's going on in his life, because I couldn't realistically do that without asking if there's been any news about his nephew. I simply couldn't bring myself to listen to the anguish in his voice.

Simon always reiterates, whenever he calls, that he's there for me, to help with anything I might need, no matter what it might be. I always thank him, and say that if there is anything, I will certainly let him know.

Like ricocheting bullets, my thoughts are still pinging in all directions and I've started losing my balance a bit now, so things appear to be stepping up. Apparently trying to treat this effectively is temporary and tricky. They can give me what's called a surgical resection, where they take away the tissue that surrounds the tumours, to enable them to be more easily targeted for radiation. Followed up by chemotherapy, all that might just stem the tide a little. I cannot be fixed, it seems, but a convoluted process of treatment can offer a bit more time.

But do I *want* more time, when all it will do is keep me suspended in my self-created torment? And even with more time, I'm still going to eventually get to a non-functioning, incoherent dribbling stage where I'm confused, delirious, unable to swallow, incontinent and progressively losing consciousness thanks to the growing inter-cranial pressure the dexamethasone will eventually give up trying to suppress.

So what happens then? Who is responsible for me then? Whether it's dying of brain herniation, seizures or a tumour haemorrhage, all straws are brutally, stupidly short. And that kind of an ending is not what I want, either for myself or for anyone who'd have to watch me or care for me, like my poor lovely mum. That really is hell on earth, and she doesn't deserve that, even if I do.

So, it appears to have come down to the choice of atoning for my actions, in short time with my dignity, or in even shorter time with my life. And as the hours roll by, as night gives way to morning while I sit here in my living room on yet another lonely night of self-reflection, with yet another dwindling bottle of whisky, I find myself leaning more towards atoning with my life.

27

Friday
- Darren -

Well, we got Mum's precious fucking curtains, which she was adamant I had to hang before I could go anywhere. Now it's all done, the room looks great, and now we just need that red rug she's dreaming about. I make a joke about stealing one to order, but she doesn't laugh, and I remind her that that's all it was – a really shit attempt at a joke.

The plod phoned today to say they still have no solid leads about Tommy, and to ask if I had any other information I hadn't already given them, or anything I'd thought of or found out since. I told them no.

I still don't feel ready to tell them the truth about where me and Tommy were the Thursday before last, and it's less to do with cowardice than feeling convinced that it just wouldn't change anything for the better, even for Tom.

The sergeant who rang me said there had been a bit of false information come in, people who said they thought they'd seen him, but it turned out to be a wild goose chase each time. Some people get off on wasting police time. Maybe it makes them feel important, to say they'd seen something they hadn't, and watch the plod go barking down a dead-end alley.

Anyway, even if the so-called sightings were genuine, they've all amounted to nothing. So Tommy could be in a completely different place than where some sick or misguided bastards have suggested the plod waste time going looking. Marla is in contact with them every day, but she's frustrated because they can't tell her anything. Every day it's the same old cracked record. 'We're doing everything we can,' they keep saying, which doesn't feel like very much at all.

I know I'm wrong for sitting on the information about where we really were and what we were doing, but I'm still hopeful that

Tom will turn up. Maybe he's just had a bump on the head or something. He might have ended up on a bus somewhere and ended up God knows where, with no phone battery to let anyone know, and no money to get back. A little voice in my head keeps saying I'm wrong, that something far less harmless has happened, but I'm still hoping that any minute I'll get a call from Marla, or from Tom himself, to say he's home safe and well. I'm hanging onto that for dear life.

And if I do confess now to where we really were, how will that change anything? I'm convinced, and so is Mum after going round there, that Tommy left that house and that something happened after that, so fingering the poor bastard for a burglary isn't going to help him when he is found, is it?

The plod have dredged the local canal, just a few hundred yards of it, and found nothing. I'm glad they didn't and so is Marla. Imagine being told they've found your kid's dead body floating in the fucking canal.

I've been dithering a bit, about going to see that woman. I toyed with the idea of going tonight, but thanks to a burst water main on the normal bus route, everything's being rerouted and taking ten times as long. It's chaos, and I'm taking it as a sign that tonight's not the right time to go. I'm determined to go tomorrow though, no matter what Mum or anyone else says about it.

28

Saturday
- Barbara -

Darren's going to see that woman at the house he and young Tom Findlay burgled a couple of weeks ago - the house I went to. I think it's a bloody big mistake, him doing that. He's going to end up locked up again, because I'm sure she won't tolerate him turning up there. The barefaced bloody cheek of him! Mind you, I'm a fine one to talk, aren't I, after pitching up there and telling lies, myself? And I do understand what he's trying to do. He just wants answers.

But there's ways of going about these things, and this is all wrong. My reaction was the right one, I think. Darren should hand himself in. No good can come of this 'withholding information' malarkey. That's no small thing. Perverting the course of justice, I think they call it, obstructing the police with their enquiries, or something, and *that* bloody caper I *know* you can go to jail for. The police take that kind of thing very seriously.

See, the thing is, with my lad, he's already been in trouble enough times. Jail's been a bit of a revolving door for him so the chances of him dodging a prison sentence for perverting the course of justice, well it's just not going to happen, is it? They'll lock him up. He says if he comes clean they'll lock him up anyway, for the burglary; but it's just another bloody burglary, isn't it? And I know that's a terrible thing to say, because no burglary is *just* a burglary is it? People's lives are badly affected by a burglary.

Thankfully, we've never been burgled, but I've got friends who have, and they say it's an awful violation. Their homes don't feel safe or clean anymore, and they lose all their trust and faith in a fair world. I know there's no such thing as a 'fair' world, and they know it too, but it's an explanation they use to try and describe how they feel.

Poor Michelle had her car broken into once, before she and her husband moved to Barcelona. The thieves bent her driver's door frame open with a crowbar and they managed to unlock it that way and take what they wanted. She lost her CD player, stuff out of the glove box, a pair of shoes, other bits and pieces. Nothing of any real value, and it was a real old banger of a car, no alarm or anything, and just a month or so left on its MOT, so when she found it broken into and called the police with the details, they didn't even bother coming out.

They gave her a crime number for her insurance but she didn't claim because the car wasn't really worth anything and she didn't want to lose her no claims bonus. Her husband bent the door frame back into shape, and the car was okay to keep using, but she couldn't get on with it, after that. She had to get rid of it. She said driving it around after that, after someone had been rifling through it all, it gave her the creeps. It didn't feel like her car anymore.

I understand how she felt. If anyone broke in here and took what little we've got of any value, I don't know if I'd want to keep living here.

No, what I meant by 'just another burglary,' well, it's Darren's form, isn't it? It's what he does. That's a different thing entirely from perverting the course of bloody justice, wasting police time, or whatever you choose to call it. Messing them about with their enquiries is a lot more serious, and so will be the penalty for him, if this all comes out.

To his credit, he did go and talk to them, and I do believe him when he says he did that to stop them from coming back to the house because he knows how much it upsets me when they turn up here unannounced. But he didn't tell them the whole truth, down there at the station, and I don't know what they'd think about that. Wrong information is worse than no information, especially if they send people up to the rec to ask around, when Darren knows full well that he was never there with that boy in the first place. Coppers haven't got time to fish for red herrings.

But despite all that, and the ongoing worry about his little friend (and let's not talk about the bloody silly, hare-brained idea of visiting that woman), he's been a different man this week. This living room looks beautiful, and it's all down to his work. I had to laugh away to myself at the look on his face when I first told him I wanted him to do the decorating. It was priceless. I've never seen horror like it, or self-doubt, and he's full of that, Lord love him. But to give him his due, he's not made a bad job of it.

He thought I was mad, when he first clapped eyes on the wallpaper, but he made a good stab at putting it up and it looks lovely. He even thinks so himself. I knew there was more to him than this petty thievery he's involved with, and that proved it. When he sets his mind to something, he just gets on with it. That's a good quality to have; I'd just like to see more of it, and less of this dossing about that seems to have taken such a strong hold of him.

He told me last week about his trips to the seaside, how it clears his head. I'm glad to know he's not always out committing crime when he's not at home. It's what I've always imagined; that whenever he's off somewhere it's to do something wrong. It's quite a comfort actually, to learn that sometimes he's just doing what any ordinary person would do given the chance; taking a walk along a beach.

That doesn't surprise me. He's too young to remember, but I took him to the seaside once, after I had a very bad row with his Dad. I stormed out of the house, dragging him along behind me, and we were both crying our eyes out. I picked him up and cuddled him, to comfort him, as I walked to the main road and flagged down a passing taxi, which you can't do nowadays, it's all phone calls or internet bookings now. But I got into a taxi and I hadn't a clue where I was going, I just needed to get away.

When the driver asked where I wanted to go, I just muttered to him 'anywhere but here,' and he took me straight to the railway station. Darren must have been around three, because I could have him on my knee and not have to pay a fare for him. The first train leaving was to the coast, so that's where we went, and we stayed at the beach for the whole afternoon, while I got my head back together.

He didn't play in the sand like I expected him to, so not having a bucket and spade for him wasn't too big a hardship. That was lucky, because I couldn't have paid for one if he'd asked me. He just sat there on a rock in the sun, quite content to listen to the sea rolling in and out, and he turned his face into the wind and giggled as it blew through his hair.

I remember that day, clear as a bell. I was expecting Michelle, just, and I remember feeling so sick about having to go back home. But there was nowhere else to bloody go, and I looked at my lovely little lad, all giggly and happy in the sunshine, and somehow that gave me the strength to go back. I knew I could take him again, if I had the chance, and it would make him happy. We never got there, though, with one thing and another.

So it's no surprise to me that he likes the sea and the beach, just that he's never mentioned it for all these years. It's like a secret part of him that nobody knew about that he's just decided to share. That's how I know things are changing.

I just hope he doesn't bugger it all up with this bloody idiot notion of not telling the police what they might need to know about his missing friend. If he ends up in jail again, that might be the end of any change. He's his own worst enemy sometimes, I swear.

I do hope they find that boy, Thomas. It's been more than two weeks now, and it's not looking hopeful that he'll just turn up, but I really wish he would. I know young lads do just run off without a word, and never look back. It's probably more common than you think, but this doesn't feel like a runaway scenario to me.

I remember Darren, at sixteen. He had a strong mind of his own, a lot of hatred for his father and every reason to run away from home, but he wouldn't have done that and gone for a week without a word.

Tom Findlay has a mum and a sister who love him, a girlfriend too, and none of them had fallen out. He'd be missing them all. He'd let them know where he was, if he could. He'd let *someone* know, wouldn't he?

It was good to finally talk frankly to Darren on the bus yesterday about what had happened between me and his Dad. It was hard to talk about, make no mistake, but since we did I feel a bit lighter about it all. Having the chance to explain myself wasn't something I thought I'd ever get with Darren. It's not like you can just wade in at the dinner table, or stop on the upstairs landing, and say, 'oh by the way, I know you never understood why I stayed with your bastard dad, but...'

You can't just start a conversation like that out of the blue. It had to wait for the right moment, and the right moment never seemed to come, so when Darren asked, I thought about it for a good few minutes then decided 'bugger it, he deserves to know', and I thought it might just help him.

And I think it has. I should have told him years ago, all that stuff, but to be honest it's still a bit sensitive even for me, even after all this time, and that conversation, once it started, well it felt a bit like picking at a scab before it's properly healed. You hate to do it because it feels horrible and looks a right mess, but you just can't stop yourself. And I know Darren didn't have much respect for me for sticking with his dad and putting up with so much shit without ever explaining myself, so he was long overdue for a proper explanation.

But like I say, without a proper platform you can't just spout out that kind of ugly family drama, all random-like. Once you start a conversation like that, you have to see it through, no matter how hard it might be. It's a proper can of worms. Once you tear the lid off, you can't put it back on. I'm just glad, for all of us, that he's given me the chance now. And I think he understood, in the end.

I did tell him, on the bus, that there were many nights when I argued with his father about the way he treated the kids. But I could never push things too far. I'd try and talk to him when he was sober, which wasn't very often, but even then I had to pick my moments, because even when he wasn't drunk, he was usually still angry and capable of ranting his silly bloody head off at the drop of a hat.

Taking him to task about how he treated his family never went down well, and I was lucky if I ever got to make a point without a row going off. I did try. But it's like trying to disarm a ticking time bomb. You've got limited time to do the job, and even when you're as careful as can be, if you just touch the wrong wire, it can all just blow up in your face.

Maybe Darren has a bit more respect for me, now he knows how hard it would have been to walk away back then. I know he's always loved me. But respect is something different. Love is unconditional in families, no matter how bad they might argue at times, but respect has to be earned. His dad demanded it and never deserved it, Darren needed it from him and never got it, and I can see I never really earned it myself from the kids, who just saw me as weak and unable to stick up for myself or for them.

It's a funny old thing, respect, and it only really works properly if it's a two-way street. It's hard to expect to get it from someone you don't have it for, and it's hard to have it for someone who doesn't have it for *you*. And it's a hard thing to fake, even for the biggest forelock-pullers out there. It's one of those things you just can't pretend to have if you don't, since people can usually see right through that. I think they call that obsequiousness, or some other grand bloody word for something basically pathetic. At any rate, whatever it's called, it's insincere and obvious to most that see it.

Some people say you can't love someone you don't respect them, either, but that's not true. I've loved my son from the minute I knew I was carrying him, but there've been many, many times when I haven't had much respect for him, and that's felt terrible to me, like a betrayal of my own child, to not respect him. But when you've done your level best to make sure your kids know right from wrong, and you know they understand what you've taught them, then they continually flout that knowledge, what do you do? When they keep doing things that are clearly wrong, that they *know* are wrong, and hurtful too, it's soul destroying.

I've never understood why Darren took that first moral U-turn in the first place, or why he didn't turn around again and get himself back on track. It's not like he didn't know, or wasn't capable of being better, so I do struggle to respect him sometimes, and I know Pat does too. Darren's selfish behaviour winds Pat up something chronic.

As a parent, you don't want to see your own kids messing their lives up, and even though you can't protect them forever, you just have to hope that the way you've brought them up will see them straighten out that backbone in the end. The light will come on and it will all sort itself out. It's the best you can hope for, and I do keep hoping. And something is definitely changing.

At least I hope it is, because I'm getting a bit fed up with being the meat in the bloody sandwich around here.

Pat and Darren don't get on, and sometimes it gets me down. I love Pat. He's a good man. He drinks a bit much sometimes, but he's *nothing* like Darren and Michelle's dad was, and he's earned the right to have a few drinks when it suits him because he works his fingers to the bloody bone in that chip shop, and he never begrudges me anything for myself or for the house. Every year we have a nice holiday that he pays for, and there's never any issue if I want something a bit special. He always takes me out to dinner somewhere lovely for my birthday. I always get red roses on Valentine's Day, and not the cheap ones, either. Proper florist ones they are, with long stems, and that lovely posh floristy smell they have.

I get spoiled rotten at Christmas too, and we always have plenty of food in the cupboards. It's more than can be said for the way we had to live when the kids were growing up. I do wish Darren could appreciate Pat's efforts a bit more sometimes. We'd be in a right mess if we only had to rely on my silly bit of money from my cleaning jobs.

Finding love again wasn't something I was expecting. I'd hoped for it, of course, because nobody really wants to be on their own, do they, even if they've been hurt before? I just never seemed to meet anyone, and I'd got to the stage of thinking it was going to just be me and the bloody cats forever more. But, when the brother of a friend of one of my ladies I clean for called round at her house, to put up some pictures, we got chatting. Pat had just bought a closed-down chippy and was doing odd jobs in the daytime until he could get it going properly. Nobody was more surprised than me, when he asked me out.

I know just how hard that man has worked to make a success of his chip shop. And I often think it would be nice if Darren could acknowledge it too, since its Pat who stocks the fridge with the beer Darren drinks when he feels like it, and Pat who pays for the Sky TV subscription Darren watches when he wants to. It's been bloody years since my son did a decent day's work himself, but that's no reason for him not to respect someone close to home who does. Pat doesn't say a lot but I know that's how he feels too, like Darren's just an ungrateful freeloader who doesn't appreciate the hand that bloody feeds him.

I can see both sides of it though. Darren doesn't really want to be here. It's just circumstances. This is his usual bail address, and even when it's not, it's his home. It has *always* been his home. I had to fight like a heavyweight boxer to keep this house, after my husband died, and I'm not going to turn my son out of his home and into the streets when he needs support.

He can't afford to go anywhere else, and that's the simple fact of it. The dole would probably pay for some rat-hole flat somewhere, but I don't want him to live like that. Living here isn't what I want for him either, but he has to live *somewhere*, and if I didn't do as right as I should have by him while he was growing up, I can do right by him now. Pat moved in here knowing what the situation was, so that's the deal.

I know he doesn't like it. He gets upset when Darren disrespects me, but he has to understand that it's not as simple as giving him ultimatums or marching orders. So a spiky sort of truce hangs over us most of the time, but occasionally Pat loses his temper, like the other night when he saw Darren in the hall at four in the bloody morning, fully dressed, sneaking towards the front door and obviously going out somewhere.

I had to explain everything that's been going on, to calm him down. He doesn't want the police knocking here at all silly hours of the night and morning either, and I don't blame him one bit for that.

So I'm constantly treading a tightrope around here. Pat doesn't hate Darren, he just wants him to man-up and stand on his own two feet, get a job, get a flat and start living like a normal person, free of crime. He wants the stress taken off me.

I get it. I also think those two would get along fine if they could just find a way to respect one another. But all they do is dance around the issues, neither one wanting to upset me, but not willing to bury the hatchet, because that would involve discussion (God forbid!), a mission to find common ground, and for both to understand that they might just be wrong about one another. If each of them gave the other a chance to prove themselves, they might find it easier to get along. They're both lovely men, but they just can't see it in each other. And of course they've both got their stupid pride. I want to bang their bloody heads together at times, but it wouldn't help to say that, so I don't.

So we're lurching along okay for now. Pat's mentioned how good a job Darren's done with the decorating, and Darren's been civil in return. It's a step forward. Too soon to say if we might be turning a corner, but I *can* sense something changing.

It's like that feeling you get, towards the end of winter when you leave the house with your coat on, then before you've taken a dozen steps you realise you should have put a lighter one on because the winter bite has gone and you can almost smell the spring starting. This thing with those two, it feels a bit like that.

Of course when spring is on its way, we tend to get a bit ahead of ourselves, don't we? We leave the winter coat on the hook, and go out in the spring one. Then, another dozen steps down the road, we realise that winter's not really over, and there's still a fair few frosts to get through before we can say it's really gone. So *I'd* best not get ahead of myself, especially since Darren seems hell-bent on seeing that woman, without caring how serious the consequences might be for him. Instead, I'll just be grateful for any thaw in the winter chill, however brief a time it bloody lasts. If he gets locked up, we'll be straight back to a blizzard, no question about it.

Talking about the weather, the sun is out, and it's just flooding into my lovely red and yellow living room. It really is so beautiful in here now, I don't even want to go to work in a morning! I just want to sit here with my feet up on my lovely new footstool, and read a glossy magazine while I sip a cup of peppermint tea like a true lady of leisure, in this lovely cheery room.

I wonder what my stroppy boys would say about *that!*

<h1 style="text-align:center">29</h1>

Saturday

- Darren -

After a stint in the bathroom, I look about as presentable as I probably ever will. I've had a shave and I've put a clean pair of jeans and a decent shirt on – long-sleeved, which covers most of my tattoos. I can't do much about the ones on my neck, and it's the first time I've ever wished I could cover them up. I'm usually pretty proud of my tatts, but I don't want to give the wrong impression today, and end up having a door slammed in my face before I've even started asking what I need to.

I give Mum a quick hug to try and reassure her, since she's standing in the hallway looking ramrod bloody straight, like someone's shoved a broomstick up her arse. She's got a right face on her, and the thickest person in the world would know she's not happy, but she does step aside as I head to the front door.

'See you in a bit, Mum.'

'You look nice, Darren. Just mind how you go, love.'

That's all she says. I know how much else she'd like to say, and I'm grateful that she doesn't. Maybe she knows it's a waste of time, because I've made up my mind now, come what may, to do this.

I jump on a bus for town and from there I make my way on foot, over to Topsham. I'm feeling like a cat on cold cobbles, all jumpy and hollow inside. I couldn't face any lunch, so my stomach's empty, which doesn't fucking help, and by the time I get to the cul-de-sac I'm feeling sick with nerves. I stand at the woman's front door, and I take a deep breath. Her car is in the driveway so I know she's home, and as I knock, I wait to hear footfalls. Nothing happens.

I give it a few seconds and knock louder. *Surely she must be here!* Across the street, a door opens and her old neighbour comes out. He makes his way across to me, and I stand there using every strand of self-restraint to not make a bolt for it.

'Are you looking for Alison?' he asks.

Alison! Her name is Alison.

'Er, yeah. Is she not here?'

'Who are you, please?'

'Er, I'm just a friend. I just want to see her for a few minutes, just to ask her something.'

The bloke looks at me, weighing me up. At length, he says 'She's not here.'

'Oh, right.'

Shit!

'How's her dog?'

The bloke's face relaxes. He clearly believes that I must indeed be a friend if I know about Alison's dog.

'Badger? Oh, a bit banged around, but he'll be alright eventually. Assholes did a right job on him, poor thing.'

Badger. Alison and Badger.

'When do you think I could come back, then?' I ask him.

'Not sure. She's out with her mother. She could be back at any minute, but it might be hours. I really don't know, lad.'

'Thanks. I might wait around for a bit, see if she comes home. Will the dog be alright?'

'Oh yes, he'll be fine, eventually.'

'Okay then, thanks again.'

'What did you say your name was?'

'I didn't, but it's Darren.'

'Right then Darren, I need to get on. Might see you again sometime.'

And with that, he is striding back towards his own house. Conversation over, and Alison is not at home. I don't know why, but seeing her is now too important to me to even think about leaving. I need to stay here, for however long it takes. I have to see this through now, no matter what it means. But if I stay here hanging around on her front doorstep, and she does come back, what will that bloke think? What will her *other* neighbours think? It's a bit of a curtain-twitching cul-de-sac, this one; everyone on neighbourhood watch.

And even if I do hang around, what will she do when she sees me? If she makes a scene or panics, I'll probably end up going down for freaking her out on her own fucking doorstep.

There's only one way to find out. I've spent the whole week psyching myself up to speak to this woman, and the only other choice is to carry on being a coward. But I just don't want to be a bloody coward anymore over Tom. He deserves better than that. I've failed him once. If it turns out that by not having the guts to try speaking to her I end up failing him again, well, there's no living with that. I know that, as surely as I'm bloody breathing.

So I'll take what comes but in the meantime, since it's not a good look loitering (without tent, as Tommy would put it) on the doorstep of someone who's not home, I decide to go for a walk for half an hour, to kill a bit of time. I wish I had a pound for every mile I've walked this past week, but I'm full of nervous energy again, and I need to walk some of it off, otherwise it's likely to be *me* who's freaking out and panicking when I speak to this woman called Alison. She's a real person now. She's not just 'that woman.' anymore. She's Alison; a real person with a real mum, a real neighbour, a real life, and a dog named Badger.

As I walk, I'm overtaken from behind by an old bloke in a tweed jacket and flat cap. He looks like a proper English gent, like he should have a fucking pheasant slung over his shoulder and a rifle in his hand. He nods but he doesn't make eye contact, probably thinks he's too good for the likes of me. A woman walks past me the other way and smiles at me, but my nerves won't let me smile back, so as she goes by me she's probably thinking I'm an ignorant twat.

I walk for about twenty minutes then I turn around and go back towards the cul-de-sac. This is a nice neighbourhood, quiet and affluent but not pretentious. Trees at the roadsides, well-kept gardens. Cars in driveways, all clean and high-end, like Beamers and Mercs, commuters home on the weekend.

Makes me wonder how Alison can afford a place around here. It's none of my sticky-beak business really, but when everyone else is so much older or in couples, all established and professional like, she somehow seems like the odd one out, a bit out of place there all on her own and still quite young. I'd say she's only in her early thirties. Maybe she's a big-shot lawyer, the sort my dad wanted me to be. That would be bloody brilliant, wouldn't it? *All I fucking need.*

I get back to within sight of her place and I see a car reversing out of the drive, with an older woman at the wheel. That must be Alison's mother. I duck down a side alleyway, not wanting her to see me. I don't really know why, I just think it will keep things less complicated if fewer people see me coming and going. I could have done without that bloody neighbour coming across, but at least he gave me the idea that Alison might not be long, and I could hang around for a bit.

It takes me a full twenty more minutes, just to get myself psyched up again, and then I walk towards her front door, and my heart thumps in my chest. As I raise my hand to knock, the door opens, and Alison is suddenly standing there staring at me. She looks tiny, fragile, not like I remember her at all. She's so pale her skin looks almost blue, and she has bloody great purple rings under her eyes, like she hasn't slept in a month. She doesn't look like she'd be capable of hitting anyone with a fucking feather, let alone a frying pan! I struggle to believe this meek bird of a woman is none other than the raving, pan-waving harridan of only a couple of weeks ago.

There's a pretty bunch of flowers, all in pinks and purples, in a vase on the sideboard in the hall.

I'm starting to think I've been totally barking up the wrong bloody tree thinking this little woman knows anything, so I'm toying with the idea of just turning around and leaving again when she opens the door a bit wider. She continues to stare at me, but she makes no move to open her mouth or call for help. It's almost as if she isn't all that surprised I'm here.

I speak quickly, in case she snaps out of her trance and starts yelling or something.

'Alison, I'm not here to hurt you. Please don't think I'm here to hurt you. I swear to God I'm not. I just want to talk to you for a few minutes, that's all. That's *all*. You don't even have to let me in. I'm not expecting to come in.' I'm acutely aware that I'm babbling a bit.

She stands there, still staring at me, and whispers 'okay.' But that's it. She doesn't say another fucking word and it's really unnerving.

I take a deep breath and plough on. 'Alison, I've come to say sorry for breaking into your house, and for hurting your dog. It was a really shit thing to do. I'm really so, so sorry.'

I speak in a rush, and I'm mortified that with the words come tears, slow, fat silent ones rolling down my face. Crying *again* I am, like a proper bloody baby. Give me ten minutes, I'll be sucking my thumb!

As she continues to stare, she reaches off to the hall table, gropes around and picks up a box of tissues, then silently hands them to me.

'I'm so sorry. If I could take it all back, I would.'

She clears her throat to speak and when she does, the first thing that strikes me is how gentle her voice is. After hearing her screaming like a banshee in her own house, just two weeks gone, I don't know what I was expecting, but it wasn't this.

'My neighbour Bill told me you'd been. He's just brought my dog home. And since you've already sent your mother to me, I suppose you'd better come in too.'

I look at her in disbelief. 'How did you know that?'

'You're Darren Davies. Your mother is Barbara. She came here last week, didn't she?'

I'm speechless. I look at her and she can see the confusion on my face.

'Bill saw her leave, and we talked. He told me her parents never lived in my house so I Googled her and found you. Social media, you know? Makes things pretty easy. I know who you both are.'

I don't know what to say. I'm tempted to comment that Bill's a fucking busybody, but I decide it won't help to say that, so I stay quiet. I've burgled her home, hurt her dog and sent my mum around to lie to her face. On top of all that she's had to find me standing here on her doorstep. She's probably just wanting to have a bit of bloody peace, but she's more likely thinking this is just the latest instalment in a chain of horrible nightmares.

She's just a normal woman, living her life, going about her business, hurting no-one and probably wondering, *why her?* As the silence comes back to settle over us again, with just the muffled sounds of more neighbours' car doors slamming as they make it home from wherever they've been, I find I'm wondering the exact same fucking thing.

'You can come in. But I am going to leave the door open, and if I ask you to leave you will have to, right away. Understood?'

I nod, and she opens the door wider and stands aside. The next thing I know I'm in her hallway. A faint whiff of bleach hits my nose, but it's gone again as quickly as I notice it. I follow her through to the living room, and she gestures for me to sit down. I pick an armchair and she picks the one opposite. We both sit and stare at one another for a minute or two. Having given my apology, I'm not sure what else to say, but since she invited me in, maybe she's got something to say to me instead.

But it seems like she doesn't quite know how to start a conversation either. It's like she's invited me in on an impulse and is now thinking '*shit, what did I just do?*'

But then she clears her throat again and just asks, simply, 'Why did you send your mother here?'

Since I've made the effort to come here, and she already knows more than I thought she would, I decide that telling the whole truth is the only real option, no matter what the result.

'I wanted to make sure your dog was alright. It's been haunting me. I've had no end of bloody nightmares about it. And I was hoping Mum could find out what might have happened to my friend Tom. He's the lad I was here with that day. I haven't seen him since I ran off from here. He's missing. Officially. I'm really worried about him. We all are.'

'All?'

'His family. His mum, his girlfriend, me. For starters.'

She's staring at me again, but not in a threatening or worrying way. It feels more like idle curiosity, like she's seen something she wants to just examine a bit more closely.

'What makes you think I'd know anything?'

A silence settles, for a minute or two, while I form an answer. Again, honesty feels like the only way forward.

'Because I feel like a complete and utter bastard for running away, like the coward I am, and leaving him, and I need to know what happened here with you and him before he left, because you might have been the last person to see him alive.'

'Like what? What do you think could have happened here?'

'I don't know. I think he probably just left, after I did, but I want to know if he said anything to you at all, about where he was going.'

'Why would he tell me where he was going?'

I look down at the floor, realising what a stupid question it is, really. After all, what did I think? That he'd have told her he had to get home for his tea, as he was running out the door with her fucking laptop?

'I dunno. I just felt I had to come here. Try and find a missing piece of the puzzle, if you know what I mean.'

Alison nods, slowly. 'I do know what you mean. But I can't help you. I'm sorry.'

She looks incredibly pale, almost haunted, and I see that as guilt. So I decide to grab the bull by the horns.

'Then why do you look guilty of something?'

She looks startled. 'Guilty? What do I look guilty of?'

I decide I can't really accuse her outright of something I'm not even sure of; something I don't even believe her capable of in fact, so I resort to trying to explain myself by saying how shocked, pale and, in fact, really *ill* she looks. 'No offence, but your eyes look like two pissholes in the whitest snow I've ever seen.'

She lets out a bit of a laugh, but it's not a funny one. She sits for a minute, almost smiling but not quite. Then she takes a deep breath, and starts to speak.

'You're pretty candid, I'll give you that. Well, let's see… I'm shocked that you and your mother have both had the nerve to show up at my door after you and your little friend tried to rob me blind. And I'm pale, yes, and sick yes, because I have a terminal illness.'

I gape at her, unsure how to respond.

She looks at me with her eyebrows raised. I don't know if she's waiting for a response or not, but I haven't a clue what to say. So the silences starts growing again and I start to fidget. After a minute or so, which feels like fucking ten, she speaks again.

'I'm sorry, that was unfair. I appreciate your reasons for coming here. Badger, my dog, will be fine when his shoulder and his nose have healed, but I'm sure your mother has already told you that. And I accept your apologies about the burglary, but I can't help you about your missing friend.'

Her tone is final. The way she speaks, she doesn't leave room for me to say anything more about Tom, or ask anything further. It's like a door slamming that you can't open again, so I have no choice but to let it go. She doesn't know anything, so I'm back to square one. It's frustrating as fuck, but what can I do?

I hear a short whimper coming from the kitchen.

'Can I please see the dog?'

She looks wary. Very reluctant.

'Please? I won't hurt him. I just want to reassure myself he'll be okay, because it's haunted me ever since it happened. Please? I'd love to give him a pat, to say sorry. And you forgiving me is only part of it. I need him to forgive me too.'

She gestures towards the kitchen, and I stand and go through to find the dog asleep in his bed in the cage by the door. He's twitching and dreaming a bit, and making a whiffling sound. I kneel down, and I pat his shaggy fur. He wakes, lifts his head to look at me with bleary eyes, and then drops it again and goes back to sleep. I can see he's doped up, probably for the pain. I find I'm tearing up again, and I reach into my pocket for one of the tissues Alison gave me at the door and I give my eyes a quick blot. I keep my hand on him, and I whisper to him gently, apologising over and over, and telling him how beautiful he is, because he really is.

When I stand up again I'm surprised to find Alison standing right behind me. It gives me a bit of a start, because I didn't hear her come in. She steps back to allow me to go back to the living room, and I sit back down again. I know I should leave, I've got the answers I came for, which are in fact no real answers at all, but somehow I just want to keep talking to her. She sits down again too.

'I do appreciate you doing that. I'm sure he appreciates it too, or at least he will when he's less drugged up on his pain relief.'

I ask her what it's like dealing with him in the state he's in, and she admits it's difficult but they're managing. She just misses their long walks. I tell her it's only a matter of time until he's on his feet again and they can go back to their walking but she just looks at me.

'I won't get to walk with him again, not like we did before. I'll be gone before he's right again.' Her words are quiet, but clear.

She is dying, this poor woman whose life me and Tom fucked up by wandering in here, thinking we had some entitlement to her stuff, and hurting her innocent dog. She's dying, and how could what we did possibly have made anything better for her? The knock-on effect is that I really *have* robbed her, haven't I? I've robbed her of the chance to walk with her dog, properly, before she dies, and that's what she misses the most, and can never have again, if what she says is true.

Like I've said already, most of the time I don't even think about the consequences of what I do, or the impact it has on other people. It's one of the things the psychologists keep wringing their hands about in jail when they keep trying to get me to see some sense on those bloody stupid, so-called 'recidivism prevention' courses that aren't worth shit. They never work, it's a waste of everyone's time.

This is the first time I've seen just how bad things can be for someone thanks to me just doing what I want, and I've never felt so uncomfortable in my whole miserable, pathetic, stupid, pointless fucked-up life. I feel like shit, wishing the ground could open up and swallow me, and I'm hoping to hell it wasn't me or what I've done that's started or triggered her terminal illness.

As if she's reading my mind, she says 'It's nothing that could have been predicted. It's a brain tumour; pure, random and simple, and it's taking me out, sooner rather than later.'

'There must be some treatment ...' I start and trail off. It's none of my business, and why would I think she'd want to talk to me about it anyway?

'Treatment, yes, but no cure. Only difficult interventions that might buy time I don't want.'

'Why don't you want time, with your dog? With your life? If you don't mind me asking...'

She explains that she doesn't want to suffer or lose her dignity. And funnily enough I can relate to that, because a few years ago I watched a programme on the telly with Mum and Michelle, about a man who had that fucking horrible motor neurone disease. He wanted help to die, but it was illegal, and I remember Mum being all upset about it and saying that if she was in that state she'd want us to do something about it so she didn't keep suffering. She'd want us to help her do away with herself.

And I promised her I would. If it ever came to the point where she couldn't speak, or go to the loo, or take enough drugs to stay free of pain, I'd help her to die, and I know what it means if I got caught. It means serious jail time; *years*, instead of a few weeks or months, but I'd still do it. She's the one person I'd happily do that kind of time for and although prison's no picnic, at least I know what it's all about. You have your shitty routine and everything's as boring as fuck, but for someone like me who can handle himself well enough, there are few big bad surprises, and there are far worse places to be in this life, if you don't have anything good going on in it.

So I understand what Alison's saying. She wants to just go, when the time comes, and not keep suffering for however long, just to have time that doesn't even have any quality. What's the point of having more time, when you're in constant pain, or shitting yourself every five minutes, or you can't remember the people you've loved all your life who suddenly seem like strangers; people to be scared of?

To fill the silence, I tell her about that programme, and she listens! This woman, whose life I threw into complete chaos, who should hate me and be throwing me out of her house about now, is listening to me as if I have something to say that's worth hearing. She has that respect for me, and I don't feel I deserve it but I tell her I understand the way she thinks about it all, because that programme changed my way of thinking too, and if I was in a car crash or something, all mangled and horrible, I wouldn't want to live either, so it's really no different. And I told her what I'd agreed with my mum, finishing off by saying that although I'm a selfish bastard for thinking it, I hope it never came to that for Mum *or* for me.

She smiles at that. 'There's nothing wrong with putting yourself first. You can't be of any help to someone else if you're not in a good place yourself, Darren.'

That was a kind thing to say, I think to myself. I didn't expect that. I'm not sure what I was expecting when I came here, but I was prepared for all kinds of shit. Kindness? No, I didn't see that coming.

'I kind of have a history of not facing up to things. Running away, not manning up, that sort of thing,' I confess.

'Well you've already said you'd man up for your mum if she needed you to. Even if you didn't want to, you would, wouldn't you? Do what she asked?'

'Yeah. Yeah, I would. For her.'

'Well then. And despite whatever consequences might have happened, like me refusing to answer the door, or slamming it in your face, or even calling the police and having you arrested, you still had the guts to come here to apologise for hurting Badger, and for breaking in here. You wanted to find out about your friend, and you even challenged me because you thought I looked guilty! So not that big a coward then.'

Well, when she puts it like that, maybe I really have got more backbone than I first thought.

'I'm sorry about your brain tumour. It's really sad, a proper fucking tragedy,' I offer, not really sure what else to say. She shrugs.

'It's the luck of the draw, the shortest straw, but someone's got to draw it, and I guess this time it's me. At some point you have to accept it, and it hasn't been easy, but I think I have now.'

'What will happen to your dog? Badger?'

'I have a friend who I trust totally, to find him a good new home.'

She looks so sad, thinking about her dog. But what amazes me is how fucking calm she is. I'm not sure I'd be that calm myself, if I got told I was on borrowed time. I find myself telling her about the animals I used to find when I was a kid, injured birds, hedgehogs and the like, and how I used to scoop them up and put them in the pocket of my parka, and take them home to mend. In my own way I guess I'm trying to tell her that hurting animals isn't really in my nature, and I think she gets it, because she smiles at me a little, and looks a bit less sad.

But I don't want to take up any more of her time, because she looks like she's about to fall asleep. She's too polite to ask me to go, but I feel sure that's what she wants, so I stand up and offer her my hand, which she takes.

'Thank you for seeing me. I'm a bastard. I don't deserve you to be nice to me, but I'm glad you have been. I just feel a bit guilty for feeling better, especially since you're so... well, sick.'

She shakes her head. 'Don't feel guilty for feeling better. It took courage for you to come here to try to make amends, and you have, so you *should* feel better. I've done things in my life that I'm still working out how to make amends for, so you're streets ahead of me.'

She lays a hand on my arm. 'Thanks for coming. I appreciate it more than I can say. But what I *can* say is don't give up on yourself. You're a decent person, worth more than the life you've chosen. You seem pretty intelligent to me. You can turn it around, if you really want to.'

I explain myself a bit. I tell her I got good grades on my A Levels, but my first job fell through and I never figured out how to pick myself up. But I also tell her that I do want to change; I just need to figure out how.

She smiled at that, and nodded. 'We've all got choices. There are always choices. Sometimes it's hard to see them, but they're always there.'

'You know, you're right. I always tell myself that I didn't choose this life, I more or less fell into it, but falling into a life of petty crime *was* a choice, wasn't it? I *chose* to take the wrong path, and stay on it. So in a way I *did* choose this life, didn't I? I am the product of my own shitty choices.'

'You're capable of better. How old are you? Twenty-two?'

I tell her I'm twenty-six, and her eyebrows shoot for her hairline. She cocks her head on one side and looks at me, more or less impassively again, as if she's looking at a specimen of something and trying to figure it out. Something has caught her attention about me, but I'm pretty sure it's not my stunning good looks and my intelligent conversation.

'You still have plenty of time to turn your life around. If you are planning to do it, just make sure it happens before you end up doing something *really* stupid, and losing the chance forever.'

I know exactly what she means. Criminal behaviour has a habit of escalating. I've been in the bang-up with guys who were doing long stretches for all kinds of things they once never thought they'd do. And most of them had started off by shoplifting, or nicking the neighbour's pot plants off the back deck, or something just as fucking silly. I knew my future was going to go one of two ways.

I end by saying I'm sorry she can't help me work out what happened to Tom. I'm still hoping, fishing for something further, some tiny clue I can latch onto, but she just closes her eyes and says nothing about it. It seems cruel to press her, and I feel a bit protective of her, somehow, even though we've only just met. It's hard to explain, but I don't want things to be any harder for her than they already are. I think we've caused her enough grief, me and Tom.

At the door, she says 'Thanks again for coming.'

From out of nowhere, I just blurt it out; 'can I visit you again?'

Suddenly I'm cringing inside, and I'm gobsmacked. I dunno where the hell that came from, and I'm standing there expecting her to tell me to just fuck off and never come back, but instead she just quietly says; 'If you like, as long as you don't ask me anything more about your friend. Like I said already, I can't help you with that.'

And there it is again, that slammed door on Tommy.

But she said I can come back. So I take her number and tell her I'll make contact before I come again, just to make sure it's still okay, and I mention that if she changes her mind about it, that will be okay too.

30

Wednesday
- Alison -

My thoughts are interrupted yet again by the arrival of another round of unwelcome, wittering visitors. This damned house has started to feel like Heathrow airport, with people coming and going, and so few of them even bothering to ask me if I mind the intrusion. They simply take it upon themselves to descend on the dying, swooping in with soup and sympathy, and often without even so much as a phone call first. I'm sick of them. In fact, I'm about to stop answering the door, and I'll be telling Mum to ignore it too.

And as far as unwelcome visitors go, I have to admit that Darren Davies showing up at my door last week was an absolute doozy. I certainly hadn't bargained on *that* happening! If someone had asked me who I'd expect to find on my doorstep, in my wildest of nightmares, I would still not have thought of him. In all fairness, if we're talking about nightmares, I'd probably have said Tom Findlay, but you get the drift.

So when Bill brought Badger back on Saturday and told me a man called Darren had been here and probably intended to come back, I was literally beside myself. When you hear something you really don't want to hear, something you've been dreading but hoping will never happen, your bowels go loose, and you can feel all sorts of other unwelcome things happening in your lower stomach; everything trying to head south, and you're engulfed by an unavoidable sense of impending doom.

That's what I felt when Bill told me that. Like the world had gone from under my feet again, and I was suddenly back in that unquantifiable place; disconnected, floating, and facing something terrible, but with no clear idea what it might be; only the certainty that I wouldn't get away with trying to dodge it.

Badger stirs, then tries to get to his feet. His pain killer has no doubt worn off (he's down to just one now; it's good progress, according to our usual vet, who I knew I had to go back to) and he whimpers a little and lies back down again. His tail wags slightly, but he looks at me sadly. Although he's well and truly on the mend, he is still in some pain.

I fetch his tablets, and I gently feed one to him wrapped up in a choice piece of ham. I lie on the floor hugging him as best I can, lightly scratching his back in his favourite spot, that universal doggy-joy place, where his tail joins his body. Then I get to my feet, open the French doors, and half walk, half carry him out into the back garden. He completes his toilet immediately, and I bring him back into the house, where he promptly falls asleep again, bless him.

My phone pings with a message, It's Darren Davies, asking if he can visit again, in about an hour. Oddly enough, in a way I could never hope to explain, he's the one person I'm interested in seeing.

I get rid of Mum and my other visitors as quickly as I can, by telling them I'm feeling overwhelmed and need to sleep. Nobody wants to deny the wishes of a dying friend, so they all scuttle off within minutes, and I'm left alone again.

I didn't know what to expect when I opened the door to him last week, but it certainly wasn't tears and remorse. As he stood there on my front porch, weeping, I sensed he really was genuinely sorry for what he'd done. I felt his shame, sweeping and swirling all around us both, like unseen autumn leaves. Remorse, guilt, and a deep desperation to be forgiven. It caught me a bit off-balance and all I could do, while my thoughts scrambled for sensibility and coherence, was stay silent.

Blessed (*or cursed?)* with a 'poker face,' I've been grateful for it as a worthy shield, at times when revealing my emotions wouldn't have helped me, and that was one of those times. Had I been the type of woman to wear my heart on my sleeve, Darren Davies could have turned the tables on me super-fast. When facing a criminal, you never know what they might be thinking, or what kind of advantage they're seeking to get. Perhaps they're a bit like dogs. Maybe they can sense and home in on fear or vulnerability, although not having known many criminals on a personal level I couldn't really say that with any certainty.

But the man seemed utterly pathetic, standing there, and I didn't get a sense of crocodile tears designed to distract or manipulate me, so I decided to take a chance. I let him in and heard him out, figuring if my judgement was that poor and he really was here to attack me and leave me for dead, he'd be doing me a bloody big favour.

It's funny what you'll do when you think you've nothing left to lose. In the not-too-distant past I'd *never* have taken a risk like that; way out of the ballpark of balanced judgement by anybody's standards. But, with so few bridges left to burn, I threw myself clean out of what passes these days for a comfort zone and took a chance on him not battering me.

And guess what? I was surprised to find that he actually seemed like a reasonable character. I was touched too, that he also asked forgiveness directly from Badger himself. That came in what he thought was a private moment between himself and the dog. He wasn't aware I'd overheard it.

I wouldn't have seen that gentle sweetness of soul, or found out that Darren Davies had any redeeming features at all, if I hadn't taken that risk, and I'm astonished to have discovered that I actually quite liked him. He was surprisingly respectful, remorseful and fundamentally honest. He was also quite humorous too, here and there, and I found that rather charming, particularly as he appeared to have no real idea of how nice, and how funny, he actually is. The quintessential rough diamond. Even with his effing and blinding, he was funny. So how could I not forgive one so sorry, and so utterly wretched, over his actions; particularly when despite my best efforts I couldn't bring myself to dislike him? And whatever kind of person he is, he's a long way from being as sorry or as wretched as *me*.

It's quite ironic (there we go again with the irony!) that I've been sitting here, hoping that my initial brief encounter with Darren Davies would lead to more. I do want to see him again, and although I can't even really explain why, I just want to know more about what goes on in that terribly interesting head of his.

It's not what you'd call an attraction, even on a cerebral level, like it has been in the past, with men I actually fancied. This, wanting to know more about a man who intrigues me, is really more of a *curiosity*, I think. But I do think he is full of potential, and if there's anything more I can do in this world that's good, after fucking up the lives of people who never deserved it, and facing a very bleak and imminent end to my own life, maybe it's helping this man to find himself and reinvent his.

Maybe him pitching up in pieces, out of the blue, was meant to happen. If anyone had told me I'd end up sitting in my living room with him, mopping him up and chatting like we'd known one another for ages, I'd never have believed it. It's the kind of farcical exchange you'd see on a dark T.V. sitcom.

So here we are, then. Life imitating art.

It's caused me to wonder, too, how often we make judgements about people without knowing the full facts behind the things they do. I wonder how many people don't get the chance to redeem themselves in even the smallest ways because we're all so busy feeling wronged and relentlessly determined to see the worst in whoever has wronged us, We deny them the chance to try to make amends; to make that one overture, to extend an olive branch that could literally turn everything around for the better, for everyone involved.

At least I did that. I did give him the chance to redeem himself, a little at least.

Often it's our own simple stubbornness that perpetuates a thorny status quo. How much helpful insight do we miss, as a result?

Darren does come again, and; albeit grudgingly, I have to say our second conversation is as interesting as the first one. When he is leaving again, he tells me he feels better for visiting. Surprisingly, I am really glad about that. He feels better, so his visits really aren't all bluster underpinned by some obscure motive. It really *has* been important to him, to be forgiven for his mistakes.

And, to be honest, it hasn't been hard to forgive him; not really. Not when you consider what I've done myself, and how much worse that is, and the fact that I've looked him in the eye and lied through my teeth to him about his friend. He doesn't appear to suspect a thing. It's nothing short of incredible. I just hope one day, when he does find out what I've done, *he* can find a way to forgive *me*.

In the overall scheme of things, what Darren Davies did to me and Badger was a small thing. Comparatively speaking, I mean. It's still a big thing, of course, particularly for poor Badger struggling away with his pain and confusion, but it falls a long way short of murder (manslaughter?), and those additional little nuggets of dead-body concealment, and dying of a brain tumour. While seeking to keep things in what passes for perspective, I think it's safe to say that it's been a hell of a month so far.

I've managed to fend off his questions, which hasn't felt very fair, but let's face it. I might be shuffling off the mortal coil in record time, and taking a risk like letting a known criminal into my home for social niceties, but I'm not stupid enough to sit there and say 'yeah, Darren, I whacked your mate with a metal skillet and – oops! – the silly boy upped and died, so I tipped him into someone else's grave.'

There's a very fine line between bravery and stupidity, and I'm not quite that stupid, or that brave. Not quite stupid enough to incur the consequences a confession like that would bring to the doorstep. Not quite brave enough to face the prospect of ending my days in an HMP infirmary.

Darren talked about cowardice, but he's got nothing on me, has he? What would he say or do to me, if he knew the real truth?

Anyway, if he feels he can talk to me in a way he can't talk to anyone else, maybe I owe him that. He certainly has some baggage, and that's probably a big part of why he's the way he is. I'm no shrink, but even I know that a chronic lack of self-esteem can push people into making unwise choices, especially if they really struggle to believe they are capable of better.

Also, from a more selfish point of view, listening to *his* tales of trial and tribulation means I can temporarily take my mind off my own. For the time that he's here, that works. The minute he's gone, of course, the despair descends once more, and I find myself back to facing the full force of my own self-loathing.

It's a welcome change to have the opportunity to sit with someone who isn't constantly making the conversation all about me and my brain tumour, or my arrangements, or my feelings, or whether I'm warm or cool enough, or hungry, or getting enough sleep, or managing my pain levels, or whether I've planned my own godforsaken funeral yet. I have enough of myself to deal with already, without talking about it all with someone else.

Darren Davies, for all his faults and sins, has already very nicely relieved me twice now, albeit temporarily, of the swinging pendulum of sufferance with lousy choices at either extreme; sitting in a smothering silence with my conscience clawing away at me, or smiling through gritted teeth at the endless drone of well-meant but ridiculous conversation from boring friends and relatives. Of the three discomforts, the least wearisome has definitely been listening to someone talking about himself and not me. I find it extraordinary, that Darren wants to keep coming.

It's not fair of me to be so mean-spirited about the people who are only trying to help, but it all just feels absurd. Mum says everyone's really only wanting to feel useful, and Darren said more or less the same thing, but since when did my terminal illness become all about others and what they want? And how does anyone think that an endless stream of inane platitudes, and declarations of sadness and frustrated indignation at the random injustice of it all, will provide me with anything positive in my remaining time on earth?

Oddly enough, for one so usually self-contained, selfishness has never been one of my faults, until now. Neither has intolerance. I've never suffered fools, but I've always given someone a fair hearing. Now though, my fuse is very short, and I find I just want to turn my back on the inane verbiage I'm getting from so many, now that word is spreading. People calling round, sounding falsely over-cheerful, and then wringing their hands in front of me with the sorrow of it all.

What can I say? I'm too pissed off to talk to people whose conversation bores me to tears. I don't remember half of what they say anyway. I never know what to say myself, and there's only so much false jollity, patronisation or doe-eyed expressions of sympathy a girl can really stand.

One so-called friend, who 'sang' a flat, murderous rendition of Monty Python's 'Bright Side of Life' at me complete with stupid 'be-doop' chorus noises, will never know just how insulting and unhelpful that was. Nor will she know how close I came to hauling myself painfully out of my chair and slapping her silly face for it.

Why *won't* she know? Because I just couldn't bring myself to tell her what an insensitive bitch she was being and, in doing so, make any aspect of my illness about *her*. In these final days or weeks, I think it *should* just be about me and what I want, even if that doesn't suit someone else.

And perhaps these uncharacteristically negative and spite-laden thoughts about well-meaning others are really just the influence of the tumours as they bend my personality in a new direction and chomp away like Pacman at what's left of my grey matter. That being the case, I stand to become a very unpredictable and bad-tempered bitch indeed, as the time slides by, and I eventually 'buy the farm.'

31

Friday
- Darren -

I'm feeling really pissed off, today. Tom's mum Marla's just phoned to say the latest update from the police has produced no new information. Nothing, again. Not one single lead, in all these bloody weeks, and those posters on lamp posts are all turning brown and curling up at the edges. Some twats have attacked one and drawn fangs, cross-eyes and a moustache and beard on one, and that really pissed me off. I'd have ripped their fucking heads off if I'd caught them doing that.

It's beyond a bloody joke, all this. Surely to God they should have found *something* by now to explain what might have happened? What are they doing? People can't just disappear, like Tom did, can they, without someone knowing something?

I think back to a morning just after he went missing, when we all met up on the rec ground, dozens of us, to look for him. There were friends, and teachers from his old school, neighbours, family members, and local pensioners, shopkeepers and other people who didn't even know him but wanted to help. There were even people from his old cub group out to pitch in, though it's been years since he's been a part of the cubs. Marla got to the point where she couldn't afford to send him, anymore.

We all thought we'd have him found by mid-morning, lunchtime at the latest. Everyone set off with high hopes and a plan, yelling ourselves hoarse, but at the end of it we had nothing. No clues, nothing, and we were all pretty disheartened. And all these weeks on, there's still no sign of him, not even the faintest fucking trace.

I'm telling myself now, as I sit here, that it might be time to start trying to accept that wherever he is, he's probably not coming back. But I can't do that. Not yet. It's too soon to accept something like that. The sadness is so strong I can't put words around it, and the guilt? It's crushing.

I went to see Alison again, after that first time, and it was odd that I found her so easy to talk to, like I've known her for years. She's a debt collector, at least she *was*. She's stopped working obviously, since she only has a limited time left, and she's on lots of drugs to keep her from having fits and falling over.

She was a little bit more shaky on her pins the second time I went, but still really calm about everything. Badger looked a bit better, too. Her vet had made a house call to check him over and she's been able to reduce his medication by half. It's really good news. I took him out into the garden to the loo for her, and I'm glad she trusted me to do it, since I really wanted to do it; my way of trying to help her, and him.

He's such a character, that dog. So good natured, in spite of his pain. Tommy's dog Button, the mad mutt, he once gashed his leg trying to jump through a barbed wire fence and if you went near him he'd snarl and try to have your hand off. This dog, he's quite the opposite. He soaks up the love like a sponge. Maybe it helps him to feel a bit less rubbish and sore.

Alison says she's forgiven me and I can't believe how lucky I am that she has. She seems like a nice woman, and one of the things she said was that her life was going to be too short to not let people off the hook who deserved it, before she kicked the bucket. Apparently I deserve it; to be let off the hook.

That's like gold, to me, from someone like her. Would I have tried to rob the woman if I'd known how nice she was? Course I wouldn't. And now that I know her, I'd paste the shit out of *anyone* who tried to hurt her, *or* her dog.

We haven't talked about Tom though. I have tried a couple of times to bring up the subject, by saying the police still have no leads on him, and saying I miss him, but whenever I mention him she acts like she hasn't fucking heard me or she just changes the subject. She does that with some skill, but I do still notice. I suppose the poor woman just doesn't want to hear bad news about anything, since she's already got enough to be thinking about, with her injured dog and her own looming death, so I talk to her mostly about good things and try all the while to ignore the massive elephant of a fucking great terminal brain tumour skulking in the shadows of the room.

But I really wish I *could* talk to her about Tommy. She's so sensible, and practical, if I could just tell her about when I went to see the plod and didn't tell them everything, and whether it would make a difference if I did, she might be able to help me decide what to do. The more I think about it and try to work it all out in my own head, on my own, the more confused I get.

The only other person I can talk to about it all is Mum, and I already know what *she* thinks, don't I? Unfortunately, I don't always feel that poor old Mum has the full take on things, and I do know she's not always right. I'm positive she's not right about me handing myself in. But if they find Tom, and things do come to light about where we were that day, I'll be more than willing to confess. I really will. I'm fed up with living like there's something in the shadows waiting to grab me.

Talking away like the clappers with someone who's dying; I never thought I'd ever be doing that. But like I say, it's not all gloom and doom. We've even managed to have a bit of a laugh a couple of times, when we've talked about my mad mum, and what she can be like sometimes. We've even managed to have a laugh about some of my prison stuff, weird conversations I've had with mad-head pad mates that were off their rockers, that kind of thing.

A woman called Daphne called in one time, when I was there, and she seemed nice as well, all excited about an up-coming wedding, but tearful too, because she knows Alison won't be there. Alison was meant to be her chief bridesmaid, I think.

It's so sad, that you can have all these plans, and then all of a sudden, wham! You find out you won't see them happen; you'll be gone before you get to go to something you've been looking forward to. You must feel really cheated.

Alison talked about some theory of the different stages of grief, how there's so much tied up in there with all kinds of feelings like disbelief and anger, resentment, and all that. But then in the end the theory says you get to a stage of acceptance, and that's where she's at. I guess you do have to get to that, or go mad with the effort, but I can't imagine being okay about dying.

That's what I find hard. Her being so calm about it all, and losing all those plans, like long walks and picnics in the park with the dog trying to scoff your sandwiches, a mate's wedding where you should have been bridesmaid. Going on the holiday you've been saving and buying new clothes for.

It's been bloody years since I went on holiday, and the only time I ever went anywhere really interesting was that first year Mum and Pat got together. They went to Tenerife, and they took me with them. Pat tried to act like a Dad, but it was way too late by then. I didn't need a Dad at that stage of my life, and everything was already a fucking mess, so him with his holiday and his cheque book, it wasn't going to make a difference by then, was it?

At least he tried though, didn't he? And I've never even acknowledged that before now. He did try, and I was an ungrateful snot-nose to him. He's been married before and he has a grown-up son I've never met, but he's banged on a few times about how we're like chalk and cheese, me and his Ben, who's always grateful for the help he gets given, never throws anything back in Pat's face, blah, blah, blah. Ben the Bastard never seems to put a foot wrong. The Golden Child.

Did I ever want to meet this gold-plated tit with a halo around his head? No way. Pat's made it more than clear that I'll never have a hope of measuring up. I don't need to be confronted with the evidence.

It's funny how you meet all kinds of people in life, and some of them you can never imagine spending real time with (like Ben!), yet others you just gel with, like Alison Jones, and you end up wanting to talk for hours on end, like there's never enough time to say everything you want to because you've got so much to say.

Words just start coming out of you. There's a trust there, and despite some of the things you're saying being awful and wrong, you just know that it's okay to say them, so you do, and nothing bad happens. All those prison shrinks trying to get me to talk, and I never trusted a single one of them, with their pens and papers, scribbling fuck knows what into some file that anyone can look at, and you have no control or clue about who sees what they've written about you, whether it's right or wrong.

Alison never writes anything down. She just listens, then she says something wise, or daft, and it just makes me want to keep talking. I told her she's my confessional, and she thought that was just hilarious. 'Tell me what you like,' she said. 'I'll take it to the grave.'

What do you say to that? I didn't know what to say. I think she saw it too, because she reassured me again that she was at peace with everything. 'Black humour,' she called it.

Oddly, I'm at peace with her dying, probably because I didn't know her before she wasn't, so I didn't get the same shock everyone else did. I know one day soon she'll be gone, and I'll never see her again. She'll be someone I once knew a bit, and spent a bit of time with, who made me feel better about myself for an hour or two, here and there.

Actually, to be honest, I don't know if I really am at peace with it, but I can't change anything for her, can I? I haven't got a magic wand to wave, to make her better. So I do have to try to get to a place where I'm okay about her dying, as much as I ever will be.

This little woman, from a completely different class, treats me like her friend, in her final weeks or months. She wouldn't say how long she has left and it feels really rude to ask, so I don't. But I do wonder.

In different circumstances, like if I'd kept my job at the call centre, I could have gone out with someone like Alison. Nowadays, with a criminal record as long as your arm, I'd be punching too far above my own weight and well out of my fucking league to even try to get the attention of a woman like her, or that lovely girl I met at the beach. But it's shown me what I *could* have had, what my life *might* have looked like, if I'd managed to stay on the right side of the law.

Is it too late to turn things around? Alison doesn't think so, but I'm not so sure. We did talk a lot, about my robbing. She's the first victim I've actually met, and when I told her that, she asked me if I'd ever thought about what some of the other people were like, that I'd stolen from. She said that while some were probably rich gits, who could probably afford to lose a few material things, most of the people I'd stolen from were probably just ordinary people, like her, who worked hard for everything they had, so it all had real meaning for them and it would have hurt to lose it.

Alison lives in a nice neighbourhood, so she looks well off, but that doesn't mean shit. She told me she bought her house with some inheritance money but she still has to earn a certain income, to pay her monthly bills. I never thought about it that way. Appearances can be deceiving, and just because someone *looks* like they could afford to lose a few things, doesn't always mean it's true.

I've learned so much from her, just in the course of talking, and it's made me think a lot more, about all kinds of stuff. We've talked about so many different things, and for once I feel like someone cares what I think, what I feel, but won't judge me for it like most of the people I know. It's why I never really talk to anyone. They all know me too well, if that makes sense. I just get judged all the time.

Alison has said more than once that she's done stuff she's not proud of either, but she won't be drawn on the details of anything. Whatever it was, it can't be as bad as some of what I've done. I bet *she's* never abandoned a friend to save her own skin. That's the one thing I can't talk about with her, because she won't let me. But everything else we've talked about, well, it's all helped me straighten my head out about a few things and, let's face it, that's what I've needed for far too fucking long.

She's losing her life, and I'm keeping mine – at least as far as I know! But I've been wasting it, and maybe I *can* change that, especially if she thinks I can.

After just a couple of visits, a couple of decent chats, Alison Jones believes I can make something of my life. I get the feeling she wouldn't say it if she didn't believe it, because she seems to be a no-bullshit kind of person. She tells it like it is. I just wish she didn't have this shadow hanging over her, this 'clutch of brain tumours' as she calls it. She looks sad all the time, kind of 'hunted,' for want of a better word, like she can't get away from the burden that's killing her. Well, she can't, can she?

So, when it comes to changing my life, what would I do, given the chance? We talked about that too, and I had to think for a while. She said; 'don't tell me what you think I should be hearing. Tell me what you really would do, given the chance.'

So I told her. I'd like to work with animals, or maybe be a chef. Both options need a lot of training though, and I think I've missed the boat on that. The interest in cheffing comes from when I worked in the kitchens for a while, in prison. There was something really cool, for me, about keeping a big kitchen all sparkling clean. And taking a load of boring ingredients and making something edible out of them; there was something really good about that too. I can make a mean rice pudding, and when I told her that, she laughed her head off. She hates rice pudding, apparently. So I told her I could make a decent soup as well, and not from dishwater either, and that made her laugh as well. 'Soup, I can do,' she said.

Maybe if I go again I can make her some. If Mum lets me anywhere near to the kitchen, that is. I think she's afraid I'll burn the place to the ground.

When I left Alison's the second time, she said she'd let me know if she wanted company again. I felt a bit like that was telling me she didn't really want me to go round again, but she reassured me it wasn't the case. She just needs a bit of time on her own to prepare for what's coming. She's getting a bit fed up with all the visitors. The 'sympathy and flowers' she keeps getting from well-wishers is starting to get her down. I told her off, for that. I'm comfortable enough with her to tell her off, although I tried to do it nicely.

But she really shouldn't begrudge people the chance to come and see her and offer their thoughts, because they're her friends, and they *will* miss her. They'll have to deal with her being gone. They'll have to pick up the pieces she leaves behind, and for some of them it will be really hard. I think about that little Daphne, at her own fucking wedding, looking at her bridesmaids and seeing the gap where Alison should be. I think about Bill, watching someone else move into this house to become his neighbour, after she's gone.

For the people who care about her, seeing her before she goes and saying things that feel important to them is a big part of the process of saying goodbye for them. I wanted her to remember that, so I told her, and to her credit, she took it on the chin.

She does need some breathing space though, I think, because she *is* really tired, and her mum's there a lot, fussing and wittering away, and that wears her down. It's finding that balance between having the space to prepare for your own end, and respecting those who are already starting their grieving over losing you.

I hope she calls me again. I would like to see her again. And maybe take her some soup.

32

Saturday
- Alison -

As far as I've always been concerned, we only have one life that we know, or can be sure about having, so whether or not we live it to the full is down to ourselves, and what we choose, or not, to do. While I've never been sure what the purpose of my life really was, and had yet to formulate personal goals that would enrich and fulfil me (unless you count buying this house I truly love), I always felt that eventually I'd get to a place where I'd look back on my life and think *'yeah, I made a meaningful contribution.'*

It occurs to me now that I've never had a plan, for what meaningful things I was going to do, that would enable me to sit there one day in my rocking chair and think that way.

And now, with everything about to be cut so brutally short, what can I say about my life to date? What have I done that actually means anything to anyone? Sadly, the list of all the things I haven't done with this precious gift of life is a hell of a lot longer than my list of achievements. I haven't raised money for charity, helped the homeless, travelled to inspiring places or sponsored an African child. I haven't given an inspirational speech, learned to ride a motorcycle, or jumped out of a perfectly good plane and trusted a few bits of string and some sewn-together pieces of nylon to get me safely to the ground.

I've always stayed firmly within my comfort zone, only stepping into uncharted water a couple of times; once, when I took on Badger, and then when I allowed a common thief to become my friend. And it occurs to me now, sitting here in the all-enveloping dark; those two forays I took outside of my personal boundaries turned out to be the ones that have brought me the greatest joy. So why didn't I push the envelope more? Why *didn't* I go to those foreign places, immerse myself in strange cultures to eat, pray and love, or volunteer to dish up Christmas dinner at the local homeless shelter? Why *didn't* I learn to speak Italian, swim with killer whales, or adopt an orphan?

They were all things that have passed through my mind in fleeting form, back in the days, just a few short weeks ago in fact, when I thought I had time to formulate goals, to discover desires, and put them into action. While I don't consider my existence to have been anything remarkable, it certainly had the potential. It *was* my life, and I always felt like I should, and eventually *would* do the best I could with it, and treat it like a gift to be cherished, somewhere down the track.

But that's the thing, isn't it? So many of us operate within a kind of self-created bubble of intangible but taken-for-granted certainty, that we will *at some obscure point in the future* have time to start experiencing life to the full; when we've got over *this* particular hump or *that* particular hurdle; when we've saved *this* much money, or reached some other specific, personal point in our lives where it feels appropriate to make significant changes. But does it *ever?* And if so, when? There's no point in wondering about it, though, is there? It's not like I'm going to find out.

We don't tend to worry too much, in the short term, about forming those goals of self-enrichment or being in service to others. At least, that's how it's always been for me, un-driven and purposeless as I have been, beyond climbing the ladder at work. It's my loss, as it turns out. I've squandered my gift of life, in fact I've written it off completely. It was nothing of note before. Now, I'm not worthy of it at all, and it's only fitting that I relinquish it.

Of all the many things I believed I would one day do, taking another person's life wasn't one of them. Nor was contemplating suicide. Taking my *own* life, or even imagining being in a place where it felt like the best option, is something I've never dwelt on. Just one more thing then, for me to consider from my exclusive place of virtual ignorance of all the fundamental life questions that really matter. I'm not the most enlightened individual, am I? While I know I love chardonnay and hate rice pudding, my lack of real, true self-awareness is beginning to appal me. Have other people always seen me the way I see myself now? 'Good evening. How are you? I'm Alison Jones, and I have had my head up my arse for my entire life.'

'*We know!*'

Would that be everyone's reaction? What do people really think of me? Darren Davies, petty thief, small-time crook, he seems to think I'm interesting enough to talk with, but I bet he'd change his tune quicker than a lightning bolt if he knew the truth about me and what I did to his poor little friend Tom Findlay. How big and fast a U-turn would that be? Someone once told me that how we see ourselves is usually very different from how others see us. If we think we're awful, others, curiously don't tend to. If we think we're absolutely bloody amazing, others think we're awful. That sort of thing.

Ah, the great philosophical questions which have kept psychologists and philosophers busy for hundreds of years, and no doubt will for hundreds more, long after the ripples in my pond are gone and long-forgotten.

Philosophy; the fundamental nature of knowledge, reality, and existence. What truly fascinating concepts to be concerned with. And one of the biggest questions of all is whether, if you had your time over, you would do anything differently. Personally, if I had *my* time over, I'd like to think I'd make very different choices indeed, but who's to say? Maybe I'd still be sitting here planning my own death before the brutality of disease takes over and calls the shots instead.

In truth, I always had some vague idea that people who killed themselves were mostly just attention-seeking cowards, unable or unwilling to take responsibility and face up to what was wrong in their lives, as the preferable alternative to actually flinging themselves off the mortal coil. I never imagined what it would feel like to get to that place in your head where nothing and no-one matters, where the only peace you can find is in oblivion, and the only place that makes sense to go, in preference to sticking around to face the music, is whatever the fuck you might find at the other end of the mortal coil.

Yet here I am. And, since the word coward keeps cropping up, I may as well wear the hat that fits me.

My heart's desire now is to do one of the few things I still have control over. I *will* end my own life and that can be the fitting finale to everything. It will be brutal for my friends, of course, not to mention my poor mother, but it's still the best alternative for all, I think; far better than watching me quickly deteriorate to a 'cabbage' state; a shambolic, pitiful point of no return. Nobody deserves the heartbreak of watching someone they love going through that, and being forced to live with that memory or being forever condemned to trying to transcend it, and cling to what was better instead. That's a lot of work.

Suicide will be easier for my mum to bear, and I'll have paid the ultimate price, albeit in the most cowardly way, for the horrible things I've done.

I'm already a coward. May as well be hung for a sheep as a lamb then. Having checked my life insurance policy I've found that now I'm a few years into it, it does indeed pay out on death by suicide. So I don't have to compromise my dignity in order to get the car paid off, and a host of other bills. There's even a small, separate funeral policy that I took out when I grew up a little and realised the full impact and magnitude of my father's untimely death for those who were left behind to scrabble to pay for the 'arrangements,' until the insurance company coughed up.

In the settled silence, there's nothing but the sound of Badger's snoring to punctuate the night. Quietly, the realisation daws that I am completely at peace with my decision and, finally, with myself. I don't dwell on how I might have thought about my own demise had I not taken the massive moral swerve that rendered my life of little value anyway. I've never had time for what-if's. Life is too short. Oh, the irony, *yet* again!

They say guilt, un-confronted, can mutate and turn to cancer. If that's the case, it seems I was 'fast-tracked.' Karma, as some would call it, came to claim me before my guilt even had full time to fester. Maybe there really is some truth in it after all, the karmic wheel, the notion that whatever folly (or monstrosity) you put out into the world gets absorbed, turned around, and then delivered back to you by way of a fate-created penalty; a universal, smack-in-the-face justice.

And maybe, just maybe, once we're dead, we get to find the answers to all those questions we have no proper answers for here on earth. Maybe there's an oracle somewhere, a great big set of encyclopaedias we get to look at, that chronicle the solutions to the world's biggest mysteries, or those that fascinated us personally, as we were growing up. Like what really happened to the dinosaurs? Are there people on other planets? Did that man the entire world will never stop talking about *really* murder the family next door? Is there really an all-forgiving God? How many years does the earth have left before it implodes or explodes under the burgeoning strain of relentless disrespect from the human race?

And which will be first past the post? World oblivion, or scientists finding a cure for *glioblastoma multiforme*?

I'm so glad now that I've done the things I've needed to do while I'm still coherent and 'of sound mind.'

The first was to write a letter to the police, explaining everything that happened. I called Evan Hunter, my solicitor, and got him to witness it, and I've charged him with making sure the police get it after I'm gone, because Tom Findlay's mother deserves to know what happened to her boy, and where he is.

I also wrote a letter to Simon Westrupp, the man who deserved as much as anyone else to get an explanation for why I hid the truth from him, from the outset, and then kept him firmly at arm's length after that fateful dinner. He was a lovely man who wanted to like me, but I gave him nothing of myself, and would only talk about superficial things, whenever he called. Just one more reason on the long list of why I'm such a disgrace, as a human being. At least he will soon understand.

I've written a letter to my mother too, asking for her forgiveness, because if there really is some kind of miserable afterlife where I'm now condemned to dwell, I may just be able to endure it if the person who always loved and understood me best still loves, understands *and* forgives me. I hope she will make it to that place, in spite of the disbelief, confusion and pain she will undoubtedly have to hack through, to get there.

Mum is very emotional. She's always ranting, crying or giggling uncontrollably at something that's going on in the world. She's the only person I know who cries at sad soap opera storylines. She's been crying endlessly over this brain tumour thing, and she's going to be desperately, immeasurably upset at the outcome as I've chosen it. She will be beyond devastated. But, as I've told her, this is my choice. It's what I really want, my heart's desire, and she mustn't beat herself up over not watching me every second. Nobody can do that, it's far too demanding.

I've made all the arrangements for the disposal of my lovely house and its contents. I know what I'm going to do with the proceeds of that, and the insurance. Evan Hunter has sorted it all out, and made it all legally binding.

And I've made arrangements for my beautiful Badger. That was the hardest plan to make, that's one the thing that gets me. Leaving my gorgeous boy. It's the only thing that hurts anymore. With his quiet gifts of patience, love and loyalty, he showed me what true love really was. How ironic, again, that at the end of everything I did, motivated purely by that love, I'm now choosing to leave him in the saddest way.

I'm entrusting Simon to ensure my beloved dog has a good home with worthy, deserving people who will cherish and adore him. Whatever his feelings towards me will be, I have no doubt that Simon is the best person possible, to do the right thing by Badger. And wherever I end up, if anywhere at all, the one thing that will come with me and stay is the gratitude I feel for having had Badger in my life. It was the greatest privilege to love him, and to have his love in return.

I hope my explanation will resonate, when the shock subsides. My solicitor, Evan, will look after my mum. That wonderful, big bear of a man will wrap her up in condolences and comfort, till the worst of the shock subsides, and he will help her to pick up the pieces, after that.

One of the hardest parts of all this, has been telling Evan that I'm dying. The sadness in his face really hit home to me, and I realised that for a brief time, I'd quite forgotten that I was more than just a client to him. He has known me since I was a child. He was a really good, trusted friend of my dad's, and since Dad died Evan has always fought my corner, stepping in when he thought I needed support with all kinds of things, not just legal matters. He's never been more than a phone call away, and I have to acknowledge that this is a devastating turn of events for him, and not just on a professional level. I couldn't tell him about my plans to take my own life, because that would have been far too unfair to him.

There will be a few surprises, when the will is read. I hope I'm weaving a positive legacy, and nobody who misses out will feel too cheated. Oh, to be a fly on the wall, when everything comes to light. Perhaps I will be. After all, with such a shaky system of belief, who's to say I won't be surprised enough to find myself hovering around, in some form, to bear witness from a different dimension, from a different room, or from just the other side of a rainbow bridge?

And so it ends, any time now. I've decided to spend my last conscious moments indulging in one of my happiest little pleasures, listening to two of my jazz idols together, Count Basie and Duke Ellington, as they tinkle and swing their way through Battle Royal on repeat play. And, as I sit here with my large, last-ever glass of cool, crisp chardonnay, waiting for the worst *(or the best?)* to happen, I find I'm at peace with it all.

Life will go on, the world will keep turning, and one day, hopefully, the people who loved me will look back on me with thoughts no more complex than that love. Once the grief and disbelief have diminished, hopefully what's left will be the simple, unsullied memory of someone unremarkable but lovable; a woman who simply made bad choices, but who made sure she paid for her crimes.

I hope that when the dust settles my legacy will carry with it an understanding that what happened was simply a series of catastrophic events, all underpinned by stupid acts and daft decisions. It wasn't an orchestrated catalogue of evil deeds that even the most twisted of people would struggle to dream up and execute. I hope those who know me will appreciate my inability to behave with such malicious intent. And those who don't know me? Well, it doesn't matter much what they think, but I hope they too will forgive me in time. It would be nice to be remembered, if not well, then certainly without rancour or judgement.

Sleep, I'm now prepared for. Pain, I'm now prepared for. Judgement? Well, I'm ready for that too, in whatever form it takes.

So no more nights then, of waking and shaking in a clammy cold sweat, with the smell of dank earth in my nostrils. No more nights of jolting awake, from the nightmare of being buried alive, and fighting through the night to get my breath back.

Badger stirs briefly in my arms and I lay my cheek against his. He doesn't feel my quiet tears as he settles back to sleep. I raise my glass gently, in a final salute to the Duke and the Count, as the drowsiness comes to claim me and it's time to say goodnight.

33

- Barbara -

Well, if you'd blown at me through a straw I'd have gone clean off the bloody chair, when that solicitor said what he did. I think I must have sat there with my mouth hanging open like some kind of half-wit. Sometimes, when words dangle in the air like that, you just want to reach out and grab them, examine them, and say them over and over again or get someone else to, to make sure they're real. I think we all wanted to do that, right then.

Everyone's reaction was the same. Voices all clashing and falling over each other, all of us wanting to know if it was a joke, just another sick thread in the wicked web of a madwoman who'd already had us all distraught with shock and grief in the days and weeks after most of what she did came to light.

Turns out it wasn't a joke at all. Alison Jones really *had* arranged for her lovely big house and all her personal effects to be sold, with the proceeds being divided equally between Tom Findlay's mother Marla, and my Darren. After being reassured that it was in fact true, we all just sat there in silence, staring at the solicitor like he had an extra head.

You could have heard a pin drop in that bloody office, even onto that thick fancy carpet, and I think the solicitor Evan Hunter expected that reaction, because he didn't seem at all ruffled by it. He smiled actually, a little bit, while the importance of what he'd told us all sank in. I don't know what he said to Alison when she gave him her instructions, whether he advised her against it or not, but I'm guessing he was privy to the knowledge about what she'd done to little Tom, too, so maybe this was all his idea. Waiting a month for the will to be read, maybe that was his idea too. We certainly needed time to let the dust settle before being able or willing to respond to a high-handed summons from her bloody solicitor.

'Whose idea was it, Mr Hunter, to do all this?' I asked.

'Oh, it was Alison's, I do assure you, Mrs Davies. These were her wishes. She wasn't influenced one way or another by anyone or anything, other than what she already had in her head as the proper thing to do. And she was, brain tumour notwithstanding, of perfectly sound mind. I am completely satisfied of that.' And he smiled in such a way that we had no doubt he was right. He was a most reassuring man, in his own efficient way.

'Is it likely to be contested?' Simon asked.

'What, the will? Absolutely not, Mr Westrupp. It will not be contested. Ms Jones *was* of perfectly sound mind, and she stipulated that no contests would be entertained. The only person who could have contested it in any case was her mother, and Alison was very clear that she wanted her mother to accept the terms of the will. I have spoken with Mrs Jones and she is in accordance with Miss Jones' wishes for the distribution of her estate.'

Silence settled again in that office, like the heaviest coat you'd ever want to wear.

Evan Hunter went on to add, 'Mr Westrupp, there is another private letter, specifically for you.' He handed Simon another letter, which Simon tucked straight away into his shirt pocket. It didn't look like he wanted to open it on the spot, which was fair enough. It was nobody else's business, what was in it.

Marla Findlay suddenly stood up. 'I'm sorry, but I can't sit here. I can't get my head around this. First I find out that my son's been bloody murdered, then I find out he's been thieving his way around the town thanks to someone far too old for him meddling in his life where he didn't belong, and now this. I need to leave. Walk. Run. Scream. Anything but bloody sit here.'

Evan Hunter nodded to her. 'I'll give you a call in the coming week, Mrs Findlay, to discuss the arrangements going forward. Thank you for coming.'

She gave him a tight little smile, and a curt nod of her head. Then, without acknowledging any of us, she tore out of the office like a fox being chased by a hound.

Darren looked at me. I could see he was absolutely speechless. He couldn't think of a single thing to say, and neither could I. If I was shocked, how must *he* be feeling? I stared back at him, shaking my head. Normally I'm a woman of enough words when it matters, but even I was at a complete loss for what to say right then. So we stared at one another, like a couple of head-shaking, clueless numpties.

Eventually the solicitor spoke again, assuring us that he would be there to answer any questions they might have, the beneficiaries, and those who'd been given direction.

That didn't include me, of course. I was only there because Darren wanted me to be. None of it was anything to do with me, really. But I'm glad he asked me to go, because as I looked across at my son, all baffled and confused, I knew he'd probably have missed picking up on half of what was said, purely through the shock of being told that he'd inherited enough money to buy himself a house, from someone he barely knew and had actually attempted to rob, who had in fact killed his friend just before she jumped on the one-way train to wherever the hell she's ended up, in whatever life comes next. You couldn't make it all up, really. So it's just as well I was there, because I knew I wouldn't forget a single thing that was said, even if Darren couldn't make sense of it.

Evan Hunter then stood up, giving us all the feeling that we'd been dismissed as summarily as we'd first been summoned, so we all stood as well and got ready to leave. He shook hands with us all and said he'd be in touch again in due course.

As we left the office I suggested to Darren and Simon that we all go across the street and get a coffee. They both agreed. With Marla Findlay long gone, no doubt struggling somewhere with her own thoughts, it was just the three of us that landed in the coffee shop to talk things over.

We ordered our coffees and sat down to wait, and still nobody said anything. It was like we were all grappling really hard, to get to grips with what had happened. We all knew how each other felt, so the silence wasn't uncomfortable, just a bit odd, as if we all knew it was too intense but none of us really knowing how to break it.

Eventually it was Simon who spoke first. 'I hope Marla's alright.' I remembered then that she was his sister, and of course he would be worried about her dashing off like that. I told him he should try to ring her on his mobile phone. He did try, but it just rang out. If it was ringing in front of her, she was ignoring it, and I couldn't say I blamed her for that. But that little interlude did manage to break the ice that had felt like it was forming and spreading all across the top of us all.

Finally having a cue to speak meant both myself and Darren piped up at the same time. We both then stopped, looked at one another, and Darren nodded to me to continue.

'I'm sure she's alright, but it's a lot to take in, isn't it, off the back of the news she's already had? The poor woman must be feeling completely swamped by all this. I can hardly get my head around it myself, and it doesn't even relate to me directly.'

Darren leaned forward. 'It does Mum, it relates to you because it relates to me, and you *were* mentioned in the letter. So she was thinking about you too. Alison, I mean.'

Alison. Alison Jones. A woman I barely knew from a bar of bloody soap, but she's put so many of us through such a ridiculous range of emotions, in such a short space of time. It feels like a pendulum swinging, from one mad extreme to the other, and all this has got me wondering if I'm losing my *own* bloody marbles.

First she kills Tom Findlay, then she covers it up, then she manages to admit to it after she's dead, and then leaves whopping great bloody legacies to make amends. No. You really *couldn't* make this up. It's the oddest thing I've ever heard of in all my years on this earth. But then, she did have a brain tumour, so who knows?

To her it probably all made sense, and how can anyone truly say they can get inside someone else's head, who's not quite right in it? Why would you even try to understand someone like that? Sometimes I think it doesn't do to dwell on these things, because it feels like being driven round the bend, in a car you can't slow down.

I watched my son, you know, as he took that call. The one from Marla Findlay on that awful Monday morning, telling him the police had been round and told her what had happened to Tom. I'll never forget watching his face as he listened to what was being said.

'Hiya Marla,' he said at first, upbeat enough, but then he went so still, so frozen, and I knew, with his face going the colour of concrete, that it was bad news. When he finally hung up the phone, after what felt like far too long, he was crying, proper like. It wasn't just a few quiet tears, but outright heaving, rasping bloody sobs, and I didn't have to ask him. I knew, right there and then, that Tom Findlay was dead.

I watched my boy crumple like a paper bag. It doesn't matter how big they get, how strong they might be, or how bloody belligerent they are at times, when your kids are in pain, there's nothing on this earth that you wouldn't do, to stop it. And I couldn't stop it. There was nothing I could say that would be able to undo or somehow make it less than what it was, this terrible, terrible thing. All I could do was sit there. I was too afraid to touch him, because there were so many emotions in those tears, and rage was one of them. I saw rage, self-loathing, and hatred so pure it literally stopped me from speaking. I felt afraid of him then, for the first time ever. I felt that if I touched him, he might just rear up and tear me to pieces.

So, what did I do? Well, I made us a cup of tea. That's what we do around here. When there's a crisis, a trauma, bad news and the like, we put the bloody kettle on, and strangely enough it usually does seem to help.

So I handed Darren a sweetened mug of tea, which I firmly advised him to drink, and he did. I half expected him to throw it at me, or at the wall instead, but he didn't, and that tea did actually have a calming effect, because by the time he'd finished it, he had his breathing under control again.

'Mum, I just can't make any sense of it. Marla says that Alison Jones killed Tom. She killed him by accident, that day we were there and I left him. She hit him with that fry pan, and she killed him, and she covered it up.

'She died on Saturday night, Mum. Alison took a massive overdose on Saturday night, right after her mum had gone out for a few hours, and she just never woke up again. She left a fucking letter for the plod, confessing to it, and telling them where to find him. They did, Mum. They found him this morning. He was buried on top of someone else, in a recent grave, in a cemetery near the National Park.'

Tears had slid down Darren's face in silent streams. But his grief, his confusion, his devastation, oh God, that was a terrible thing for any mother to have to witness.

Sometimes watching the range of human emotions on someone's face can be a bit like watching a film. Different moods and feelings come and go, and you get a glimpse of what the character is dealing with. They're actors, in films, and they're clever enough to portray the right range of emotions so the viewer can understand what they're really thinking as they're playing their parts.

My son's face was just full of emotions, all fighting for top spot, but that was no act. What I saw that morning was conflict, mostly. Like trying to look at both sides of a coin at the same time, trying to figure out how you could do it, or what the point of it would even be. Just conflict and confusion, as he struggled to make sense of what he'd been told.

I knew he'd got to know Alison, visiting her at home a couple of times. I don't think the two of them were what you'd class as 'close' in any way, but I sensed that he'd mended a fence, in a manner of speaking. She'd forgiven him, which meant the world to him, I know, and he found her interesting to talk to. He knew she had a brain tumour, and she'd told him there was no coming back from it, and it was killing her pretty fast.

But she didn't tell him she was planning to take her own life, and that's what she did, in the end. It was a big shock to him, on the back of everything else, and we learned later how painful, strung-out and frightening her death must have been. Even when you choose it in full knowledge of the facts, dying like she did in agony from all those tablets, and all alone, it's a truly terrible thing. To choose that option, over dying in relative comfort in a warm supportive hospice, that woman must have been in absolute torment.

At first I thought it was fitting. When we first got the news of her death and what she'd done to that poor lad, and were struggling to digest what we'd been told, I just thought Alison Jones was the world's biggest coward. As for Darren, he wanted to go to the morgue, find her body and tear the arms and legs from it and smash her over the head with them, even though she was already dead. He said he felt like he could do that physically, like he had so much energy it was the only thing he wanted to do. He didn't know how else to use it.

Later on, when I'd had a fair few quiet moments to really think about it all, I just found the whole situation unbearably sad for all concerned, even for her. I think Darren did too, once his rage gave way to grief, and not just for poor Tom Findlay.

Now, a year down the line, I can only describe the feelings I have about it all as bittersweet. How else could you describe something as tragic and wonderful all at the same time? Bittersweet; it's the only word that works.

I know how deeply betrayed Darren first felt by Alison. She was someone he'd come to like, in the brief times they spent together talking about God knows what. She'd always waved away his attempts to talk about Tom Findlay or that day he and Darren were at the house. But Darren let her off the hook, because of the brain tumour. He didn't want to push it, in case it distressed her or made things worse. But now we both know why she kept refusing to talk about it. She was well and truly *on* the bloody hook, wasn't she? And she would've known what everybody else knows; that most crimes eventually get discovered. Her heart must have been in her mouth, that Darren might twig and somehow see through all that smoke and bloody mirrors.

They've got all kinds of sophisticated stuff going on now, like DNA and all those other scientific comings and goings, and they can link criminals to crimes a lot easier nowadays than they ever used to, even crimes that were committed years ago. It's amazing really.

Alison Jones probably knew her time at the crossroads was coming, and maybe she just couldn't face the race, with the win being one of two outcomes; discovery, or a one-way descent into death. She knew she only had one other choice and she took it. She took her own life because she didn't want anyone's pity, scorn, or condemnation. She was already condemned, so she wanted to go out on her own terms. Cowardly or not, I can't say I blame her for that.

Brain tumour or no brain tumour, I do think prison is a better alternative than losing or taking your life over something you did wrong, though, no matter how bad it was. I think any kind of life is better than no life, but what do I know? I've never been faced with that kind of choice. I can't imagine doing anything like what

Alison did to Tom, but I bet there was a time when she didn't think she could either. So who's to say what *any* of us might do in the same situation? If I'd done something like that, if I was in her position, how would I want to play it, especially if I was staring down the barrel of a horrid death in any case?

I think I'd have done exactly what she did. I'd have ended it on my own terms.

Forgiveness is a wonderful thing, and the world needs a lot more of it. We all have a choice about whether or not to forgive those who have sinned against us, just like the Lord's Prayer invites us to do. Some are better at the whole forgiveness thing than others.

Marla Findlay is the most amazing example of that. She forgave my boy for abandoning hers, and leaving him to meet his fate. And she forgave Alison Jones for what she did. I don't know how she managed all that, I really don't. It's more than I could have done in her position. Even though it was manslaughter, and not outright murder (Alison didn't intend to kill the lad, and I do believe that), it's still a massive stretch, to expect to be forgiven for that and what came after.

Maybe it was easier for Marla to forgive her for it because she's dead. The only loser, nursing a grudge against someone who's dead, is yourself really. It's pointless, isn't it, all that bitterness? It just turns to bloody cancer for people who can't let go of it.

Marla Findlay made a conscious decision to forgive her trespassers, those who'd let her down in the worst possible way. I met her for the first time at Evan Hunter's office, and even thought she was clearly still grieving hard for her little boy, she seemed to be at peace with not expecting to ever achieve much in life. Until she stormed off (being literally unable to sit next to Darren, as one reason I think), my impression of her was a quiet, gentle woman, who'd had the thin end of a wedge for a long time, but who'd more or less accepted it.

But Alison Jones' legacy changed all that. Once she'd got over her disbelief and shock, Marla stood up straight and true, came up with an idea, and put it into action with a speed and a zeal I've not seen in anyone for a very long time. It was like someone had put a bomb under the woman.

The result was the Tom Findlay Foundation for Missing Persons, set up in what used to be an abandoned storehouse near to the town centre. Marla bought it for that purpose. After she'd forgiven Darren, he'd mentioned to her that I was good at colour schemes, so she got me to go down there and give some advice about decorating the place once the builders had left. She said she didn't have much imagination for that kind of thing, herself. I didn't believe that for one minute, but I could see she was already occupied with a million other things, so I stepped in and did everything I could to help. I even went down there and made tea all weekend long for the gang of volunteers that were all painting, sewing curtains, making rag rugs and everything on the working bee, before the opening day.

It was such an amazing atmosphere that weekend, happy music playing, everyone cheerful and slogging away like pit-ponies, to make sure everything would be perfect and ready. By the time the opening day rolled around, I'd signed up myself as a volunteer at the Centre.

That was a great day. A monumental day for Tom Findlay, God rest his soul. Thanks to his mother, that lad lives on now, in the hearts of so many other hopeful families who are searching for loved ones. Most of those cases do have a positive outcome I'm pleased to say, in terms of life versus death, even if a found person chooses to stay away.

I just do three days a week down there, and Marla actually pays me for doing it. Most of the staff consists of volunteers but she offered me a paid part time post, as Volunteer Co-ordinator, and I was thrilled to accept.

As well as helping the families, I also organise the roster of volunteers for the various tasks they all get to share, like cleaning or admin, or putting up posters and the like. Some even go door-to-door in some areas. I look forward to going to work each day, which is more than most people can say, and I've met some truly lovely people.

For the other two days of the week, I'm doing an interior design diploma by distance learning. It's a lot of work, but I'm really enjoying it. The money Marla pays me covers the cost of the course, and once I've got my diploma I can hopefully get some work doing that. In the past few months I've had my whole house decorated, thanks to Darren and Pat, and now Pat's on about selling up and moving somewhere a bit nicer, just to suit the two of us, now that Darren's moved out.

Maybe a new place would be a good idea. I'm thinking about it. A year or eighteen months ago I'd have bitten his hand off, because our house was so tatty and horrible, and full of bloody ghosts. But now it's lovely, all nicely redecorated, and I feel like it's a new place anyway, so we'll have to see.

Darren's come on so much in the past year. He's like a different bloke altogether these days. Training as a vet, thanks to arrangements Alison put in place for that too, has been the making of him, and that dog, Badger, is the love of his life.

It's funny how things turn out. When Simon offered Badger to Darren, we all thought he was having a bloody laugh. But he was serious. I think that nice man knew exactly what Darren needed. Not just a home, but a companion, someone to love, someone to need *him*. It was way too soon for him to have a woman in his life, in my opinion, but a dog? Perfect solution, especially since Darren was buying a flat and dog ownership's not the same kind of problem for owners as it is for tenants.

He and Badger come for their tea on Friday nights after work, and they stop by Pat's chippy on the way to pick it up. There's always a sausage for that lovely dog and a spring roll for me, and my boy always reaches over, counts out six chips, puts them on a plate and watches me eat them, then he piles dozens more onto the plate and laughs at me as I tuck into them too. It's a little ritual we seem to have started. I know it's only temporary, that his Friday nights are only on loan to me until he meets a nice girl, when his weekends will then be taken up with different things. But for now, I'm just grateful for what I have of him. Maybe if he meets the right girl, we can still have a few Friday nights together, and *all* have fish and chips.

He seems happy, and as settled as he can be, in his new life. I'm so proud of how he's turned things around. I'm sad sometimes, of course, that it took what it took to make that happen. I wouldn't be human if I wasn't, would I? But I've also learned that sometimes people do have to go through a fire, to have all the surface shit burned off them, and come out all shiny and new. Like the phoenix rising from the ashes! Darren is ten times the man he was before the Tom Findlay incident. Would he have found his way without all that happening? I doubt it. Would something else have happened that turned him around? It's impossible to say.

What we have is what we have, and I think it's safe to say that those of us left standing, in the aftermath of Tom Findlay going missing, and being found and properly put to rest, are all better people for it. Alison Jones sprinkled a bit of magic around us when she died. She did a truly terrible thing, but she more than made up for it, and when I look around me, at how Darren's, Marla's, and even *my* life has changed, there's so much promise now, so much potential that wasn't there before, and maybe never would have been.

Even Simon Westrupp says he's a better man for honouring the last wishes of a woman he'd only known for a very short time. He took the leap of faith she begged him to, and gave a broken man the opportunity to better himself in a truly meaningful way. Because he did that, Darren is well on his way to having the kind of life he always dreamed of but once thought he'd never be able to have. And Simon's watched his sister come into her own too, doing something really meaningful, and on a really big scale.

They say that everything happens for a reason. Maybe Alison Jones was never meant to have a future, and maybe Tom Findlay wasn't either. In the grand scheme of things, maybe what happened was what *needed* to happen, for those who were languishing in lives half-lived, to be able to stand up straight and see over the wall. Perhaps it was all pre-written in the stars, or the cards, or whatever belief you might have would suggest. Destiny, for want of a better word?

Many times, I've tried to put myself in Alison Jones' position. She didn't have a family of her own, her dog was her 'cherished one,' like my kids are mine, like any mother's kids are hers. Badger was Alison's baby, and although I do love my cat, I've never felt passionate about an animal myself. I do have childless friends who treat their pets like the children they never had, and as much as I can't imagine it for myself, I've seen enough of it going on, and I do understand it. You feel what you feel. You love what you love, and I can imagine how it must feel if that's your 'child' and you realise someone's hurt it.

Would I go at someone with a heavy metal object who had hurt my children? Damn right I bloody would, with no hesitation. Show me a mother who *wouldn't* take someone apart for hurting her child. So why would a dog be any different to its owner who loved it as much as a child? I don't suppose it would. Just because I can't imagine feeling a love like that for an animal, that doesn't mean it isn't real to the people who do, and who am I to imply that it's not as important just because it's not a human child? That's just arrogance, and I might have a lot of bloody faults, but that's not one of them. I've never presumed to know more than anybody else about anything at all, or behave as if I did.

So it's not what Alison did, that I have a problem with, because I understand that. What I really struggled with, in the beginning (and sometimes I still find it hard to believe, even now) was what she did after. I know that panic set in and she stopped thinking clearly, and who knows whether the brain tumour had any influence over that? Again, I don't have the right to judge how she felt, or what she did, or why. All I know is she paid the biggest price possible and before she bowed out of her life she did everything in her power to leave a legacy that mattered. She did have a moral conscience. The letters she wrote made that very clear.

What's more, the positives that have come out of this for so many of us make everything easier to bear. That's what Marla says, and if she can get to that place, after everything she has lost, there's no reason why the rest of us can't. Tom was her baby and she couldn't protect him, and I can't imagine what hell she still goes through about that, on certain dark nights when she's alone with her thoughts and feelings. But she found it in her heart to forgive, and she said what we've all been thinking, that as much as we'd like to hate Alison Jones for what she did, it's not very easy to do that, because the outcomes have been so good for so many people.

But there is a bit of sadness that will never truly leave us. It's that bitter-sweetness, a poignant feeling, as we all learn to let go of the worst of what happened, and give thanks for where we are now.

34

- Simon -

After we left Evan Hunter's office that day he read Alison's will to us all, I could feel her letter burning a hole in my shirt pocket. I couldn't bring myself to open it, in front of people I didn't know. I needed to be alone with it, so I could open it in the privacy of my own space.

Truth was, I didn't know how I felt about Alison Jones. Initially ignorant of her actions, I was certainly saddened by her illness and her death. It all popped up, and was here and gone, so quickly. We'd barely got to know one another and then, all of a sudden, it was crystal clear that we were never going to, and then she was gone. I'd been excited at the idea of having a new woman to spend time with. I had no clue what the possibilities were, no expectations of where it might lead. It just looked like being fun, and interesting, and I was looking forward to getting to know her better.

When I first found out what she'd done, it took me a very long time to get my head around it. The brutal coincidence of it involving my nephew was just part of the issue for me. Although I never really got to know Alison, I'd never have picked her as the sort who'd kill someone, even by accident, and cover it up. She seemed like a fairly calm person, not overly warm, but I had the feeling that she probably would be, once she got to know someone.

It had always been clear to me that she had endless love for Badger, her dog, and it seemed to me that a woman who could love an animal like that, with all the commitment a heart and soul could offer; well, someone like that couldn't be all bad.

That's what I kept clinging to, while my head tried to process what she'd done to Tom and, by default, to my whole family. Marla is making a decent fist of things, with the new foundation, but our parents will never get over losing Tommy. He was a loveable little rogue, and he certainly had his faults, but he was the light of their lives. I kept trying to reinforce for myself the images I had of Alison that showed the love she had for Badger, and the intentions behind the provisions she later put in place in her will, to try and make amends for her actions.

I didn't want to hate her for robbing our family of someone so unique and special, which is what little Tom was to us all. I wanted to be better than that, but I knew I wouldn't be able to resist letting the hate consume me if I didn't keep focussing on the good stuff about her that I somehow needed to keep reminding myself about, to counterbalance what she did and what it meant. I didn't want to go mad with rage, and grief that my poor little nephew had lost his life the way he did.

I also kept trying to tell myself, for a long time, that it was nothing to do with my lack of discernment, that I'm not such an appalling judge of character that I failed to see what was right under my nose. I kept telling myself there was nothing to see, and when I finally got to the point where I could let myself off the hook, I realised it actually was the truth. Even sociopaths and relentless serial killers have had wives or mothers that never had an inkling of the depth of their depravity, even when they lived under the same roof!

I had a vague notion that I knew what was in Alison's letter because we'd talked about her friend, Darren Davies. As I later found out, he'd been Tom's mate too, and he was pretty much the last person to see Tom alive, if you don't count Alison stuffing the poor little bugger into a cupboard.

Darren had been to see her a couple of times, I knew that much, but at the time I didn't know how she knew him, or what their relationship was. It never occurred to me to ask; it was none of my business really. But I often wonder, what if I *had* asked? Would she have told me everything? If I hadn't been so bloody determined to mind my own business, and had just asked her, would she have found the courage to confess, to ask me for help?

It was already far too late for poor Tom by then, but it might not have been for Alison, even with her terminal cancer. Instead of committing suicide in the loneliest, most horribly painful way, she could have had the chance to die in absolution, in comfort, in a hospice perhaps, with the people she cared for around her. She could have said goodbye properly to the people who loved her if she'd had the opportunity to ask for help. Did I deny her all that, in not asking her who Darren Davies actually was?

But I didn't ask, and she didn't say. Whenever I rang her, we talked about fairly innocuous things, like the plans she'd once had for her garden, and what was in the daily papers. All she ever said about Darren was that they were friends, and then she explained that he needed a break in life, he was the sort of bloke who'd appreciate a helping hand to make something of his life, and he had a deep love of animals. She asked me if I'd consider training him to be a vet. In all of those phone calls we had, she never once told me she'd been the victim of a burglary by anyone at all, let alone that one of those burglars was Darren, and the other was none other than my own nephew Tom!

It was Darren himself who filled in most of the gaps for me, after Alison died and Marla had been told by the police about her letter of confession. At first I just couldn't take it all in. It seemed incomprehensible to me that as an on-call vet, the dog I was called out to assess and treat had in fact been a victim of that burglary.

It seemed even more incomprehensible that she'd killed our Tom, and concealed the fact. I don't know if he was already dead, there in her under-stairs cupboard, when I went to her house that first time, but maybe not. Maybe that thump I recall hearing in the hallway was Tom's last plea for help. Maybe, all tied up and gagged in there, he heard or recognised my voice and tried to alert me the only way he could, by banging against the door.

How could I have known what had happened, though, or who'd been involved? How could I have had the faintest idea, when all I was there for, on call, was to assess and treat an injured animal? I had no clue about the person, the house, the circumstances, or anything else, and I couldn't have been expected to.

Alison seemed like a normal enough woman when I got there that night, not that I profess to be an expert on women. She seemed a little rattled, but who wouldn't be, on coming home to find their dog in that state? She was very emotional, and I just put that down to the shock of finding him like that. I'd be pretty upset myself, if it was me. Being devastated and acting on edge would be par for the course, wouldn't it? How could I possibly have known what was really going on in that house?

I can justify my actions fully, I know that now. But it did take a long time for me to get that place in my head where I could live with myself for not knowing. The simple fact was that nobody could foresee such a random, freakish set of coincidences. The knowledge will never relieve the desperate, endless sadness I feel, that my nephew was dead or dying just steps away from where I was standing, and I had no idea. That's something I'll never stop finding hard to live with.

I've had to really work, to equate Alison Jones with the acts she committed, even though I'd only met her a few times. A light impromptu plate of pasta with her once at her house couldn't really be classed as a 'date,' and on our first proper one we'd barely got talking when she collapsed at the table in the pub and ended up in hospital, diagnosed with a brain tumour! So it shouldn't have rocked me as hard as it did, that someone I hardly knew went and did what *she* did. But, somehow, it did. And it has meant a lot of soul searching for me.

I often wonder if it was realising that Tom Findlay was my nephew that tipped the balance for her, there in that restaurant. With a brain tumour, I don't suppose you can ever tell what influences behaviour, or when. Maybe she'd still have slid to the ground and had that fit if I'd sat there and said nothing much at all about anything. Who's to say?

People ask me if I feel relieved that we never got any further than we did before I found out what she'd done, but I never know how to respond to that. I know where they're coming from, and I suppose in some way they're implying I might have had a lucky escape. They may be right about that but personally, I don't see it that way.

I see that whole series of events as a monumental tragedy, not just for Tom, but for Alison too. She was an ordinary enough woman with an ordinary enough life, and then something extraordinary happened and she handled it badly. The end result was a devastating, tragic testament to a catastrophic lapse in moral judgement. Panic makes people do stupid things. Stress triggers people to make stupid mistakes. I know that. And she had a bloody brain tumour, so surely there has to be an element of forgiveness, somewhere, in all that. Maybe, in doing what she did, she was under the influence of a cancer that had already started eating away the rational part of her brain; the part that would otherwise have stopped her in her tracks and allowed her to consider different choices.

If only she'd confided in me when I first got there, about what had really happened, on that awful day. But common sense tells me she wouldn't have done something like that. We didn't even know each other.

If only Tom had been doing something else instead, on that day. If only she'd been stuck in traffic for another ten minutes and missed the lads entirely. If only they hadn't hurt Badger. My head still swims sometimes, with so many pointless 'if-only's,' even though they never help me reconcile anything. *If only, if only, the woodpecker sighs, the bark on the trees was as soft as the skies.*

So when I did finally open Alison's letter, I wasn't all that surprised at what it said.

'Dear Simon

I know you must hate me right now for what I've done, and I don't blame you. I've robbed you of your nephew, and when I hit him with that skillet, it never even occurred to me that he was a loved member of someone's family; that someone, somewhere, would be angry about what I did. I wasn't thinking at all. Blind rage had got the better of me.

I never meant for Tom to die. I really didn't, and I told the police that. All I wanted to do was give him a fright, but it backfired on us both in the worst possible way. Tom overpaid grotesquely, for the simple crime of being a burglar and a thief. He paid with his life, which is way too much, and I'm not sure that paying with mine would even up the balance even just a little a bit, but I want to bow out having left something worthwhile in my wake, not just the bitter taste of loss and betrayal. I want to heal that if I can, at least in some small way, and you'll know by now, the way in which I want to do it.

We talked a bit about Darren, you and I, in the phone calls we had, before I left, and I planted the seed with you about giving him a decent shot in life, a chance to make something of himself.

I got to know him a bit in my last couple of weeks. He came to visit a couple of times, and we talked about a lot of things, including what his life was like growing up and how he ended up on the wrong side of the law. It was all just a series of unhappy circumstances for him, Simon. Circumstances and stupid choices that had disastrous consequences and, of course, I know all about that.

Darren's not a bad man at all. He's just lost, and he needs someone to give him a break. I remember what you said about getting your inheritance, and how it paved the way for you to get out of the rut your life would otherwise have been. You got to train, to do something you really love, and I remember you telling me how great that felt.

Maybe you could pay that forward and give someone else that chance. I do believe Darren would make a good vet, and although I know I'm not in a position to ask for or expect anything from you, let me stress to you that this isn't about me. It's about offering a leg-up to someone who needs it, about putting something back in place of what I've taken; something that can enable a man adrift to make a useful contribution to society and reclaim his self-esteem in the process. You can do that. You're a good enough man to do that, and I think you would want to do it, for someone, if you could. Could you do it for your nephew's friend Darren? He loved Tom, I think, in his own way, not that he was capable of understanding or saying that.

I'm not talking about you bankrolling anything. I'm organising enough money to pay for Darren's training, if you would employ him alongside it, even part time, to encourage him to be the best he can be. Mentor him, Simon, and maybe one day he can be as lovely and meaningful a man as you are. I have a feeling that's possible, but we'll never know if we don't give it a shot. This is me begging for something, by the way. Begging is something I've never done before, other than begging all whose lives I've ruined, along with a God I've never been sure I actually believed in, for forgiveness for my sins.

Please, Simon, try not to remember the worst of me. If you choose to remember at all, please would you try to remember what's good? Remember me for loving my dog, which is how all this mess started. Remember me for liking animals more than

I thought long and hard about what she'd asked for, and I questioned everything about myself in the process. Did I really want a reminder of this strange, unfathomable woman, staring me in the face every day for the foreseeable future, at my workplace? Would I not be better to just turn my back on the whole horrible, wretched matter? Should I not just lay Tom to rest for good in my mind, and try to move forward? Would that even be possible?

Or could I find it within myself to salvage what I could for the truly tormented man, the self-confessed messed-up coward who ran off to save himself, leaving my nephew alone to die in a strange place? Could I help to heal his heartbreak, and could that help to heal my own heart in the process?

In the weeks that followed the revelations, I spent a lot of time with Marla, talking things through, and we covered a lot of the same ground many times. It felt endlessly sad and it was a real struggle, going over the same stuff over and over again.

But I came to realise that going over the same ground, however many times you feel the need to, really does help you to eventually process things properly. It's a form of therapy for post-traumatic stress, or so I've been told, and I think we were both feeling a lot of that, and Tom's sister Jenna was as well. We all cried so much in those early weeks, for all that we'd lost, for all that we wish we'd known or could have done, and for the fact that it was all too late to matter.

Rehashing everything hurt like hell every time we did it but we somehow needed to *keep* doing it until, eventually, it started to feel less horrible, and hurt a little less, and we found ourselves able to start remembering Tom more from a place of love than loss.

When I told Marla what Alison wanted for Darren, she didn't say anything for a long time, but when she finally pulled her gaze back from the middle distance and focussed on me again, she said something so profound it hit home to me in a way nothing she'd ever said to me before in our whole lives had ever done.

'I believe, Simon, that when there's a trauma or a tragedy that hurts us, we have to focus on ourselves, be accountable, and do all the soul-searching, the self-analysis, the counselling or whatever we need to do to get the healing process underway. I think that is critical but I do believe it only takes us so far, towards healing ourselves. I think what gets us the rest of the way to being healed is the perspective we gain from helping others who can suffer less themselves, if we give them what help we can.'

When I thought about it, I realised she was right. At some stage, you have to stop licking your own wounds and try and create something meaningful out of whatever's left, otherwise a terrible event would remain exactly what it was in its rawest form; a family tragedy, forever frozen in time, with a bitterness-laden heartache at its centre that would never go away.

I also realised that Alison Jones had known that too. So I resolved to try and have a meaningful talk with Darren Davies.

After getting his number from the solicitor, Evan Hunter, I rang Darren one night at home. He was surprised to hear from me, but we arranged for him to come to my practice the following lunchtime.

I asked him a lot of questions at that meeting, about himself mostly and about his life, and to give him his due he didn't hold back. He was candid about everything, especially about his mistakes, and he admitted that until he received Alison's legacy, he'd been under no illusions that life was going to treat him well, because he'd already stuffed things up for himself pretty badly.

When he said that he wanted to use Alison's money to buy a little place of his own, he brightened considerably. It was like watching a light bulb come on. He clearly valued the opportunity she'd given him, now that the truth of it had finally sunk in, and he wanted to make the most of it. There was no talk about fast cars, holidays abroad, new tattoos and nights in the pub getting legless. Instead, he talked about how he didn't want to let her down, or Tom, by squandering his one decent chance, and as he talked I began to see that with the right opportunities this man really could potentially make something of himself. I saw what Alison saw, and then I understood why it mattered.

I asked Darren about Badger and he literally flinched. Again though, he talked openly about what he'd done to the dog and I was surprised to see that he was trying not to cry. He was clearly completely disgusted with himself for hurting Badger. He felt so bad about it, the remorse was literally oozing out of his pores. He told me he'd have done anything at all to be able to take that back. And I believed him.

He told me that he struggled mightily at times with his ambivalence about Alison, but he wanted to 'come down on the right side of it all,' No fancy words, not exactly articulate, but the spoken thoughts of someone who had also done a lot of soul searching, just like the rest of us. None of us knew, in those early days, quite how to feel about Alison Jones, so I knew exactly what he meant.

So I did what Alison asked me, I took a leap of faith, and offered Darren the chance to train with me to become a vet. I explained to him that it meant years of hard training that he would have to pay for, but I would provide the practical, hands-on element and something of a wage, if he wanted the opportunity. He did cry then, this tough, tattooed man, and I could see how much it meant to him to have the chance to prove to someone in authority who believed in him, that he could in fact be successful at something.

He told me about his call centre work, being laid off, ending up dossing around and being unable to find his way back. I got a sense of how alone he was. Despite having a mum who obviously loved him, the relationship struggled because he found it hard to get on with her partner and all living under one roof had been difficult. He said that things had improved a bit lately, and that his mum's partner was in fact helping him to buy a good little flat. The sale was going through, so it seemed like the perfect time to offer him the chance to come and work at the practice. I suggested he work for a month, on full time minimum wage, to see if he even liked the work, then if he did, we could get him enrolled on the degree course and start his hands-on training at the practice, if that felt like what he'd want.

As he was leaving, he shook my hand and promised he wouldn't let me down. I had a very strong feeling he'd be true to his word, and he has been. For the past year, he's steadily learned and grown very well into the job, and eventually he'll be a qualified vet. If he stays on after he qualifies, I think we'll be lucky to have him. The look on his face, when I told him that, has so far been one of the greatest rewards of my life.

I also offered him Badger, who had been living with me but still needed a permanent home, which I was really too busy to give him. I wasn't sure what Alison would have thought about that, but it somehow felt like the right choice, in spite of what had gone before. Darren was a lonely man, about to start living in a flat by himself, an hour away from his mum and her partner, and without a decent circle of friends yet. When I asked him what he thought, he said he needed a bit of time to think about it. He wasn't sure whether the dog would be a constant reminder of everything he needed to try and put behind him.

But the following morning when he came into work, he said he did want to take him, explaining that he'd been awake most of the night thinking it over and had come to the conclusion that it was another opportunity to make amends to Alison and to Badger himself, by loving him as best he could and giving him the best home he could, and that I could bear witness to it if I'd let him bring Badger to work. So it was settled. A year on, and the two are inseparable.

Darren still doesn't have a big circle of friends, but he has met one or two decent-sounding people locally that he has the occasional pint with. For now, he is concentrating on his work and his studies. He's a credit to himself, and in the space of one year I've gone from doubting my own sanity over employing and training him, to feeling incredibly privileged to be a part of the journey of someone who is turning out to be a very gifted and remarkable man. His affinity with animals is extraordinary.

Employing Darren Davies has been as near to a perfect choice as I could ever have hoped for.

When I told him that, he stood in front of me with tears in his eyes. And I realised then, that despite all her faults, Alison had seen in Darren what he couldn't see in himself; potential. She'd been remarkably astute in her assessment of him. She'd been a debt collector, highly trained to get the measure of people quickly. She'd been bang on the money about Darren, and that made me lean just a little more to admiring her than condemning her. Sometimes, it's a fence I still struggle to choose not to sit on, even now.

Marla's centre, The Tom Findlay Foundation for Missing Persons, is also doing really well. It's still a new facility, in terms of its establishment, but it has already achieved national recognition for the work the team does, mostly through volunteering, in locating and reuniting missing persons with their families and friends.

Initially, immobilized by pain, grief and shock, my sister withdrew into an almost catatonic, barely functional state. Tom's funeral was desperately sad, and from there she descended into her own little world, and didn't look like coming back out. Friends, family, none of us had a clue how to get her to snap out of it. My niece Jenna came to stay with me for a while, because it was just too difficult for her to be at home with her mother in that state, because she was dealing with her own grieving process too. It really was the most difficult time we've ever gone through, as a family.

Overnight however, without any warning, Marla seemed to snap out of her fug of misery. My doorbell rang at seven o'clock one morning, and she was there on the doorstep, large as life. She'd showered, dressed, got made up, and was carrying brown paper bags. She announced she'd brought breakfast for us all, and would then run Jenna to school, before heading into Evan Hunter's office to 'talk turkey,' as she put it. She wouldn't say anything more.

A month later, she'd bought the little old storehouse in Division Street. Twelve weeks on from that, she had the builders in, and within the next two months the whole place was fully functioning with office spaces, meeting spaces, a leisure area, bedrooms and showers. The Tom Findlay Foundation for Missing Persons was officially up and running.

From that moment on, my sister was a force to be reckoned with. Gone was the careworn, directionless woman from before. In her place was a driven, dedicated powerhouse of purpose and resolve. The transformation was nothing short of incredible.

Marla has found her 'ecological niche' and, with it, the dedication to try to ensure that others going through the torment of wondering if their loved ones were safe could have support and encouragement not to believe the worst, until they had no choice.

Another lovely development for my sister was the arrival of an unexpected romance. Sergeant Eddie Pegg, who initially went to the house in the last hour of his day's shift with the news contained in Alison's letter to the police, found himself putting the kettle on for a distraught mother and sister and staying for most of the evening while they absorbed what they'd been told. The police had already sent a team out to the gravesite, to verify the letter's information, and they exhumed Tom and took his body to the morgue, where it was cleaned up and given some dignity. Marla was asked if she wanted to formally identify Tom, but she couldn't bring herself to do it, so I went.

That was the hardest thing I've ever had to do. Nobody wants to identify a body, especially one younger than themselves, with so much life left to live that they've been brutally robbed of. After seeing Tom like that, I didn't think I'd ever be able to swallow down the lump in my throat. It all felt so wrong somehow to see my lovely little nephew, usually so full of life and cheek, all still and silent, black and blue and barely recognisable as someone I'd loved for sixteen years.

Anyway, Sergeant Pegg started calling at the house on his way home from work, and I think he was a big part of Marla's recovery. It's funny how nothing happens for a long time, then everything happens at once. After years on her own, Marla was like a rudderless ship; going through the motions but without any real sense of purpose, other than raising her two kids by herself. She had no idea what life might offer her, beyond that. Then, as soon as she got underway with the Centre, Eddie Pegg was also in the new frame of her life.

I saw the easy friendship Eddie and Marla had, and how respectful and relaxed Eddie was with young Jenna. They all enjoyed one another's company, so when the heaving boat started righting itself, so to speak, it was clear to me that Eddie had an ongoing role to play in their lives, and that they were happy for him to do it.

There's talk of a wedding in the coming spring, with me as Best Man. It will be seven or eight months from now, so roughly two years from when Tom left our lives. Eddie has two daughters from his previous marriage, but they're both in their twenties, and they've been away from home for a while now. It'll be nice for Jenna to have a couple of older step-sisters for a bit of extra guidance if and when she needs it, but without having to live with too many strangers at once. So much has already happened too fast, for that young lass.

Wherever Alison Jones is now, I hope she can see the end results of the web she wove. I don't know what she envisaged at the time, but she certainly couldn't be unhappy with the outcomes we have now. Lives have been transformed in the best ways possible, out of the worst kind of tragedy. A true silver lining.

Am I sorry I met her? I don't know if I'll ever be able to honestly answer that question. It could have been any vet that was called to her house that day. It would still have been my nephew, killed and concealed, my family ripped apart, but I would not have been involved, other than as an informed relative. It would have been a completely different experience.

So many questions, to which there are no answers, and probably never will be. Another thing we all have to live with, as best we can.

You can torture yourself forever with what-ifs, but what we have now, like it or not, are a series of outcomes that would never have occurred if Tom hadn't lost his life. So it's a fools' errand, trying to predict how things would be if the events that brought us all to these points in our lives hadn't happened.

We all meet up once a month, Darren, Badger, Barbara, Pat, Marla, Eddie, Jenna and me. We have a pub dinner and a couple of beers somewhere dog-friendly, and each time we do, it gets a little easier to be happy. Each time we meet, a few more of our backstage, drag-down demons get laid to rest, and our smiles are just that little bit more heartfelt, our goodbye hugs just that little bit tighter.

Having these new people in my life has made it richer and more meaningful, and that's *my* slice of Alison's legacy. I think she knew that helping Darren would give my own life more meaning. I think she would also be happy to know how big a gift it is to me, to see my sister so changed for the better, with purpose and love in her life.

It's all in the way you choose to view it. In the beginning, I was so angry and confused I literally couldn't speak about it all. But time softens sharp edges and heals hard wounds, and if my sister can forgive another woman the worst of sins, what kind of man would I be if I couldn't at least try to follow her example? It's been a journey of peaks and troughs, and one I'd never wish to repeat. But I'm profoundly grateful for it, in so many ways.

As a family, we'll miss Tom forever, but I think it's safe to say that the silver lining within the dark cloud of that terrible summer is truly remarkable. The sun has come up, and the show will go on, and we are all better people for having been through the storm.

Rest in peace, Alison Jones. I think I've managed to get myself to a place where I do think you deserve that.

35

- Darren -

I could sit here all day, staring out at the ocean. Some days I do spend hours, just sitting, watching the waves crashing onto the rocks. It gives me a peace I once thought I'd never have.

There's no beach at this end of the bay, only rocks, but it's not far of a walk to a decent stretch of sand. I find that sometimes it's enough just to have a window open in my flat, to hear the crashing sea, hear the gulls, and smell the salty air, and I don't need to go out and walk. I don't feel as driven and restless as I used to. Nowadays I can sit still, and that's enough.

It's not enough for Badger though, who's always up for 'just one more' walk or run along the beach. One of the neighbours here reckons it's no good, having a dog like this in a first floor flat, but she can sod off, the interfering old bag. Badger's as happy as a pig in shit, and everyone else loves him to bits.

He's the darling of the block. This Christmas gone, he had so many chews, marrowbones, pigs' ears, squeaky bloody toys and the like, off the neighbours. Some of them even wrapped them up in Christmas paper for him! Bonkers, they are, but in the best way. Every Monday night Badger gets at least one bone or pile of scraps from someone's Sunday roast around here. Spoiled rotten he is, and it's all good. I think Alison would be chuffed.

He's a really good dog, very loyal, and great company. I'd be lost without him, now. He's my best friend in all the world. Being able to take him to work is a real bonus, and that was the deal breaker really. You really *can't* have a dog in a first floor flat if you're going to leave it alone all day, but Simon welcomed me to take him in with me.

It's an hour on the train each way, to both the university and the surgery and back, so the days are long, and my evenings and weekend are all tied up with study and revision, but I can't believe what I'm learning.

On average, a dog has 320 bones in its body, half again as much as a human. Even cats have more bones than humans. It's incredible. I never knew how many complaints an animal can suffer from, either, so I'm always amazed by what comes through the door at the practice. On the days when I'm at the surgery, no two are ever alike and they all fly by so quickly. I'm usually told its home-time hours before I feel ready to go, and Simon always laughs at me, saying I'd still be there at midnight if they let me.

He's right. I bloody would. Friday always comes around so fast. I don't know where the time goes, but it's so absorbing. Whoever it was that said 'time flies when you're having fun' wasn't wrong.

But don't get *me* wrong. It's heartbreaking sometimes, like when an animal has to be put down, or you have to tell the owner it's not going to get better and its days are numbered. It's Simon or one of the other vets who does that. I'm a long way from being qualified or ready yet to take on that kind of responsibility. It's hard enough seeing pets and injured wildlife in such a state that putting them down is the only kind thing left to do. It still hurts to hear the words, 'there's nothing more we can do.' Saying them to someone about to lose their best friend in all the world, and watching their faces fold in on themselves, is still way beyond me, just yet.

Uni is hard too, because I'm a mature student, and I spent the entire first semester sitting in the lecture halls feeling like a rabbit in the headlights, and doubting whether I'd ever be clever enough to get a degree. But I got into stride in term two, and hooked up with a couple of other older students and we study together sometimes, and that helps a lot. Its long, hard and complex, but I'm loving it.

Simon gave me an appraisal a few weeks ago, said he was 'delighted' with my progress! He explained some plans the practice has for expansion, and he wants me to stay on after I've qualified because he thinks I'll be a valuable asset to the practice! Me! A valuable asset! Imagine that.

It was a good appraisal. He made me think that anything is possible, and he wouldn't do that if he really didn't think it was. He was true to his word, and now I'm well on my way to becoming a professional veterinary surgeon with a permanent job waiting for me at the end of my training. Already! Me! Imagine that.

I've never had anyone believe in me as much as Simon does. I know Mum believes in me, but that's what mothers are supposed to do, so it doesn't count for the same as someone professional telling you they think you've got the potential to be every bit as good as they are.

He's paying me a decent part time wage and overseeing my training. Simon's a really good bloke, and I've got all the respect in the world for him, because he's giving me a real future, with proper prospects. And he respects *me*. In the appraisal he actually asked me what *I* thought about how the training and the job's going.

Nobody's ever asked me anything like that before, how I feel about things. Nobody's ever wanted to know whether I needed something more than what I already had, whether I was happy, whether there was anything more that could be done to help me. All it ever used to be, was people telling me what to do, how I *should* feel, what I *ought* to fucking want.

I told Simon I'd like to do more with farm animals, and maybe wildlife too. We've had a few wild animals brought in, usually by drivers that have found them or hit them. Some birds of prey, a couple of owls, the odd fox or badger, and one woman came in distraught, with a baby fox that her dog had found and attacked. It didn't survive, despite our efforts, but for a while I felt the true privilege of trying to help it to live. I was gutted that we couldn't save it, and I thought about how much some people hate foxes, how others hunt them for sport even though they're not supposed to, and how few champions wild animals really have, as they keep trying to live alongside the people who've mostly just stolen their habitats and then started resenting the poor little sods for trying to hang on.

This is a completely new way of life, a life where I have a real role to play. I'm not a waste of space anymore. I have a *place* in this life, a purpose, a reason for being. If you'd said to me a year ago, that this is where I'd be, I'd have walked away from you, laughing my arse off.

There was only ever one sticky point really, at the beginning, when Simon pointed out that I had a foul mouth and it needed to change. He was right, and I knew it. It's been said before enough times, but I'd never taken any notice, and it *is* a really bad habit. You pick up all sorts in prison, and on the streets with the kind of lowlifes I was hanging out with.

A gutter-mouth is the least of what you pick up, and even the professional workers in the jail start doing it over time, effing and blinding all over the place, but it really has become the worst kind of habit, when you get to the point where you don't even realise that every other word out of your mouth is an effing swear word. Well, I couldn't talk to customers like that, could I?

It's not easy to change, but I'm working on it. Simon started off with a swear box at the practice, and he got all the other staff to join in, in putting a post-it note into a jar every time I said fuck, or worse. He explained that it wasn't about being ganged up on. He just wanted me to see how bad I was, and that was a proper way of measuring it. After the first day, I was embarrassed enough, but after a week they could hardly fit any more post-it's in the bloody jar, and I could appreciate then, just how bad I was.

It did help. Knowing how bad you are is the first step to changing yourself, and I'm doing better now than I did all those months ago. Now I hardly ever say fuck out loud at all, and I don't seem to be thinking it so much either, anymore.

Back at the flat, I put the kettle on for a cup of tea. A nice bottle of whisky looks at me from the shelf in the kitchen. It's less of a luxury these days; I can afford a bottle of something decent once a month or so, and I'll just have a nip or two in the evenings as I'm watching TV, and unwinding a bit from work.

Tom looks out at me from a silver frame on the mantelpiece. It's a picture his mum took. He's laughing, mad bugger, 'forever fifteen,' with a goofy look on his face like he's just been told the joke of the bloody century. Marla gave me the photo (and the frame, as a housewarming present), which she said was taken about a year before I met him. It's a great photo. I can't look at it without smiling back at it. He's got his arm around his little sister Jenna, and they're both laughing at the camera like whoever took the photo had said something really funny. I often wonder what it was.

I think about him a lot, Tom. I miss him, but I have him to thank for this new life, so he's got pride of place on the mantelpiece.

This flat is tiny but cosy. You couldn't swing a bloody cat in it, to be honest, but I don't care. It's mine, and the best thing about it is that it's far enough away from all those drop-kick bastards I used to hang out with, waiting to see me fall and wanting to know who the fuck I thought I was, for daring to take a chance at a better bloody life.

This place is Victorian, with some interesting bits ('embellishments,' Mum calls them) on the outside of the block. It used to be a hotel back in the day. Looking at the big staircase at the foot of the communal entranceway, fancy tiled floor and real wood panelling everywhere you look, it's obvious that it must've been something special, in its day.

When we found this place, it was priced at ten thousand more than I got it for, and I didn't think I had a cat in hell's chance. Posh building, sea views from every window, who the fuck *did* I think I was, imagining I could have something like that? I'd never haggled in my life before and didn't even know where to start but, as it turns out, Patrick Michael McDonagh, my mum's chip-shop Prince Charming, is exactly that – a very charming negotiator!

'Robo-haggler' came in here with me, took one very quick look around, and told the agent it needed complete modernisation. The agent babbled something back about it being reflected in the asking price, but Pat wasn't having any of that. He went in with an offer of twenty thousand less, and I really thought the agent was going to bloody lamp him for his cheek.

But he took the offer to the owners, who came back and offered to knock five thousand off so Pat - ever the cheeky bastard - asked for fifteen, and they settled on ten for a quick sale, cash buyer, no chain, all that jargon Pat knew about and spouted forth to the agent, making me look like the buyer of the bloody century. They bit our hand off, in the end.

I learned a lot in that process, and when we started decorating I also learned how patient a man Pat was. Him offering to help me decorate just blew me away, and the care he took with the details was unbelievable. He's a stickler for detail, is Pat, and it paid off because this place looks great. He keeps telling me I should have it valued again for insurance purposes, and I guess he's right. He's right about most things, as it happens, and there's a time in the not-too-distant past where you'd never have heard me admitting that. We've come a long way, me and him.

We had a right game getting the bloody bathroom upgraded. I've kept the old roll-top bath but we had to send it away for recoating, and it took weeks to come back. I had to go to Mum's on the way home most nights for a shower, which meant we never got home much before nine o'clock, and usually with extra bags, thanks to her shopping for tartan curtains and matching bloody cushions and the like. She's cushion-obsessed, my mum. I thought about putting saddlebags on Badger, but I could imagine Alison's outrage at turning a perfectly decent dog into some kind of soft furnishings pack-horse.

Mum and I also went round a few reclamation yards to look for bits and bobs, like the grate for the fireplace and some old brass doorknobs, and we went to kitchen places to shop in sales for old-style taps and stuff, modern versions but still in keeping with the age of the place. Since she took that Interior Decorating course, she's developed a really good eye for what goes with what. This place looks terrific, and it's mostly down to her. I really liked the old central heating radiators, so we kept them, painted them up nice in a kind of silver paint, and they're a real feature of this little place now.

And for all that ferreting around for olde-worlde style stuff and keeping some of the original bits that were already in here, the flat doesn't look old fashioned. It looks 'chic,' as Marla Findlay says, possibly helped by the cream leather sofa and footstool with nice solid rosewood feet, that I picked up at Mum's beloved charity furniture shop for a hundred quid. People get rid of the oddest things. Perfectly good sofa and footrest, probably only a couple of years old, and they just gave it all away. A year ago, if I had a hundred quid, I'd have spent it on tattoos and whisky, or a new pair of jeans.

Pat also found a big second-hand gas cooker and range hood, thanks to one of his mates in the catering trade. It's replaced the knackered old thing that was barely usable in here, and we put some new doors on the kitchen cupboards. One has glass in it, and looks proper up-market, since Pat put an LED light in it. With a lick of paint here and there (no wallpaper for me, sorry Mum, does my head in good and fucking proper, that), it all came up a treat, and my mortgage is so tiny I could actually afford it on the dole. But I'm never going back *there*.

I didn't need a mortgage at all, in fact, as Alison had left enough to more than cover the cost of the place, and enough money to cover my vet training costs for the full five fucking years, but Pat advised me that it might be good for my credit status if I had a bit of one. That felt bloody huge, let me tell you. *A credit status! A mortgage!* Me! Dodgy Darren Davies from the wrong side of the tracks, living in a Victorian seaside flat with a dog, a car, a proper grown-up's bank account, a credit status and a fucking *mortgage!*

Yeah, a car; that was the other thing. I decided to have some driving lessons and take my test. It took me three goes (kept failing on hesitation at roundabouts, eff-eff-ess), but I did eventually pass it, and now I'm looking for a car. It needs to be something reliable, that I can drive to work in, and go see Mum, and take her out in. It needs to be good for Badger too, something he can get in and out of, so not a two-seater.

I'm thinking about an estate, just a small one. I've limited money that I want to spend on something, so I'm still waiting but Marla's bloke (sodding plod, would you believe it?), has had a tip-off about one coming up that I can probably afford, so I'm waiting to hear.

Life sometimes makes you laugh, and I'm laughing at the fact that the plod are helping me buy a fucking car. Wasn't so long ago they'd have arrested me and chucked me in the lock-up just for looking inside one. I guess this way, getting me one to buy, they know I won't be after stealing any.

Well my days of being tangled up with the plod are over. The next encounter I have with them, once we've got the car all bought and paid for, might just be Marla's wedding. It's mad how things work out sometimes. Turns out one of the officers who went to inform Marla about what had happened to Tommy was Eddie Pegg, a bloke she'd been at school with. They hadn't really known each other except by sight and name, but something sparked between them at that meeting, in spite of the awful news he was bringing, and they ended up getting together. Now they're talking about getting wed, once his divorce comes through.

Marla looks happy. There's a spring in her step and a twinkle in her eye. She's been robbed of her son, her baby boy, but she's got a nice bloke now, and a couple of step-daughters in waiting too, I believe. So her life goes on, just in a different direction than she probably ever thought it would.

I often wonder what Tom would have said about that. Whether he'd have loved or hated having a copper for a step-dad, I think he'd be pleased that his mum's found happiness with a decent sort. And he might have hated the idea of step-sisters, but he'd be glad his own his sister won't be lonely.

I think he'd be proud too, of the Tom Findlay Foundation for Missing Persons, that Marla used Alison's money to set up. She bought a derelict storehouse at auction and had it fixed up really nice. She's linked up to other agencies across the country, with computers, video links and everything, and they all provide support to family and friends of the missing, as well as advice and efforts to trying to locate them. Eddie helps as much as he can with advice, and with the police contacts he's able to use.

Most missing persons don't end up dead, as it turns out. Most eventually are found, and while some want to come home, just as many don't. The main thing is that people know what's happened and why. As Marla says, even if their loved ones choose not to come home, at least the families have peace of mind knowing they're not trafficked for the sex trade, locked in some pervert's bloody basement, dead in a ditch somewhere or buried under a mound of dirt in someone else's fucking grave.

A lot of the work Marla and her team do involves trying to persuade a located person to just call their family once a week to let them know they're okay. They can even go into the centre, to do it, if they're local. The centre does amazing work. They're reuniting families, in one way or another, all the time. Mum has a bit of a job there too, and she loves it.

It's a nice place to go and hang out, with bright cheery rooms and some comfy furniture. It has a kitchen where families can get a cup of tea or heat up a bowl of soup, and there's even a couple of bedrooms and little shower room for someone who might rock up as a missing person who might need a bit of encouragement or support to go home proper.

Pat and I decorated all that too, and I'm really proud of the work we did there. I'm getting quite good at this decorating malarkey. I can always do a bit of moonlighting with it. Someone always needs something painted.

Sometimes when I'm out with Badger, I fancy I can feel Alison zipping along with us, in her own spirit way. She was cremated, and I don't know where her ashes were scattered, because I was too pissed off with her at the time to want to find out. I do regret that now, and I've thought about finding her mother, and asking her. But I dunno whether that might be the worst thing I could do, like ripping the scab off a wound she'll probably be forever trying to heal already, with it being a suicide and all. Might just be better to let sleeping dogs lie, so to speak.

Alison said she didn't want a memorial to her life, since she'd squandered it so recklessly. She didn't think she deserved to be remembered.

I think she was too hard on herself. In the beginning I wanted her to be brought back to life just so I could kill her myself for what she did to Tommy, and I did wonder whether I could ever forgive her for lying about it, and betraying my trust in her, sitting there talking to me about this, that and the next thing, all the while knowing she'd killed my mate.

But time passes, and when I realised the legacy she wanted to leave, and how significant that really was, I saw it from a different angle. Someone once said to me, 'it's not what happens, but how you deal with it that counts,' and although Alison was the worst form of coward in many ways, I understand it, because it's not that long since I was a fucking great coward myself, is it, weaving a mess I couldn't work out how to unravel? And she tried so hard, in the end, to make something good come out of the whole horrible mess, and she managed it. So what kind of bloke would I be if I didn't try to do the same? Just the same old coward I always used to be, that's who.

While I was inside I met a lot of lads who'd done stupid things, then tried to cover them up, and ended up making things worse for themselves. God knows, I've done some stupid things myself. Let's not forget that if I hadn't had the bright idea of robbing Alison Jones in the first place, in her posh house, and if I hadn't run off and left my mate to face unknown consequences with her, she'd still be dead but none of the other unspeakable stuff would have happened. But there again, none of us would be where we are now, would we? All of us are in a better place than we once thought we'd ever be.

Was what she did that much worse than what I did? On most levels, you have to say it was, but it's all just the result of circumstance.

She always steered the conversation away from Tommy whenever I tried to talk about him. That was the coward in *her* I suppose, but there's a coward in all of us isn't there? And I liked her, before I knew what she'd done. That stays, underneath all the anger and betrayal, the disbelief, and the confusion about what she did, and who or what that made her. What I've learned is that when all that stuff finally falls away, what you're left with is what was there to bloody start with. And I liked her.

It might sound daft but I sometimes talk to Alison. I talk to her when I'm walking along the beach with Badger, and I ask her when I'm about to make decisions about him, like whether to try him on different food or get him a new collar. *'What do you think, Alison?'*

I sometimes talk to her at night when I'm lying in bed, listening to the waves as they crash over the rocks just a stone's throw from my window. I talk to her when something amazing happens, like the appraisal that has led to me being able to go so much further than I once thought I ever could. I talk to her when I visit Marla's centre. *'Look at what you made happen!'*

And I tell her, now and then, that I understand the love she had for her dog, and why she was so enraged when she found him unconscious in her kitchen. I'd have done the same thing she did. Whether I'd have carried on down the path she took, I don't know. Unless you're in that position, how could you *ever* know what you might do?

As the time passes I find I'm really humble, and grateful to Alison Jones, for so many things. She did a bad deed, but she did what she could, after, to make sure something good came out of it.

Not everyone would have done that. She could have gone to her grave carrying the secret of what happened to Tommy, but she chose to come clean and say sorry in the best way she knew how. And it wasn't about any religious thing, like wiping the slate clean to get into heaven, or any kind of shit like that.

Alison had a conscience, and a kind heart in the end, in wanting the people who cared about Tom to know what happened to him. She gave up what was left of her own life to atone for it, and she left everything she had to be used as wisely as we knew how, to make things better. She called herself a coward, but I think in some ways she was really brave.

Some might see that differently, but not me. I'm where I am today because of her. She might have taken away my friend, but she gave me the kind of life I would probably never have come to if she *hadn't* taken him away.

Tom's life is over, but his name lives on, in the hearts of the people who loved him, and in the centre Marla's built that offers so much support and hope to others who have no idea where their loved ones have gone. It lives on through me, and I thank him every bloody day, as he sits there atop my mantelpiece, laughing like he hasn't a care in the world. I hope, wherever he is now, he's laughing that hard all the time, and he never has a minute's pain or worry, ever again.

He was just a kid. It took me a long time to shake that vision out of my head, him scared shitless, choking and dying in a dark cupboard where nobody could hear him. What that must have been like for him, I can't imagine. But the vicar at his funeral told us all to focus on the things we liked and loved about Tom, and not to dwell on that one horrible part of it all, or the fact that some of us might feel we'd let him down, because torturing ourselves with all that would only stop us from ever being able to be happy that we'd known him, and he wouldn't want us to be sad. He was a happy boy, and he'd want his friends and family to be happy. *I'm* so happy, that I knew him.

It's amazing what you can let go of, when you try. I've had some counselling, thanks to the plod's Victim Support scheme. It's kind of funny, how after years of being a stupid criminal creating victims willy-nilly myself, I somehow ended up worthy of victim support. But this time, when counselling was offered to me, I actually used it the way I was meant to and it did help. I'm still amazed that they treated me as a victim, even after everything came out in the wash, including what I did, and what I hadn't said when I should have.

I struggled for a long time with the guilt of leaving Tom, because he *would* be alive today if I'd grabbed him on the way out. But I'm coming to accept that while what I did was selfish and cowardly, that wasn't what got him killed.

Alison Jones had choices. She wasn't mad, or bad. She just opted for the wrong choice, the really, really stupid one, when she was half crazy with worry and panic. I had no control over what she did, and no idea she could even do such a thing, and the consequences were what they were. I still feel sorry I left him, but how can you stay sorry for something that happened when the outcome of it turned your life into something so much better than you once ever dreamed was possible?

We've all got our demons to live with and for me, one of mine will always be regret about leaving that day, even with the outcome as it is. Another will be feeling glad, in so many ways, for the fact that him dying gave me this second chance at a meaningful life. It feels like being disloyal to someone who didn't deserve to be let down. But Tom was the kind of kid who would have said 'go for it, mate,' to anyone who had a golden opportunity. He would never have chosen to die, but he did die, and his mum says that we have to thank him for the opportunities we now have, to reach out and help others in distress, whether animal or human, because of his passing. We have to honour him, by making it count.

The work we do needs to matter. She's right about that, and Alison was too. It needs to matter, so that Tommy lives on through it.

In the beginning, all I did was cry. I never knew I was even capable of crying so much. I never knew *anyone* could cry like that. I'd hoped against all hope, for weeks, that Tom would turn up but I did know, somewhere in my heart of hearts, that something really bad had happened to him. Somehow, despite what I kept trying to tell myself, I just couldn't shake the feeling, a real darkness deep down inside me, that he wasn't coming home. I just fought really hard against accepting it, and giving in to those thoughts. It felt like giving up on *him*, and I didn't want to. He didn't deserve people giving up. I'd abandoned him. I wasn't going to give up on him as well.

Then when we got the news, I had no option. All hope was gone. Hope's the hardest thing of all, to let go of, but when you get no option it does make you sick to your stomach and your bones. And when I started crying, it felt like I'd never be able to stop. It was proper anguish, like falling into a well so deep you felt you were going to drown in it before you could ever get out, and such a big part of you didn't even *want* to get out.

Mum stayed with me, all the time I cried; hours, it was. She held me like I was a kid again, and that's what I felt like; a little kid, all helpless and screaming, wanting the truth to not be the truth. She said, part way through it, she thought the tears were about more than just Tom.

She was right, as it happens. As I sobbed, with a sadness that seemed to swallow up my whole body, I realised I was crying for myself too, for the stupid fucked-up mess I called a life, for the awfulness of all those early years we all somehow managed to get through. I was crying for my mum, for *her* wasted life with my fucked-up shit of a father, and I cried for Marla Findlay, as well as her boy, my little lost friend Tommy. I cried for Badger and his pain, and all my stupid mistakes, all the horrible things I'd done, all the time I wasted behaving like a dickhead, and it seemed to go on and on and on, forever, an endless grief, a tide I had no way of stopping.

At the end of it all I was exhausted, so tired I could hardly lift my head. Mum made me a sandwich and a cup of tea and told me to go to bed. She gave me a couple of pain killers, and I just did what I was told, meek as a lamb. I didn't have an ounce of fight left in me. That night I did sleep but it was all peppered with frying pans and funerals, and the endless sound of someone sobbing that didn't sound like me.

Now that the biggest dust-storm of all time has finally settled, we all feel a bit less bereft. We're all just getting on with things, because that's what life is all about. Picking yourself up, dusting yourself off, and moving on. Marla said to me that life pushes us forward, whether we want it to or not, and it's only when we kick against the process that we start to have problems. She also told me it was okay, in fact it was *time*, to forgive myself and move on.

So I don't force anything, but I don't do nothing, either. Simply, I just take each day as it hits me. Some days I'm sad, some days I'm just grateful, especially when I think about Marla Findlay's amazing ability to forgive the very worst of things that people do to one another. The world needs a lot more people like her in it.

I'm grateful when I look at Badger. I feel so thankful that I've had a chance to make it up to him properly for what I did to him. He's my dog now, and I've never felt so much love for *anything*. Something inside me has been unlocked because of this dog, it's the only way I can describe it. Loving him has allowed me to see through different eyes, to appreciate the other love around me, from my mum, and even from Pat.

I hope that someday, a nice woman will turn up that I will actually be worthy of. Until she does I'll just concentrate on being the best I can be for Badger, and Mum and Pat, and even my sister Michelle, who I hadn't talked to in years before all this. We've reconnected, and I hope to get out to Barcelona some time over the next year or so, to see her and her husband Paolo, and meet my two little nieces. And, of course, I'll concentrate on doing as well as I can in my new career; doing something that really matters.

My second chance is so huge, I struggle sometimes to believe it. As time moves us all forward and we feel the edges blurring around the trauma of everything that happened, the sharpness of it all is fading. It's caused me to wonder, now and then, if that means I'll also one day forget about Tom.

But then I get a hold of myself. Given the way my life's turned out, how could I ever really forget Tom Findlay, or Alison Jones? And even if I could, why would I? People come and people go. Some don't leave much of an impression, but others do, and well beyond what you ever might imagine.

Last weekend while I was in one of the cafe-cum-tourist shops along the sea front I saw a little plaque, one of those daft bloody things you hang up somewhere in your house. It reads; *'Some people come into our lives and leave footprints on our hearts, and we are never quite the same.'*

I bought that plaque. It's sitting there on the mantelpiece, next to Tommy's photo, and if anything more really needed to be said, about him or Alison or all that's happened, that plaque says it, like nothing else could.

Acknowledgements

From a concept in my head, this book became a reality, thanks to the following people:

Dr Rose Bosnell, Neurology and Stroke Consultant, for her invaluable advice and guidance about the diagnosis, manifestation and management of brain tumours.

Aisha Jamil, Graphic Designer, for creating so perfectly the vision I've had in my mind for a very long time, for the cover of *A Moral Swerve*.

Gwen Morrison from PublishNation, for getting the final formatted draft completed in record time.

Kerry Purvis for the endless support and encouragement to persevere against the odds with getting this book pushed through to publication. Only he knows what I went through, and how close I came to giving up, before I got here.

To my readers and fans across the world whose praise and encouragement to keep writing stories means everything to me.

This book would not be what it is without any of you.

Also by Annie Cook...

No Small Change
A Teapot Cottage Tale (#1)

**The 'change of life' means menopause.
But what if it also means reinvention, with the help of a
little bit of magic?**

Adie Bostock is a self-confessed 'basket-case.' She's fifty-two,
at the mercy of her haphazard hormones, and struggling to face
the end of her marriage. Alone for Christmas and fed up with
family drama, she lands at Teapot Cottage where she plans to
wallow in guilt and self-pity in private.

But the cottage, with its mysterious healing energy, has other
plans for Adie and she soon finds out that it takes more than one
person to make things fall apart, and more than one to put them
back together.

Confirmed widower Mark Raven is a rough-edged farmer
determined to hide his heart. He's battling with grief and ageing,
and keeping his rather dreamy daughter at least partly in the real
world. Romance is not on his radar.

Adie and Mark want to keep things purely platonic, but an unseen
influence is nudging them in a different direction. Then Adie's
husband decides he wants her back. It's what she's been praying
for, but is it still what she really wants?

**Escape to the Lakes District, with this magical, life-affirming
story about overcoming adversity and finding love again
later in life.**

The Power of Notes and Spells
A Teapot Cottage Tale (#2)

**Every woman dreams of finding the love of her life.
But what do you do when yours brings baggage that can
hurt you and your family?**

Feen Raven is often described as more than just a little bit barmy.
The young 'white witch' has finally found her soulmate, but old
family wounds are opened again when she finds out who he's
involved with.

Gavin Black is on an unhappy errand that forces him to reconnect
with his estranged mother. All he wants is to claim what's his
and go home again, without any complications.

Carla Walton can't let go of a grudge. After a lifetime of pushing
everyone away, she is isolated, bitter, and blaming everyone else
for her problems. She wants to be left alone so she can keep
ignoring her demons.

But Teapot Cottage, with its mysterious ability to heal the
broken-hearted, always has a more complicated agenda for
people who don't want to rake up the past. Pretty soon, Gavin,
Feen and Carla come to question everything they think they do
and don't want in life.

Will love and a little bit of magic help them find a way forward?
Or will old family fractures be too hard to heal?

**Come to the Lake District, to a gentle place where a beautiful
blend of music and magic can heal the hardest hearts.**

When It's Meant To Happen
A Teapot Cottage Tale (#3)

**Having a baby is something most women dream of
and plan for. But what does it mean if you can't make
it happen, no matter how hard you try?**

Meet Darren and Debby Davies.

Debby longs for a family of her own, and is desperate to have a baby with the husband she adores. But fruitless years of trying to conceive have started to make her crazy, that she can't seem to achieve the one thing she always felt destined to do.

Darren is at his wits' end with his wife. She is changing in ways that really scare him, and the way her parents treat him is starting to take its toll. He's beginning to doubt that their marriage can survive a never-ending series of storms.

As their doubts take hold, that their love can survive, Debby and Darren know they're in the last chance saloon. But Teapot Cottage, with its mystical way of pouring balm on battered souls, gently guides them towards a life they could never have imagined.

Can they stay together and face a very different future from the one they had planned, or will they find the challenges too great, and go their separate ways?

Come and spend some time in the Lake District town of Torley, where lives can change and anything can happen!